Discoucia

A Victorianish Fairytale

By Nicholas Lovelock

Clink Street

London | New York

Published by Clink Street Publishing 2017

Copyright © 2017

First edition.

The author asserts the moral right under the Copyright, Designs and Patents Act 1988 to be identified as the author of this work.

ISBN:
978-1-911525-82-0 paperback
978-1-911525-83-7 ebook

*'Just on the border, of your waking mind, there lies another time.
Where darkness, and light, are one. And as you tread the halls
of sanity, you feel so glad that you are unable to go beyond.'*

Discoucia

PART I

A Chance Meeting

'Dreaming is a phenomenon we all experience many times in our lives; some have passing dreams that are forgotten several seconds after we leave them. Some are so vivid that they remain with us until we die, and their details are imprinted on our minds forever. However if the particular journey through our nightly picture show isn't merely what we see, then there is a whole world playing out in our minds completely unknown to us.'
– Desiderius Erasmus Von Rotterdam (probably)

Silence ruled the air, and the sleepy road that ran through the middle of the Acacia Forest glistened with the now melting frost from the night before. The spring sun sat high in the sky as three men stole through the thick undergrowth that bordered the road and lay beneath the canopy of the trees. They were wearing purple coloured armour that was so opaque it made them nearly invisible in the dark shrubs. On their backs they carried brown cloaks, which were presumably for when they would come across a town or village and would want to remain inconspicuous. They carried an ornate pistol on their belts in a black leather holster, and their blond haired leader gestured for them to stop. They watched the road and apart from a pigeon breaking through the leaves and flying off in the distance, nothing could be heard.

Then one man put his hand to the ground and felt a faint vibration, then smiled. What the men could not see was a figure above them in the canopy that remained quiet and motionless. It stretched its leg out to balance on a branch but that branch was old and snapped under the weight, which led the figure to fall straight into the middle of the three men in a plume of leaves and dust. The figure was knocked unconscious, and the two normal men pulled out their knives to make sure this little inconvenience didn't disturb them. The blond leader however saw this as an opportunity to guarantee that whatever was coming up the road would stop so he picked up the stricken figure, who was wearing various colours of green so they were perfectly camouflaged.

He threw them out of the bushes and into the middle of the path, right out into the open. The leader saw that their target was now advancing up the road. The bow of a majestic ship floated along the road, its sails catching the breeze and its blue flag with the symbol of a crowned golden lion above three crashing waves danced. It came to a stop directly over the body and remained stationary about 10ft above the ground. The men watched intently at this tense situation waiting for the ship to move, or for someone to come and pick up the figure. The hull above the body suddenly opened up and another figure swung down on a rope and grabbed the unconscious body, then just as quickly returned to the ship and the hull doors shut.

And then several things happened. The men grabbed their guns and shot blindly at the space where the body used to be; and out of the top of the ship came a large gun, which had seven barrels in a hexagonal pattern. It quickly opened fire and the men ran as far as they could through the splinters of acacia wood that flew through the air like missiles. The sails on the ship retracted and the Nostradamus blasted its engines and the whole ship flew like a bullet along the road.

It reached the ruins of the Sandy Fortress and stopped, floated up and landed on a stone platform. The ship was now nestled about 30ft above the canopy of the forest, and the sun rose higher into the sky above a sprawling green sea. Sir Arthur Pageon the spy, adventurer and explorer laid the unconscious figure on his bed and removed the strips of green fabric from their face. He was stunned to see that the figures long flowing platinum hair balloon out behind her, and laid her peacefully down on the bed. He wandered off downstairs into the living room of the ship.

The Nostradamus was an extremely ornate ship, and Arthur had done everything he could to make it feel like home. Downstairs he had made a sitting room complete with bookcases, a desk, a table, a settee, paintings on the walls and green velvet curtains. Arthur walked out of the door, and out onto the sprawling deck. There was another person standing on the right hand side that was inspecting some rather nasty bullet holes in the wooden banister and returned with him to the sitting room.

"Afternoon Corky, did they do much damage to the old girl?" said Arthur. The man had a dusty beard and wore black overalls. He was about 5ft tall, and carried a spanner in one hand and a cup of tea in one hand.

"They couldn't put a hole deeper than an inch with those pea shooters," he replied.

"Oh good, and please tell me that that is just tea and that it doesn't have any other added ingredients," said Arthur.

"This time it's just tea, on principle I don't drink anything alcoholic until after three. And who is that pretty little thing you rescued from the road?" he asked taking a swig of tea.

"If I'm not mistaken it's Princess Josephine, and if it is I think I'll need a cup of 'tea' too when she wakes up," he said jokingly.

"Very well you arrogant little upstart," he replied, and disappeared through a hatch in the floor. Arthur was about to reply, but he heard movement in his bedroom and looked up to the ceiling in a worried fashion.

Josephine woke up and was still a bit dizzy. She instinctively remembered that she was tracking purple hunters and went for her sword. When she found that it wasn't there she looked around at her surroundings. She was in an ornate bedroom with blue velvet curtains, and at the end of the room were two doors, and they had no windows in them so she could not see what was inside. She went to the right door and it opened to reveal a landing, and she heard footsteps coming up them. She ran to the other door which she found was locked after a few tries.

"Good afternoon Princess Josephine, it's a pleasure to see you again," said Arthur.

"Sir Arthur Pageon? Am I on the Nostradamus?" she asked.

"Yes and welcome to my ship, what is it that you were doing out in the middle of the Acacia forest?" he asked.

"I was following the purple hunters that were following you."

"Well they're gone now so will you come with me to see your father?" he asked.

"Why does my father want to see you?" she asked.

"No idea, I'm sure he does this so I can't refuse him since I'm dying to know what he needs me for."

Arthur opened the curtains and saw that Jo was wearing green shorts, and a long sleeved shirt in a darker green. She was also wearing green shoes, and her long silky platinum hair was held back by a green hair band. Jo saw that Arthur was wearing a dark blue suit with a bright blue embroidered waistcoat, and he wore light blue shoes which matched the rest of his ensemble. Arthur had curly brown hair that grew down to his shoulders, and had bright blue eyes that Jo felt lost in, which was strange because she felt that there was more to Arthur than she thought.

Jo got up and felt around for her hunting sword but it wasn't in its hilt, nor was it anywhere to be seen. "Where is my sword?" she asked in a suspicious tone.

"It's downstairs, I didn't want you sleeping on it as that would have been uncomfortable. Don't want a member of the royal family falling on their sword now do we?" he replied.

"Oh, very well then let's go and see my father and find out what he wants you for," she said.

Arthur led Jo out of the bedroom and down into the sitting room. "I shall inform my driver that we are ready to leave; you don't mind walking do you only I don't want to park my ship in the Sky Port. Too many people want to find out how everything on this ship works," he asked.

"Not at all, it's only half a mile to the city walls and from there it's another mile to the Azure Hall through all of the tunnels, corridors and passageways," she said.

"I know, let's go," he said.

Arthur and Jo left the ship and walked down the old worn steps of the ruined fortress. One would expect the place to be evil looking, with scarred ruins and dead trees poking out of every dark crevice but the old fortress was covered in fruit trees and flowers growing in the cracks of the old mosaic floors. When the two had left the old ruined gates they walked across the Sky River Bridge, which had been restored after it was destroyed by the Great Uprising. They came to the massive oak forest that surrounded the mountain that Evermore was built upon thousands of years ago.

"So, what do you think of my father," she asked.

"He's an interesting fellow and loves his country which is a refreshing change from all the previous kings we've had, why?" he asked.

"I was just wondering, you know, trying to make some conversation so this little walk isn't boring," she replied.

"Oh, um, in that case what do you want to talk about?"

"What was in the room behind the door on the left?" she asked.

"That would be my wardrobe; I also keep some other things in there just to make the rest of the ship tidier," he replied.

"But why lock it?" she asked.

"So no one blunders in there and starts asking stupid questions" he replied. "What kind of stupid questions?" she asked.

"If you ever go in there, you can find out," he replied, and Jo now stopped asking questions and thought about what could possibly be in there.

"Well I suppose it could be clothes since it's a wardrobe, but surely you wouldn't lock if it's normal clothes like what you're wearing right now. So is it other kinds of clothes?" she asked.

"Oh for crying out loud," said Arthur quietly.

"I'm just using logical thinking to answer the question, but wait a second if I remember rightly there was always that rumour that you did that thing in Chene," she said.

"Why does everyone make fun of that when they aren't even sure about what really happened, I got knighted so it must have been something heroic," he said.

"Yes Sir Arthur, if you believe it to be heroic then you carry on," she said, smiling in a way that she hadn't done for a long time.

"It's in the past now and I kinda regret it so please just drop it," he said.

"Please don't be offended by my curiosity, it's just that it was a big thing when we heard about it. Also that you met a god," she said.

"That is not true, look we're almost there," he said.

They walked into an open area that was clear of trees, and they saw that they stood above a great valley and a river ran through the middle, the source being a great stone gate that the water flowed out with a mighty roar. Arthur looked over to the other side and saw with his keen eyes that a man was standing and waving. He was dressed completely in white, and had brown hair almost identical to Arthurs. Arthur waved back, and Jo saw him too.

"Who is that?" she asked.

"No idea, but he's waving so I'll wave back" he replied. Then, a strange thing happened; Arthur felt something in his jacket pocket that wasn't there before. When Jo wasn't looking he took it out and saw that it was a letter. He opened it and his eyes widened. He put it back in his jacket pocket again so it was out of sight but its contents were far from out of Arthur's mind. Arthur then walked down the stone stairs that led to the valley floor and the main gate.

"Just out of interest Sir Arthur, how old are you?" asked Jo.

"I'm 210, finally old enough to get into gentlemen's clubs," he said.

"Ah, I'm only 204 but for women we're allowed anywhere" she replied. In Alavonia a person who is 210 would be 21 on Earth. They live to 1000 as a person would live to 100 in our world and as such the year is 20144 and runs on a very different time line than anything we're used to.

"So, do you know the way?" asked Jo.

"Yes but I'll let you lead," said Arthur.

The gate was open and the two guards did not bat an eyelid when the two walked past. Through the gate they walked down a great wide corridor, which had a glass covered channel with the water running through at tremendous speed. On the right about a third of the way in was a large corridor which had a red floor, and they saw people milling about at the end. Opposite to this was a passageway that was covered over by a shiny metal grate. The sound of rushing water could be heard at the end of the short passageway.

"Is that the water system?" asked Arthur. "It is, the people have a thing about seeing all the mechanisms that transport water around and it means that if there is a problem, some engineers can get to it much more quickly" she replied.

"I see; well I've heard that your water system here is the best one in the kingdom since you have so much water pass through here," said Arthur.

When they reached the stairs that led up, Arthur couldn't help going to a passageway to the left, and Jo tried to resist but had to follow him. It was a small tunnel but Arthur didn't have to crouch because he was only about 6ft tall. The passage went to the right, and the torch lights on the wall flickered as they passed. Arthur walked down and he saw what he wanted to see.

Jo found Arthur looking down at the sand covered paths that were cut into the very rock, and the flickering firelights made out of Darkworld stone burned. They were a very rare mineral because once they were lit, they never went out. Arthur could see down into the depths of the mines and saw a glimpse of the Great Underground Desert, which was created when a vast natural cavern was discovered deep below Evermore and was used to dump the sandy deposits that were found during mining.

"What are you looking for?" she asked.

"I'm not looking for anything; I'm just amazed at what we have created underneath our capital city," he replied.

"In comparison to what's actually down there you'd be amazed ten times as much, but let's go and meet my father," she said.

They returned to the main corridor, and walked up the large stone stairs to the covered courtyard. If Arthur had not followed Jo, he may have got lost, as beneath the Azure Hall was a labyrinth of corridors, and they met various different courtiers that were engaged in a game of Hide and Find, as in Find the way out before the Finder finds you.

Jo led Arthur up a set of stairs and they opened up into a vast hall with sandstone walls and blue stone ceilings and massive glass windows, which let a large amount of light through but barely illuminated the inside of the hall.

9

A large table ran through the middle and people were sat in different places, but since there were not many this appeared to be a time when nothing important was going on. They walked over to the end of the hall where the giant throne stood, a testament to the workmanship of the first Discoucian's. It was built out of a huge block of serpentine that was discovered to be even more unbreakable than obsidian and the bedrock that is found beneath the deep lava pools underground.

"Come here my dear, and bring your companion with you," called a voice from nearby. It was High King Olandine, who wore the ceremonial white robe that all past kings had worn before him.

"Hello daddy, how are you?" she asked, hugging him.

"Personally I'm old and unfortunately I get every ailment that comes with it, but enough about me since I see you've bought me Sir Arthur," he replied.

"How may I help you my king?" he asked, bowing.

"Firstly I'm glad you two are acquainted because I'm making you partners, as this particular mission requires two," he said.

"Daddy I really don't think this is a good idea, I don't need him," said Jo.

Arthur remained quiet as he knew that when the King had made up his mind, then nothing would sway him. Actually he was restraining a lot of anger because he didn't even know Josephine and she didn't know him, so to make the assumption that she didn't need him after falling into the middle of a trio of purple hunters wasn't very fair at all.

"That is my final word on the subject and I wish for you to respect it daughter of mine," he said.

"Yes Daddy," she grudgingly replied.

"Secondly, what I'm about to tell you must remain secret. There is a power that seeks to destroy the kingdom by bringing down the cities one by one. We are not dealing with the general massive armies that we have fought in the past, but with new and terrifying technology that is completely unknown to us." he explained.

"What kind of technology?" asked Jo.

"In the far north-west of Discoucia is the Karga peninsula, beyond the lights of Chene where it sits in the dark shrouded by a mysterious fog," he said.

"What makes this fog mysterious?" asked Arthur.

"It's hot," replied the King bluntly.

"That's impossible; fog is caused by cold temperatures and cannot exist in hot areas, as is my understanding," he replied.

"The fog itself is hot, but the outside temperature is cold, which makes the fog even warmer," he said.

"Now this I have to see," said Arthur.

"What is Karga like?" asked Jo.

"It was once ruled by a very rich family whose name escapes me, but they lost all of their money and their castle was left to decay in the elements. The forests all around the land are hugely overgrown since there is no one there to tend them and they're now home to all sorts of dangerous creatures," he explained.

"Very well, we can check it out if it is your wish," said Arthur.

"Yes Daddy we shall go...together," said Jo grudgingly.

The King walked over to his two advisors, and that appeared to be the cue for Arthur and Jo to leave.

"You know how the family in Karga lost all their money right?" asked Arthur.

"No, how?" asked Jo.

"Your father many years ago found out that they were funnelling money to Neo Firmania in a tax avoidance scheme and all the money they had left they had to pay back. Once again you can never escape taxes," he replied.

"I doubt my father would have left them destitute," said Jo.

"No idea about that, maybe they went back to Neo Firmania to get their money," said Arthur.

They returned to the Nostradamus as quickly as they could, and Jo was given a guided tour of Arthur's ship.

A short stop

The ship lifted off then sailed into the north east, and Arthur sat at his desk while Jo looked at the various books that filled the bookshelves. "So where did you get this ship?" asked Jo.

"I stole it from my father just before our house was demolished and he went on an insane rampage," replied Arthur.

"Of course, it was your father that caused the Great Uprising, but then that means..."

"Queen Lilia the Young, most dangerous threat to the nation and warlady of Harrha Island, is my twin sister. The person we have been sent to arrest is my dear sibling who took a much different path in life than I did. Please don't probe too far into it as it's a topic I don't really like to discuss," he replied.

"Ok but can we take a look inside your wardrobe? I have rather a lot of clothes and it would be a lot easier for me to put them in there rather than leaving them all over your bedroom floor," she asked.

"Very well if you insist, then I will show you," he said.

They both climbed the stairs and entered Arthur's bedroom which had several white suitcases in a pile next to the bed.

"Do you really need that many clothes?" he asked.

"Yes, next question?" she asked sarcastically.

Arthur didn't answer but unlocked the door to the wardrobe and turned on the long light that hung above. Jo was amazed to see rows of clothes all neatly in hangers, and others hanging out of boxes that were placed in irregular areas all across the floor.

"This place is a mess," said Jo.

I haven't had a chance to clean up or sort everything out, maybe you should stay out of here if you find the place messy," he replied.

"You know, I heard that my father once assigned you to discover who was smuggling in the old Chene Harem, and since the only men allowed in there were King Jassuer and his advisor, how did you get in?" she asked.

"I guess I can't avoid this any longer so take a wild guess," he replied sarcastically.

"I'm going to go with blue ballroom dress and bright blonde wig, since Jassuer really liked blondes," she replied.

"He was politely asked to stop smuggling in illegal poisonous Blue Whisky in return for the public not finding out that his new favourite girl wasn't actually a girl" replied Arthur.

"That's a story to tell the children I suppose, but you have rather a lot of dresses and this one wouldn't even fit you" she said, lifting an old purple dress.

"No that was my sister's; when I left, all this was in the ship, which I believe meant that my mother intended to leave with her" he replied.

"What happened to your mother?" asked Jo.

"She was killed by a falling piece of masonry when an Evermore gunboat destroyed our house, they never found her body. I was told that by one of the servant's years later since I wanted to leave all that behind" he said sadly.

"I'm sorry, that was an unfair question to ask" she replied.

"Oh well it's in the past now, but if you don't mind we're flying over Fina and I would like to visit my house like I do every year" he asked.

"May I come with you?" she asked.

"I was rather hoping you would," replied Arthur.

The ship sped past the vast gleaming walls of Evermore and flew across the great valley that lay between it and the ruins of Fina. They were similar to the ruins of the Sandy Fortress, and they were built upon one of the few mountains in the centre of the Discoucian continent. This surprisingly flat mountain was a strange place because in a valley surrounded by a wall of rock were iron sculptures of people, left over statues of lords, ladies, kings and queens that had been overthrown and their likenesses discarded here. Fina lay much closer to Evermore than it did to the sea city of Cesta.

The ship landed outside the walls of a once magnificent building. The wall they had landed by had flowers growing out of its many cracks, which made for an oddly pleasant sight. The gates had gone, ripped out many years ago which made it easier for the two to gain access to the old Pageon estate.

"Do you still own the land?" asked Jo.

"On a legal level since I am a second older than my sister, I own Fina but what do I want with a gloomy desolate mountain range," he said.

"I see. Shall we go to the house?" she asked.

They continued up the desolate drive to the manor, which stood as a decayed tree stump sticking out of the ground. "Do you have pleasant memories of here before, you know..?" she asked, but Arthur was deep in thought. He pictured the house as it was before, white plaster walls and ornate red ceilings, the curtains billowing in with the summer breeze, and him running from his sister who wielded a wooden sword. In Arthur's mind the walls fell down and the ceilings collapsed. This bought him back to reality as Jo tapped him on the back.

"Sorry, an attack of nostalgia," he said.

"Are you ready to go? I mean all this memory stuff is delightful but we should be heading for Karga," she said.

"Of course, race you back" he said, and ran. Jo for a second didn't take him seriously, and when she saw that he was in fact running, she ran too. Arthur was winning, until Jo streaked past him, her hair flowing behind her. They jumped over the high wall and landed on the deck simultaneously, and both breathed hard.

"I thought you were joking!" she angrily panted.

"I know, but you nearly beat me," he replied, also out of breath.

They re-entered the ship and it began to fly across the sky, leaving behind the mountain which was swallowed up by the night. "I have a question for you, Jo" he said while sitting at his desk.

"Go for it," she replied, lying on the settee with her feet up.

"What's your sister like?" he asked.

"Alex? She is very devoted to the Order of the Tangerine, and I only see her on Daddy's birthday, because that's the only time she deems important enough to leave the Order's Monastery in Thorisea, why?"

"I was just wondering, I've never really met her, so I have no idea what she looks like," he replied.

"Like me, only slightly older," she said.

They were interrupted by Corky, who knocked and entered. "What is it?" asked Arthur. "And a good evening to you too boyo, I just came to tell you that were about an hour from Karga, and with your permission I'll park her on the beach outside the forest and turn in for the night," he said.

"No problem, I'll see you in the morning," replied Arthur.

"And if you don't mind I'll park as far away from the forest as is possible, after what I've heard," he said cryptically.

"What are you talking about?" asked Jo.

"That creature miss, with the iron teeth and glowing yellow eyes," said Corky.

"I don't believe you, but if there is a monster then after this we'll go to Proceur and you can have a weekend holiday," said Pageon.

"An esteemed thank you for the vote of confidence sir, and on that note I'll say goodnight," he said, and left.

Out of the window Jo could see the bright lights of Chene quickly pass by. "Why do you call him Corky?" she asked.

"Two reasons mainly, his full name is Cornelius Undergast, and he's also a fan of the drink," he replied.

"Has he been with you long?" asked Jo.

"He was my father's driver, how old do you think he is?" he said.

"I'd say he was over 600," replied Jo.

"He's 348," he said.

"I don't believe you" she replied.

Arthur and Jo sat at the desk, Jo in a chair opposite Arthur's that she had pulled up from the corner of the sitting room, and they began to have dinner together. Corky had stopped off in a small town and Arthur got some Fire Island takeaway, which he eyed suspiciously but Jo ate quite happily.

"So tell me, Arthur, about this whole travelling lifestyle, it tells me that you have an inability to settle down," said Jo quite savagely.

"It's true, and from the way you believed you could handle this alone and going as far as questioning your king's judgement, I have to guess that you are jealous of your sister," he said.

"I have no idea what you mean," she said.

"Your sister is never at home and despite the fact that she could be doing terribly you know your father wouldn't know. So that means you have to compete with someone that is constantly showing you up despite never being there. This is your second mission as a member of the Discoucian Secret Service and after rescuing you from what could have been an early end to your promising career I have to ask why you thought you could take care of this on your own," he asked.

"You may think you're this great adventurer who travels the world for the glory of the empire, but I fail to see what right you have to criticise me," she said.

"Are you sure this is the right vocation for you Princess?" he asked.

"There are things I can do that you surely cannot, and as much as I believe that I can complete this mission on my own it doesn't mean that I am over-confident," she replied.

"Still wouldn't you be better suited to another job, maybe doing royal visits and opening new buildings?" he asked.

"You know you complain about me sounding arrogant, but as much as you would hate to admit it, you're not comfortable at all with me being your partner either," she said.

"I never said anything of the sort," he said.

"What do you think it would do to your reputation, having to rely on a princess?" she asked sarcastically.

"I see that you and I are going to have a very fun time, though if I promise to not question your lifestyle choice, then I suppose you will extend me the same courtesy?" he asked.

"I don't know how long this partnership is going to last, but until then I think we should work together and afterwards continue with whatever that just was," she replied.

The Fog

"Am I sleeping upstairs?" asked Jo.

"Of course, I rarely sleep since it's a condition I inherited from my ancestors," he replied.

"I'll see you in the morning then," she said.

"Goodnight Josephine," he replied.

"Please call me Jo," she said.

"Then call me Artie, it sounds less formal. Goodnight Jo," he replied.

"Goodnight Artie," she said, and disappeared upstairs. Arthur settled down at his desk with the letter he found, and began to read it properly.

"'To my brother, Arthur

I would like to inform you that I am planning to do something that you would consider stupid and unethical but it has to be done. As much as I would like to spare you from it, only you can accomplish that. Stay out of my way and you won't meet an untimely death at the hands of my army. As much as I would like to see you again after a new world has been established I would hate for it to be as a corpse. Your dear sister, Queen Lilia the Young.'

"I'll get you one day Lilia, one day I'll get you," he said to himself, and then took a book from the shelf that read '*Karga, A History*'. ""So Karga is home to all kinds of strange flora and fauna, but the notion of it being haunted or that it has any ties with the supernatural can be dismissed instantly since after being banned in the 170th century, witchcraft has never been witnessed there',"" he read. "Well, I don't much like the way that's worded but it seems that the monster isn't an old thing," he said, relaxing in his chair.

The ship now sped over the sea, and past hundreds of little fishing boats and tiny lamp-lit villages that lay around the coves and beaches of Discoucia. They flew closer and closer to the fogbound shores of Karga, and all the adventures that waited for them...

Voices in the Fog

Jo was dreaming. She was wandering through a dark forest and the fog was up to her ankles. She was completely alone, the forest was silent and every footstep she made echoed all around the trees. Walking in one direction, she felt that she was heading for something but had no idea what. Then, from far behind her she heard the sound of something crunching its way through the trees. She tried to run but her feet stayed walking and didn't change pace. She could not see what was behind her but knew that she had to hide. She looked ahead and saw what remained of a castle, but she couldn't tell its height because of the dark canopy of trees. Her path led her up to a rotting oak door which she pushed open with a creak. She stared into the gloom and two luminous yellow eyes stared back at her. With the prospect of being attacked from both sides, Jo fainted and landed on the floor of Arthur's bedroom.

She looked around and for a second she forgot why she was there, and then remembered everything as the memories came flooding back. She got dressed and hurried down to the sitting room, expecting to see Arthur passed out on the settee. When she looked out of the windows she couldn't see anything, as the fog her father had told her about had completely enveloped the ship.

"Artie! Artie!" she shouted when she walked onto the deck.

"What!" echoed a voice from out in the murky distance.

"Where are you?" she shouted.

"Down here, on the beach," he shouted back.

Jo walked down onto a bewildering sight. Arthur and Corky were playing golf in the sand. "Good morning. Pleasant sleep?" he asked, taking a shot at the hole they had dug into the sand. He missed and Corky sniggered so quietly that Jo could not hear but Arthur heard, and nearly threw his club at him. But then he breathed heavily, calmed down and composed himself.

"Yes, your bed is extremely comfy," she replied.

"Thanks, anyway are you ready to go monster hunting?" he asked.

"Ready when you are," she said.

They walked over to the borders of the forest which was thick with brambles and nettles. Visibility ahead was practically zero but Arthur seemed to know which way he was going.

"Have you ever been here before?" asked Jo.

"No, I walked around this morning to see if there was a way in," he replied.

Arthur led Jo to an opening in the tree line, where all the weeds and plants had been crushed and the branches were broken and torn from the trees.

"I suppose this is the best place to start, mysterious looking place wouldn't you say?" asked Arthur, with a hint of excitement in his voice.

"You first," she said.

"I thought you were the strong independent woman and what kind of gentleman would I be if I didn't let you go first?" he replied.

"Just go" she said, smiling as Arthur passed her and led them through.

The forest was so dark that it could have been the middle of the night and there would be no difference to the light levels. The fog wound its way all around the trees and across the path. The duo's hair hung lank on their shoulders as they pushed on along the path that passed through random outcrops of rocks and large untended hedgerows. Patches of grass grew beneath the massive birch trees whose silver bark glistened in the damp but warm atmosphere.

"How far is the castle from here?" whispered Jo.

"I believe that it's about half a mile in this direction," he whispered back.

They walked past a sundial which was covered in ivy, and the remains of a stone path. They reached a small field of rapidly wilting honeysuckle and pushed on through. Ahead Arthur saw that a dark path cut through a hill, and had two large hedges that grew over it. A dull crunching sound echoed deep from within and seemed to flood out like a voice.

"Are we going in there?" asked Jo.

"No, we're not going into the incredibly scary looking tunnel that obviously has something nasty at the end," he replied sarcastically.

"We have guns" she replied, taking out hers.

"You know, this may send a bad message to anyone who we tell but I feel so much more confident when I have a gun in my hand," he said.

"You're right, it is a bad message, but at this point I think we should take them anyway and leave this part out," she replied.

Jo had now forgotten her previous anxiety about entering the tunnel and followed Arthur along with a newly found confidence; not because she was now armed, but after the way he reduced the situation to a joke and did not seem to take it as seriously as she did. However she was noticing some stark similarities between the layout of the forest and the one in her dream.

They had reached about halfway through the tunnel, and Jo saw through the steaming mist that the walls were made out of old stones, placed on top of each other and not in any particular pattern. Arthur walked a bit further on and felt the floor underneath him change to hard stone. The fog was absolutely stifling and Arthur had to take his jacket off, which was now soggy.

"Look at that, vintage Eve of Saint Lara and soaked," he said.

"I didn't know you had such a high class taste in fashion" said Jo.

"What else am I going to spend my money on?" he asked.

"I don't know, a home and a wife," she replied.

"You give me way too much credit as far as my life is concerned, I'm an orphan so if you don't mind I'd like to get off the subject," he said.

"What does being an orphan have to do with it?" she asked.

"I didn't have a stable family life and it didn't prepare me for adulthood," he said.

21

"It's a bit late to be complaining about that now, here of all places," she replied.

"Maybe I shouldn't have mentioned it, I barely know you," he said.

"And I barely know you but we're not going to get anywhere if you don't want to be co-operative," she replied.

"I thought you didn't need co-operation?" he asked.

"What are you talking about?" she asked.

"Never mind," he replied, walking further along the path.

He looked around and saw that they had entered an old courtyard, which had several trees poking out of the floor, and all around the floor was covered with the odd patch of moss. "We're not that far away from the castle, in fact if I'm not mistaken that little blinking light off in the distance is the main hall" he said.

"You mean the old and ruined castle that has not been inhabited for centuries?" asked Jo, obviously hinting at the fact that something wasn't right.

"Yes, I see what you mean. There's a way down through those trees and I think that we go to the left then straight to the castle walls," he replied.

They climbed down the old stone stairs that had once had beautiful stone carvings, but now vines curled their stalks around in effort to choke the life out of the solid pink granite. After reaching the bottom it became clear to Arthur that he had walked out into the open, and he sensed that something was coming towards him from the left. He and Jo ducked down below the stone banister and for a tense few seconds they peered through the holes in the vines out into the gloomy clearing. Jo watched, shaking slightly, and Arthur held her hand. For a second she felt quite safe and then remembered that she had only just met him, along with their heated discussion last night she decided to take her hand back.

There was a loud crash and out of the trees to the left came a tall black figure with glowing yellow eyes. It turned to the stone banister, and out of nowhere came a fist swishing down above them, then a spray of dust as chunks of stone flew everywhere. Arthur grabbed Jo and ran past the figure, which had got its arm lodged in the stone. He stopped at the hole where the figure had burst out, and Jo ran in past him. He picked up a stone and threw it at the figure, which seemed to be wreathed in darkness. "Metal, that figures," he said to himself. He left the figure to struggle while catching Jo up, and saw that she had made it to the castle walls. They loomed up into the fog, pinnacles of slime covered stone, while Jo was standing outside a wooden door.

"Why aren't you going in?" he asked. She didn't reply but stayed rooted to the spot. Arthur grabbed Jo's hand and pulled her into the now open doorway. He slammed the door shut and ran up the stone spiral staircase with Jo trailing behind. They turned round the stairs three times and it was pleasant to be out of the stifling fog for a moment. They reached the top and entered a vast courtyard that spread out as far as they could see - which was not very far, as the fog was so much thicker here.

The stone floor was uneven, and weeds were growing out of the multiple cracks. "I can just about see that light," said Arthur.

"Me too, and you can let go of me now," she replied, and Arthur let go straight away and seemed a little embarrassed but thanks to the fog he was spared Jo noticing.

"What happened back there," he asked.

"I don't know, I'm sorry," she replied.

"Don't apologise, it can happen to anyone. Listen, I have an idea and I want you to go around the building and climb on the roof. I'll go straight through the front door and you can watch from above what goes on," he explained.

"I don't think that will be much of a problem, I'll keep an eye on you," she replied.

They split up, and Arthur drew his pistol. He walked across the courtyard half expecting another creature to jump out at him, but this didn't happen. The main building was mostly intact and a big oak door separated Arthur from what was inside; he opened the door and couldn't believe the sight that greeted him in this decaying ruin...

An unlikely answer to a puzzling scenario

Arthur walked into what was once the great hall of the castle, and he saw rotting green drapes on the broken glass windows. However it was what lay in the centre of the room that drew his attention. It was a beautiful-looking machine that whirred and whizzed with bright lights glaring from various different bulbs around its polished brass frame. It was bulb-shaped with a large tube extending out of the top and into a hole in the ceiling. There were various wires connecting different parts of the machine, and a control box in the centre, with dials of numbers running up and down.

"You are beautiful," said Arthur.

"She is, isn't she," said a voice from behind him.

Arthur spun around and saw that three men were watching him; the one in the centre wore a fancy purple uniform with silver epaulettes, and had shiny slicked black hair and a short smart moustache. The one to his left wore a simple purple uniform, and the one to the right wore a white lab coat and had goggles tangled in his frizzy brown hair.

"Good evening, and who is that I have the honour of addressing?" asked Arthur.

"Commander Norso, at your service," he said smartly.

"Can I have a cup of tea?" he asked.

"Excuse me?" asked Norso quizzically.

"You said you were at my service," replied Arthur. Jo silently laughed from her hiding place above, and she now saw that Arthur was a little braver than she thought.

"If that is your idea of a joke...?" asked Norso, not changing his expression.

"It was, but since I don't hear any laughter we won't dwell on it. So tell me, I understand that you have a machine that can generate fog, though I cannot fathom why," said Arthur.

"Please, Sir Arthur, have a guess, I would love for you to figure this one out," said the small brown haired man.

"Will you please introduce yourself, sir," said Arthur.

"I am Professor Claudio, an authority on the weather of the world," he replied.

"Of course now I remember, you're the professor that resigned from Evermore University along with Dr Dayton when you both blew up your laboratory," he replied.

"Yes, he went freelance while I joined Queen Lilia since the King wouldn't allow me to continue our experiments," he said.

"Oh, I think I can make an educated guess at why you would want to generate artificial fog, I mean it has so many uses. You can use it to scare superstitious locals, you can rob palaces and escape into the fog and you can move entire armies without anyone seeing. I have to say that that is a brilliant idea," he said.

"Not just an idea, but a reality!" he shouted maniacally.

"So is this a prototype?" asked Arthur.

"It's a tester and since it works, we can now depart for Harrha but we won't need it as I have all of the plans with me, ready to mass produce," he said.

"One more question, is that your guard dog outside? As it seemed to be a little stuck when it demolished a granite banister," he said.

"That is one of Queen Lilia's new soldiers which still has a few problems but when we take it back to her, she can make it more powerful than ever before," he explained.

"I see, so what are you going to do now?" asked Arthur.

"I'll field that question," said a voice from behind. Arthur was about to turn around but was knocked unconscious by a rifle butt.

Arthur awoke to find himself strapped to a chair, facing the Fog Machine, which now had another component attached to it. It was a red box with four slowly rotating dials that read 0369, but then clicked over to 0368, and Arthur instantly recognised it as a bomb. The men were all gone and he was left alone in the hall, watching the dials inexorably click down to zero. "Whenever you're ready my dear, I'm waiting right here," shouted Arthur.

Jo swung down from the roof and landed right in front of Arthur. "In case you didn't notice that bomb will be going off soon, and I would appreciate it if you untied me," said Arthur calmly.

"I don't know, I kinda like the idea of you subdued and tied up," said Jo in a cocky tone.

"This really isn't the time or place for wherever you're going with this Jo. Can we get out of here now? I have to report this to your father," said Arthur.

"All righty then," she said, cutting the ropes binding Arthur's arms and he stood up, still staring at the machine. "Are you coming, or are you just going to stand next to a ticking time bomb?" she asked, exasperated. Arthur didn't answer, but he walked behind the machine and was heard unscrewing something.

Arthur shouted "Eureka!" and ran with Jo out of the hall, clutching an object that Jo didn't see. They ran down the stairs and out of the old oak door, and into the courtyard where they had last seen the creature.

"Where has it gone?" asked Jo. "No idea, they probably took it with them," said Arthur.

There was an explosive bang that lit up the night sky, and in seconds the fog dissipated, and they both saw the land for what it really looked like. The overgrown arches and columns all looked so beautiful; for the first time since they arrived in Evermore they saw the huge pink moon that was now above them, making it as light as day in the moonlight.

"Let's get back to the ship, I'll message your father and I owe Corky one fully paid trip to Proceur," said Arthur.

"Hopefully this time I can have a good night's sleep," she replied. Arthur then took out a piece of paper from his pocket and Jo walked over to Arthur to read it too.

"'Order of 1,000 prisoners from I to H within the next month'," read Arthur.

They both walked back through the forest which now seemed cool and calm after the fog and the lingering threat of a monster had gone. They climbed aboard the ship and it lifted off then sped across the land to the east, where they would not find a calm holiday but another extension to their already strange adventure.

An Icy Reception

"So what do the letters mean?" asked Jo.

"I guess when you mention prisoners and the letter 'I' it probably means Icester," he said.

"Oh no I'm not going there, it's freezing like all the time," she said.

"I think that's why they called it Icester dear," he replied.

"Have you got anything warm to wear?" she asked.

"Since I can tell you've been dying to go in there again, check my wardrobe. There's a ton of stuff in there," he replied. Jo went upstairs followed by Arthur to look for something that would keep them warm in the frozen wastes and mountains of Icester.

"You have so much stuff and it's everywhere, one day we'll sort it out," said Jo.

"I know, I just haven't had the chance lately," he replied. Jo pushed past various jackets, and then dresses, and then she finally got to a strange looking fur coat. It was green velvet with tufts of fur coming out of the collar, wrists and bottom. The inside was fur as well and it looked perfect for the purpose they had in mind. Jo put it on and she instantly warmed up.

"I'll take this one," she called to Arthur who had found a blue one that was just the same.

"I'll take this one then, if I remember rightly I got these from Icester a long time ago when Lady Argrecius ruled, and she insisted that all the guards wore colour coded uniforms," he explained.

They left the wardrobe, and when they looked out of the windows they saw that they were passing Chene. It was still night so the city was lit up beautifully. "It looks lovely, doesn't it?" asked Arthur.

"Yes, a real miracle," replied Jo. They then flew over another tributary of the Sky River and they saw ahead; looming out of the darkness, were the peaks of the Icicle Mountains.

Tiny snowflakes began to fill the air and settle on the deck, but it was too warm for them to settle so they melted straight away. The ship began to fly higher and higher, since the only safe place to land in the mountains was a sheltered valley that looked down onto Icester Prison from high above the clouds. "Have you ever been to Icester before?" asked Arthur.

"No I haven't to be honest with you, members of the royal family wouldn't be welcomed much since when your appointed to Icester as a Lord or Lady, then 300 days of the year it's pretty much a death sentence," said Jo.

"We may have to change your name then, you can be my assistant," he said. "I'll get you for this Arthur," she said.

"OK then, *Miss Daisy,*" he replied.

"OK I have to agree with you that name is inspired, not a touch of royalty about it," she said.

"Nope it's just a lovely normal name," said Arthur.

"Actually that was mean, to all Daisies in the world, you have a lovely name," she said.

"Who are you talking to?" asked Arthur.

"No one," said Jo who followed Arthur out onto the deck.

The second they left the ship the cold hit them instantly, all their exposed skin was jabbed by tiny invisible icicles but with the fur coats it wasn't as bad as it could have been. They flew through ghastly looking mountain passes and past jutting cliffs that were slightly obscured by the snow.

There suddenly came a colossal moaning sound from deep in the mountains, and Jo clutched Arthur, and Arthur clutched back. After the sound subsided, the two got back to their senses and continued their conversation. "Probably the wind," said Arthur.

"Echoing through a cave," said Jo.

"Yes, couldn't possibly be anything else," said Arthur.

"Can we go back inside now?" asked Jo.

"Yes, yes we can," said Arthur in a hurried voice.

The ship sped through the snowstorm, and finally came to a small sheltered valley that was only big enough for the ship to land and then a little walking space between the ship and a 1000ft drop. The Nostradamus landed with a crunch on the snow covered ground, and out of the sides came four hydraulic metal spikes, two on each side. They dug into the ground and the ship was now stable against the howling wind.

Arthur was packing everything he needed to survive a downhill climb and an uphill climb on the way back. "So Corky, all you have to do is activate the snow defences when we leave the ship," said Arthur.

"Then I can get back to inventing a new engine for the ship," he replied.

"Yes, and do anything you want, just don't get cabin fever while you're up here all alone," said Arthur.

"I don't know about that, I've got enough things to do," said Corky.

"In that case, carry on," said Arthur, who walked outside with Jo.

"Carry on? I got a leaky oil spewing pile of carry on for you right here," he muttered under his breath. When they left the sitting room the whole ship changed. Steel shutters came down over the windows and the valley which had been previously lit by the ship now went dark, and Jo wanted to leave as soon as possible.

"Why do we have to park all the way up here, when it would make so much more sense if we parked in Icester's Sky Port like everyone else?" asked Jo.

"For three reasons really. This way we're high up and away from anything bad that could happen. Secondly, I don't have to pay for parking this way and don't look so judgemental, everyone does it," he explained.

"And the third?" she asked. Arthur jumped over the banister of the ship and shuffled through the snow over to a rock wall. Jo looked at him quizzically until he pushed on the wall, and it opened like a door.

31

"Oh I see and that makes perfect sense now," she said. Jo followed Arthur through the door, which closed behind her. The ship was left like a scene in a snow globe, lonely and covered in a blanket of powdery snow.

Arthur and Jo made their way along a pitch black tunnel; it was surprisingly warm after the bitter cold of outside.

"Arthur, where are you?" asked Jo, who couldn't see a thing and was strangely amazed at the crystal echoes of her voice.

"In front of you, just keep walking," he replied. There was a light ahead, a pale blue light that they quickened their pace to get to. At the end of the dark tunnel was a large chamber, which was lit by blue glowing crystals poking out of the walls.

"You know, I never actually mentioned before but you have a beautiful voice," said Arthur.

"Are you paying me a compliment?" she asked.

"Yes your majesty, I was. You don't have to make such a big deal about it," he replied.

"It's just weird that after all the things you've done, all the tales people at court tell about you and you compliment me," she said.

"Is this just a stream of consciousness or are you leading up to something?" he asked.

"I'm still not one hundred percent on you Arthur; I mean you appear all perfect but I bet you are someone completely different when I get to know you," she replied.

"I guess you can find out, now come on," he replied, walking along the frozen path and trying not to slip.

"This place is beautiful, how did you know about it?" she asked. "When I was trying to capture Jeff the Cracker, the escaped mass murderer, I followed him through these tunnels; unfortunately for him he fell down one of the many random holes in the floor and was impaled on a crystal stalagmite" said Arthur.

"That doesn't sound pleasant by any means," said Jo.

"It wasn't, but it was so cold down there that his body is still preserved on the crystal," said Arthur.

"You left him there?" she asked.

"Yes because it would be very difficult to get him down and it would serve as an example to any other prisoners," said Arthur.

They walked along a frozen bridge that spanned an immense cavern with stalagmites made from ice poking out of the floor, and Jo was glad that Arthur had given her special shoes with small iron spikes on the soles; that way, she could walk on the slippery floor without looking stupid. After they had walked along the bridge they came to a large cave, and the floor descended down as far as the two could see.

"It's downhill from here," said Arthur.

"How are we supposed to get down?" asked Jo.

Arthur walked over to the wall by the entrance, and there was a pile of wooden boards. Arthur picked up one, and threw it to Jo. "What are we going to do with these?" she asked.

"Really big snowy downhill cavern, wooden boards, any of this adding up for you?" he asked.

"Oh, we're going down together right?" she asked.

"In a sense," he replied. Arthur took his board and ran for the slope; he placed the board on floor and slid down.

"This is wrong, this is wrong, this is wrong," she shouted, and followed Arthur down the slope.

Arthur slid down the slope, dodging snow covered ropes as he descended. The cold wind blew on his face but he didn't notice it, instead he was focusing on not crashing into any obstacles. Then Jo whizzed past him and he saw that she was quite good at this. "I thought you were scared!" he shouted.

"I thought you were fast!" she retorted.

Arthur shook his head and leant down to gain more speed. The cave then became a tunnel that was in a perfect circular shape. Arthur saw Jo up ahead and pushed his foot on the floor to pick up more speed. He saw his chance and he undulated up the wall past Jo and overtook her. She gasped as he had come out of nowhere, and she instantly tried to catch him up. Arthur then began to slow down and large drifts of small ice particles flew up in Jo's face.

They emerged into a huge ice cavern and Jo saw her chance for revenge. She swiped her hand across a snow covered rock and collected some. She then fashioned it into a ball and threw it. It sailed over Arthur and missed completely. "Missed," he shouted. The ball hit a mass of snow that hung above the entrance to another tunnel ahead, and knocked it down. Arthur then took a not-so-pleasurable snow shower. He sailed through the frozen rain and it stopped just as Jo entered.

She was beginning to get the hang of it as they entered another tunnel. The walls were a beautiful shade of blue, and everything was lit by the ice crystals that were either frozen in the ice or hung from the ceiling. They then sailed out of the tunnel and there was a large rock right in front of the exit. Arthur flew at it, and Jo then flew into him. The rock didn't block the entrance; however, it did stop them from flying down about 30ft into a chasm.

There was a snow-covered path that led around the large circular chamber, but it was what lay at the end of the path that caught their attention. The circular chamber was part of an even greater cavern which was filled with buildings, all made of wood, and they were all lit up like a Christmas village.

"It's a subterranean town, but what is it doing below Icester?" asked Arthur.

"There's only one way to find out," said Jo, who slid down the circular path before Arthur could stop her. He watched Jo slide down, and then slide straight into a guard who was standing outside the wooden walls of the city. She was grabbed and taken in, and then the gates were locked.

"Oh dear, now I'm going to have to rescue her, 'Miss I don't need him' says what?" he said.

Ice Diamonds and Snow Gold

Arthur made his way slowly down to the fence, climbed up and looked around. This part of the town was empty so he jumped over and hid behind a fence. All the wooden shacks were empty so Arthur pushed on, trying to find Jo. He climbed up onto the roof of a house and saw that at the end of the immense cavern was a large building; that rose above all the others. Arthur figured that this was the place he should head for since it was the only place with lights. He ran across the roofs of the houses and made his way to the building.

"You're putting a lot of effort into saving someone you believe you don't really care about" he said to himself. "She's a member of the royal family, doing nothing would be like treason by proxy, or something" he replied to himself. "You can believe that all you want, but you're beginning to like her" he said. "When did I start talking to myself?!" he shouted, and realised that he had probably alerted the whole town. Nothing stirred and he pushed on, thinking he must be going mad.

When Arthur reached the building he saw that is was as badly built as the others. He climbed up to the window and saw that in a room was Jo, tied to a chair. There were two other people in the room, a nasty looking guard and another person who was wearing similar clothes to Norso. Arthur couldn't hear what they were saying so he climbed over to another window, and saw a room with no one in it. He opened the window and climbed in. He closed the window and turned around.

The room was full of sacks, and Arthur took out his knife and ripped one open. He reached in and he felt rocks that were cold to the touch. He pulled them out and they were diamonds, but ice cold diamonds. He looked over the sacks and saw that there were bars of a white metal. Arthur put the handful of diamonds into his pocket and walked over to the bars. They were purely white, and he picked one up. It was gold, but snowy coloured gold. He put one of the bars into his other pocket. He heard someone coming out of the door and he ducked behind one of the larger sacks.

The two people walked out, and Arthur saw that the man had a straight dark beard and slicked-back hair. He wore a purple commander's uniform, and had silver epaulettes too. The man that walked behind him was a purple guard, and had on the usual obsidian armour. Arthur watched as the commander started talking to the guard. "You stay here and guard her, lost mountain climber my backside, she knows more than she's saying and looks just like Princess Josephine," he said, and walked off. The guard stood there in front of the door. Arthur thought about it, and then stood up.

"Good evening, how are you today?"asked Arthur. The guard was taken completely by surprise, and didn't know what to do. He went for his pistol, but Arthur punched him as hard as he could. The guard fell to the floor, but to Arthur's surprise he got back up and used his pistol to hit Arthur on the shoulder. Jo was tied up but she heard the sound of crashing outside the door, and wondered what was going on. Arthur barged the guard over to the door and grabbed a bar of snow gold, which he threw at the guard. It flew through the air and caught him square on the head. The guard flew back and smashed through the door, right to the feet of Jo.

Arthur walked through and leaned in the doorway. He had a black eye and his lip was bleeding.

"Hey, how are you?" he asked.

"Better than you I see," she said. Arthur untied Jo and tied up the guard. He took her to the room full of gold and sacks of diamonds. "What on earth do they have all these for, do you have any idea how rare these diamonds are?" she said.

"They're the second rarest and second most expensive gem there is," said Arthur.

"There's only one jewel that beats it, and that's Chrysalidium," said Jo.

"Yes, but I've never seen any of that before," said Arthur.

Jo put her hand in her chest and pulled out her necklace. It was a white glowing gem surrounded by gold, and was about the size of a grape. "Oh, I thought you were about to...never mind, that's beautiful and it must be worth a fortune," said Arthur.

"It is but we'll talk about it later we need to be getting out of here" said Jo.

Arthur couldn't leave all this wealth behind so he took as much as he could carry as did Jo, then with her help they hid it below the floorboards in another room and left it just in case they returned.

They ran for the door and ran straight for the roofs. Arthur ran as fast as he could and Jo followed him, surprised at how agile he was. Down underground it wasn't as dark as they would have expected, however it was not the temperature that was bothering Arthur but the thought of climbing up to the Nostradamus again. Arthur stopped, and changed his direction as he had seen something.

They ran between the place they had entered and the large building to the back of the cave. Arthur saw what appeared to be a tower which was lit up in the darkness, but in fact it was something else entirely. They got closer and Jo saw that it was a huge elevator, and Arthur was making for it because it seemed so much easier than climbing.

They reached the building that was built into the side of the cliff, and snaked up into the dark cave roof. Arthur looked around and saw that the lift was at the bottom of the cave, and the commander that they saw in the big building was going up. "He's going up and so are we, break down that metal grate and climb in the shaft." said Arthur.

"We're going on the top?" asked Jo.

"Yes, now, quickly before we get stranded down here," he said.

Jo pulled the grate off the cage that the elevator went up and down in. Arthur then slipped in and Jo followed. They stood on a ledge watching the rope shake as the people got in.

"Now when it comes right to us, you don't want them to hear us jumping on it," said Arthur.

"I know," said Jo.

The rope went taut, and it started to move upwards. When it got to them, they walked on it as quietly as they could. The lift carried on ascending, and as they looked out they could see the whole cave, and all the tiny houses and shacks that lay on the floor.

Below them they heard the sound of two people talking. Arthur listened in, and he heard the conversation they were having. "So tell me again what all the ice diamonds and snow gold is for," said one.

"It's for cold fusion fuel; her majesty thinks that by fusing cold diamonds together and using the gold as a snowy insulator, then it will create a super fuel for the machine," said the other.

"Oh, well I guess that makes sense," he said.

Then the conversation got really interesting. "She's going to go nuts if she finds out that Princess Josephine was here and that she escaped. Not to mention Sir Arthur Pageon," said the guard.

"Nobody tells her, as far as we know nothing happened here and she'll get her delivery of ice diamonds and snow gold," said the commander.

They arrived at the top, and Arthur saw that there was a large vent that was blowing cold air. Arthur pointed up, and Jo nodded. They climbed up the vent, with Jo going first and Arthur going behind. The vent was at a diagonal angle, and they climbed for about ten minutes until the vent levelled out. They continued going until they reached the end; Jo pushed on the frozen vent and found that they had ended up outside the walls of Icester.

"Up there, there's some stairs so we can climb up and get back to the ship," said Arthur.

"OK but you lead, since you've been here before," said Jo. They walked across some flat wasteland, and found that here the snowstorm was worse. They reached the mountains, and Arthur found the old frozen staircase. Suddenly they heard the moaning sound again, and it echoed through the mountains.

"Umm, still think that that's the wind?" asked Jo.

"If I said it was a snow monster, then you would probably overreact," said Arthur.

"Why did you have to say snow monster?" asked Jo, now trembling, but not from the cold. They continued up the stairs, and to take her mind off snow monsters, she began to count the steps. When she reached two hundred with no end in sight she started to worry.

"You know, you can take that idea that I'm a defenceless rich girl out of your head right now," said Jo.

"I'm sorry?" he asked.

"If there was a chance of there being a snow monster out there then it's perfectly logical to be alert, or in my case just a little frightened" she replied.

"I never said a word, but maybe you should ask yourself what you are really afraid of," said Arthur cryptically. Jo couldn't think of an appropriate reply so she remained quiet.

"How much further is it?" asked Jo.

"We're about halfway, are you getting tired?" he asked.

"No I'm good, I was just wondering since we've been climbing for a while," she replied. They continued up the stairs that were carved into the rock wall, and which offered no protection from the sheer drop on the other side. They suddenly heard the moan again, however this time it sounded more like a roar and it seemed closer. Jo was now very frightened, and she clutched onto Arthur as tightly as she could, and wouldn't move. "I'm not moving," she said.

"We're not that far away now, come on," he said.

"Why aren't you scared?" she asked.

"There's a cave over there, let's go in and we can talk," he said.

Inside the cave, they sat down by the wall, while Arthur lit a small fire.

"So tell me, why aren't you scared?" she asked.

"If I was scared then we would both be sunk. At least with me not losing hope, you won't completely lose yours," he replied.

"So you're being a tough guy for me?" she asked.

"Yes, I am, now tell me why you're so scared," he said.

"When I was little I had a rather traumatic experience at the dance school in Ashin," she said.

"Tell me about it," said Arthur.

39

"I was in a room with two other students, Lady Julia and Lady Josette, this was before she became the ruler of the city of Adlin," she explained.

"How old were you at the time?" he asked.

"I was 130, that's the only age you could study at the school until it changed," she said.

"Did you know about the Red Coven then?" he asked.

"I'm getting to that," said Jo.

"OK, carry on," said Arthur, who was happy that Jo didn't seem as scared as she was before.

"Anyway, they kept telling me scary stories, and one night I woke up to find that they had all gone. Being young and impressionable at the time I went to look for them. There was something funny about the way the place was, it was painted in really stark colours and all the fixtures were too high to reach," she explained.

"So, did you find them?" he asked.

"No, the rest of that night is a bit of a blank, though I remember seeing a horrible face, it was all furry and had big red eyes and fangs," she said.

"So you're worried about a similar creature being up here in these mountains?" he asked.

Just as he asked, they heard the roar and crunching sounds from outside the cave. Arthur kicked the fire out and covered Jo, who was so scared that she hid her head in Arthur's coat. She heard the sound of something entering the room, but didn't dare to look up. She then heard the sound of it leaving the room, and then she finally looked up. "Is it gone?" she asked, but Arthur was just staring at the cave entrance. "What was it?" she asked.

"I, I, I don't know, it was too dark," he said.

"We need to leave, now" she said. They both got up and slowly moved out of the cave. Any footprints were gone from the path, due to the snow.

After climbing up the rest of the stairs they made it to the Nostradamus, and Jo couldn't wait to get back in. They climbed up to the banister, but something horrifying had happened. Part of the banister had been ripped off, and now all that was left was bits of wood and some deep footprints in the snow.

"That thing was up here; let's get out of these mountains while we still have the chance" said Jo, who scrambled through the snow for the door. She banged on the door but there was no reply from Corky. "Corky it's us, you can open up" shouted Jo. Arthur was standing by the broken banister looking at the damage when he heard the sound of roaring coming from the path.

Corky opened the door, holding a blunderbuss. "Come in quickly, before that thing comes back," said Corky. Jo ran inside but Arthur stayed outside. "This is no time for heroics sir, let's leave this accursed place now," said Corky.

"Give me the gun, and start the ship so were ready to lift off" said Arthur. Corky handed the single barrelled gun to Arthur and ran into the cabin. Arthur waited for the creature to come up the path again, and he felt the ship whirr to life.

Jo ran out to join him. "What are you going to do?" she asked.

"Get over to that searchlight, turn it on but don't point it until I say," he said. Jo ran over and activated the large light which warmed up and cast its light onto the floor.

Arthur waited, and when he saw a black shadow in the darkness over by the path he shouted for Jo to turn the light. She did and the ship began to take off, because Corky had misunderstood Arthur's command. For a split second Jo and Arthur saw a large black furry shape with glowing red eyes. It put its arms up to shield its eyes from the light and as they pulled farther and farther away, the less they could see.

Back in the ship Arthur dusted the snow off and put the gun back on the mantelpiece where it belonged. "You see, it is real!" shouted Jo.

"I still doubt that there could be a monster there, it was probably someone in a costume," said Arthur.

"How can you still not believe what you have seen with your own eyes?" she asked. "Any creature like that would be constantly seen moving about or stalking its prey. I just don't believe in anything like that actually existing without anyone knowing or seeing it," he replied.

"And what do you mean costume, nobody is that stupid to dress up like a monster," said Jo.

"You'd be surprised," replied Arthur, as they left the mountains and flew south over the Acacia Forest to Proceur.

The Panicked Populace of Proceur

The city of Proceur was founded in the Green Shade Valley by some former inhabitants of Gard that wanted to leave the smoke-polluted mining city and live a more harmonious existence with nature. They built a large wall around the mouth of the valley and built acacia wood houses, since at the time there was no law against cutting down the trees. They began with planting simple crops but soon discovered that the soil was perfect for growing grapes, barley, hops and wheat so they turned into a brewing city. After building the largest brewery in Discoucia they became famous for their Nature's Ale and their other export, Blue Whisky. The people became prosperous, but they used the money to build new waterways and alternative technology that didn't pollute or belch out foul smoke.

The main street of Proceur stretches up to the main bridge and in the other direction is the main gate that has a road along it on the other side, and then the Acacia Forest stretches far off into the distance like a green ocean. Either side of the main street are the houses where the residents of Proceur live. Their houses have the most beautiful gardens, which have the most fragrant flowers used in the fermentation of Blue Whisky. The City is ruled by Lord Artlintone, or at least it was the last time Arthur visited the city, and he lives in the majestic Hilltop House, which is built out of blue and white marble similar to the city of Adlin in the north.

The Nostradamus landed in the massive cobblestone square near the main gate. The place was deserted, and Arthur walked out onto the deck and scanned around. It was a long trip from Icester and the sun was setting in the east, behind the mountains, and the streetlights were beginning to illuminate the empty street.

"So, that component you removed from the back of the machine, why did it lead us here," asked Jo.

"That's something I thought I covered on our long trip," replied Arthur.

"For the readers Artie," she said sarcastically.

"Oh right, well on the back it read that this was one of two, and since Professor Claudio said that it was to be used to scare superstitious locals, then where better than the forcefully undeveloped city of Proceur?" he asked.

"I can't think of anywhere to be honest," she replied.

"In that case, I assume that all the locals have retired, and that fog bank creeping its way across the floor and up the street may have something to do with it," said Arthur. Sure enough the fog was creeping closer to the ship, but seemed to be staying about a foot high, and not going everywhere like in Karga.

"What do you suppose we do?" asked Jo.

"I don't know about you, but I'm going for a walk," he said.

"I'll stay here and wait for you, I've got some tidying up to do" she said.

Arthur vaulted over the wooden banister and rolled onto the cobblestone street, causing wisps of fog to roll around him. He stood up, dusted himself off and walked down the street. He stopped, and Jo watched as Arthur knelt down and waved his hand through the fog. "It's warm," he shouted. Jo waved back and walked into the sitting room. Arthur continued to walk down the street and disappeared out of Jo's sight.

She looked around the sitting room and pulled out a book on 'Horticultural Engineering' but it stuck halfway out and clicked. The bookcase slipped open, and she found that a safe was built into the wall behind it. At this point Jo saw a potential challenge and put her ear to the safe and clicked the dial. When she heard two clicks she opened it up and she saw that the size of the door bore no relation to the size of the actual inside of the safe. There were ten gold bars, and a blue silk bag that was filled with jewels. What attracted Jo's attention were the papers that lay beneath the gold and platinum jewellery. She pulled out one of them, and it was a letter from someone only known as 'A'. She read the letter and her eyes widened as she discovered something about Arthur that she never would have guessed.

"Jo! I need help now!" came Arthur's voice from outside. She threw the paper back in and slammed the safe door shut, and closed the bookcase. After running outside onto the deck, she saw Arthur running down the street clutching someone in his arms.

"What? What is it?" she shouted back. Arthur reached the ship and pushed the person up, who was revealed to be a young girl of about 80. Jo pulled her up and Arthur stayed standing, looking down the street.

"What were you running from?" she asked the girl.

"A Monster!" she replied, shaking.

"Did it have glowing yellow eyes? asked Jo.

"It was so tall! Look, there it is!" said the girl, and Jo saw that a figure just like the one she saw in Karga was slowly advancing up the street. It stopped about five feet from Arthur, and just stood there, its body indistinguishable from the darkness that enveloped it.

"So, who might you be?" asked Jo, as Arthur climbed aboard.

"This is Dahlia, who was breaking this new curfew law put in place by Lady Elain, who replaced Lord Artlintone," explained Arthur.

"I didn't think he had any family," said Jo.

"He didn't, that's why I am a little suspicious of this whole setup," he replied.

"So what do we do now?" asked Jo.

"Do you want to go home, Dahlia?" asked Arthur.

"Yes, but how? That thing is guarding the road," she replied.

"Then I'll distract it while you and Jo go over the rooftops" he said.

"Are you mad? That will never work," said Jo.

"Do you have a better idea? It's made out of cast iron and by my reckoning it can withstand a bullet, so I really can't think of anything else to do," he explained.

"How are you going to distract it?" asked Jo.

"I'll be back in a second," he said, and walked into the sitting room leaving the two girls watching the black figure. Arthur returned with a powerful looking rifle, and he rested it on the decking aimed at the figure.

"I thought you said that bullets wouldn't work." said Dahlia.

"Sometimes, when you're facing an adversary that thinks it's invulnerable, a large dent in its armour will have to do," he said.

"Is that a metaphor?" asked Jo.

"Well, if someone knows that you're going to fight instead of being scared of what they put in front of you, they become less of a barrier and more cautious of you," he replied.

And with that Arthur aimed directly at the head of the creature, and pulled the trigger. The gun kicked, a bang filled the silent air and echoed all around the valley. The creature was hit on the top of its head and the bullet caused what appeared to be a helmet to fly off, exposing the inside. The creature walked forward, then backward, and then fell onto the floor with lights sparking out of its eyes.

"I wasn't expecting that," said Arthur.

"You killed it!" said Dahlia.

"I'm not really sure that it was alive in the first place, do I look like a murderer?" replied Arthur.

"You're the one holding the gun," she replied.

"I like her," said Jo.

By now a crowd of people streamed out of their houses to see the fallen creature. "Grandpa!" shouted Dahlia. She climbed down from the ship and ran to a man who was looking at the creature. Arthur ran down too, and Jo saw them talking to each other. Arthur pointed at the creature and four men helped him carry it into a hall at the end of one side of the street. Jo decided to lock the door of the sitting room and follow Arthur to the hall.

Jo walked into the hall and saw several villagers crowding around something in the centre of the room. She wandered over to Arthur's side and saw that he was disconnecting several wires from the creature's head. In the bright light of the hall the creature could be clearly seen. It was in the shape of a man, and its body was made

46

of metal, painted in black. There were hundreds of rivets holding it together, and it was 10 ft tall from its feet to its head. Arthur yanked out a long thick copper wire from its head, and the creature jolted. Apart from Jo and Arthur all the villagers jumped back, but saw that it was just a nervous twitch.

"So, it's a robot?" asked Jo.

"Just like one of those clockwork toys from when I was a kid," said Arthur.

"Only this one can smash granite," said Jo.

"You see, the copper wire that was connected to a brain seems to be part of a remote control, and whoever is controlling it must be somewhere up high, so they can have a better signal, and so they can see what they are doing," said Arthur.

"Explain what you mean by 'remote control'" said Dahlia's grandfather, who was nicknamed Magpie since he had a habit of finding silver when they were digging over a new field. He was also Lord Artlintone's head gardener, and was seen as a head man in the city.

"Well, it means that someone could be standing all the way on the other side of the valley, and be controlling this here by pressing a load of buttons. They wouldn't have to be close, and by extension they wouldn't be implicated in any crime that was committed. But it seems that the only thing that this little devil was being used for was keeping you in at night," explained Arthur.

"I see, so what do we do now?" asked Magpie.

"Dismantle this thing so it can't be reactivated, and I suppose there really isn't much we can do until the morning so I'll say goodnight and meet you outside my ship about 6.00," said Arthur.

"That's fine with me, I'll bring all my best men, and hopefully we can sort things out once and for all," said Magpie.

Arthur and Jo left and walked back to the ship.

An Uprising Down South

The sun rose above the verdant valley, and the flowers were blooming in the beautiful gardens. However, this would be a different day than one the people of Proceur were used to, as a group of men walked towards the Nostradamus. Jo descended the stairs and entered the sitting room, where Arthur was sat at his desk. He was tinkering with a pile of gears and wires, but didn't seem to be getting anywhere with them.

"What are you doing?" asked Jo.

"Nothing really, I got bored; I think we should go to Chene after this, I need a laugh," said Arthur.

"I would love that, I haven't been there for years," she replied.

"Oh good, is there anywhere you want to see?" he asked.

"I always wanted to stay at The Paradise Hotel and to visit Princess Mona, since she will only see royalty," said Jo.

"Why does she do that?" asked Arthur.

"I think that she's very stuck up, which is strange for someone so young," she explained.

"Would she see me?" asked Arthur.

"I don't know to be honest, there's only one way to find out," she replied.

"Okay, it's Chene next then," said Arthur.

"Sir Pageon, were ready," shouted Magpie from outside. Arthur joined all the men outside, and they planned what they were going to

49

do. Arthur looked into the distance and saw Hilltop House, and asked them about what they knew.

"One night they moved in, they came with three flying ships and the next thing we knew, we were under the rule of Lady Elain," said Magpie.

"So what happened to Lord Artlintone?" asked Jo.

"He died quietly in the night, but there was no funeral, and he was taken away, and we began to be ruled with curfews and forced work," he explained.

"I want to go there, but I guess that it's guarded," said Arthur.

"Of course, there is no way to get in," said Magpie.

"Well that's really not true, I have an idea but I would like you to create a big disturbance that will cause as many of the guards as possible to leave the house," said Arthur.

"And what are you going to do?" asked Magpie.

"I'm going to leave, and fly off into the North," he said.

"You're leaving us?!" asked Magpie, stunned.

"As far as Lady Elain and her guards are concerned, I shall leave, and that way I'm no longer a threat," replied Arthur.

"Then what are you going to do?" he asked.

"You'll see, all you need to do is focus on distracting the guards, I'll leave you to think of something interesting," replied Arthur.

Arthur climbed aboard the ship, and she lifted off the ground, blowing dust everywhere. They watched as the ship flew north, across the green ocean of acacia trees until it was out of sight.

Jo was left with the people, and she helped them in their plans for distraction. It was mid afternoon when they exacted their plan. A guard walked past the large stone stairs that extended up to Hilltop House, and didn't at all expect the potato that flew through the air and cracked him square on the side of the head. Since the guards were not used to the citizens fighting them, they both turned around to see that a large amount of people were standing in the streets around them. They didn't know what to do, and one of the guards decided to run up the stairs, shouting for other guards to help. The other guard just stood, aiming his rifle at different people in a worried fashion.

Magpie and Jo walked forward, and stared at the frightened guard. "We want to see Lady Elain" said Jo.

"You can't!" he replied.

"Why?" asked Magpie

"You just can't, now return to your homes!" he shouted.

"No, not until we see Lady Elain," said Jo.

At this point a battalion of guards appeared down the stairs, all carrying rifles, and wearing white uniforms.

"By order of Lady Elain, you people must disperse" shouted one of the guards that had recently turned up.

"Make us" shouted Magpie.

"I will shoot!" he shouted, and all of the men cocked their rifles.

"If you shoot any one of these people, then the 200 of us will take down the 20 of you, and those gun's aren't instantly reloadable, so what chance do you think you possibly have?" asked Jo. The guards shuffled nervously as the truth of what Jo said slowly hit them like a flying potato.

Above them, a large explosion was heard, and The Nostradamus flew out from behind the house, and was followed by another ship. They had a duel in the sky, and the ships whizzed around firing side cannons at each other, but they missed each time. The Nostradamus flew out over the walls and out over the flatland that led to the mountains. The ship fired at its enemy, and its back engines blew out, causing it to fly at the mountains. It skidded onto a slope, and all of the crew jumped out and ran just before the ship exploded. The Nostradamus flew back, and all the guards ran back up the stairs. The people watched as another ship flew out from behind the house, and once the guards had gone out of sight another appeared, and followed the other into the east, as the sun was now dimming and the pink moon rose. They were parallel to the mountains, and once they were reduced to tiny dots on the horizon they were gone.

Out above the wastes Arthur and the other ship nearly collided, and he ran out as Corky steered it expertly so that the two ships never touched. Arthur drew his sword and pistol that he hardly ever used and was greeted by the seldom seen Lady Elain who jumped from her ship to his. She wore a similar ensemble to Jo, but hers was much looser and was mainly blue.

"You shouldn't have come here Sir Arthur!" she shouted, staring him down while her curly blonde hair flew like a flag behind her.

"I was under the impression that you were a lady, but you fight like a man!" he shouted back as the clash of steel was drowned out by the roar of the ships engines.

"Maybe you should be more focused on what your opponent is doing instead of what she should be doing!" she shouted, and lashed at him with her rapier.

Gravity then took over as Corky tilted the ship and Arthur felt the fine tip of the blade graze his left eyelash. He however was holding on to the banister but she fell down into the open air beneath, only to smash straight into the gunship as it flew over and off to the west and the still lingering darkness of the moon.

A cheer went up from the people, and Magpie, accompanied by Jo ascended the stairs of the now deserted house. They found that Arthur had docked the ship and with the help of Corky had taken something from Lady Elain's room. The house was in a mess, with bottles and other rubbish strewn across the floor. Doors were knocked off their hinges and interior windows were broken. The wall paper was torn and some of the paintings were either thrown on the floor in the corridors or had large holes in them.

"Look at the state of the place, Lord Artlintone would be turning in his grave," said Magpie.

"Not exactly," said Arthur, who appeared out of a dark room. He turned the light on, and they saw that Lord Artlintone was laid in bed, fast asleep.

"They drugged him I think," said Arthur.

"Have they really gone?" asked Magpie.

"I believe so, and when he wakes up you can tell him that the evil that was holding your city is now gone," said Arthur.

"How can we repay you for setting our town free?" he asked.

"A crate of Blue Whisky wouldn't go amiss, if I'm honest," said Arthur.

"Consider it done," said Magpie.

"Oh, and there's one more thing, but can I discuss it with you in private?" asked Arthur.

"Yes of course" said Magpie. They closed the door and Jo heard them muttering something indistinguishable, and Jo just caught Magpie saying, "It's the least we can do." They opened the door, and said their goodbyes to Magpie and Dahlia.

"So what did you get from Lady Elain's bedroom?" asked Jo.

"Follow me upstairs," said Arthur. They ascended the stairs and Arthur took Jo into the expansive wardrobe, and she saw what he had taken from it.

"You took her personal wardrobe?" she asked.

"That's what she was spending the money on, the money that she got from selling the ale and whisky" said Arthur.

"What did you get it for?" she asked.

"I got it for you," he said. Jo was speechless; she didn't expect Arthur to do something like this.

"Won't the people in Proceur be annoyed?" she asked.

"Actually, Magpie said it would be a good idea to get rid of them, since it would only make everyone angrier than they already were," he replied.

"Thank you so much, I never expected this. But this still doesn't mean that I fully trust you," she said.

"If you say so, you get acquainted with your new present, and I'm going downstairs to write a report for your father," said Arthur.

"Where are we going to next?" she asked.

"I found this in the house," said Arthur. Jo took the piece of paper that Arthur had, and she began to read it aloud. "'Commander Elsius to oversee conversion in Starfall Academy'," she read.

"So, were going to Starfall Academy for the rich and intelligent to find out what's going on," said Arthur.

"OK, that sounds like it's going to be another chapter in our already strange adventure," said Jo.

The ship flew off to Gard, leaving the City of Proceur peaceful once again, and all of its inhabitants grateful for the timely intervention of Sir Arthur Pageon and Princess Josephine.

Starfall Academy

The ship flew around the edge of the Southern Mountains, and since it was getting dark, they saw the lights of Gard ahead. The city of Gard is known for its many fantastic buildings, and its even more fantastic mines. After settling on the mountains the settlers from Elowe began to mine. They prospered much more because they could settle above while the people of Elowe had Evermore above them. The city grew fast and is known to have the greatest army, and the greatest wealth of all the cities. It is currently ruled by Lord Yage, who has plenty of women, though only had the one wife. Lady Sylvia divorced him when Yage threw a bottle at her, which missed but it didn't matter as the damage was done. Sylvia left for Seraphale Island and has begun to build her castle which she has named Alectrona Castle. Taking her nineteen daughters and a third of Lord Yage's fortune, she and her next fifty descendants will be wealthy no matter what.

The main landmarks of Gard are the palace, which is incredibly huge and beneath it is the treasure vault, and Starfall Academy. However the academy doesn't really belong to Gard as it sits above the city, nestled between the thunder scarred peaks. It silently stares down to the city below while its purple bricks are illuminated every night by the many lights of the city. It is an academy for the very rich and the very intelligent, two things that rarely go hand in hand. The academy has been very quiet lately, darkened windows and silence all around the valley.

No trees grow there and it is the site of a much older town that was demolished for the building of the academy. It was known as Dark City and was home to some rather odd people that disappeared overnight and the next day the whole place was empty. Not much evidence was left for the few people that went there looking for an explanation aside from the lack of personal items suggesting a mass exodus, but a mass exodus from what?

"What's your plan then? How are we supposed to get into the academy?" asked Jo.

"I don't know to be honest, this one's going to be tough," said Arthur. The ship landed on the far left side of the valley, and it sat, about half a mile from the academy, but about 20 feet from the cliff edge that descended down to Gard.

"We need to think of something," said Jo.

"I think I'm going to do what I always do in these situations," said Arthur.

"Go on," she said. "

I'm going for a walk on my own, that way I can think of something to do and it's not because of you since I think better on my own," he said.

"Okay, I'm going to look through Lady Elain's wardrobe," she said.

"I'll see you later," he replied, and walked off outside.

It was very warm, since they were in the south in midsummer, and Arthur walked over to the newly repaired banister then jumped over to the ground. It was very rocky but Arthur was experienced at climbing, so he ambled across the landscape to a large rocky outcrop that rose up out of the ground, and gave him a good view of the academy.

After walking for about twenty minutes, he reached the base of the rock, and looked up. One side was illuminated by the bright lights of Gard, and he swore that he saw a girl at the top. After rubbing his eyes and thinking that he must be dreaming he began to climb. The stone had lots of places to climb, and he found it quite enjoyable to reach the summit. After a while climbing, he reached a small plateau, and a warm breeze blew over it. He then saw the girl, who was sitting on a rock, quite pleasantly.

"Good evening," he said.

"Good evening," she replied.

"How did you get up here?" he asked.

"I flew," she replied, walking out of the shadows so that Arthur could see her better. She had long light brown hair and wore a simple blue dress with a big white bow on the front.

"Oh, and do you plan on flying back Miss?" he asked.

"Archie; it's nice to meet you, Sir Arthur," she replied.

"Are you a witch?" he asked.

"I'm not holding a broomstick you know, anyway I have a present for you and Princess Josephine" she said, holding out a blue box with a white bow on it.

"Oh, is this a bomb?" he asked.

"Is it ticking?" she asked.

"No, it's sloshing," he replied.

"Have you ever heard of nitro-glycerine? It's a liquid explosive and shaking it could blow your head off," she said, without a note of concern on her face.

"On the bright side if it goes, we both go," he replied.

"I think I'm gonna like you, Arthur. My full name is Archaelia D'Angelo Mysterioso but call me Archie," she said.

"That's a guy's name, though I suppose it's short for Archaelia" he said.

"Look, I just wanted to give you this and now I have to go, unobtainable, unreachable and unnecessarily enigmatic. We'll meet again and you'll probably want to know more," she said, stepping away from Arthur.

"I barely know you, and I have problems enough with that stuck up strawberry field's bimbo down there," he said.

"That's no way to talk about your partner, besides I guess she doesn't talk about you the same way to other people," she said.

"If you would have been watching the previous couple of weeks you would have seen how much of a pretentious do-nothing condescending..." but Archie put her hand on his shoulder and he suddenly felt funny. He felt as though all his anger was a red cloud and was slowly changing to blue cool waters.

The girl then faded out of view right in front of Arthur. He felt like this was all a dream, and looked at the box quizzically. After shaking it up and down he heard the sound of water sloshing around inside a bottle. He slipped it into his jacket pocket and looked down for a way to get back to the ship.

Arthur made his way back to the ship and he saw that it was still very dark. This was a special time in the Discoucian year, when the sun would not rise for three days. The whole world would be in darkness until the sun rose again though it was hard to tell when, since most of the clocks in Discoucia were based around the sun. "I was only gone for about an hour," he thought to himself as he climbed back aboard the ship, but when he looked at his watch which was powered by a solar crystal, it had in fact been several hours. When he got back into the cabin Jo was fast asleep on the settee.

Arthur sat down at his desk and began to open the box. Jo awoke to the sound of Arthur sitting down, and she walked over to him sleepily. "Where were you? It's been ages, but it's a little hard to tell since it's Tridark Time again," she said.

"I was looking around from above at the academy and I could see no lights, and I met a witch up there," he said.

"Oh, you did, did you? Is that the reason you took so long?" she asked.

"I think so, she gave me this," said Arthur, unravelling the bow.

He opened the box, and inside was a small blue bottle and a piece of paper. Jo took the bottle and studied it, while Arthur read the note. "I got this idea from Alice in Wonderland though I've changed it a bit to suit the situation, but it will help you get into the academy without sticking out too badly. Drink one teaspoon of the liquid but don't waste it, and when you're finished take another teaspoon and you shall be back to normal, A'."

"So this is the gift from your witch, and what do we do?" asked Jo.

"I think she could be the real deal, because I never mentioned anything about what were going to do, and she disappeared into thin air. Also when you asked me if I had met a god before, I have," said Arthur.

"I knew it, and was this witch the same person?" she asked.

"She looked similar, though she was accompanied by a young girl the first time and had longer hair," he explained.

"And we should trust her for no reason, right? It could be poison," she said.

"Why would she want to poison me? Look I'll take it first and that way if it is poison you can tell your father and he can catch her for murder, deal?" asked Arthur.

"I wouldn't ask this of anyone, not even Lilia, but if you're willing to risk your life for this" she said, and handed Arthur a teaspoon from the side. Arthur poured the liquid carefully out and put the bottle back on the desk. He drank the bright blue drink and it tasted like sweet fruits and was so nice that he wanted more, but knew he couldn't.

After a couple of seconds Arthur looked at Jo, who looked at him astonished, and he saw that she had begun to grow taller.

"Arthur, you're, you're, cute," she said.

"Huh what are you talking about, when did you get taller?" he asked, looking around.

Jo then confirmed the obvious. "I'm not taller, you're shorter," she replied.

Arthur walked over to a mirror and saw that he had become younger, about 100 years younger. His clothes were too big for him, and he pulled his trousers up, which made Jo laugh.

"This is perfect, you drink it and we'll be kids again and we can fit into the academy like the other students!" he said.

"Hmm, the chance to be young again for a couple of days, try and stop me," she said, picking up the teaspoon.

"Wait a second, I think I should get changed first, and then I'll get my sisters old dress from when she was 100, and you can wear that. It's probably the only thing that will not be too big for you anyway," he said.

"Go on then, but be quick, I can't wait," she replied.

Arthur carefully made his way upstairs, and after about five minutes came down again in a smaller version of his blue ensemble carrying the purple dress for Jo.

"Now go outside," she said.

"Whatever you say" he said and walked outside, and had to reach up to the door handle which was higher than before. As Arthur walked out he was met by Corky.

"Hello lad, are you from the academy?" he asked.

"Guess again, Cornelius," replied Arthur in a deadpan sarcastic tone.

"Well I've seen some strange things while I've been your driver but this beats them all, what have you done now?" he asked.

"Well, since were infiltrating Starfall Academy we needed to be kids, and a witch gave me the means to do that. Absurd, I know, but there you go," he said.

"Ok, is Princess Josephine a child too?" he asked.

"Yes, she is," said a much younger Jo, who walked out of the cabin and stood next to Arthur. Jo was wearing the purple dress that Lilia used to have, and it fitted her perfectly.

"You two do whatever this is and I'll see you in the morning," he said.

"That's three days away and I trust your going to one of the pubs in Gard?" he said.

"Obviously," replied Corky.

"In that case, I'll fly the ship away if anything happens," said Arthur.

"See you later, little sir" replied Corky, who set off down the path to the streets of Gard.

"What a pleasant fellow he is," said Arthur

Discoucian Horror Story

Arthur and Jo began to walk towards Starfall Academy. "What do you know of the academy?" asked Jo.

"Nothing much, it was built about fifty years ago and has been a secretive place ever since. But all the students that attend come out as geniuses at the end of their education so they must be doing something right," said Arthur.

"Don't you think that this is all a bit surreal? I mean, were kids again and that's great but when you really look at it, it's a little strange," said Jo.

"Yes I agree with what you're saying, but if we question everything that goes on it loses some of its magic don't you think?" he asked.

"I suppose so, how does it feel to you?" she asked.

"Since I know everything I did when I was older, it feels weird being a kid and an adult at the same time," he said.

They were getting closer to the school and they saw that it had a porch surrounding the whole bottom floor, and the roof of the porch was held up by purple brick columns that shone in the reflected light of Gard. Behind the porch were the dark windows that had no light at all and looked out at the two walkers like cold, empty eyes.

"This place looks a bit evil don't you think?" asked Jo.

"Yes but thankfully were both sensible adults that won't be put off by mere appearances," replied Arthur.

"Are we?" she asked.

"Yes, yes we are," he replied, and they carried on walking to the building. When they reached the front door, Jo was about to knock, but Arthur stopped her.

"We're trying to sneak in," he said.

"Oh, so we go in round the back?" she asked.

They walked along the porch and past the windows. Arthur put his hand to the window and tried to see in but it was all black inside. "Either the room is empty, or there are tinted windows," said Arthur.

"And if they are tinted windows, then you may have just peered in on a class full of kids and not known it," she replied.

"Yes, you're quite right, and if you are in fact right then we're through the looking glass here," he said.

"Thanks for the cheery conversation," she said.

They continued along the porch until they were out of the light and it began to become pitch black, now that they had lost the light of Gard. "Here's a door, but how do we get in?" asked Jo.

"It's probably locked," said Arthur.

"I can't think of a reason why it would be unlocked," said Jo. The door then creaked ominously open, and inside was as dark as outside.

"You first," said Jo.

"Why me? I thought it was ladies first," said Arthur.

"That's only in safe situations now get in there boy," she said.

"Yes girl, if you insist," he replied, and was about to walk in.

"You know this just proves my point that," but she couldn't finish as Arthur pulled her into the corridor.

It was warmer in the corridor, but that made it no less eerie. Arthur looked around, but didn't want to turn a torch on for fear of alerting someone. He walked along the dark corridor, and heard a click! It was only Jo closing the door behind her. Arthur put his finger to his lips in a gesture to be quiet. Jo nodded in the gloom, and she tiptoed along the floor to join Arthur. From what they could see the corridor was small, and there were multiple doors on either side. Arthur tried a door handle and it was stuck. The whole building was quiet; however there was a sound, a very quiet sound, and Arthur put his head to the ground to listen. Jo walked straight into him and fell on top, and instead of shouting, she began to hear the sound as well. It was a humming, and it seemed to be coming from below the floor. They got up, and carried on down the stuffy corridor. There was no light coming from anywhere, and the whole place was an overload of creepy.

After walking slowly along the corridor they felt that they had entered a larger room, since it was cooler in here. Arthur's eyes were beginning to get adjusted to the gloom, and he could make out a staircase, and that he was standing on a carpet. The windows let in no light, and it was pitch black all around, for Jo at least. She was beginning to get a seed of fear, and it was starting to grow. Arthur looked over, and thought he saw something moving at the top of the staircase. It was so dark that he couldn't be sure, as he couldn't hear anything. In the dark all his other senses were sharpened, but the humming was the only constant sound he could hear.

Jo had now become more frightened, and she grabbed Arthur's hand. Though she didn't remember his hand being so knobbly, and she squeezed it.

"Arthur," she whispered, but she didn't get the reply she wanted. She felt something hiss on her face and ran blindly into the open. "ARTHUR!!!" she shouted, and the silence was broken by an ear-splitting gunshot, and the shattering of glass. Light poured in from outside, and for a second Jo saw what she had taken the hand of. It was a short creature with black eyes and long arms, and at the first sign of light it ran up the stairs. "Arthur, come here!" she shouted. Arthur walked over and she grabbed him and didn't let go.

"Come on, it's gone now," said Arthur.

"Let's get out of here" she said.

"Yes, but were coming back, and next time we'll be better equipped" he said. Arthur jumped out of the window, and was surprised about how much more energy he had, and Jo followed who was just as surprised. They ran back to the ship, and as they did, two glowing yellow eyes watched them from an upper window.

Back in the ship, Arthur was getting every portable torch he had, and Jo was sat on the settee, shivering. "I'm not going back there," she said.

"Then by all means stay in the ship, but are you really going to leave me to go in all on my own?" he asked.

"I'll think about it," she said.

"If you want to wait until morning, you will be in for a long wait, and besides, it was probably a student in a goofy costume," he said.

"It seemed real to me. What about that creature in the Icicle Mountains? That seemed real enough," asked Jo.

"I have no idea what that was, and I'm sure there's a perfectly logical explanation for it," said Arthur.

"I'm sure that was a dope in a costume as well," she said.

"I don't know why someone would be haunting somewhere as remote as there, but I'm sure we'll figure it out one day," said Arthur.

"Yes, but not with me hopefully," said Jo.

"What an oddly ominous thing to say," said Arthur.

"I didn't mean it like that," she said.

"No, of course not. But on a completely unrelated note, I'm ready," he said.

Arthur had made a backpack for Jo, which had two torches that extended out of it and rested on her shoulders. "Push this button and they will turn on, and you will light the place up, just remember to stand in a corner," he said.

"That way I'll light up the whole room?" she asked.

"You got it," he replied.

"And do I get to take my gun?" asked Jo.

"Sorry but they're little kids, evil little kids but little kids all the same. If you accidentally shoot one then you try explaining that one," he said.

"Once again you're right. Well can I at least take a bat?" she asked.

"We're all kids now, so I never said anything about not hitting them," he said. Jo pulled a bat from behind the settee, used for Zutorni, a sport invented in Evermore which involves hitting a ball as hard as you can in a confined arena, and then dodging the highly bouncy ball as it flies in all directions. If it goes through a small hole at the top of one of the walls, then the game is won. However, if a person is hit by the ball, their team loses ten points. If they dodge the ball successfully, they gain five points. The game leads to a lot of bruises.

Arthur and Jo walked to Starfall Academy once more, now much better prepared for the horrors that waited.

"Are you sure you're ready for this?" asked Arthur. Jo just patted the bat in her open palm, and Arthur knew that someone was going to get hurt. They finally reached the academy, and they saw that the window had been fixed, and there was no sign of it being broken.

"That was quick," said Arthur.

"You're telling me. Shall we go around the back?" asked Jo.

"I suppose we have to, I know we've lost the element of surprise, but at least we know which way we're going," he replied. Arthur led Jo around the back and the opened the door. The corridor was as dark as ever, but this time they were prepared for it.

"Turn yourself on, Jo," said Arthur.

"Just like normal then," she said, and pressed the button that extended from the backpack.

The corridor was lit up, and they both saw that they were walking through a large room, a very large room, and the walls were fake. They were wooden boards being held up by wooden planks. "This doesn't make much sense," said Jo.

"It does and it doesn't," said Arthur.

"Don't be enigmatic, it's very irritating," she said.

"Come on, let's see what's in the rest of this funhouse," said Arthur. They walked down the corridor and found that the bigger room they were last in didn't look so scary in the light.

"So, where did you see it?" asked Arthur.

"Over there by the staircase," said Jo.

Just as Jo finished talking, something ran down the stairs. It was big and made a horrible screaming noise. The only thing that they saw was its glowing yellow eyes. Jo instinctively swung her bat, but Arthur pulled her out of the way, and the light went everywhere. They heard a crashing sound and Arthur swung Jo around to see, and they saw another black robot, which had embedded itself into the wall. It was twitching, but not really moving.

Arthur reacted like lightning. He ran over to the robot and climbed up to its head. He then yanked off the plate behind its head and pulled out its brain, and Jo saw a load of wires sticking out. The robot then collapsed in an undignified heap on the floor. Jo walked over to it, and without warning she smashed the head even more with her bat, with Arthur standing with his eyes wide open.

"I'm sorry to shatter your revenge fantasy Josephine, but the thing that attacked you had black eyes and leathery green skin, and claws," he said.

"I know, I'm just taking my anger out on something else, I hated that one in Karga and I'm making up for lost time," she said.

"Whatever helps you sleep at night," he replied.

After Jo had been smashing for a while, Arthur looked around for a light switch. He found one, and the whole of the bottom floor lit up. The lights hurt their eyes, since they were slightly accustomed to the dark now. The second floor looked pretty dark so Arthur decided to check the upper floors. Jo went first this time because she had the light source. She knew that she would have to go first, but she preferred to be in charge of the light source. They climbed up the staircase, and the corridor they entered was as bad as the first. Arthur tried the first door, but it was locked. "Oh I've had enough of locked doors," he said, and took a run up, and bashed through the door. It gave way almost instantly, and the two were greeted with a strange sight.

The room was obviously a bedroom, and in the corner was a dejected looking girl. "Hello," said Arthur.

"Please, the light!" she shouted weakly. Jo turned the light off, and closed the door behind her. "

Who are you?" asked Jo.

"I'm Lady Rhylia, daughter of Lord Yage, who are you?" she replied.

"Sir Arthur Pageon and this is Princess Josephine," replied Arthur.

"You can't be, you're my age" she replied.

"We'll explain that to you later, right now we're here to help you," said Jo.

"What are you doing chained up?" asked Arthur, breaking off her manacles.

"Commander Elsius, she's mad, she's brainwashing us into being monsters," she said.

"Look Rhylia, I'm taking you to my ship and I want you to tell me all about it," said Arthur.

"I'm too weak to walk," she said.

"Then I'll carry you, are there any more people on this floor?" he asked.

"No, I'm the only one who hasn't succumbed yet, any other monsters in the academy are just students in costumes but they think that they are really monsters and so will be as dangerous," said Rhylia.

"Aren't you going to say I told you so?" asked Jo.

"No, I'm just thinking that we'll just have to chance it downstairs," said Arthur.

They left the room, and they heard the sound of something running down the corridor behind them. Arthur ran with Rhylia, and Jo ran behind him. They reached the staircase, and saw that the light had been turned off.

"Light up, Jo," said Arthur.

The light spread across the room, and for a split second, the room was full of monsters. They all looked different, some were ghostly creatures, and other's just looked horrible in general, but Arthur didn't stop to find out; he ran down the corridor and out with Rhylia still in his arms.

"Were out now, look at the beautiful lights of Gard," said Arthur. Rhylia was about 90, and she had light brown hair, and a white complexion due to being chained up in the dark. Her clothes were reduced to rags, and she tried to look, but the light hurt her now sensitive eyes.

"Take your time, you will get used to it," said Jo. Arthur picked her up and carried her to the ship. He pressed a button on the side that Jo had never noticed before, and a side panel opened. Arthur carried her into the ship and then up some stairs to the deck. Jo closed the door behind her and followed Arthur up the stairs to the deck. Arthur took Rhylia to the sitting room and laid her on the settee. Arthur didn't turn the lights on; he left the light of Gard to light the place up.

"I'm finally out of there," she said.

"So please explain what is going on, because this whole plot doesn't make much sense," said Arthur.

"It all began about a week ago; they have been fast, really fast. We were visited by Commander Elsius and we thought that she was just part of the army from Gard, since they often come to see what we were doing. Our head teacher, Miss Torcent, disappeared soon after and Elsius replaced her," explained Rhylia.

"So she took over that easily? How?" asked Jo.

"There were a couple of students that wanted power, and she promised them that which made them a little crazy. I tried to call home, but my father doesn't care; ever since he divorced my mother, he doesn't care about what any of his children do. It's mostly out of spite, and I was supposed to join her on Seraphale but I guess she wanted me to finish my studies first," said Rhylia.

"When we find out what is going on I'll take you to your mother," said Arthur.

"But you're my age, how is this even possible?" she asked.

"Just go with it," said Jo.

"I'm not going back in there!" said Rhylia.

"No you're not, I just need to know where I would likely be able to find Elsius," said Arthur.

"In the cellar, there's a lab there and they've been doing something down there all week," she said.

"You stay here with her Jo, and I'll go alone, that way if I get caught Rhylia here can still go to her mother," said Arthur.

"That's very noble of you" said Jo.

"It's the sort of things heroes do, stupid for the sake of stupid and when it works it's hailed as being heroic" he said.

"And when it fails?" she asked.

"Then you take Rhylia to her mother," he replied.

"Touché Arthur," she said.

"You can fly, can't you, Jo?" asked Arthur.

"I took my test a bit late but yes I can, why?" she replied.

"Here's what I want you to do," said Arthur, who began to relate the plan to her and Rhylia. Arthur ran out of the cabin, now filled with courage, and he left Rhylia in the capable care of Jo.

Arthur walked once more to the building; however this time he wanted to get to the cellar and looked around for a way to get in. He was looking by the chimney when he found what he was looking for; a metal grate that led to a set of stone stairs. Arthur then formulated a plan, and smiled inwardly about how clever he was. He opened the creaky grate and walked down. He jammed a screw in the hinge, so that the grate couldn't be shut after he entered. He walked down the dark stairs and saw that the door was open to the cellar. He walked in, and it was silent, except the humming was louder now that he was underground.

He leaned over for the light switch, and turned it on. The room lit up and a black shape ran upstairs. Arthur then went over to the light switch and pulled out a strange device of his own making. It was a portable welder and since the switches were metal, he welded it so it was permanently on. He tried the bulky switch but it wouldn't budge. He locked the door behind him and walked across the cellar. It was empty, though the humming sound seemed to be coming from a door over in the corner.

After seeing that the door was locked, he decided to have some fun with this house of horrors, and walked over to the stairs. There was a light switch, and Arthur turned it on. The stairway lit up and the shadow ran away again. "Where are you going to run when I've turned on all the lights?" asked Arthur in a calm and confident voice. He heard a hissing sound ahead, but still carried on, melting the light switch as he continued on. He made his way into the main room with the staircase, and turned the light switch on. The robot was still there, lying on the floor with wires sticking out of its head. Arthur fused the switch, and then saw that there were three possible places for him to go, the left, the right, or upstairs. He decided to light up the bottom floor, and walked to the sitting room.

The light switch was on the left of the doorway, and he found it quite easily. He turned it on and found that a 'monster' was asleep on the floor. It was not the one that Jo had seen before, but had four arms and a horrible -ooking face. He tied it up with some of the large reel of rope, and then pulled its face off. It was a young boy, with messy hair, and large bushy eyebrows. Arthur unlocked the main doors, and left him on the porch. He then closed the doors, so no other little monster could free him. Arthur walked into what had been the kitchen, and turned the light on, which revealed a foul sight. There was food strewn everywhere, and it was apparent what happens when you leave rich children on their own for a week. Arthur heard the sound of something moving, and he ran to the sound, and opened the door that led to the fake corridor that he had first entered. The light switch was incredibly easy to find, and Arthur really thought nothing of it, but someone was watching him.

Arthur heard something behind the fake corridor walls. He ran around, and someone was huddled in the centre, trying to hide from the light.

"Good evening," said Arthur.

"Get away from me!" she said. It was a female voice, and she was dressed as an old witch.

"I can't do that, what's your name?" he asked.

"Lady Susan," she said.

"From Cesta?" he asked.

"Yes," she said.

"Come on, obviously being a witch doesn't suit you, I'm taking everyone home," he said.

"Why?" she asked.

"Because it's the right thing to do, and I want to have a word with Elsius," he said.

"I'm the least of your worries here, you'll have to watch out of Corlio, all this power has gone to his head," she said.

"Oh, you mean Lord Yage's son, I hear he can be as temperamental as his father," said Arthur. The girl took her mask off, and she was actually quite beautiful, with long blonde hair, and a pale complexion just like Rhylia.

"Come on, let's get out of this mad house, you can join Rhylia and Lady Josephine aboard my ship, I've caught one of your friends already," explained Arthur.

Arthur led Susan through the kitchen and through the foyer. He opened the door and walked her out into the fresh air. The boy had been taken to the ship, and was now tied to the banister.

"So, two down, how many to go Rhylia?" he asked.

"There's three more, this is Faltaine, and he's cataleptic," she said.

"I'll be out in a minute," he said, and walked back in.

"Thanks for the help Susan," said Rhylia sarcastically.

"I was brainwashed, so totally no blame on me," replied Susan, as Arthur disappeared into the school.

At this point Arthur had finished on the ground floor and he decided to go to the first floor, which is where they had found Rhylia. Jo and Rhylia stood on the deck, and suddenly Rhylia's window smashed, and out of it sailed a suitcase. It landed on the deck, and Rhylia instantly recognised it as hers.

"I'm going to get changed, I'm feeling better already," said Rhylia who took the suitcase into the cabin.

Back upstairs, Arthur was bashing every door down, trying to find any more monsters. He bashed the last door in the corridor, and then regretted it. There was another monster, but this one was completely black, and was only a shape of a person. It jumped on Arthur and he had to hit it as hard as he could. Arthur then found out that it was another boy, who was covered in black fabric, and was presumably going for the shadow look. He dragged him downstairs and out onto the porch.

"Who is this one?" asked Arthur.

"Gregory," said Rhylia, who had changed into a simple green dress, and out of the rags she had on before. Arthur pulled him onto the ship, and he was tied next to Faltaine, who was still asleep.

Arthur now knew that he had only two more monsters left. He walked around the first floor, and saw that there was a set of stairs leading to the second floor, and he ran upstairs, and turned the lights on. He was confronted by a girl, who was dressed as something he had never seen before. She had horns, long black hair and glowing yellow eyes. She also had fangs, dark blue skin, and large black wings.

"Hello, my name's Arthur, what's yours?" he asked.

"What are you doing here?" she asked.

"Oh you know, transfer student," said Arthur.

"I'm Corlio's sister, and he doesn't want to see anyone," said the girl.

"Well I want to see him, and then Elsius, and then I'm done, but I see that you're the deluded type," he said.

"How dare you speak to me like that!" she said.

"Oh what are you going to do?" asked Arthur.

71

"I will destroy you!" she shouted, and lunged for Arthur. He dodged out of the way, and she flew through the doorway, gliding on her wings. They then got caught between the door frame, and she was stuck.

"So you see, I'm going to see your brother and you can just cool off and pretend to be a door instead of a horrific demon," he said. She dangled there helpless, and Arthur walked up the next set of stairs to the attic.

"Hello," said Arthur. He heard the hissing sound, and continued up.

"So, you must be Corlio, son of Lord Yage, actually, I should say unwanted son," he said.

"Shut up!" shouted the voice, which Arthur still couldn't see.

"I think that you should come out, and rescue your sister from being stuck downstairs," said Arthur.

"Leave me alone!" he said. Arthur turned the lights on, and he saw Corlio, sat on an old armchair, without any costume.

"So, are you ready to go home?" asked Arthur.

"Why would I want to go home?" he asked.

"Well, to be honest I don't know, I mean, you're rich enough to do what you want so if you don't mind, I'm going to relieve Commander Elsius of her command," said Arthur.

"She gave me servants, so I can't allow that," he said.

"Fair enough," said Arthur, who ran at Corlio, and Corlio ran at him. Arthur was surprised at how weak Corlio was, and he managed to subdue him quite easily.

Arthur walked downstairs with Corlio on his back, and saw that the creepy looking girl was still stuck. He grabbed her as well, and she struggled as much as she did when she was stuck. Arthur took them out to the ship and he tied Corlio up first, and then with the help of Jo and Rhylia, they tied the girl to the banister, who Rhylia identified as Lady Tryssa, her younger sister and the really spoilt and stuck-up daughter of Lady Sylvia.

"So we have all the kids, but what are we going to do now?" asked Arthur.

"I think I'll go and find out what Commander Elsius is up to, and you can keep an eye on everyone here," said Jo.

72

"If that's what you want then you can go ahead, Rhylia and I will stay here," he said. Jo took off her backpack and she took her two gold pistols and her hunting sword, plus something else, which she put into her pocket, and jumped over the banister, doing a tuck and roll as she landed.

Arthur slowly moved over to Lady Tryssa and sat next to her, beginning a very interesting conversation.

The Granite Tunnel

Jo walked down to the cellar, and looked around for the sound of the humming. She saw that it was coming from behind a door at the far right of the room. Jo walked up to the door and tried it, and she saw that it was locked. Jo then pulled out her hairpin and began to move it around in the keyhole. After five minutes of fumbling with the lock, she still couldn't open it. "Oh god help me," she said, and sighed. The door then creaked open, and Jo looked around nervously. She then opened the door, and saw that carved into the back were two words: 'You're welcome', it said. Jo was now quite worried, but continued on down the stairway. In here the humming sound was louder, that it was clearly audible. It was a rhythmic sound that continued to get louder as she walked further down the stairs. Jo saw a light at the end of the spiralling staircase, and had walked down about a hundred steps, so she knew that she was beneath the cliff.

When she reached the light she had come to a door that was letting a bit of light in. She pushed it, and she was blinded by the light that poured onto her. "Good evening...wait a minute, you're not Sir Pageon, who are you?" asked someone, a woman by the sound of the voice.

"Who's asking?" asked Jo.

"Commander Elsius, head mistress of this school," she said.

"Could you turn the lights off, it's a little hard to talk when you're being blinded," said Jo. The lights were turned down, and Jo saw three people, a woman in a purple and silver dress, and two others in normal purple guard uniforms.

"Now, who are you?" asked Elsius.

"I'm just a lost kid; I was out walking in the mountains when I came across this place. I heard the sound of humming coming from down here so I came," explained Jo, who was amazed at how easily she could lie.

"You weren't attacked when you came here?" asked Elsius.

"By what?" asked Jo.

"Never mind, do you always carry two pistols and a sword with you?" asked Elsius.

"Safest way for a woman to travel through the mountains," she said.

"What is your name?" asked Elsius.

"Clarissa," said Jo, remembering that that was the fake name Arthur used in Chene.

"Very well Clarissa, allow me to show you around," said Elsius.

"If you insist," said Jo.

"What are you doing?" whispered one of the guards to Elsius.

"If she sees nothing going on, then she won't tell anyone," whispered Elsius back.

Jo was taken around the tunnel that was being dug, and she saw that it was very unstable, and if one of the supports were gone, then chunks of unbreakable granite would fall into the tunnel, blocking it forever. Jo felt the outside of her pocket, which was bulging from the object that she had taken from Arthur's desk drawer. They reached the end of the tunnel, and Jo saw what the humming sound was. It was a complicated drilling machine, and the humming was coming from the generator.

"We're just mining; this academy doesn't get much in revenue, so by mining we get more money to improve the conditions for our students," said Elsius.

In a split second, Jo now finally understood the mystery. The kids dressed as monsters, they were just guard dogs, to keep people away from what was really going on down here. Elsius was obviously unhinged to do that to kids, but she obviously wanted to get something down here. Diamonds or gold would be pointless; there's plenty more places to mine for those in Discoucia, and they'd be easier too. If she remembered right, they were about 100ft down, and the tunnel went even further down than that, and the cliff was about 50ft high, so what are they trying to reach? The Green Coven, the richest one of all four and it has the greatest collection of land holdings and documents too; so it's a robbery and a big one too. They must nearly be there by now, Jo had to something about it.

"So, that's all you need to see," said Elsius. Jo then came up with a plan, completely stupid, but she was back to being a child, so she could get away with it.

She started to shake, and then shouted, "I have claustrophobia; I have to get out of here!" Jo then ran back down the tunnel so fast, that for about a minute the guards didn't know what to do.

Jo ran to a pillar that was out of sight, and pulled the object out of her pocket. It was a bomb, with a 30 second fuse. She hid it behind the pillar, and carried on running until she reached the entrance, where she stopped and stood with her hand on a table, catching her breath. The two guards came running, along with Elsius. "I'm sorry, I just couldn't stay, it was getting to me," said Jo.

"That's OK, what did you think of our tunnel?" she asked.

"It was lovely, I hope you find what you're looking for," said Jo.

"KABOOM!!!" the bomb detonated.

The guards jumped behind the light with Elsius as the whole tunnel collapsed, and when they got up Jo had disappeared.

Jo ran up the stairs as fast as she could, and when she nearly reached the door, she said a prayer. "Please god, lock the door after I leave" Jo ran out and the door swung shut and clicked. Jo saw that there was something carved into the front of the door that wasn't there before.

"'Once again you're welcome, but don't refer to me as god, who knows who else might be listening'," she read aloud, then the door began to shudder, and she saw that it was locked.

Arthur and Rhylia were looking around for what caused the small earthquake, but couldn't find anything at all. Jo ran out of the academy, and shouted something that the two couldn't hear.

"Are we ready to go?" asked Arthur.

"Go, go now!" shouted Jo.

Jo jumped on and the ship lifted off. It flew across the rooftops of Gard, and when they picked up Corky from a rooftop pub, they headed straight for the royal palace.

The royal palace was huge beyond reckoning and would take a whole chapter to describe, however it was a small balcony that the ship was heading for. They stopped just outside, suspended in mid-air. They were here to take Corlio back, and he walked off the ship still tied up.

Inside there was a party going on, and the whole room was lit up brilliantly. "Off you go, Corlio, and tell your father Sir Arthur Pageon sent you," he said. Corlio had no idea who Arthur was, and when he heard this he stood staring in disbelief. The ship pulled off to its next destination, the outskirts of Cesta.

When the ship had reached Cesta, it was lit up too, and looked beautiful next to the sea. They dropped off Lady Susan in a clearing on the other side of the Sky River and she walked home. They then flew past Evermore, and Arthur carried a still asleep Faltaine and placed him in the windowsill of his mother Kate's house. And after giving a letter to the White Guard about what was going on in Starfall Academy, they continued to drop the children off. They then flew along to Adlin, where they dropped off Gregory, who was happy to be home, and with only Lady Rhylia and a still-foul-tempered Lady Tryssa left, they set off for Seraphale Island, which was empty apart from Alectrona Castle.

"Before we get there, do you think we should return to normal?" asked Jo.

"Good idea, I've never met Lady Sylvia before and I want to give her a good impression of me," said Arthur.

"We'll take turns, you go first and I'll wait here," said Jo.

"What are you two talking about?" asked Rhylia.

"How old do you think we are Rhylia?" asked Jo.

"Just a bit older than me?" she asked.

"I'm 219, and Arthur is 220," said Jo.

"Wouldn't you be taller if that was true?" asked Rhylia.

"They're lying, sister," said Tryssa.

"Honestly, what is your problem?" asked an older Arthur who walked down the stairs.

"I don't believe this!" said Rhylia.

"We didn't either but if you could keep it yourself, Rhylia, we would be very grateful. I know Tryssa won't, but then again nobody will believe her," said Arthur, as Jo went upstairs.

"I won't say a word, you saved me from hell so it's the least I can do," she said.

Tryssa was just sat on the settee getting madder and madder.

"Though to be honest, she does have the handicap of being implicated in kidnapping," said Arthur, sat at his desk.

"What do you mean?" asked Rhylia. Tryssa now stopped trying to break out of her ropes and listened.

"Well, you were being held against your will and Tryssa here, your own sister did nothing to free you," said Arthur.

"That's true," said Rhylia, staring at her sister.

"So if she says one thing about it, she will then have to tell the whole story and if she does she's only making it worse for herself," explained Arthur.

"I never thought about it that way," said Rhylia, looking at Tryssa angrily now.

"I'm done, how far are we from Seraphale?" asked Jo.

"We're nearly there actually, how much of the potion is left?" he asked.

"About half the bottle. I think we should keep it, in case we need it again," said Jo. They were flying across the sea, and they had thankfully avoided strafing the Icicle Mountains, because there was a particularly nasty storm brewing, and Jo was telling Rhylia about the creature in the snow.

"I don't believe that," said Tryssa.

"They were just our age, and in a second they aged 100 years, what is there not to believe anymore?" asked Rhylia.

"There is no snow creature living in the Icicle Mountains," said Tryssa.

"Quiet, we're here," said Arthur.

Alectrona Castle had been finished, and it looked amazing. It was huge, and sat beneath a massive mountain range that was fogbound even in the summer. The castle was built from pink bricks, and the windows were letting out yellow light, which made the whole scene look like a fairytale. "Here you go, home time," said Arthur.

"Please meet my mother, she would love to thank you personally," said Rhylia.

The ship landed outside the huge doors, and the whole outside beyond the castle walls was wasteland, until it reached the trees of a large forest. Rhylia ran over to the door and banged on it. It opened and a guard appeared.

"Can I help you Miss?" he asked.

"Could you get Jeffrey, the head butler and tell him that Lady Rhylia and Lady Tryssa have come home," she said.

"Very well. If you could wait in your ship I'll get him for you," he said. Rhylia ran back to the ship, and she packed her suitcase ready to go. Arthur carried Tryssa and they were met at the gate by Jeffrey, a man of about 500 who wore a black tuxedo.

"It's lovely to see you home my Lady, but why may I ask have you come home early?" he asked.

"It's a long story, I'll tell you about it later, and where is my mother?" she asked.

"She is in the Fantasy Room since it's Tridark, and she doesn't like the dark," said Jeffrey.

"Then take us to her, and don't mind Tryssa she will be carried by Sir Pageon," said Arthur.

As they walked into the grounds, Arthur and Jo didn't realise that Lady Rhylia had taken the blue bottle, and she had revenge on her mind.

The castle was brilliantly lit inside, and the main colour scheme seemed to be pink, purple and dark red. They were being led to the centre of the castle, and they walked along a corridor that had paintings of all the children that Lady Sylvia had brought with her to Seraphale. They came to a large door that was made of dark wood, and Jeffrey knocked on it.

"Enter," said a voice from within. Jeffrey opened the door and he saw why it was called the Fantasy Room.

They walked into a forest, though the trees were not real, and there were waterways that had bridges over them. The room was like a landscaped garden, and there was also a large lawn area where a group of children and one woman were having a picnic. It was a stark contrast to the horribleness of Starfall Academy, and it was so light here that it was like daytime. The woman waved at the group, and Rhylia ran to her. Arthur and Jo followed with Jeffrey, across the bridge and onto the lawn.

"Why is my daughter tied up?" asked the woman. Rhylia whispered in her mother's ear, and she nodded. "Thank you for bringing my daughters back. Please, Sir Arthur, walk with me, and bring my daughter," she said. Jo was left with Rhylia, and she met all of the children, all seventeen of them.

"So, Sir Pageon, if you could please not let this get out I would be most grateful," she said.

"Don't worry, I won't say a word. You have a lovely home here," he said.

"Anything to get my children away from my ex-husband," she said.

"Yes, I would think so, but you seem to have everything you need here," he said.

"With a fortune of three hundred and ninety seven trillion, I can afford to," she said.

"Ah, right, well you definitely have a pleasant colour scheme," he said, as they ascended the stairs. Lady Tryssa wasn't saying a word, and she remained silent as her mother carried on talking.

"We're nearly at my daughter's room; she will stay in there until daylight," said Sylvia.

"I'm sure she'll be fine with that," said Arthur.

When they got to the door, Sylvia opened it and Arthur saw that it was huge. There was a large bed, and he laid Tryssa on it. There was a red drink sitting on the table, and when she was untied she ran for it. Arthur watched as she downed it in one go. "What is that?" he asked.

"Strawberry juice, she loves it," said Sylvia.

"Pardon the question, but how old is Tryssa?" asked Arthur.

"She will be 114 in November," said Sylvia. Then something happened that defied belief. Tryssa began to shrink. Arthur then instantly thought of the potion, and he did the maths in his head, and Tryssa was now back to being 14.

"Oh dear, this is terrible!" he said.

"What have you done?!" shouted Sylvia.

"Not me, but I know who," said Arthur. He opened the door, and all of the children who had been listening in fell onto the floor. "Rhylia, why did you do that?" asked Arthur.

"She left me manacled to a wall for a week, she deserved it!" shouted Rhylia.

"Look, Lady Sylvia, I am so sorry, but a new experimental potion that I have been tinkering with causes a person to become 100 years younger, and it seems that Lady Rhylia here has given some to Lady Tryssa and now she's 14 again," said Arthur.

"Funnily enough, I always wanted to go back in time with this one, I'm sure that she's such a monster because I was never there, so I should thank you. I could do with being 100 years younger" she said.

"Pass me the bottle, Rhylia," said Arthur. She handed over the bottle to Arthur, and he saw that there was a teaspoon left.

"Here, consider it a gift from a friend," he said, handing it to her.

"Thank you, I don't know how I shall ever repay you," she said, downing the bottle, and then picking up the now much smaller Tryssa. Sylvia then became much younger, she was about 350, and now she was 250.

"You'll find a way," he said, and walked off with Jo down the corridor and out of the castle. On Tryssa's balcony, all of the children waved goodbye to the two travellers, who made their way south to Evermore, now having met the Four Commanders of Queen Lilia.

"This has been a strange adventure hasn't it?" asked Jo.

"Stranger than most, but what did you think of Seraphale?" asked Arthur.

"I liked it, it seemed like a nice place to live," said Jo.

"Maybe one day I'll retire there," he said.

"When do you think you'll be doing that?" she asked.

"I don't know, in the future some time," he replied.

"You're going to have a stately home or a castle right?" she asked.

"That's the plan," he replied.

"A big old house, sounds quite lonely," she said.

"Do you want a drink?" he asked. "Go on then, I've had enough of running away from monsters" she said, and they settled down to a comfortable return to Evermore.

"Now that we've been on four missions, can you tell me something?" asked Jo.

"Ask away," he said.

"Have you ever had a girlfriend?" she asked.

"I have never had the time," he replied.

"Oh, I always thought that you were the dashing explorer," she said.

"Well I kind of am, sorry for sounding big-headed," said Arthur.

"I know that now, but I thought hundreds of girls were on your arm all the time," she said.

"I'm not interested," he said.

"So you're not into girls? I had a cousin, Lady Lynda, who wasn't in to boys, and..." said Jo, but she was stopped by Arthur.

"No! No, I'm into girls, but I've not had any time lately, what with my megalomaniac sister and all," he explained.

"OK," she said, sipping her drink.

"Why do you ask?" he asked.

"I was just curious," she replied, downing it.

A Purple Invitation

It was in the Azure Hall that the two found the High King again, only this time he was sitting and not standing as he was before. "So, you two have done well, you've blown up the Castle at Karga, though that place was a dangerous ruin so you've probably done a public service to the kingdom. You saved Lord Artlintone, who by now must be older than anyone else I know, and I hope he makes plenty more interesting business decisions in the near future. You discovered a whole wooden city below Icester that funnily enough had none of the ice diamonds or snow gold you mention. Then you as members of the secret service acted like a school bus and returned psychotic children to their homes. But I hope that you found out something about what Queen Lilia is planning, so this whole endeavour wasn't a complete waste of time," explained the King.

"Apart from generally scaring locals and using what appears to be a fog generator to hide an army...not much," replied Arthur.

"Are you sure about this?!" he asked.

"Quite sure Daddy, it's all true," said Jo.

"In that case you had better see this; it was brought to me by one of her messengers and is addressed to me personally," said the King, handing a purple piece of paper to Arthur.

'To my dear High King Olandine, I bid you a heartfelt sadness at your current condition, and I offer you chance at being well again. All I ask is that you or one of your family members graces my humble island with their presence. I will expect you in two months from the date this letter reaches you.

 Sincerely yours,

Queen Lilia the Young

P.S. I will be having my birthday celebration at the time, and since I shall also be inviting guests from all over the kingdom, nothing underhanded will befall you or your family.'

"It's obviously a trap," said Jo.

"Of course it is, but what would you suggest I do?" asked the King.

"I think your daughter should go since she knows what she's doing," said Arthur.

"And you would accompany her of course," said the King.

"She's my sister, she'll recognise me in a second," said Arthur.

"No she won't," said Jo.

Both Arthur and the High King looked at Jo, but she wasn't going to answer. "I'll leave it to you, but you have two months so I would like one of you two to do a little favour for me," he asked.

"Of course, Daddy," said Jo.

"I'm not feeling as strong as I used to be so I have two tasks that I would like you to do," he said.

"Do you want us to do them together or separately?" asked Jo.

"It will be quicker if you did them separately, and since you want to go to Chene before you go to Harrha it makes more sense," said the King.

"So where are we going?" asked Arthur.

"I would like one of you to fetch a herbal honey drink from Lady Josette in Adlin," he explained.

"Considering that the city of Adlin is only open to women, I think we know who is going where" said Jo.

"I always wanted to see the mine workings, plus I can see more of Evermore while you are gone," said Arthur.

"Good, in that case I shall see you soon," said the King.

Jo went to go but Arthur was held back by the King. "There is more to being courageous than fighting villains and rescuing my daughter," he said.

"What do you mean Sir?" he asked.

Jo grabbed Arthur and took him to another door that he hadn't used before in the right hand centre of the hall. She led him into a courtyard, and then across a stone bridge that crossed over a street where hundreds of people were milling around. Ahead he saw a huge building with large windows, and through the windows he saw gleaming piles of gold.

"That's not Evermore's gold reserve, is it?" asked Arthur.

"No, we have an incredibly huge amount of treasure beneath the city, in a place where no robber would ever be able to go," she explained. They descended a set of stairs and came to another courtyard, where children were playing beneath the well tended trees and splashing in the fountains that poured from holes in the walls into large marble fonts.

The day was becoming evening, and the stars twinkled in the gaps between the towers that extended into the sky. There was a staircase that led down to a large open courtyard, and in the distance they could see the lit up ruins of The Sandy Fortress. Walking along the main wall of Evermore, they saw the oak forest that made up a first defence for the city. The trees were swaying in the breeze, and deer could be seen running through the holes in the canopy.

The ramparts led through a couple of towers, and then to a maze of battlement walls which in turn led to more towers. Then they finally came to a huge courtyard that was missing some parts of the floor. They were one level above the floor, and the level they were on didn't look at all stable.

"Just one little question, why on earth is the city so beautifully maintained but this area looks like it's falling apart?" asked Arthur.

"It looks quite deceiving, but it's as stable as the rest of the city. It is used by everyone as a kind of assault course, and that way they don't become fat and lazy courtiers like the ones in Chene," she replied.

"And why are we here?" asked Arthur.

"I need your help to carry something from my bedroom; I told Cornelius to fly the ship to right above my ceiling," she said.

"Nice to see that you've commandeered my driver," said Arthur.

"Our driver Artie," she said with a smile.

They navigated their way around, and found that they had made their way to a balcony above the reception hall. There were people standing in groups around the hall, but none of them noticed the two as they returned to the courtyard since there was no way of getting any higher from the reception hall.

They walked all around the courtyard's second level, which seemed to be intact, and climbed a ladder that led to the third level. "Oh good, we can get to my bedroom from here, though it won't be easy, as there more holes in the floor than there were before," she said. The carpet in the corridors was a black and blue checked pattern, and there were indeed more holes in the floor than before.

They reached the end and entered a large room whose walls were covered in paintings. Outside a window Arthur saw the inhabited part of Evermore, and all the houses had acacia wood roofs and tall red brick chimneys that puffed out smoke. The city looked beautiful in the dark, with its many tiny lights twinkling like an extension of the night sky.

"Come on Artie, we're nearly there, said Jo, grabbing his arm and dragging him away from the window. They came to a long corridor that looked out onto the city like the other did; only the city looked so much bigger and brighter from this angle. Jo opened a door in the centre of the corridor, and she took Arthur in with her.

"So, this is my room," said Jo. Her room was massive, befitting a princess of Evermore, but it was not the size of the room that caught Arthur's attention. It was more the large amount of clothes that were strewn everywhere.

"You didn't tidy up before we left to go to Karga did you?" asked Arthur.

"No, but my room is like this pretty much all the time," she replied.

"So what was it you wanted to get?" he asked.

"I wanted to get some money, so that I can pay for some of the stuff in Chene," she replied.

"But we're not going there for a while, why do you need it now?" he asked.

"I was hoping you would let me use the ship to go to Adlin, since it's nearly impossible to get to by foot or by horse, and then I was going to put this in your safe," she replied.

"How do you know I have a safe?" he asked.

"I accidently discovered it when I was getting a book on 'Horticultural Engineering' from your middle bookcase," she replied.

"Did you go in it?" he asked.

"No, I couldn't figure out the combination," she said.

"I thought you might, well, in that case the code is 6-7-1-9-6-7," he said.

"OK, I'll put it in on the way there while you're making your way below the city," she replied.

They finished in Jo's bedroom and made their way to the top of the building, which was covered in flowers and Arthur saw that Jo had a garden above her bedroom. He waved goodbye to her as she sailed off into the west, and he walked back to the Azure Hall to meet the High King.

"Now that my daughter is gone, tell me if you think she is ready for a life outside the palace," he said.

"I guess; is it really up to me to decide that?" asked Arthur.

"Well, you've spent a lot of time with her and she's a bit of a handful. She needs to have a constructive influence and seems to have changed during her time with you," he said.

"I don't know about that, but if I'm helping then that's all that matters," replied Arthur.

"Take care of her on when you go to Harrha, as much as Lilia is your sister there's not much either of us can do about the evidence," he said.

The Dark Chasm Creature

Arthur looked out at the scene he had witnessed with Jo weeks before, and he felt different somehow. Before his mind had been filled with thoughts of the beauty that people had created down here in the dark, carving massive stone corridors out of the rock, and lighting them up so it seemed like the sun was shining on this underground kingdom.

He walked down the stairs; that winded around the rock columns like a spiral staircase. Arthur noticed that the path led down to the shores of the Great Underground Desert, which confused him because a desert is supposed to be hot, however the temperature in a wide open space was chilly. "Thank god it's not hot down here, this combo gets unbearable sometimes," he said, taking off his blue jacket and slinging it over his shoulder.

Arthur carried on walking and was so absorbed in the scenery that he didn't hear the sound of someone walk up behind him. They tapped him on the shoulder and Arthur was so surprised that he awkwardly spun round and tripped on nothing. He crashed into the shape and they both flew off the side of the landing and onto the sand dunes.

"I'm so sorry," he said quickly, then looked at who he had pulled down with him. It was a giant teddy bear, and it pulled off its head to reveal the woman Arthur had met on top of the rock outside Starfall Academy. "You!" he shouted, and it echoed around the massive cavern.

"Archie actually but I've been called worse," she said.

"Who are you exactly?" asked Arthur.

"Well first off maybe we should climb back up, I've got fur in my sand...wait that's not right," she said.

"You're not even a real bear, who are you and where do you come from?" he asked as they made it up to the landing. She sat down and dusted herself off while Arthur put his jacket back on and folded his arms.

"I come from a place far away, and you wouldn't believe anything I tell you about myself if I told you" she said.

"I'm fairly open minded and I have seen many strange things in my life so please tell me and I will make my own decision," said Arthur.

"Very well Sir Arthur, I am the god Authos and I have created this world with the power given to me by The Great Creator himself. There are four elemental gods and I am the Goddess of Water. I wish to help you in any way that I can and am prepared to give you some evidence that what I say is true," she replied.

"Well I am prepared to believe you if your intentions are honourable. Why would a god want to help me?" asked Arthur.

"I helped you once before if you remember rightly, I want you to have the best chance against evil, though this isn't the standard struggle I can assume," she said.

"So you know that it is my sister that is the person I am fighting," said Arthur.

"I do and I think we should bring her back down to earth before she does something stupid," said Archie.

"And see her imprisoned for all the evil she has committed?" asked Arthur. "Oh goodness no, she doesn't really deserve that," said Archie.

"So what would you suggest we do?" he asked.

"Rescue her and take her with you on your next adventure so she can be brought back to reality," she replied.

"That was my intention but nobody would ever let that happen," he said.

"We could try, I'll give you all the help I can," she said.

"I suppose with a god I can't lose," he said.

"I wouldn't bank on me being very reliable, though, since I disappear at strange times and have a really stifling personality," she said.

"If we're going to be friends then it's something I'll deal with. Now can we go to the Dark Chasm?" he asked.

"Of course," she replied.

Arthur and Archie walked along the terrace that was built between the desert sands and the massive rock wall. They finally came to the South Gate of Elowe; it looked out onto the desert as a castle above ground would look over the flatlands. They walked through the massive marble arch that had the most intricate carvings that Arthur had ever seen. "Look, it's a huge carving of what they think Evere looks like," said Archie.

"It looks normal," replied Arthur.

"It's missing a set of wings, and its horns need to be a lot bigger," said Archie.

"Have you ever seen her?" asked Arthur.

"It's a long story, shall we go?" she asked.

They walked along the tunnel, and either side of it they saw that trees were growing out of the sandy soil beneath the huge lamps that lit up the tunnel. "Why do they have trees down here?" asked Arthur.

"It's quite brilliant to be honest; you see, trees produce oxygen above ground, and down here there is a distinct lack of it, so you see, this tunnel and the Forest of Black Light are Elowe's oxygen factories. They produce enough oxygen that it removes the need to build airshafts," she explained.

"You know an awful lot about this stuff," replied Arthur.

"I read a lot, and I write a lot, then I go and stop evil people from destroying the balance of the world," she replied.

"So you're an author?" asked Arthur.

"Yes, you could say that," she replied.

"In that case, I'm going to call you 'The Author', since that is what you are," said Arthur.

"You called it not me, but could you call me Archie, that's my name," she replied.

"If you insist, but why did you say, 'I called it'?" he asked.

"Nothing. Shall we push on?" asked Archie.

They walked along the floor, which was covered in sand, and from the walls, more sand was flowing out. "Those are the small tunnels that the sand from mining flows out of; it comes into here, and then flows out into the desert out there," she explained.

"I see, and how far is the Chasm from here?" asked Arthur.

"It's a mile down the main sandy tunnel," said Archie.

"How did you know that? You said you didn't know the way," said Arthur suspiciously.

"It's on the map over there," said Archie, pointing to the wall. Arthur looked around and saw that there was indeed a map on the wall, one that he didn't see before.

"That map wasn't there before," he said.

"No, I just magically made it appear," said Archie.

"Funny, I just didn't notice," said Arthur.

"Anyway, it's a mile away, so should we press on?" asked Archie.

The road to the Dark Chasm went past several natural landmarks that were breathtaking to behold. They saw one of the many black glass bridges in the distance that spanned the Dark River. The water wasn't a different colour, but since it was as black as night in areas without light then there was no other name it could have. They saw the edge of the Forest of Black Light; at the top of a small cliff, the roots of the massive trees poke themselves through the solid rock. They also went past an entrance that read 'The Cave of Lost Dreams' on top of it, and even though Arthur wanted to go in, he looked at Archie, and then decided not to.

"Don't worry, you'll get a chance to go there one day," she said.

"How do you know? Are you clairvoyant too?" asked Arthur.

"You don't trust me, do you?" she asked.

"I just find it very strange that you appeared out of nowhere," said Arthur.

"I didn't come out of nowhere, and if you want to know my real name, it's Archie because I like Bubblegum Pop, and I come from over the hills and far away, if you must know" she said.

"Are you even from Discoucia?" he asked.

"No. I tell you what, when we get to the Dark Chasm River, we can talk all about this," she replied.

"If you say so, how far are we away?" he asked.

"Just follow me; we can make the time fly by with pleasant conversation," replied Archie.

"How old are you?" asked Arthur.

"That's not pleasant conversation, try again," said Archie.

"You start the conversation then," replied Arthur.

"Tell me, do you have a wife?" asked Archie.

"No, I don't", he replied.

"Then who was the girl I saw you with outside the main gate?" asked Archie.

"That was Princess Josephine, she's my partner," said Arthur.

"I see. Well she seemed nice," said Archie.

"Yeah, she is," said Arthur in a dazed tone.

"There's something I should show you about me Arthur," said Archie.

"I thought you were going to wait until we got to the Dark Chasm Bridge," said Arthur.

"Look, we are at the bridge," said Archie.

Much to Arthur's amazement, they had reached the bridge. The Chasm was so large that Arthur's eyes had trouble adjusting to it. The Bridge spanned halfway across, and in the light Arthur saw that the side that the bridge began from was dull, but the side they aimed for was twinkling and that was apparently the gems that they were aiming to mine.

"So what did you want to show me?" asked Arthur, who spun around expecting to see the teddy bear. Instead it was the girl about the same age as him, wearing the same white and blue dress with light brown hair down to her waist. Her dress had a white bow around her waist, and there were two blue butterflies holding her hair out of her face. She seemed to be glowing in this shadowy netherworld and made Arthur feel safe.

"Wha...who are you?" he asked.

"It's the same me, only this is my favourite form, and the reason you didn't know that we had arrived here so fast is because of the trees. If you want to know why the people are disappearing, then the trees are where you need to start. I'll see you in Chene when you have finished here," said Archie, who faded out of view, and Arthur was left alone on the natural terrace.

"Hey, whoever you are I'd get off that terrace, unless you want to get a sand bath!" shouted someone below. Arthur climbed up a rusted ladder to another terrace, and stood next to a group of workmen who pulled a large chain, and a mass of sand flowed out of a small hole beneath the platform, and out to where Arthur had been standing.

"Wait, the person I was with is still down there somewhere," he said.

"Sir, we saw you standing there for about five minutes talking to yourself," said one of the men.

"Talking to myself?" asked Arthur.

"Yes. Who are you anyway?" he asked.

"Sir Arthur Pageon, I'm here to help with your missing person's problem," said Arthur.

"I don't know what you think you can do, but you should probably go and see the site manager, he's in his office next to the bridge," he said.

"Thank you!" shouted Arthur, who walked up some stairs, and strolled across a large open corridor, and saw the vast expanse below. He made his way to the railway track, which was a double track, and a couple of mine carts were moving up and down.

"Can I help you sir?" asked a man standing in a mine cart.

"Yes, I'm here to see the manager, I'm on business from the King," said Arthur.

"I can take you to him, but he's in a very bad mood at the moment, so you will have to be tactful," he replied.

"Very well, I'll take my chances," said Arthur. He climbed aboard, and they zoomed down the wooden lattice structure that supported both the tracks and across the flatland which was covered in stalagmites, some as large as the trees that grew between them.

"So tell me what you know," said Arthur.

"Seventeen men have disappeared in the last two weeks, and they have all been on their own, they walk off and just disappear," he explained.

They came to a small building with a wooden painted sign saying 'Office'. "Here you go, good luck sir," he said, and the cart pulled off down the track towards the bridge. Arthur entered the office, and dodged a flying piece of metal.

"I said knock when you want to enter!" shouted the manager from behind his desk.

"Sorry about that, only when seventeen of your miners go disappearing then I see that as exceptional circumstances," said Arthur.

"Who the heck are you?" he asked, now slightly subdued.

"Sir Arthur Pageon, representing the High King," he said.

"Well that's all nice, but what do you think you're going to do?" he asked.

"What have you been doing to prevent it yourself?" asked Arthur, now leaning on the manager's desk.

"We've set traps for it, but we can never catch the damn thing," he said.

"What does it look like?" asked Arthur.

"No idea, we've never actually seen it, but when men go over to the east dump, they never come back again," he explained.

"And what are you dumping?" asked Arthur.

"Sand, bits of dead tree, rocks. Nothing that his majesty would consider illegal to dump," he replied.

"The bits of dead tree, are they from any tree in particular?" asked Arthur.

"They're from acacia trees, those trees won't grow down here like the others do. I mean, birch trees and oak trees grow down here perfectly, but acacia is different," he explained.

"I'd like to take a trip to the east dump, you've blocked it off I hope?" asked Arthur.

"Yes, it made sense. Now no one goes there but if you're going, then I'll go too, the men's morale is low enough as it is" he said.

They both left the office, and walked through the forest of stalagmites on a road that had been carved through. They reached the east dump, which had a wooden wall with a patchwork metal gate, and a yellow sign saying 'Danger' written on it.

"You mix around the letters in that, you get 'Garden'," said Arthur.

"Excuse me?" said the manager, who was fumbling with the lock.

"Just trying to lighten the mood," said Arthur, just as the manager opened the door.

The east dump had a wall around most of it, but part of it backed onto a cliff, and over that cliff was The Dark Chasm River. They walked along the open space, and Arthur saw something move in the dark. "Did you see that?" asked Arthur.

"Yes, but not clearly," said the manager. They came a lot closer to the edge of the cliff, and heard the river flow invisibly past. Arthur threw a rock and they waited thirty seconds until they heard a splash.

"There it is, it's out there, in the dark," said a very frightened manager.

"Look, I can't see anything," said Arthur. Then the manager did something completely unexpected: he screamed, and ran for the gate, but then stopped, and ran for the river. Arthur tried to grab him, but he jumped so fast that nothing could stop him plummeting down into the darkness. Arthur drew his gun, and took out a device that he had been tinkering with, a portable torch. He clicked a button on its end and a spark illuminated the various crystals inside the tube, and a flash of light showed Arthur the Creature for what it really was. A miner, clothes ripped, frothing at the mouth and a wild look in this eyes, charged at Arthur, but was repelled by the light of the torch. Arthur ran for the gate, and the miner followed him. Arthur flashed the light again, and it recoiled, it ran towards the cliff edge. It lost its balance, and slid off, with a terrible holler as it plummeted down, to join the other seventeen men it had sent down there. Arthur looked around and picked up a root that was sticking out of a pile of sand. He tucked it into his pocket and walked off.

Arthur reached the manager's office, and a crowd of miners had gathered. "What happened to the chief?" asked one of them.

"He fell. The creature was one of your lot and he had rabies, that's why whenever you brought lights over there he attacked, and it seems that all of your men jumped over the edge of the cliff. Either out of terror or of being infected," explained Arthur.

"Is the creature gone now?" asked another.

"He fell, into the river, and hopefully that's the last of it, but do you have any idea who it could have been?" asked Arthur.

"It could have been Langdon; he was always disappearing to explore caves after we'd finished work," he said.

"In that case, I'll alert the King and you all stay together. I'd build a wall around the camp, just in case," said Arthur.

"Thanks, I suppose. Are we going to get overtime for this?" asked another miner.

"That's something you should bring up with your new manager. Is there anyone who can take me to the surface?" asked Arthur.

"I can, we'll use the new elevator," he said.

Arthur was slowly winched up to the surface, slightly disturbed after what he had seen down here in the dark, and wondering how someone could have caught rabies all the way down here; then he got his answer. He saw out of the elevator, much to the surprise of himself and the man with him, a wolf, running across the tracks, and being chased by a load of miners.

"Don't touch it!" shouted Arthur, but he heard the sound of gunshots and the miners killed the infected animal.

"I suppose you'll sleep better tonight," said Arthur.

"Yes, but I didn't think we had wolves in Discoucia," he said.

"Only in Evermore's zoo. I wonder if one escaped," said Arthur, just as they reached the top of the shaft.

Arthur left the underground, not wanting to go there alone again, and he made his way to the Azure Hall, to meet up with the King and to report to him about the infected animal.

A Trip to Chene

Arthur had missed Jo, not that he cared to admit it, and found it good to see her again. Unbeknownst to him she felt the same way, but she didn't care to admit either.

"So, how was your trip?" asked Jo.

"I got attacked by a crazed rabies-infected miner and nearly died by falling into a chasm, but other than that it was fine. How was your trip?" asked Arthur.

"I nearly got poisoned by Lady Josette, then I had to sit for three hours listening to her babble on about how she has such a better life with no men around." she replied.

"We have different ideas of what danger is, I suppose," said Arthur.

"So tell me about the wood you found," she replied.

"Well this is a root from an acacia tree, and I found that when it is cut, spores are released into the air, and they are hallucinogenic," he explained.

"So they're a drug?" asked Jo.

"In a sense yes, and since we've stopped cutting down acacia trees none of this would happen above ground. I would assume that the wind would blow the spores away before someone inhaled them, but deep underground there is a distinct lack of wind so the miners would breathe in the spores and see what they expected to see, a monster," he replied.

"That's brilliant, if not rather creepy," she replied.

"Your father will make sure that all of the acacia trees that were planted down there are gone and hopefully this won't happen again," said Arthur.

"That still doesn't explain how a wolf managed to get all the way down to the Dark Chasm Bridge without anyone noticing," said Jo.

"Maybe it found a cave that we don't know about, and it could have remained hidden for days, but I would like to know where it came from," he said.

"You don't think it could have been your sister, do you?" asked Jo.

"I sincerely hope not," said Arthur.

"But anyway, at least we're on our way to Chene now, good old clean Chene full of bright lights and normal rich people who are so stuck up I'm surprised they're not floating," said Jo, rubbing Arthur's back as he was laying his head on his desk.

"I suppose so," he said.

"Good, then I'll take you out for dinner at the Seven Wonders restaurant and we can talk about my idea for getting you into Harrha without your sister noticing," she said.

"OK, I'm good with that, but first I'm going outside as I'd rather like to see the sky and the land and feel the air," he said.

"I'm going to bed, I'll see you in the morning," she said, and walked up the stairs while Arthur walked out onto the deck.

He watched the dark shapes of mountains loom past, and the tiny lights of villages. He wondered to himself about what the lives of the people in those villages must be like, not having to worry about anything other than their own little problems, and he thought that he wanted a simple life like that, with a family of his own. An image of Jo popped into his head, and he tried to think of something else, then an image of children with curly platinum hair came into his head. He decided to do something that would take his mind off these thoughts, so he decided to go and see Corky on the bridge.

Arthur climbed up a ladder that led up to the bridge, which was above Arthur's bedroom, and had a simple wooden wheel to steer the ship. Corky was smoking a cigar, and was surprised to see Arthur.

"Is everything okay sir?" he asked.

"Not really Corky, I think I'm in love," he said.

"I know" he replied bluntly.

"What do you mean you know?" asked Arthur.

"I'd have to be blind, or blind drunk not to notice sir, I think you should go for it. After everything I've seen you need a woman," he said.

"I don't need anyone, I did perfectly well on my own before," said Arthur.

"She's buying you dinner in Chene, she wouldn't stop asking questions about you all the way to and back from Adlin, and she's already moved in so what more proof do you need?" asked Corky.

"I suppose you're right, but she's a Princess of Discoucia," he said.

"And you're a Sir of Discoucia, an honour you don't inherit but get given after you've proved that you're worthy of the title," said Corky.

"And considering that my father was a traitor and my sister one too, will the High King want Lilia as an in-law?" he asked.

"Something tells me that things may turn out differently, but we're nearly there and if it's OK with you, I'd like to get thoroughly hammered tonight since Adlin had no alcohol," said Corky.

"If that's how you want to spend your time then go ahead, have fun and thanks," he said, climbing back down to the sitting room. Unknown to him, Jo had heard every word through an open window, and she fell asleep straight away.

The city of Chene was truly a wonderful and majestic sight to see, lying on a flat land that borders Icester, Evermore, Fina, Cesta, and the mountains that divide Discoucia from the lands of Obsatia, Kharoon, Karga, and The Echoing Mountains. In the day the city stands gleaming in the sunlight, and at night it can be seen from all the borders of the cities like a guiding light on a dark sea voyage.

The ship landed on Chene's massive Sky Port above the train station, and Arthur decided to go for a walk since there was no one around and the streets were so well lit that he felt quite safe after the horror he had previously experienced underground. He walked down Upper Heaven Street and made his way to the Garden of Eden, which was a park where all kinds of exotic flowers grew, and cool crystal clear water flowed from magnificent fountains.

"Good evening Arthur," said Archie, who was sitting on a park bench alone, and holding nothing. Arthur sat down next to her and didn't reply. "How was the flight here?" she asked.

"You said that you wanted to help me, first I meet you as a Teddy Bear in the underground, and you change into the witch I met above Starfall Academy," said Arthur.

"Aren't we supposed to talk about something trivial before we get into the meaningful stuff?" she asked.

"Are you a hallucination?" asked Arthur.

"Yes and no," she replied.

"Very well, I'll play your game. Tell me why you are not a hallucination," he said. Archie didn't speak, but instead she smacked Arthur on the back of the head.

"Oh very good, If you were a hallucination I wouldn't have felt that," he replied.

"Very good," said Archie, who stood up and changed her size to 10ft tall, and walked over to a tree to get an apple, and then she returned to normal.

"I see. Are you a magician?" he asked.

"I was for a while, but then I became an author," she replied.

"Can I ask you a personal question?" he said.

"Go ahead," replied Archie eating the apple.

"This is probably the most surreal experience of my life," he said.

"In comparison to how your life was before, you will have to get used to these surreal moments," said Archie.

"Okay so if you are a god, then tell me about yourself and what you mean when you say that you are an author?" he asked.

"This is not a conversation that we should be having now; I don't even know why I appeared to you this early, there must be something special about you," she explained.

"Thank you, but do you mean that we are going to meet again?" asked Arthur.

"Of course I shall see you, Jo and um, never mind. Next time you need me, then I shall meet you again but just try to look surprised," she replied.

"Are you going? What am I going to do for the rest of the night?" he asked.

"When you're with me time distorts, so as you can see it's morning now," she replied.

"That's impossible," said Arthur.

"Well anyway before I go, I should probably tell you something else," said Archie, who told something to Arthur before fading away.

Sure enough, the sun rose behind the trees and Arthur was left alone in the park, holding the apple with a large bite out of it. "Hey Artie! There you are, I've been looking for you everywhere," shouted Jo.

"Oh, sorry I was just talking to someone but they've gone now. How did you sleep?" he asked.

"Oh, I felt a bit lonely considering I couldn't find you this morning," she said.

"Right, where do you want to go today then?" he asked. "I want to go swimming, and later on I would like to go to that fancy dress shop I saw on Miracle Boulevard," she replied.

"Oh you mean Madame Arrietta's?" asked Arthur.

"Yes, have you been before?" she asked.

"Many times, and she knows me so we'll get better service than anyone else," he replied.

"Good, then we can go out for dinner at the Seven Wonders," she said.

"Sounds brilliant, are we going swimming in the Paradise Hotel?" asked Arthur.

"Yes but there's something I have to do first, could you wait for me in the ship?" asked Jo.

"If you insist. I'll see you in a while," he said, walking off around the corner of the street.

Arthur had no intention of going back to the ship as he knew that Jo had been through his safe, so he decided to follow her. She walked along Upper Heaven Street and round the corner to the business district. She came to the big red brick building that extended up to the sky. This was the centre of agriculture and what Jo was doing in there was a mystery, so Arthur watched as she entered the building. "What is she doing?" asked Arthur to himself. He walked up to the window and saw that she entered a side room, but there was no one around for her to see.

He walked around to the main entrance and walked in. It was a Saturday so no one was working, and apart from a guard who was probably down the pub no one was guarding it. Arthur walked to the door of the room that Jo entered, and saw that it was opulently decorated with three big paintings on the wall. One had a burning skull, the second had a small cottage and a beautiful sky, and the third represented the levels of hell in Discoucian mythology. Arthur looked around and Jo had disappeared from the room, though there was no way for her to leave; only the door she had come in. He looked suspiciously at the painting of the cottage which seemed to be rather large, and the door looked very realistic even for a painting.

The Yellow Coven

Arthur reached out for the doorknob, and it was real! He turned it and the door opened. Arthur stumbled into a corridor which was coloured yellow, and the floor was made from a peculiar kind of brick which was dark red. There was no place for Arthur to hide so he crept down the corridor. He could not hear anything apart from talking coming from far off down the corridor. He came to the end where the corridor went down underground, and then it split to the left and right. Arthur heard talking down the left corridor, but didn't hear anything from the left. He peered out and saw that the left corridor led to a larger room, and there were a load of bookcases that he saw from his vantage point. He then heard the voices getting louder to the right, and then walked slowly along the left-hand corridor.

The room he came into was huge and was surrounded by bookcases, with the Discoucian power symbol carved into the floor and two entrances, one going straight on and the other leading to the right, but he couldn't see what it led to. He decided to walk across the room and find out where the corridor to the right led. There was no place for him to hide if someone did come, and Arthur felt as though he was being watched.

"There's not much I can do about it," he thought to himself. The bright yellow walls made him feel slightly dizzy, but he carried on walking. He entered another room, and saw that it had a hole in its centre, and the hole was glowing. His curiosity got the better of him and he walked over to stare down the hole. It was a lava pit, and at the bottom of it was the churning molten rock, about 30ft down.

"Who are you and why do you trespass in the Yellow Coven?" said a voice rasping from behind. Arthur turned around and nearly fell down the hole, as he saw a girl who looked positively hideous. She had a warped face with pointed teeth and glowing green eyes, and scrawny red hair tied in a bun, though this was pointless because most of the hair was escaping to the sides. She wore a tarnished dress and dull red gloves that were ripped, exposing her long fingernails. She was wearing old red shoes that matched the rest of her ensemble, and she looked absolutely ghastly.

"Um...good morning?" replied Arthur, a little worried but trying to maintain composure.

"Answer the question!" she shouted, her mouth dripping saliva. Arthur took her hand off his arm and walked over to a bookcase, while she watched in disbelief.

"If this is the Yellow Coven, then I've heard that its rich members dress up as ugly people. Since there is a big lack of ugly people in Discoucia, then the question should be who you are," he said calmly.

"I hate that mind of yours," she said, standing up normally. "

"OK, what...the duck," said Arthur. "I'd give you a ten out of ten for the costume Jo, you nearly had me, but it takes a lot to get past Sir Arthur Pageon."

"Unfortunately with Coven rules I can't really take it off until I'm out of here, but I don't know what I'm going to do with you," she replied.

"Is there any other way out of here?" he asked.

"No, I'll try to distract some of the other members, while you go down the main corridor and out into the warehouse," she said.

It was strange for Arthur to see someone so repulsive have such a beautiful voice. "Yeah OK, I'll meet you in the fancy dress shop and please don't wear that there, it might scare some people," he replied.

"Oh shut up!" she shouted in the same rasping voice she had in the beginning.

She limped down the corridor, staying in character, and Arthur hid behind the corner and saw two other people dressed in similarly hideous costumes walking past. He waited until they were gone, and heard a crackling sound behind him. The stone doorway he had seen earlier in the room, which was made of a blue and purple coloured stone, now had a swirling red pattern inside it. Arthur walked up to it, and a hand reached out to take Arthur's hand, which he gave. Arthur was pulled through into a world that he couldn't believe.

He stood on a platform in the weirdest cave he had ever seen. The walls were made from blue stone, and the floor was on fire in some places, but the fire was blue and made the place seem cold, and it was cold as the floor was covered in ice below the sandstone platform. "Where are we exactly?" asked Arthur, now extremely cold.

"Welcome to a version of Hell, Arthur, I was going to meet you later but it seems that you needed a hand," said Archie.

"This is Hell; wait a minute what the hell is hell?" he asked.

"In your myths and legends, what does it specifically state about where you go when you die?" she asked.

"If you intentionally murder, not counting wars or accidents, then you go somewhere and never return. However, if you've led a life of good deeds that have erased any bad ones you've done, then you go above the clouds, to a high place not reachable by any ship," he replied.

"That's kind of beautiful but here is the place that spawned the myth, It has yet to have a name, why don't you name it?" she said.

"Why not Erthyana?" he asked.

"No, we are not naming this dark cold netherworld after your mother," she said.

"How did you know that? Oh wait, god," he replied.

"Think of something different," she replied.

"I can't think of anything," he said in a tired voice.

"Very well, do you want me to take you back to the coven?" she asked.

"Please do, but honestly, what is going on with them? I'm curious," he asked.

"Look I'll do you a favour, for an hour you and I will be invisible and we can go for a walk around the Yellow Coven without them being any the wiser, sound good?" she asked.

"A chance to be invisible, I'll take it," he said. They passed through the same portal that Arthur had originally entered and they left this strange place, but it wouldn't be the last time that Arthur would visit...

"Are we invisible now?" asked Arthur.

"Walk up to Jo and find out, she's still got that ridiculous costume on," replied Archie.

Arthur walked over to Jo, who was looking at a bookcase, and waved his hand in front of her horrible looking face, but she didn't register at all. "See, she doesn't see you at all," said Archie, walking over to the two.

"I have an idea," said Arthur. He pulled out a book from the bookcase and placed it on the top of the bookcase, which he did while Jo wasn't looking. She turned around, and saw that the book was out of place, and she put it back. Arthur pulled it out, and put it back on the top in the same place. She turned around to see that the book was out again, and she could conceive of no way that could possibly happen.

"Come on Arthur, Is that really necessary?" asked Archie.

"Yes, she tried to scare me earlier so this is payback," he replied.

Jo walked off to a doorway and the two 'ghosts' followed her. She walked up the corridor that Arthur was going to go down, but his curiosity had led him to this. The corridor led up, then into a large room, where a blazing fire was roaring in between blue sand mounds. "The blue sand came from the other world, and this coven is linked to the others," said Archie.

"I know this sounds strange that I'm asking this now, and not when I first got here but what's a coven?" he asked.

"Broadly speaking, it's a group of witches that exist as a group with one leader and several lower members. You see, in my world a coven is a much more dangerous prospect than one is in yours. Here it is just an exclusive club where rich people dress up in horrific costumes and do god knows what, but in my world it exists to harm and to cause general misfortune," she explained.

"And you said that there is more than one coven, how many are there?" he asked.

"There are technically five. The Yellow Coven of Chene, The Red Coven of Ashin, The Blue Coven of Cesta and the Green Coven of Gard" she said.

"What's the fifth?" he asked.

"The White Coven of Evermore," she said.

"Do you want to know something?" she asked, as they watched Jo walk into a room with a large cage in it.

"What might that be?" asked Arthur.

"How old can a Discoucian live to?" she asked.

"The general age limit is 1000, but people have been breaking that record all the time," he said.

"In my world the age limit is about 100, you have ten times the age others do," she said.

"That's horrible, living to only 100, how do you get anything done?" he asked.

"Well, you see, your 220, in another world you would be 22, and time flows differently in this world. It flows ten times as slow in your world, but the actual time flow doesn't go any slower, which is a hard concept to grasp," she said.

"I think I understand, it's like walking to a destination which is the other world, and then flying to a destination, which is your world. We travel at vastly different speeds, but we arrive at the same time," he explained.

"Congratulations Arthur you may be the smartest person I've met," said Archie.

"Obviously, though I still don't believe it," he said.

"You don't have to believe it, you understand it, and that's more than I can say for anyone else," she said.

After following Jo, they were walking down a huge grand staircase. "OK, so this Coven is for Evere, The Blue Coven is for Seashorelle, The Red Coven is for Ignatio and the Green Coven is for Altatia?" he asked.

"Correct," she replied.

"So the White Coven is for you?" he asked.

"It was for me, but I told them to stop, as they were becoming too powerful. I mean, their god actually spoke to them, so they tried

111

to take over the different Covens. They did stop, but most of their temple still exists far below Evermore, and I haven't been there for years," she replied.

"Did they do the same stuff that happens here?" he asked.

"No, this is just limited to Chene and in the spirit of their God they have a load of places to fly," said Archie.

Jo reached the bottom of the stairs and still felt like someone was following her. She was now in the grandest area of the Coven, which was below the huge circular window that was in the centre of Chene. From the surface it looked like a dome, covered by a really ornate metal frame, which seemed to be made so no one could go near it and find the world below. The glass was opaque, so no one could see through.

"You know, this seems like a strange but interesting place to hang out, but I believe that they have some odd rules here," she said.

"You're a god, you can do anything," he said.

"Yes, but that's a bit of a grey area. Yes, I can do anything, but I don't want to live in a marble palace being godly and judgemental, I'd rather share in an adventure with you, it's way more interesting," she said.

"Oh, I feel honoured," he said.

"Please don't do that," she said.

"If you insist," he replied.

"You see, when I start travelling back in time and changing history, it becomes a whole mess that I end up leaving," she said.

"Can you travel in time?" he asked.

"Yes, sometimes I go backwards and watch great events, or I peek into some people's futures," she said.

"Have you seen my future?" he asked.

"Sort of," she replied simply.

"Can you tell me about it?" he asked.

"Not really, but since it's you, I'll let you ask one question, and I shall give you an honest answer" she said.

"Okay, umm, what is my daughter's name?" he asked.

"I can't answer that," she said.

"You promised you would," he said.

"The reason is because the answer is another question," said Archie.

"Then what is it?" he asked.

"Which daughter's name?" she asked.

"Oh, I see," he said, and now Arthur's mind went into double thinking overdrive. "OK, I have one more question, but it isn't about the future," said Arthur.

"Then ask away," said Archie.

"Is Archie your real name?" he asked.

"No it isn't," she replied.

Jo wandered off to a group of people; one was a woman dressed as a siren. She has long white hair that was so bunched up, it looked awful. Her mouth was so large, that it had to be fake, since it was huge, a gaping hole with long teeth. The long shiny green dress she wore was tarnished at the bottom, but hid her feet. She also wore gloves similar to Jo's; however they didn't end in claws. There was a man, who wore a long cloak, and had a horrible-looking face, with long twisted horns. He held a trident, and had white hair like the siren, but not as long. The third was a girl who had a pink dress, and wrinkled grey skin. Her face was bent into a torturous grin, and her eyes were wide open, with black accentuated eyebrows. Her hair was scraggly blonde, and she had claws like Jo, only she didn't wear gloves, exposing her grey wrinkled hands.

"Jesus, they all look like monsters from a television program, but I cannot figure out what," said Archie.

"What's that?" asked Arthur.

"A television program is something pretty exclusive to my world, and we haven't got time for me to explain what television is," she replied.

"Look, they're going, what do we do now?" he asked, but Archie couldn't help staring at the people.

"Wait a minute, they are from what I think they are from. The woman in pink is Aphrodite. And Jo is The Ghost Girl; I don't know how I missed this, but how did these characters get into Discoucia?" she asked rhetorically.

"Because this is all a dream you are having and soon you'll wake up realising that you have no powers!" shouted Arthur.

"Oh come on be serious," replied Archie

"I don't know, shall I ask Jo?" asked Arthur.

"Yes please, wait till she's alone and then grab her," she said.

The group walked off, and Jo walked back in their direction. Arthur was about to grab her, but Archie grabbed him before he could. "Not now and not right in the middle of the room, follow her and go for it when she's near a small room," said Archie. They followed her up the stairs, and when they reached the room with the sand fire, they saw Jo walk into a narrow corridor. They grabbed Jo, pulled her into a room, and locked the door. Arthur held her, while Archie held her mouth, though was quite scared by the sharp fangs that Jo's mask had.

"What is this!? A poltergeist kidnapping!?" she shouted. Archie blinked twice, and they both faded into view. "Arthur! What are you doing...invisible!" she shouted, now returning to normal voice.

"It's a long story but Josephine, I give you The Fifth God...Archie," he announced.

"Who the heck are you?" asked Jo, now defensive since there was another woman in the room.

"Oh don't think of me as a threat Princess Josephine Archaelia Olandine, I'm actually a really pleasant fellow," she said.

"Your middle name is Archaelia?" asked Arthur.

"How did you know that, may I ask?" she said.

"Look, take the mask off then we can talk," she replied. Jo pulled her fake face off and her beautiful platinum hair bounced out.

"There, happy now?" she asked.

"Very. Now where did you get the idea for that costume?" asked Archie.

"From the head of our coven, she's new and has some interesting new ideas," said Jo.

"What's her name?" asked Archie.

"Professor Cordelia Paradise," said Jo.

With the sound of that name, Archie felt a feeling of dread flow through her and all of time felt like it slowed down. Arthur and Jo stared at her blankly.

"Do you know her?" asked Jo.

"Not anyone of that name, that's what worries me," said Archie.

"What is she talking about?" asked Jo.

"Look, I'm a little perplexed myself, but it seems that she is indeed the god Authos and has power over everything," said Arthur.

"Actually, since I'm talking to you two, I'll outline the fact that I do have a few constraints on my powers" she said.

"Like what?" asked Arthur.

"Well, firstly I cannot see into the future since that power belongs to someone else. I on the other hand control water since I am the water goddess," said Archie.

"Is that why you wear blue all the time?" asked Arthur.

"I have to coordinate don't I?" she replied.

"Is there anything else a little more helpful you can do?" asked Jo.

"Now that you mention it I can bestow basic elemental powers on humans. I shall be doing that on the three of you," she replied.

"Apart from you there are only two of us" said Arthur.

"Oh, you're right; well, it only proves that I don't have the power of foresight," she said.

"What else can't you do?" asked Jo.

"I can't control the sea on a whole since that's Seashorelle's territory, and even though we're friends I don't think she would like it" she said.

"Seashorelle is a she?" asked Arthur.

"Yes, so is Altatia, but she's the loveliest god of all. However she has it in for Lilia and will get her if she ever leaves Harrha and then returns," she said.

"Why would she have to leave and then return for the god of nature to seek revenge?" asked Jo.

"One of those odd conditions, like I only help men who have experienced life as both genders. One of the strange conditions but you were my guy Arthur" said Archie.

"Absolutely hilarious your godliness," he said sarcastically.

"You've met all of these deities" asked Jo.

"Yes. Yes I have. They are merely the legendary beasts that the Discoucian people used to worship but there is always another human-like god behind them. But you still believe that I'm mad or that I'm a fraud, right Josephine?" she asked.

Jo was taken aback by this, as she indeed did not trust this new person. "Turn Arthur into a newt, then I'll believe you," she said. The second she said it, she felt like she was becoming smaller, and the room was getting bigger.

"Oh dear, she's a newt" said Arthur, picking up the now fully-changed Jo. "Can you change her back?" he asked.

Just as he finished Jo changed back, however she ended up in Arthur's arms which caused him to drop her to the floor.

"Look I have to leave, I've lingered here too long and I'm going to look for this Paradise chick, where is she?" he asked.

"She is in The Green Coven in Gard," said Jo, putting her mask back on.

"I'll see you in Lesiga when the time comes; it was nice meeting you Jo and if you really need me just feel it in your heart and I will come," she said.

"Goodbye," said Jo, still not trusting Archie one bit.

"Bye Archie, see you soon hopefully," said Arthur.

Archie changed into her male form, and seemed to resemble someone Arthur distantly remembered from somewhere.

"She's a he?" asked Jo.

"It's a little complicated, you see, the Fifth God is a representation of two sides of the Discoucian Population. By that logic, she is both a she and a he at the same time," said Arthur.

"That's ridiculous," she said.

"She's not the one in the insanely hideous costume," said Arthur.

"Touché" she replied.

"Anyway, now that she's gone, are we going to get back to lunch in the Seven Wonders?" asked Arthur.

"I almost forgot. I'll meet you outside in a minute, you can leave through that door in the roof," she said. Above them was a trapdoor, and it was accessible by a ladder that was built into the wall.

"OK, see you in a minute then," he said.

If I live to see the...

Jo walked off, and Arthur climbed up the trapdoor. He pulled down a lever, and the trapdoor clicked down on a large cog, and when it was fully opened, he climbed up. He was in a storage room, and pulled the lever so that it closed again. Arthur looked around for a door, and when he found one, he walked out of the door, into the kitchen of the Seven Wonders Restaurant!

"Excuse me sir, are you lost?" asked a cook, who was cutting some fish.

"Yes, um, how do I get out of here? he asked.

"Take a left down the aisle, and go through the green door," he said, and hacked at the fish with a meat cleaver. Arthur walked through the green door, and saw Jo sitting at a table surrounded by plants. It was on its own, and looked quite private.

"Hello," said Arthur.

"Sit down please," she said in a forceful tone.

"Was going to do that anyway," said Arthur, who was feeling that he'd done something wrong but had no idea what.

"Look I want to know, why did you follow me? Do you not trust me?" she asked.

"Why did you go through my safe?" he retorted.

"I, I," she stuttered.

"Look I was curious, just like you were and this has nothing to do with trust," he said.

"So, you don't think it's weird that I belong to a coven like what's beneath us?" she said.

"Not really, whatever float's your boat I suppose," he replied.

"You really are the exponent of tolerance aren't you?" she said.

"I hope you are too, I'm no angel myself and are we ready to leave this particular thread of conversation?" he asked.

"Alright then. Shall I tell you of my plan to get both of us into Harrha?" she asked.

"Go for it," he said, as the waiter brought them their lunch.

"Well, you see, the invitation said that the High King must attend and if not him some other members of his family," she said.

"Yes, carry on," said Arthur.

"There are only three of us. My Father, myself, and Princess Alexandra" she explained.

"Right, continue," he said.

"Well unfortunately we don't have any male members of the family except for the King, so the only candidate I'm afraid is Alexandra," she said.

"Candidate for...I don't like where this is going" he said, chewing on some celery.

"Do you want to go and stop your sister or not?" she asked.

"The things we do for duty," he replied.

"So after lunch we'll go to the fancy dress shop and get you sorted," she replied.

"The Uncommon Bird you mean?" he asked.

"Yes, that one," she said.

"Is there anything else you want to talk about?" he asked.

"I want to talk about this Archie person," she replied.

"What do you want to know?" he asked.

"Where did you first meet her?" she asked.

"First was outside Starfall, then in the underground desert I spent some more time with her," he replied.

"And at that point was she normal?" she asked.

"At that point she was quite enigmatic, but I didn't mind since I had a travelling companion through the road to The Dark Chasm," he replied.

"And is she a magician or a fully fledged god?" she asked.

"I think she is the real deal but hates to be regarded as one," replied Arthur.

"Yes, well I still don't trust her, did she say anything about me?" she asked.

"Well when I was joking around with you, when I kept pulling the books out and you kept putting it back she told me not to, I think because she was concerned for you," he replied. "I don't think it was very fair to do that considering I couldn't see you," she said.

"Shall we go, and get this over with as soon as possible," he asked.

"Okay, follow me; I have an appointment with Madame Arrietta at 3.00, and since this is diplomatic, she is going to empty the whole shop and close it, so we shall be completely alone," she replied.

"Yayy!" he replied sarcastically. They left their table and walked out into the bustling street outside. People were milling around, and all the shops were open. They walked to the bottom of Miracle Boulevard and saw that The Uncommon Bird was indeed closed. A man was heard outside saying, "Closed on a Saturday, what is this city coming to." Jo knocked on the door three times, then four times. The door opened, and they entered. The door was locked behind them, and now they were alone.

The Uncommon Bird was filled with every possible costume that could be conceived. They hung on racks that extended all around the room. Above the racks were hats of all different kinds and in another room every accessory was to be found. "Arture! You've come back!" shouted a voice from another room.

"Hello Delphine, how are you doing?" he replied.

Madame Arrietta was a large woman, who wore a red and black dress and had frizzy ginger hair. She had too much makeup on, but since she had a surplus of it no one took much notice. Arthur knew her after years of coming here, and had sort of a family relationship despite the fact that they were not related at all.

"Good afternoon Madame, we're here for the fitting," said Jo.

"Yes, please explain what you wish to do," she said.

"This is urgent business for the High King," she said.

"Look Princess, I cater to every fantasy of nearly every Lord, Lady and Royal in Discoucia and beyond, so I'm aware that the reason you didn't want anyone in here apart from us three is because you want it to remain private," she explained.

"I'm glad we got that one out of the way," said Arthur.

"So what is it that you want?" Delphine asked, walking over to Arthur and putting her hands on his shoulders.

"Well, this is going to sound a little strange, but I need you to turn Arthur into my sister Princess Alexandra," she asked.

"Arthur, you're not planning what I think you are, are you?" she asked in a worried voice.

"Sorry?" he asked.

Jo whispered something into his ear, and Arthur's eyes widened. He put his hands over his mouth and shuddered.

"No, that's not what I meant," she said.

"Oh, oh good, no, that's not why," said Arthur.

"Then why would you possibly want to look like Princess Alexandra?" asked Delphine.

"We need to get into Harrha Island and considering Arthur and Lilia are brother and sister you see our dilemma," explained Jo.

"Oh, in that case I've got everything you're going to need," she said.

"I already know this isn't going to be pleasant," said Arthur.

"What colour hair does she have? The same as yours?" asked Delphine.

"Yes, she has more light blonde hair that changes to platinum in the dark," she said.

"I'll just give you platinum, and how long will it have to be?" asked Delphine.

"About three inches above the waist, at least that was how long it was the last time anyone saw her," said Jo.

"Has this all been arranged with the real Alexandra? You don't want the real one turning up," she said.

"Yes, Alex won't leave the monastery until we've finished," said Jo.

"And the High King has sent a message back to Lilia that he will be sending his two daughters," said Arthur, sitting on a chair and reading a book that was left by one of the mirrors.

Delphine left to get the platinum wig, while Jo looked around for something that would fit Arthur. "So how long have you known Delphine?" asked Jo.

"I guess since I left Fina all those years ago. When the uprising started Chene was always safe from attack due to its massively high walls and the personnel of King Jassuer," he replied.

"Why did he call himself a king?" asked Jo.

"He declared that Chene was a separate kingdom but as long as he didn't smuggle, your father said he could do what he wanted," explained Arthur.

"I see, and you busted him for that but how come he remained a king," she asked.

"I don't know, probably because people would ask why he had changed his title which would lead to more questions and then it would bring the whole affair out into the open," he explained.

"That makes sense," she said.

"Didn't you learn about this stuff when you grew up?" asked Arthur. There was a puff of smoke above Jo, and a piece of paper floated down. Jo caught it and read it out loud. 'Please tell Arthur not to force you to break the fourth wall, once is enough so please don't let it happen again...A' she read.

"She can hear us?" asked Jo.

"I think we should just not talk about it and carry on with the matter at hand," he replied.

"This doesn't freak you out?" asked Jo.

"Not really, just run with it like I'm doing with this," he said.

"Here we go," said Delphine, plonking a heavy platinum wig on Arthur's head. Arthur instantly looked like a girl, and the hair colour suited his bright blue eyes. The wig had a large yellow bow attached to a black hair band.

"We'll take it, when were done could you put it in a hat box?" asked Jo.

"No problem, we'll leave it on 'Alexandra' for a bit," said Delphine.

"What colour would you suggest for a dress?" asked Jo.

"Light blue, since it would match his eyes," said Delphine. Arthur was left sitting down, while the other two looked for a dress. Another cloud appeared, and another piece of paper floated down onto Arthur's lap. "'Since I'm the first one, I shall say to you the second one there, I hope you're having fun'" he read. "Yes Archie, lots of fun" he said into the mirror.

121

Suddenly Archie's face appeared in the mirror, but it was dark as if she was in the night while they were in the middle of the day. "Archie?!" he whispered.

"I haven't got long," she said.

"Where are you?" he asked.

"I'm home, my dwelling place is the Twilight Vale where it's twilight all the time and I have everything I could possibly want," she replied.

"Why are you here?" he asked.

"I just wanted to tell you that if you wanted to stop off at Illumination Island, then my friend Seashorelle will say hello," she said.

"The God of the Sea will say hello!?" he asked.

"Yes, you see she owes me a favour; you look good by the way... seriously," she said.

"How would you possibly want me to respond to that?" he asked.

"I don't know to be honest but you have fun," she said, and disappeared out of the mirror leaving Arthur staring into the mirror.

"Are you that vain?" asked Jo, who had walked behind Arthur.

"Of course I'm not, I was just talking to...never mind, but I got another message from Archie; she said to go to Illumination Island before we go to Harrha. It's two hours from there to Harrha, so I won't have to be Alex before hand, right?" asked Arthur.

"I don't know, if we see anyone that's already going to Harrha then how do we explain that?" she asked.

"Oh great this is just perfect," he said.

"Why does she want us to go to Illumination Island anyway?" asked Jo.

"You'll see," he said.

"I got you a dress and so did Delphine, so try them both on and we'll see which looks better," she said. Arthur took the two dresses over to the changing room while Jo stared into the mirror.

"BOO!" shouted Archie who appeared in the mirror with a screaming face while Jo screamed and fell backwards.

"What happened?" asked Arthur, peering out from behind the curtain.

"I am going to murder her, god or not" she said. Arthur went back, now feeling better that Jo wasn't having such a disturbingly good time.

Arthur walked out, and personally he felt ridiculous. "That looks amazing," said Delphine.

"Try the other one, then we can choose between the two," said Jo. He returned again, and they both agreed that the first one looked better than the one he wore now.

"Try the first one again," they said. Arthur walked out with the first dress which was bright blue and had a silver coloured design on it and ran down to Arthur's wrists.

"Right, now put these on," said Jo, handing him a pair of long silvery gloves.

"Now, you need some shoes, and I know that were dancing around the subject, but what is he going to wear...underneath?" asked Delphine.

"I'll sort that out and I'll give him some shoes too," said Jo.

In Thorisea's Tangerine Monastery Princess Alexandra was meditating in her large room when she suddenly shuddered. "What was that? Like someone just walked over my grave or someone mentioned my name. If they did my ears would be burning so they were probably doing more than just talking about me," she said to herself.

"I suppose were done then, I'll pack everything up and have it delivered to your ship, is there anywhere else you are going before you leave for Harrha?" asked Delphine, taking the wig off Arthur's head.

"We're going swimming," said Jo.

"That's lovely, it's good that you're going somewhere as a couple," she said.

After an awkward silence Arthur was the one who broke it. "Oh no, were not a couple," he said.

"Oh I'm sorry. Well enjoy yourselves," she said.

"We will, thanks for the help," said Jo.

Jo walked out, and Arthur was pulled back by Delphine. "She didn't say anything, you did," she replied.

"What do you mean?" he asked.

"She likes you Arthur," she said.

"I'm on it, but I can't be the one to be going after her," he replied, and walked out into the sunshine.

After going swimming, they went back to the ship, and saw that all the packages were placed on the table in the centre of the sitting room. "There's your costume, or disguise or whatever, are we going to leave now?" asked Jo.

"It's too late to leave now and besides, we need to go to Cesta first, mainly because the ship needs to be repainted. Also I want to visit the Blue Coven before we go to Harrha, since I have something to tell them," he explained.

"There are so many questions for that statement that I don't know where to start," she said.

"Have you ever visited the Blue Coven before?" asked Arthur.

"No, have you?" she asked.

"When I was very young, I think I must have been 35 but I remember standing in front of the huge glass screen that looks out across the ocean and my father picking me up and putting me on his shoulder," he said.

"That must be a fond memory for you," she said.

"It is," he replied.

"How did you get in?" she asked.

"I'm a noble of Fina, and I had an interest in the sea back then, and I still do now, plus it was my birthday," said Arthur.

"I see, and they will let you in now?" asked Jo.

"Of course, and you too, they love to have high profile people there, but there is something about it you should know," he said.

"They don't dress up as fish do they?" she asked, sarcastically.

"No, there's a lot of running water, and the only light comes from the large windows that are built underneath the sea and rivers. You have to see it since it's a marvel of engineering, and that's an understatement," he said.

They both went to sleep, even Arthur who had disturbing dreams of walking all around Evermore in a bright pink dress, while Jo's dreams were infinitely more interesting.

She was walking down a tunnel, and above was a blue light reflected through the windows in the ceiling. She saw that hundreds of fish were swimming above her, and she walked along the tunnel, all the while looking up. She walked across a metal grate, and below she heard the sound of rushing water. She woke up; it was still dark. The clock on the wall read 1:00.

She tip toed down the stairs and past Arthur, who was snoring in an undignified position on the settee, with his legs bent over the back of the arms and his head nearly touching the carpet. She ran out to go to the Sky Port bathroom, then came back and went to sleep again.

This time she was riding a whale through the ocean like a horse. It was swimming gracefully, and she heard it sing. She saw another whale, and Arthur was riding it. She tried to shout him, but blew bubbles instead. "You're underwater, he can't hear you," said the whale. Jo nodded and let the whale glide across a large empty expanse of sand, and it blew it up in a vast cloud. She then saw another whale, and Archie was riding it.

"You know Josephine, you just have to ask and I can make this happen," she said.

Jo mumbled something, and Archie replied "Just remember a piece of advice I got from Lupin the Third, 'The key to enjoying life is doing as many foolish things as possible', remember that Josephine," she said. Jo woke up again. This time the clock read 3:00.

She crept downstairs and now Arthur was laid on his front, with his arms over the left arm and his feet over the edge of the right arm. He was still snoring when she came back from the bathroom a second time. She went to sleep again, but her strange night wasn't over.

Jo was walking past the largest glass screen she had seen, and she saw thousands of fish swim past it. When they had dispersed, she saw the most beautiful scene she had ever seen. The coral was so colourful that it hurt her eyes to see it. Tiny fish were congregating around red, blue, green, orange and purple sea anemones. She then saw something else; a creature so large that its sheer size was enough to scare Jo. It swam and encircled the rainbow amphitheatre, and then swam straight for Jo. She was a tiny speck in the shadow of this leviathan. She woke up, and it was 4:00.

She walked downstairs, and now Arthur was now upside down, with his hair all spread out on the carpet. His legs were bent backwards over the back of the settee, and he was still snoring. When she returned, he was lying on the floor, with his back arched up, and Jo was completely at a loss as to how Arthur was comfortable in that position. She picked him up, and laid him on the settee, and covered him in the blanket that lay on the back.

"Sleep well, Artie," she said.

The sun rose in the east, and Jo awoke after a peaceful sleep. Today she would see a wonder, and if it was anything like her dreams, then she couldn't wait.

On the windswept island of Harrha in Queen Lilia's castle, someone had just finished a painting of Archie. The shadowy figure then put it on the wall and stepped back. The painting then became peppered with darts as the dark figure stepped into the light. Lilia was not happy at all.

The City of Cesta was built on the site of a seaside village that was destroyed by Seashorelle, when they tried to catch her with a fleet of ships. Ever since then it has grown differently, and instead of 100% fishing, they mine sapphires from beneath the ocean, but they are so deep that they don't affect the seabed. The city is built with avenues for streets, and when the city floods, they fill with water and people travel through them on boats. When the water level drops, they walk along them as normal.

Arthur woke up quite cosy on the settee, and tried to remember if he had put the blanket on himself or not. "Who else would have done it?" he thought to himself.

Jo walked downstairs, and found that Arthur was tidying up before they left. This time Jo was wearing a dark blue version of her earlier green ensemble. She and Arthur matched each other perfectly, since Arthur was wearing light blue. "It looks nice, how did you sleep?" he asked.

"Some strange dreams, but otherwise it was pleasant," she replied.

"Right, were off as soon as Corky can get the Emerald Engine stoked," he said. Just as he finished, a shudder was felt through the ship.

126

"There we go, I'm going on the deck, and I want to see the Chene from the air in the daylight," he said.

"Me too," she said.

Chene did look beautiful from the air, and as they lifted to 200ft above the ground, the place looked so much smaller, and Arthur couldn't believe that the huge expanse of the Yellow Coven lay beneath all the streets and buildings. They flew south, and Jo saw that the huge expanse of wasteland outside of the City of Chene was so large, that she couldn't see the western shore and the largest part of the Sky River that flowed out into the Infinite Sea. They flew over the vast wasteland and the shadow of the Nostradamus was a tiny black dot on an otherwise blank canvas.

"As my Uncle Philip used to say, the best place to see the world is from above," said Arthur.

"You had an Uncle Philip?" she asked.

"Yes, he built The Nostradamus, and taught me how to fly it if I ever needed to, and it seems that he knew what was going to happen," he replied.

"How many members are there in your family?" she asked.

"There's Lilia and I, then there was my mother and father, my mother's brother Philip and my father's two sisters Julia and Bianca. Then there's my Grandfather Lucian, and his wife Iris. And then there's my Grandmother Calsyne and her husband Tristan. Then finally there's my Great Grandmother Helatia, and finally, my Great Aunt Maude," he explained.

"I see that you have a rather extensive family, what happened to your Uncle Phillip?" she asked.

"He was hit on the head with a mace by my father after a very big argument, but he didn't die. He wandered around the forests beneath the peaks of Fina for days. He is the only Pageon apart from me and Lilia to still live, although it's not much of an existence living in Hemlock Asylum," he said.

"Your Uncle Philip is in Hemlock Asylum?" she asked, shocked.

"Yes, I've tried to get him out, but even if I did what would I do with him?" he asked.

"That's the sad truth I suppose," she said.

"Anyway, I'd rather talk about something else," he replied.

"Why don't we just not talk about anything, and enjoy the beautiful scenery," she replied.

Jo put her arm around Arthur's waist, and she pulled him closer. Arthur was so caught up in the scenery that he didn't notice, and Jo laid her head on his shoulder as they flew south, where the weather is warmer and the wonders of the Blue Coven awaited.

They flew across several areas of farmland, which had large square fields bordered by old stone walls and the odd tree growing over a gate. They saw that it was harvest time, and that some people were pulling a cart that was filled with a huge mass of hay, and some farm houses, with barns that were painted red with white roofs. They then passed over random clumps of trees that had turned to fiery red fires in the wake of autumn. The grass had turned to yellow, and it looked surprisingly beautiful. They passed over stately homes outside small villages, which were all different, were surrounded by walls and had their own flying ships anchored outside.

"I always wanted a house like that, a stately home with a big red brick wall around it, and big fruit trees in the orchard. A pond where ducks are swimming and a big garden where I can play catch with my kids. And in the snow we can build a snowman and then pelt each other with snowballs. Do you ever dream about the future?" he asked.

"I'm a princess of Discoucia, and when my father dies Alex and I become the new advisors," she replied.

"That's not very fair," he said.

"My future is pretty much assured," she said. The ship stopped slowly, until it came to a complete stop above a grove of trees. A puff of smoke appeared above Jo and a piece of paper floated down to her.

"Don't count on that, A'," she read.

"I don't know what to say to that, except maybe we should go inside," said Arthur. They both walked into the sitting room, and the ship started off again as suddenly as it stopped. Back in the cabin, they both sat down on the settee.

"You know, she said that she couldn't see the future, though I don't believe that," said Jo.

"Maybe not, but if you think about it, she has given you hope," replied Arthur.

"I guess she has," said Jo.

"Anyway, were nearly there, and when we get to Cesta, I'll take you out for dinner, after we've visited the Blue Coven that is," he said. Jo leant on Arthur, and began to drift off to sleep, since she had so many interruptions last night.

The Sea Hag of Cesta

Corky walked in on Jo sleeping soundly on Arthur's lap, and Arthur looking at him with wide eyes. "What's the matter sir, situation not perfect enough for you?" whispered Corky sarcastically.

"What do I do? She's fallen asleep on me, literally!" he whispered back loudly.

"Shall I turn on the Barry White sir?" he asked.

"What in the heck are you talking about?!" he asked.

"No idea, your friend Archie told me to say it if this situation ever arose, personally I don't know what she was talking about," said Corky.

"Look, you know what to do, it's nearly dark, and so tomorrow morning we get the ship repainted white, like an Evermore Peace Ship, and then were going to stay here for tomorrow, and the morning after that we'll go to Illumination Island, and from there to Harrha, understand?" he asked, still whispering.

"Yes sir, I'll leave you to what is considered an unanswerable riddle...get out of that without moving," he said, and disappeared through the door.

Arthur carried Jo upstairs, and tucked her into bed, and he went downstairs, wrote a letter which he left on the desk for her, and walked out into the streets of Cesta.

Jo awoke on her own to the sound of seagulls and the sound of people talking outside her window. She looked out to see that a group of people were painting the ship. "Artie! Artie! What's going on?" she shouted as she walked down the stairs. There was no answer, and she found the piece of parchment on the table. "Jo, I've gone to the Blue Coven since I couldn't sleep, and I'll meet you in the entrance, the old abandoned lighthouse of St Helio'," she read.

She left the sitting room and saw that most of the ship was white, and that they were just finishing. She looked at the floor, and saw that it was still wet. She jumped off the ship in a spectacular display of acrobatics, and saw that when she put her hands on the banister to propel herself through the air, they were wet too, and she now had white paint on her hands and shoes. She walked down the stairs that led down from the Sky Port and walked over to the huge fountain in the centre of the city that was shaded by a massive acacia tree.

She washed the paint off and looked down into the water at the reflection, and thought about what Arthur had said. What future did she really dream of? One that was exactly as Arthur had described. She kept staring at her reflection, and saw Arthur's face in the water. She turned around and saw that there was no one near her, but the usual number of people running around. She looked back into the pool and he was still there, only now he was smiling.

She put her hand into the water and saw that the bottom of the fountain was made of glass. She felt across the glass, and saw that she couldn't see Arthur anymore, because the water rippled. She waited until it calmed and she saw Arthur say something but she couldn't hear him. He disappeared, and she was left alone again.

"Strangest thing is, I miss him," she said to herself. She got up, and walked over to the acacia tree, which had a plaque that she read aloud. "'This was the only tree to survive the disastrous flood of Seashorelle, and will forever remain as a testament to the foolishness of the people of the time',"

"Are you looking for something?" asked a young boy, who was smartly dressed.

"Yes, is that the Lighthouse of St Helio?" she asked, pointing at a large lighthouse that rose above the rest of the buildings. It was in a good state, and there was a stone staircase on the outside leading to the top, which wasn't in bad shape either.

"Nope, that's the current one, that's the Lighthouse of St Helio."

he replied, pointing up to the south. On top of a grey cliff with rain clouds and thunder, was a black shape poking up into the sky.

"Oh come on, the evil looking old abandoned lighthouse? This is like out of a book" she said.

"What an odd thing to say," he replied.

"Who are you exactly?" she asked.

"I'm Hylele, Hylele Aquatine, son of the current Lord Aquatine," he said.

"Lady Josephine Olandine, nice to meet you Hylele," she replied.

"You're the daughter of the High King?! Oh that's brilliant, there's now someone in the city that I can't boss around," he said.

"Umm, OK. Take me to the lighthouse," she said.

"Follow me," he said, and walked across the square in the direction of the lighthouse.

"OK then," said Jo, who was surprised at how easy this was.

They walked along a street that was filled with stalls selling a variety of different fish, which were all different colours, however Jo didn't notice, because her attention was focused on the stupidly scary looking building surrounded by crows circling its top. "It's not that far, but why would you possibly want to go there?" he asked.

"Umm, it was on the tourist route, and I wanted to go to the scariest place in Cesta for a laugh," said Jo.

"You're joking right?" he asked.

"Why do you think I'm going there?" she asked.

"You're going to the Blue Coven? Why didn't you just use the main entrance in my house?" he asked.

"Because I had no idea that there was one, and also because my friend is obviously planning something, and that's why I'm going. I'm new to all this you know," she said.

"Why didn't you fly there?" he asked.

"The ship's being painted," she replied.

"How big is your ship?" he asked.

"Normal skyship size, why?" she asked.

"My father is having a new ship commissioned, it's going to be larger than normal ships, and will have several rooms on it, so we can go on holiday and won't have to stay in hotels," he said.

"Good for you," she said.

They were now out of the city and came to a bridge that spanned another outlet of the Sky River. It was so strange to be warm and sunny here, but at the top of the hill it was dark and gloomy. "None of this seems odd to you, the weather I mean?" she said.

"No, should it?" he asked.

"No, I mean nothing makes much sense anyway, so why should the weather be any different" she replied, shrugging. They walked across the well trod path that led to the lighthouse that now pierced the sky like a demonic stalagmite. The windows were shattered and the wood was rotting. She walked up to the door and saw that Hylele had stopped. "Thank you for taking me here, tell your father I said hello," she said.

"OK, have fun," he said, and ran off down the hill.

"My God look at me, what has become of Princess Josephine?" she asked herself, and pushed on the old shuttered door.

The Lighthouse was as dilapidated as it could possibly be, but the stairs looked in good shape. "Arthur!" she shouted up the stairs. She heard the sound of someone upstairs, and saw a black shape moving. "You know, if I think about this logically, the entrance to the Blue Coven must be somewhere down, not up, so there is no reason for me to go upstairs and investigate that sound," she said. A puff of smoke appeared above her, and her eyes followed the piece of paper that floated down. "Honestly, when is it ever that simple" she read aloud. "OK, I guess we're doing this," she said, and walked over the stairs. She stepped up, and the stairs creaked as she stepped on them.

"1, 2, 3, 4, 5, 6, 7, 8, 9," she counted the number of steps and the number of creaks, which were the same. "I walk up nine steps and every one of them creaks, isn't that a bit of a cliché?" she asked rhetorically, and put her hand out ready to receive another note. A puff of smoke appeared and she again read it aloud. "'Funny, but I would be more concerned about what's waiting for you at the top of the stairs'" she read.

"Okay, let's go then," said Jo.

She reached the first floor, and dodged a chain that was flung down at her, and heard the sound of cackling above her; however it was a female cackling, which made her wonder. "Artie, are you practising a female voice? Because if you are, it needs a lot of work!" she shouted. A cloud of dust descended from the ceiling, and then several floor boards, and Jo was greeted by The Sea Hag. She had old wrinkled skin, her eyes were glowing green, and she was covered in seaweed that was spread out across the old rags that were once clothes.

"GEETTT OUUUTTT!!!" she shouted, displaying a set of decaying yellow teeth.

"OK, your creepy costume looks way better than mine, and your whole act is really quite terrifying," she said.

"I SAID GET OUUUTTT!!" she shouted again.

"Seriously, I gave up when you figured out it was me," she said. The Hag ran at her and swiped with her long fingernails. "Okay, very funny," she said, stepping backwards towards the stairs. She ran down them, pursued by the Hag, and straight through the door. "NEVER RETUUURNNN!!!!" she shouted, and slammed the door.

Jo stood staring at the lighthouse, and scratched her head. "If that was Arthur, then he's done his homework," she said.

"I thought you were going to the Blue Coven, what happened?" asked Hylele, who had appeared out of nowhere.

"Where did you spring from?" she asked.

"I was down by the river, to see those fish that were laying in the dirty water dying," he said. Jo held out her hand, and the smoke, and the piece of paper floated down.

"Have they got you hypnotised?" she read.

"No, not really," he replied.

"Puff of smoke, letter appearing out of nowhere, like I said before, any of this odd to you?" asked Jo.

"Like I said before, no," he said.

"Right, well, I'm going to take this, and go back in there," she said, picking up a large stick.

"You're going to use a stick against the Sea Hag?" he asked.

"You got any better suggestions?" she asked angrily.

"No no, carry on princess," he replied.

Hylele watched as Jo walked up again to the lighthouse. He waited at the bottom of the hill and heard a load of hammering and crashing

135

sounds coming from the first floor. He then saw a window smash and the stick flew through it, sailed through the air and landed on the floor. A puff of smoke appeared above him and he read it aloud. "'I told her it wouldn't be this simple'," he said.

Jo ran out of the lighthouse and back to Hylele.

"I have one question, the entrance to the Blue Coven is right as you enter, and it's a trapdoor, why didn't you just go in and avoid the Sea Hag all together?" he asked.

"Listen Hylele, when you get older, you'll understand that as a matter of principle I have to capture the Sea Hag and find out who she really is," she explained.

"She's a Sea Hag, why would you possibly think that she's anyone else," he said.

"Real Sea Hags don't have glowing green eyes and cover themselves in rotting seaweed," she replied.

"Ah, that makes sense, so what's your third plan of attack?" he asked.

"Usually I would point a gun at her, but for three reasons I won't. People may find it offensive, it doesn't convey a good message to children like yourself and because where's the fun in it?" she explained.

"What people?" he asked.

"The people who find it offensive," she said.

"You're being patronising," he said.

"No I'm not, child," she said, and ruffled his thick brown hair. She walked off again for a third crack at the Sea Hag.

Jo decided this time she was going to climb around the back and surprise her. She made the shaky ascent and reached the first floor. The Sea Hag had gone, and she climbed higher to the second floor. The Sea Hag was not there either, and she decided to climb to the lamp room on the third floor, and surmised that the Sea Hag must be up there. She reached the top and saw that she was, and she was looking through some of the boxes that littered the place. She found what she was looking for, a blue key, and she walked down the stairs.

Jo vaulted over the wooden banister and sneaked to the stairs. When the Sea Hag was on the second floor she walked over to a safe. "Finally, the treasure!" it shouted, and unlocked the safe. Jo slid down the banister as fast as she could, and smashed straight into the Sea Hag. She knocked her out, and she lay in an undignified pile on the floor.

"So Artie, what is it you wanted to keep me away from?" she asked, and saw that the safe was full of platinum bars.

"Jo? What is taking you so flippin' long?!" said Arthur, climbing up the stairs.

"I'm solving the mystery of why you disguised yourself as the Sea Hag" she replied.

"Solving the mystery of the what now?" he replied. Jo turned around and saw that Arthur was standing at the top of the stairs with Hylele.

"What are you doing there? You're supposed to be knocked out on the floor over here" she said.

"Well, who have you got tied up on the floor?" he asked.

"I haven't tied her up yet," replied Jo.

Arthur ran over to the Sea Hag and tied her up with some rope that he found. "Rule number one, Jo, always tie up the bad guy, and then find out what they are doing," he said.

"Right, now let's find out who The Sea Hag really is," said Jo, who pulled off The Sea Hag mask, and Hylele was the one who spoke up.

"Father!? What are you doing?" he asked. The all looked at the stricken form of Lord Aquatine, with his long moustache and his grey goatee beard.

"Okay, well I'm at a loss here," said Arthur.

"I caught a fake monster, I'm happy with myself," said Jo.

"The worst thing is, we can't do anything, and it's his city, so he can do what he wants," said Arthur.

"I've got an idea, but only if Hylele doesn't mind," she said.

Aquatine woke up, to find that he was tied to a chair, and that his son was sat on the first step of the stairs, and either side of him was Lady Josephine and Sir Arthur Pageon. "I got caught, didn't I?" he asked.

"Oh yeah, I got you good," said Jo.

"Well I rule this city, so you can untie me," he said.

"One question, why did you want those bars of platinum? You're rich enough to not need them, right?" asked Arthur.

"I'm a very greedy person," he replied.

"Ah, in that case Hylele will sort you out," replied Arthur, and Jo followed him downstairs.

Arthur and Jo walked over to the trapdoor and climbed down to the spiral staircase that led beneath the cliff. Hylele walked through the streets of Cesta pulling a small cart, with the Sea Hag tied up behind him. He was running as fast as he could to his home, considering it was his father that he was pulling behind him.

The Blue Coven

The spiral staircase led down deep under the lighthouse, and the two descended down, illuminated by torches that hung from the blue walls. "OK, so have you been down here the whole time?" she asked.

"Mostly, I heard that there was a Sea Hag haunting the lighthouse, but I didn't expect you to go for it, I thought you would come down here straight away," he said.

"Yeah, some things got in the way, but I found it quite fun solving a mystery," she replied.

"It's why I started travelling," he replied.

They reached the bottom of the spiral staircase, and entered a blue corridor, which was about 10ft long. They heard the sound of running water, and Jo emerged on a beautiful scene. They were about 50ft below ground, and the main entrance to the Coven was built inside a natural cave. The water was coming out of holes in the wall and flowed into magnificently carved pools. It was the crystals that were growing out of the walls that caught Jo's eye. They were red, blue, green, yellow, orange, violet and white colours, and Jo found them far more beautiful than the gems that she had a surplus of in Evermore. There were also some flowers growing out of the rock walls, and Jo felt as though she was in a dream, and nearly drifted away to the soothing sound of the slow flowing water.

Arthur took her hand and led her along another corridor, and Jo looked above and saw that she was below the Sky River, and her dream had come true. The River was so large, that she saw huge fish were swimming gracefully through the water, and she saw salmon that were swimming upstream against the current and she thought the whole scene looked achingly beautiful.

They reached the end of the corridor and the whole of the Coven opened up in front of them. The place was sparsely lit, but the main source of light was the huge glass screen that looked out onto the ocean scene outside.

Geographically they were beneath the city harbour, and Jo saw that either side of the screen was the two stone harbour walls. In the centre of the floor was the symbol of Seashorelle, and it was illuminated by the pale light coming through the screen. "This is amazing, how on earth did they build it?" she asked.

"Well, when they knew that there was about a foot of rock between the wall of the Coven and the harbour floor, then they basically built the screen first and then broke the wall down," he explained.

"It really is a miracle of engineering isn't it?" she asked. A puff of smoke appeared by Arthur, and he caught the piece of paper that floated down. "'You're welcome'," he read.

"She was sending me those when I was upstairs," said Jo.

"Did she say anything interesting?" he asked.

"She made me laugh," said Jo.

"No easy task," he replied.

"I want to get closer," said Jo.

They walked up to the huge screen, and there were other people standing with it, and they all looked rather important. Jo put her hands on the glass and stared out at the majesty of the ocean. She saw what she saw in her dream, only it was thousands of times more beautiful now, because she was actually there. The walls of the harbour were covered in coral formations that were all the colours of the rainbow. It was beginning to get dark, and the whole picturesque vision was lit up, and all the multicoloured fish were swimming around the safe reef, while the bigger fish were swimming between the seaweed covered rocks in the centre. A shark swam close, and all the fish hid. It swam away and they all returned to normal.

"I shudder to think what Lilia will do here if she invades the kingdom," said Arthur.

"For the sake of everyone who can experience this, she needs to be stopped," said Jo.

"Or convinced to take a different outlook on life," said Arthur.

"I know she's your sister, and you love her, but if we can't convince her, then we have to face reality," said Jo.

"Have a little faith," said Arthur.

"So what else do they have here?" asked Jo.

"There's the Tidal Rock Pools, and they are pretty spectacular," said Arthur.

"Then let's go," she said.

They followed the floor pattern that led to a large blue arch that in turn led down a corridor that descended down to a wide open space. The Tidal Rock Pools consisted of a large flat area which was peppered with rock pools, and water was slowly rising. The pools were home to hundreds of tiny sea creatures, and Jo saw a lobster clamber from a small pool into a larger one.

"The tide is coming in, so soon the door will be locked and the room will fill with water," he said.

"This place really is amazing," said Jo.

"All the covens are different, and since this one is dedicated to the sea and Seashorelle, I think they're doing a good job," he replied. They returned to the main room, and decided to walk back to the other entrance, and on the way they would see some more wonders.

"So what does Seashorelle actually look like?" asked Jo.

"I have no idea to be honest; we might bump into her on the way to Harrha, and then you can find out for yourself," he said.

"I doubt that will happen," said Jo, who didn't know what Arthur knew. They passed through another tunnel whose floor was made of a metal grate, and beneath a river flowed.

"That's part of the Sky River; it flows all the way from Evermore, and picks up more water from Fina and ends up here," explained Arthur.

They reached a small room that had a glass panel in the floor running through it. "I suppose that this is part of the river, running underneath the room" said Jo.

"Like you said, miracle of engineering," said Arthur.

"Where are we going after this?" she asked.

"I'm taking you out for dinner at the best seafood restaurant in Cesta, 'The 5,000 Fish Fingers of Dr Sea'," he said.

"Umm, that's the strangest name I've ever heard," she said. A puff of smoke appeared and Jo read the note that fell down.

"I couldn't say "The Crab-net of Dr Calamari"; otherwise Hanna-Barbera would sue, not that I'm saying they definitely would, but it's an in-the-event-of," read Jo.

"Does she ever listen to herself?" she asked.

Jo turned the paper over, and read the next bit. "'I drift in and out'," she read.

"I agree, she's quite funny," said Arthur.

"So lead on," said Jo.

There was a set of stairs at the end of the corridor, and Jo walked first, and Arthur followed her. They walked up for about five minutes, and came to a well lit room with a pair of ornate polished oak doors on the other side to where they came in. They opened the doors, and were met by Hylele.

"Welcome to my home, Princess Josephine" he said. The room they had entered was so beautifully furnished and so filled with things, from globes to a telescope, a desk with various measuring instruments on it, and a bookcase that was locked with a glass cover.

"Umm, where is your father?" asked Jo, keeping in a laugh.

"He's in bed, convalescing from a bash on the head," replied Hylele.

"I see. Well we'll be on our way unless there's anything else," said Arthur.

"Nope, I'll keep an eye on the house," he said.

"You don't have to boast and order people around you know, it doesn't make you any real friends, and doesn't make you a better person," said Jo.

"And what if I like it?" asked Hylele.

"Your father dressed up as The Sea Hag because he liked platinum, so where do you think you'll end up?" asked Arthur.

"I'll bear it in mind, have a nice time wherever you're going." he said, and disappeared through a door to the right.

"We're going left, so follow me, and when we get to the Sky Port the ship should be ready,". They left the magnificence of the mansion of Lord Aquatine, and made their way to the ship, so they could get changed for dinner.

"You know Artie, I just had a thought, Lord Aquatine saw you, and he's going to Harrha too, so I need to be seen with Alex," she said.

"I hate it when you're right," he replied.

"So, were going to have to put off dinner, since you're not ready," she said.

"If I can't fool a restaurant full of people then what chance do I have with my own sister?" he asked.

"I hate it when you're right as well," she replied.

"Anyway, I practised my voice while you were running around in the lighthouse," he replied.

"Prove it," she replied.

"How's this sis?" he asked in a perfect impression of a girl.

"Okay that has got to be the creepiest thing I have ever heard," she said. "Is it that bad?" he asked, still in the same voice.

"No, it's perfect, that's what is so creepy and you sound just like my sister," she replied.

"Oh good, then let's get changed and go to dinner," he replied, in his normal voice this time.

They climbed the stairs to the Sky Port, and the ship was waiting, painted white with blue stripes. "It looks like one of my father's ships, and soon his two daughters will be travelling on a peace mission," said Jo.

"If your sister ever finds out about this then she's gonna kill me," he said.

"Oh I don't know, for all her faults she has a good sense of humour," replied Jo.

"OK young princess, turn off your mind and relax," said a monk in orange robes. Alexandra then began to slowly levitate when she felt like her ears were on fire.

"Arrgghh!" she shouted and collapsed on the floor.

In the ships wardrobe Jo was putting makeup on Arthur's face, and he wasn't keeping still."Look all you need is some chalk dust and you'll look perfect," she said.

143

"It's not my fault that I tan well you know," he replied.

"Right, look in the mirror," she said. Arthur looked in the mirror, and he saw that Jo did do a good job, and that he now looked like the picture she had showed him of Princess Alexandra.

"Oh god has it really come to this?" he said.

"Oh don't look so sad, this way even I have trouble recognising you," she replied.

"I suppose so," he replied.

"Stand up and walk around, how does everything feel?" she asked.

"Surprisingly comfortable to be honest," he replied.

"That's the spirit; I mean you can enjoy this whole little experience if you want, it's not every day you get to wear the most comfortable underwear in the kingdom," she said.

A puff of smoke appeared about a foot away from Arthur, and he tried to grab the falling piece of paper, but fell over when he tripped on his new shoes. "OK, I need some more practice with that, but what does Archie say?" he asked rhetorically.

"'She's right you know'," he read aloud. Jo laughed at this, and she had begun to form a completely different opinion of Archie altogether.

"I just want you to know that I don't want to take this up as a full time thing. Then again if I seem to be acting totally normal, you know like a female and all, then don't be surprised," said Arthur.

"There are certain things that happen on assignment that need to stay on assignment and this is one of them. I won't think any less of you and I'm much more comfortable with you now that you're slightly incapacitated," she replied.

"There's something I want to ask you Jo, sister to sister," said Arthur, looking into Jo's eyes.

"What is it?" she asked.

"Would you do me the honour of untying my corset just a little bit, I feel a rib just popped," he said.

"Oh, yeah, sorry," she said, dazed.

Jo then set up a blackboard in front of Arthur, who was sat on a chair staring at it. "So your father is Thomas Olandine, which you only call him when nobody is around because it's one of those closely guarded secrets that makes no sense. Secondly you were born where?" she asked.

"In Adlin hospital, not really sure if someone's going to be asking me about that but hey," replied Arthur.

"Correct, next question, what is your favourite colour?" she asked.

"Tangerine orange," replied Arthur.

"Correct, who was your first love?" she asked.

"Umm, Sir Arole, until I became the head of The Order of the Tangerine," he said uncomfortably.

"You are annoyed by one thing, just one little thing, what is it?" she asked.

"People calling me Ally," he replied.

"You're ready," said Jo.

"That seemed easy," said Arthur.

"My sister is the most boring person on Alavonia; you'll have no problem if you don't do anything vaguely interesting," replied Jo.

"So from now on I'm going to refer to you as Alex, and you can refer to me as Jo. You should have no trouble calling me Jo, since you do anyway," she said.

"OK, Jo, and I'll let you do most of the talking, since I've been in a monastery for ages," replied Arthur.

"Oh and Archie, if you could say Alex instead of Arthur, it would confuse a lot less," she said, holding out her hand and the cloud and the piece of paper appeared.

"Thank you for the tip," she read.

"What's going on?" asked Alex.

"Since she's rectified it then I suppose it doesn't matter," replied Jo.

"I think I've got the whole walking thing," said Alex.

"Good, then you go wait downstairs while I get ready," she replied.

"I thought since we were sisters I could stick around," she said.

"But then we would become inseparable," said Jo, becoming very serious and moving closer.

"Huh?!" said a now startled Alex.

"You're not the only one who can act, now get!" she shouted. Alex ran downstairs, and Corky was waiting.

"Excuse me miss but have you seen Sir Arthur upstairs?" he asked.

"I love it that you refer to me as Sir Arthur to other people, if you want I can refer to you as Cornelius?" she asked.

"You do any such thing and I'll set this ship to spin the next time you get drunk," he replied.

"Yes but on the occasion I have a night off like now, you have one too so we'll both be in hell," she replied.

"Touché, so I can have the night off Miss?" he asked.

"Yes, but don't get too drunk since we're flying to Illumination Island in the morning and I want to get there without any slight detours," she replied.

"Firstly, that happened once and we both know it was the monkey's fault, secondly, I'll only have a few and thirdly I'm just gonna come out and say it, why are you dressed like a Princess?" he asked.

"Practice for Harrha, if you must know, and if anyone asks, you're taking Princess Josephine and Princess Alexandra to Harrha tomorrow," she replied.

"Whatever, though if you gonna do anything...odd tonight make sure you close the curtains this time," he said, and walked out.

"I was curious and thought blonde was a good look for me, the rest just happened organically," said Alex.

Alex sat down on the settee and put her feet up on the table and started reading a newspaper. There was a portrait of Lilia on the front, and the headline read 'Public Enemy Number 1!' From the way Alex was sat you could see that she was wearing bright blue tights and had bright silver shoes on. "She always wanted to be the centre of attention," said Alex.

Jo walked down the stairs wearing a green dress, and had her hair down, and it reflected all the lights in the room. "Looks nice, now come on, I'm starving," said Alex.

"Me too, what do they have?" she asked.

"I'm going to have the Sunken Seafood Platter, since it's massive," she replied.

"As long as they have big portions, then I'm good," said Jo. They left the ship and decided to take the lift, since Jo didn't want to risk Alex having a mishap on the way down.

"How are you doing?" asked Jo.

"Fine, how are you?" she asked.

"It's you I'm worried about," she replied.

"You know, if you really want to know I am perfectly fine and I don't see this as any different from what I normally do on a mission," said Alex.

"Honestly I didn't think you would be this blasé about this, it takes the fun out of it," she said.

"I was fine when I did this in Chene, I just haven't had a lot of practice" replied Alex. They reached the main square, which was full of people, and they saw that The 5,000 Fish Fingers of Dr Sea was open, and there was a queue outside. Jo walked right up to the front with Alex, and was instantly let in. They were taken to a special table next to an ornate fish tank.

"Isn't there a law against impersonating princesses?" asked Alex when the waiters had disappeared.

"Daddy said it was fine and if anything happens which I hope it won't, I'll smooth it out," she replied.

"While I end up looking like a complete dope, will 'Daddy' come to my aide then?" said Alex, looking at the menu. It kept slipping out of her hands and Jo saw that Alex had no experience with silk gloves.

"Grip it in one place with your four fingers and thumb while propping it on the table," said Jo.

"These things were not designed for this," said Alex.

"Well of course not, we're women and we're expected to look nice not actually do stuff," replied Jo.

"Oh I'm sorry, I shouldn't worry my pretty little head about it," said Alex sarcastically.

"I don't know, what's the biggest thing they have?" asked Jo.

"There's the Shipwreck Special, which is all you can eat so it should fill you up," replied Alex.

"There's something that I should warn you about, Alex; when it comes to food I get a little, um, ravenous," she said.

"Don't worry, there's nothing you can do that would possibly embarrass me," said Alex, sipping a glass of Blue Champagne and trying to stop the glass from slipping.

After about ten minutes, Alex's dinner arrived and they also came with a large plate for Jo, and told her to go up to the buffet table and get all the food she wanted. Jo left Alex sitting at the table, and she stuck as much food as she possibly could n the plate and returned to the table.

"You're not possibly going to eat all of that," said Alex.

"Is that a challenge?" she asked.

"No, it's just not very ladylike," replied Alex.

"And that's coming from you," she said.

Alex watched in disbelief as Jo demolished the plate of food, and then went up for seconds. "I wonder if I should tell her that she's got barbecue sauce all around her mouth," thought Alex.

Jo came back, with the same size plate stacked with just as much food. "Problem?" she asked.

"No, not at all but when you said you were ravenous I didn't expect that you would be that hungry," replied Alex.

"To be honest, as far as people are aware, I've only eaten in The Seven Wonders and so have you," she said.

"Good point, but thankfully Chene has a lot of places to get take away food," said Alex.

"So what are we to expect in Harrha?" asked Jo.

"I have no idea, to be honest; I haven't ever been there, it's the one place in Discoucia I have never been," she said.

"How old is your sister?" she asked.

"Same age as me, 210," she replied.

"She's done quite well in that time," said Jo.

"Yes, she was always the mathematical one, where I was the outgoing one," she said.

"Though from what I read in the Green Library in Evermore, the one thing that doesn't make sense is how all the buildings were made in a year considering that obsidian is hard to mine; and from the looks of it, she managed to build it in record time," said Jo.

"I think you should have clarification here, you see, it wasn't Lilia who built the fortifications on Harrha, it was our father. Though the thing that no one knows is how he died of old age when he was only 560," she explained.

"Some people just go, I suppose," replied Jo, finishing her second plate.

"I don't know, you see my father wasn't one for giving up so easily," said Alex.

"I'm done and I'm tired, I want to go back to the ship," said Jo, who had difficulty getting up. Alex was getting better at walking in heels and they both left the restaurant.

"Oh my god Ally?!" shouted someone. Alex froze up as did Jo, and a young girl ran up to them.

"Please don't call me that," said Alex.

"Would you prefer I called you Your Royal Highness Princess of All Discoucia?" came the reply.

"Evelyn, what are you doing here?" asked Jo.

"I was having dinner with Sir Arole, he feels terrible about what happened and wants to see you again," she replied.

"Well I don't want to see him, it was because of him that I swore off relationships in the first place," said Alex, making most of this up since she was petrified.

"Your Majesty, I'm sorry but I just had to come and see you, please join me outside," said a man who Alex assumed was Sir Arole. Jo was pulled away by Evelyn before she could stop what was happening. Alex was pulled out onto the moonlit balcony overlooking the ocean while Sir Arole delicately held her hand not knowing whose hand he was really holding.

"I don't expect you to forgive me, but I want you to know that I deeply regret what happened," he said, trying to look into her eyes but she was looking elsewhere.

"I've had a lot of therapy lately, what exactly did happen?" she asked.

"When you believed that the pretentious weirdo Sir Arthur was sending you all those letters, it was actually me," he said.

"So let me get this straight, because of you I hate Sir Arthur Pageon who's just a little miss-understood and not weird?" she asked.

"What difference would that make, look I'm sorry for what I did," he said.

"Frankly I would forgive you for sending me explicit letters but your sheer venom in the way you talk about others is enough for me to say that this conversation is over," said Alex, and she left him on the balcony while rejoining Jo.

"Come on sister I'm paying!" she shouted, walking out into the foyer.

"So you have an account at every restaurant in Discoucia?" asked Jo.

"Yes, I visit them all the time and I hardly touch my account in Gard," she said.

"How much money do you have exactly?" she asked.

"Enough, but I'd rather not think about it; plus for every successful mission your father pays me so it just keeps getting bigger and bigger," she replied.

"Our father Alex, our father," said Jo.

"Right, still working on that. Anyway I fooled a whole restaurant so I'm ready for Harrha," she said. They got to the Sky Port, and Alex did something a little strange from Jo's perspective. She picked Jo up in her arms and carried her up the stairs.

"What are you doing?" said Jo, smiling and laughing.

"Proving that I can walk up stairs in heels," she replied.

When they reached the top of the stairs Alex put her down and they climbed up to the ship. "I know I should have mentioned this earlier, but why are there hand prints on the banister?" she asked.

"I had a little accident this morning," replied Jo, turning red.

"Oh, as long as it was you and not anyone else," replied Alex.

"Now I'm going to bed, are you going to sleep?" she asked.

"No, I've got a better idea and I'll tell you about it tomorrow," replied Alex.

"Oh okay, goodnight," said Jo.

"There's one thing I need to get from the wardrobe," she said. Alex ran upstairs and came back down with a mirror.

"What do you need that for?" she asked.

"Never mind what I need it for, I'll see you tomorrow," said Alex.

"OK" said Jo, slightly perplexed. She left her 'sister' downstairs, and went off to bed.

Mirror-Phone Line

Alex propped the mirror on the desk and she sat on the chair staring out it. "Archie, I need your help" she said. The mirror changed colour, and it danced with hundreds of different colours, and Alex saw Archie's face appear.

"Yes, what is it Alex?" she asked.

"You can call me Arthur now, Jo's gone to bed," he replied.

"Oh good, then what is it Arthur?" she asked.

"I'm worried, once we get to Harrha I have no idea what I'm going to do," he explained.

"Before you carry on, how was dinner?" she asked.

"Jo overeats, and I was perfect at being a princess for an evening," he said.

"Out of context that would sound a bit strange but carrying on, what do you think you would do?" asked Archie, who was eating an apple.

"I would go to her study in the Obsidian Castle," he replied.

"Right, that's a step in the right direction; what are you going to do in there once you are in?" she asked.

"That's where I'm stuck. You see she has a massive army and the High King hasn't mobilised anything, what does he expect me to do, dismantle the whole army by myself? I don't have a hundred years of time, right?" he asked.

"Yes that's true, but considering every Lord and Lady in Discoucia was sent a message that offered them something irresistible then his only course of action was to send you," said Archie.

"So, you're saying that I'm the only hope?" he asked.

"You and Jo, there are two of you remember," she replied.

"What can two of us do?" he asked.

"Usually as the God of God only knows, I'd give you a big speech about how the two of you can beat this but then you won't really believe it, will you?" she asked.

"Could you please come here?" he asked.

"I'll make a deal with you; I shall appear only to you for one day, and then after that you must go on without me until we meet again without any use of power," she replied.

"Deal," said Arthur, and Archie's face disappeared from the mirror.

Arthur looked around for Archie but could not see her. "Archie?" he called, getting up from his seat and looking around.

"Right behind you miss," said a voice.

"Oh, there you are," replied Arthur. Archie was sat in the chair that Arthur had just got up from. She was wearing the white tuxedo that Arthur had seen in the caves of Elowe.

"So you're a girl now?" she asked.

"And you're dressed as a guy so in conclusion this is a very strange situation," replied Arthur.

"I could switch my clothes if you want?" asked Archie, who faded away, and changed to a more feminine appearance, and wore the same dress as she had done in Yellow Coven.

"To be honest, I think it makes more sense for you to be in that form, since you've been like that longest," replied Arthur.

"So you're worried about the future, who isn't?" she asked.

"I see what you mean, but I don't think the whole of the kingdom is at stake for most people," said Arthur.

"You just need someone to talk to, right?" she asked.

"Don't be patronising," he replied.

"I'm not, why else would you want me here? You just need a friend and from the looks of it, you haven't had one in a while," she said.

"Yes I suppose I do, not that I like to admit it," he replied.

"Nobody does," said Archie, sitting on the settee.

"What's the problem, tell your new pal Archie," she said.

"Firstly, just to get this out I'm not comfortable with...this," he said, pointing at himself.

"There's nothing you can really do about it, so just run with it," she replied.

"Okay next thing since you're a people person, does Jo like me," he said.

"Sorry Arthur but you'd have to be blind not to see that," she replied.

"So far so good, the last thing is can my sister change?" he asked.

"Everyone can be reached, just do what you think is right and everything will turn out how it will," said Archie.

"What, how it will for me or not?" he asked.

"You see this pebble?" said Archie, taking it out of her pocket.

"Yes, what about it?" he asked.

"I'm going to throw it at your mirror," said Archie, who threw the pebble. It sailed at the mirror, and just in time Arthur grabbed it before it could smash the glass into thousands of pieces.

"Why would you do that?" he asked, the pebble slipping out of his hand, due to the silk glove.

"You see the pebble hitting the mirror was a possible outcome, you could have stayed there and let it hit. However you stopped it from hitting thereby changing the course of the pebble and also changing history at the same time," she explained.

"Oh I see, but that was my mother's," he replied.

"I know, that's how I knew that you would catch it," she replied.

"Right, so what else are we going to do tonight?" he asked.

"That sounds like a vague euphemism but were going to kit you out for a mission, which I believe you have forgot to do," said Archie.

"What would you suggest?" he asked.

Archie clicked her fingers and they both disappeared from the sitting room and reappeared in the wardrobe. "Are you mad, she'll hear us!" said Arthur in a loud whisper. Archie sighed, and clicked her fingers again, and the walls lit up with a pale purple light, and then the light disappeared.

"There, the room is now soundproof, so you could play Moby Dick on the drums and she wouldn't hear you," said Archie.

"That sounds rude," he said.

"I assure you it isn't," replied Archie.

"So what do you want to do?" he asked.

"Hold on, I just realised that my name, it's Archie," she said.

"Huh?" he asked, confused.

"Sugar sugar... ohhh honey honey... You are my candy girl..." sang Archie, oblivious to everything around her.

"I don't understand what's going on," he said.

"Right, I'm back with you, let's get you ready for Harrha," she said.

"What first?" he asked.

"Take that dress off and put another one, or find one you want to wear to Harrha and we'll use that," said Archie.

Arthur found his old blue dress that he wore to the Harem in Chene before it was closed down and became the Paradise Hotel. "This one has a pair of exploding, umm, you know," he said.

"Yeah, I think everyone knows what you're talking about," she replied.

"What do you mean everyone?" he asked.

"You're not running with it," she replied.

"Right sorry, so what can I do with this?" asked Arthur.

"Hmm, what about a gun somewhere?" he replied.

"It's a bit of a cliché, why not something a bit more imaginative?" she said.

"How about sticking some rope somewhere?" he asked.

"It's practical, so how about putting it in the lining below your waist, and that way it won't be seen and if you need it, then it's one more thing to have on your side" she said.

"Literally," said Arthur.

"Well the moon is on my side, and the rope is on yours I suppose," she said.

"That's a strange thing to say," said Arthur.

"I really miss my iPod, being a god is good but without music it's just pointless," she replied.

"So explain to me what an iPod is, in terms I'll understand this time," he said.

"Basically, it's a storage device for thousands of songs and other music, and you can listen to it whenever you want, though such a device would be pointless considering you don't have music here," she said.

"We have music," he said.

"Not my kind of music. You'll get there eventually, you're about 200 years away; what year is it?" she asked.

"14673," he replied.

"Let's see, by my calculations your world parallels mine when it was the year 1767, so strike that, you should be 1,827 years off popular music," she said.

"I'm not going to ask, but having all that at your disposal must be amazing," he replied.

"You don't know the half of it; we also have hand held devices that can access any piece of information on the planet, and we can learn anything," she explained.

"So it's like the largest encyclopaedia in the palm of your hand?" he said.

"Yes, but very few of us use it to the advantage that you would believe, to be honest. A person like you would use it fully, because you haven't grown up with it, but my people won't use it properly because they have never really been deprived of it," she said.

"Freedom is only meaningful to those who have been deprived of it," said Arthur.

"That's why prisoners that stay in for longer are less likely to commit another crime, in most cases that is," she said.

"Anyway, what else are we going to do, since time behaves differently with you," he said.

"You need a notepad and a pencil, in case there is anything you want to write down," she said.

"So where are we going to stick it?" he asked.

"How about in your sleeve, then if you need to whack someone, you've got a concealed weapon that doesn't fire bullets," she replied.

"You don't like guns do you?" he asked.

"No, they're messy, and I never saw Fred Jones use a shotgun to solve a mystery," she said.

"Fred Jones?" he asked.

"Great track record in solving mysteries, probably a terrible shot," she replied.

"OK, well are we done yet?" he asked.

"Yes, you haven't got any weapons of any kind, which is perfect," she said.

"That doesn't make much sense," he replied.

"It will," said Archie.

Arthur proceeded outside, followed by Archie, and Jo was still asleep, and sunlight was streaming in. Jo woke up and saw Arthur sneaking out of the wardrobe. "Good Morning?" she said.

"Oh hey, I was... just..." he said, but trailed off.

"How did you manage to get in there without passing me?" she asked.

"Um..." he said, but couldn't think of anything to say.

"Is Archie here?" she asked.

"Can you see her?" he asked.

"No, is she downstairs?" asked Jo.

In fact, Archie was laid next to Jo on top of the covers, while Jo was still in bed.

"No, she's not here," said Arthur. Archie put her hands behind her head and relaxed back.

"So it's time to go to Harrha," said Jo.

"Yes, but first we're going to Illumination Island, and then in the evening we'll get to the party, not that I'm looking forward to it," he said.

"I'll be down in a minute," said Jo. With that, Archie got up and followed Arthur downstairs.

The Great and Humorous Sea-shorelle

"Why are we going to Illumination Island anyway?" asked Jo.

"It's a surprise, you'll see when we get there," said Alex, who had changed back to the female voice. The ship took off, and it sailed off to the east across the sea. The sea was raging, since it was nearly winter; and the whole of nature had changed in nearly every way. The sea was thrashing, the clouds were dark and there was a foul cold wind blowing from the north.

"You picked the perfect day for this," said Jo, standing outside. Arthur was staying outside, since he was paranoid that his wig would fly away. "Just ask," said Archie.

"To do what?" asked Arthur.

"I have unlimited power Arthur, so I could either turn you into your costume, but that technically means that you would be female, and so that is really up to you. However I could just turn that wig into your actual hair, and that way it won't blow off, which seems to be what you are paranoid about," she replied.

"Umm, I'll go for option two," he said.

"I thought you might," said Archie, putting her hand on Arthur's head.

Arthur didn't feel anything, and when Archie stepped away, he felt his new hair. "This is brilliant, I'm going outside," he said.

Arthur ran outside and joined Jo. Archie watched as she ran her fingers through his new hair. She then stormed in. "Archie! I know you're there," she shouted. A puff of smoke appeared and a piece of paper fell into Jo's hand. "'Congratulations Sherlock'," she read aloud. "Get out here now," she shouted. She got another message, which appeared in the same place. "'Wish for it, it's the only thing that works'," read Jo. "I'm not doing that," she said.

"What's going on?" asked Arthur, who had re-entered the sitting room.

"Archie's here and I want her to appear," said Jo.

"All she has to do is wish," said Archie to Arthur.

"She says all you have to do is wish, so get on with it," said Arthur.

"I'm not doing it," she said.

"No wishing, no seeing," said Archie.

"She says no wishing, no seeing and can you two stop, I feel like I'm at home again passing messages between mum and dad," said Arthur.

"Now you know how the Narrator feels in Fight Club," said Archie.

"This isn't the time for literary references," said Arthur.

"How did you know that it was a book?" she asked.

"What else is it going to be?" he asked.

"A movie?" she asked.

"I still don't know what that means," said Arthur. Jo was just standing there, watching in disbelief as Arthur was having an argument with thin air.

"I'll explain it to you in simpler terms next time you ask me about the general nonsense I'm referencing from my world, and I can't stress that enough, please don't sue," said Archie.

"And there it is again, who is going to sue you; You're a god, you can just melt them for your sake," he retorted.

"Ha," said Jo, who had sat down on the settee and was enjoying the show. "Who would even sue you anyway?" asked Arthur.

"People. They would say that by me saying a certain phrase or lyric, that by saying it here I would be copying them and claiming it as my own. When in reality I am just referencing them because

I really like what they did. So with that out of the way, can I get on with this?" she asked.

"Why would they sue you? You only get sued when you're writing a book," said Arthur. There was an awkward silence, where Archie stayed silent, and it appeared that Arthur had touched a nerve. There was a blinding light, and Archie disappeared.

"What did I say?" he asked Jo.

"Something that she didn't like I suppose, but on another note I think that you two should go on stage, that was brilliant," she replied.

"I've angered a God, and she made this my real hair," said Arthur feeling if it had changed, which it hadn't. Jo suddenly realised what he meant and burst into uncontrollable laughter.

"Oh that's so funny; you now have beautiful long platinum hair? And it's permanent, that's even better!" said Jo, who was laid on the settee trying to breathe.

"This isn't funny, this is terrible and I've got long luxurious hair," he shouted.

"Did she do anything...else?" asked Jo.

"NO! I opted out of that when she asked," said Arthur.

"I call it a perfect disguise, personally," said Jo.

"Somehow I don't suspect we'll be hearing anything of Archie, and you can go back to being Alex," said Jo.

"I really don't want to do this now, but if you insist, I'll resume being your sister. Now follow me, were near Illumination Island so let's go outside and watch as we get there," said Alex.

They walked outside and looked across the sea to a sparsely forested island with a magnificent lighthouse. It was built with several lamp rooms at different levels, and they were arranged so that there was never one above another, and they rose high into the sky. With their strange pyramid shape they were almost immovable, and in their 2000 years of service, only one tower had had any problems, and that was when Thunder Lord Logious was testing a new weapon that made a huge obsidian boulder appear out of nowhere inside one of the towers. There was a huge hole, but it all happened almost instantly, and the engineers had no idea how it happened.

"So what is it that you have done," asked Jo.

"Follow me," said Alex. The two left the ship, which had parked on the open space above one of the towers. Illumination Island was indeed huge, and a tribute to the people who built it, as most of it was out in the sea. However, they were very skilled, and that kind of skill is now put to use in the underground. They walked over to a large balcony, and for a second they stared out at the immense ocean, that which actually looked quite scary, the whole size of it.

"Come on, I'm waiting," she said.

"SEASHORELLE, WE'RE HERE!" shouted Alex as loud as she could out into the ocean. Jo looked doubtful, until everything happened at once. The ocean swirled around into a massive whirlpool, and a storm raged above it. Jo took a step back, but Alex grabbed her and pulled her close. "We face the beast of the sea together!" she said.

Underneath the water of the huge whirlpool came an immense black shape, and then a large scaly body, it's back covered in fins protruded from the water, which lapped around it. Then it reared up, and from out of the water closest to the balcony came the head, which was gigantic. The head had two yellow eyes on stalks, and tentacles coming from its head that resembled hair. The mouth was full of sharp teeth, and they gave off a dull glow in the partial sunlight. Its arms also appeared; they were like tree trunks, and its hands were webbed, about the size of ships. It was blue, and its belly was light green.

For a moment there was a tense silence, and Jo was nearly dead with fright. "Who disturbs my slumber?" it said, in a remarkably soothing, lyrical voice.

"Archie didn't tell you?" shouted Alex.

"She told me that I would meet some friends of hers, so the question stands," it replied.

"Princess Josephine Olandine and Princess Alexandra Olandine!" shouted Jo, who saw that wasn't just a mindless monster.

"In that case how are you doing?" it asked, leaning on the wall of the lighthouse rather casually.

"OK, how are you?" asked Alex.

"Oh you know, can't complain," said Seashorelle, who was now lying on the lighthouse wall and relaxing on it.

"Won't people see this?" asked Jo.

"I suspended time, so as far as anyone knows, I was never here," she replied.

"Do all gods have power over time?" asked Alex.

"In one way or another. I forget the details, but when we were all created we had a choice of powers," she said.

"Who created you?" asked Jo.

"Do you really want me to answer that?" asked Seashorelle, looking at her seriously for once.

"Yes, I want to know," said Jo.

"Your new friend Archie is so much more powerful than you could possibly imagine, she has the power to create and destroy, though she prefers to create rather than destroy. She created Alavonia and all the other planets in the solar system. And I know that is hard to believe, but she has shown you a small amount of her power I believe. You don't expect her to admit to being so powerful because you would ask her for everything and ask her to justify the problems humans created," she explained.

"I refuse to believe that, no one should have that kind of power," said Jo.

"She knows that, that's probably why she met you, she can be normal around you," she said.

"I angered the creator of all things," said Alex, putting her hands over her face.

"Oh yeah, she doesn't like being wrong, though she does have a forgiving side, so I wouldn't read too much into it," said Seashorelle, who grabbed a shark out of the sea and ate it in one go.

"So do I apologise to her?" asked Alex.

"No, she'll get over it," said Seashorelle, who was picking bones out of her teeth.

After several minutes of strange conversation, Seashorelle was ready to leave. "I must leave now, I have some fishermen I'm supposed to frighten from afar," she said.

"Sounds fun. Will we ever see you again?" asked Alex.

"Maybe, only Archie would know the definite answer to that," she replied.

"It was nice meeting you," said Jo.

"You too, and I hope that you have success in the task ahead of you," she replied. Seashorelle sank down into the sea, her webbed hand waving as she descended, and when she had gone, it began to rain. They ran back to the ship, and it lifted off, and flew in the direction of Harrha Island.

"That was surreal, even more so than when I met Archie for the first time in the Yellow Coven," said Jo, who had sunk down onto the settee.

"Meeting gods seems to be normal for us these days, though I wouldn't want to meet Ignatio; out of all the gods he seems to be the angriest. Earthquakes and the like right?" said Alex, who sat down at the desk.

"Do you think Seashorelle could be convinced to fight on our side if the situation arose?" she asked.

"I don't think so, Archie said that she wasn't going to get involved, so why would any of the others?" asked Alex.

"I suppose so, and I shudder to think what kind of war would warrant engagement by gods," said Jo.

"One that we would be hard pressed to win," replied Alex.

"What else did Archie give you?" she asked.

"She gave me the confidence to stare down lightning," replied Alex.

"Was that through magic?" asked Jo.

"None at all," she replied.

"She must have known what you needed," said Jo.

"She can't read our thoughts can she?" asked Alex.

"Is there anything you're thinking that you wouldn't want anyone knowing?" she asked.

"I'm not thinking about it; if I do, then I'm thinking about it," replied Alex.

There was a puff of red smoke, and a burning piece of paper fell onto the floor. Jo put the fire out and read the note aloud. "I can't read your thoughts, only Evere has that power and he's here in the Twilight Vale with me," she read, before the note burst into flames and the black powder fell onto the floor.

"She's really mad now," said Jo.

"You don't seem that worried," said Alex.

"I wasn't the one who started it," she replied.

"You're not helping," said Alex, banging her head on the desk.

"You're about to take on your sister in her evil fortress with innumerable forces at her disposal, and the power to crush the kingdom, but you're worried about annoying Archie?" she asked.

"Makes Lilia seem a bit of a smaller issue to be honest," said Alex.

"She's taken the fright away, hasn't she," said Jo.

"I don't think she meant for this to be a distraction, she looked and sounded pretty mad," said Alex.

As it began to get dark, the horizon was lit up ahead by a bright purple light, and above the raging sea, The Nostradamus was joined by several different ships, all different, and in different colours too. Then out of the south came a huge ship, red and gold, which undercut most of the smaller ships and flew straight for Harrha ahead of all the others. Jo and Alex ran out into the cold air to watch the ship, which couldn't keep in a straight line, but insisted on doing acrobatics instead.

"That has to be Lord Yage's ship; he always has to show off," said Jo.

"If he goes any faster, he'll stall, and then have to sail the rest of the way," said Alex.

And just as she said it, a plume of black smoke erupted from the engines and the ship dropped. There was a spray of water, and the ship bobbed in the sea like a cork.

"Thankfully it's a large ship, and the rough sea won't topple it," said Alex.

"This is what happens when you show off without the proper driving skills," said Jo.

Harrha was lit up magnificently; the place was covered in balloons, banners and lanterns. People from all over Discoucia were here, there were dignitaries from small villages and towns, who were all attended to by an army of servants. The leaders from the bigger cities were surrounded by people, since they were the most important in attendance. The ship landed high up in the Sky Port, along with several others, and all the people disembarked. Jo had just covered Alex in chalk powder, and was still amazed that the long platinum hair was real. Corky stood on deck wearing a white tuxedo, as did all the other drivers from all the other ships, no one noticed anything wrong. They followed everyone else to the main gate of the Sky Port, where two guards were waiting...

Queen Lilia's Celebration Day

"She really has done well for herself hasn't she?" asked Jo, who was walking and holding Alex's arm in hers.

"It's amazing what you can accomplish in next to no time at all," said Alex.

"Are you sure you're ready for this?" asked Jo.

"No, but what are you going to do," she replied. Jo took Alex down a huge corridor that was lined with ornately carved obsidian columns. There was a large number of people walking towards the huge square that was adjacent to the sea, so a cold sea breeze blew; however, the walls were high enough that the wind didn't affect the party. Jo and Alex walked into a scene that completely betrayed its surroundings.

Everyone was having a good time, there were important people getting drunk with village elders, and dignitaries really losing their dignity. "Look over there, holding her sister back from that waiter, it's Lady Josette and that person she's holding back is Lady Annabella," said Alex.

"Why is she holding back her sister?" asked Jo.

"Well, you see, Lady Annabella is a little bit odd, and have you ever played Chrysso?" asked Alex.

"Yes but I was never any good at it, I could never hold the cue properly," she replied.

"If you sand down the balls, you get dust. Inhale that dust and you're out of it," explained Alex.

"Out of what, I don't understand," she replied.

"One day, we'll do it, and you can find out for yourself," said Alex.

"I'm not sure I want to," said Jo.

"I didn't either, but I have my sister to thank for that. One night she came in with a pack of dust that she had sanded down from one of my father's sets. He went ballistic but we were in no state to care," she explained.

"What does it do exactly?" she asked.

"You go on a wild, mystical journey, and it all happens while you're sitting still. If you move around then Archie help you," said Alex.

They moved around the party, and Alex was attacked, not literally of course by a woman in a shimmering yellow dress. "Ally, it's so good to see you again," she said. Alex panicked, as she still had no idea who she was talking to.

"Vicki, I see you've met my sister," said Jo, who had been god knows where.

"She seems a bit different from the last time I saw her," said Vicki, who eyed Alex suspiciously.

"Please don't call me Ally," said Alex.

"I'm mistaken, you are the same Alexandra," she said.

"So how have you been, Vicki?" asked Jo.

"My Daddy said that we're here for peaceable reasons, though he has always cared too much about gold," she said.

"You own one of the largest private goldmines in the Luminosity Archipelago, why would your father want more gold?" asked Jo.

"No idea, but when you're rich you want to get richer I suppose," she replied.

"I never had that problem," replied Jo.

"So what are you doing now? I heard that you were travelling with Sir Pageon, though I thought that that was impossible since he doesn't normally travel with people," she said.

"I was travelling with him, but I left him in Cesta when I joined Alex," she said.

"Oh, so tell me, are those rumours about him true?" asked Vicki.

"What rumours?" asked Alex.

"Well apparently there was this time in Chene, when King Jassuer ruled there and..." she said, but was cut off by Jo.

"Oh yes I heard that, though I never noticed anything like that," she replied.

"Oh, well that's no fun," said Vicki.

"What do you mean it's no fun?" asked Alex.

"He's interesting and it's a refreshing change from all the boring socialites that I meet every day," she replied.

"Sorry to burst your bubble, but he's just an ordinary boring explorer and adventurer," said Jo.

They left Vicki, who went to attack some other unfortunate newcomer, and moved further around the party. "Is that Lady Blastone?!" asked Jo, shocked. There was a lady, who had black matted hair and dark tanned skin, who was getting very drunk with another person, whom the two didn't recognise.

"I have no idea who that is but whoever it is, they're getting very close to her," said Jo.

"She's the biggest producer of TNT in the land, so any budding mine baron will try to get a contract with her," said Alex.

"Right, I'm going to look around. I don't see anything suspicious yet, but you never know," said Alex, who disappeared into the crowd. Jo was left on her own, and she decided to look around too, but when she was about to leave, there was a loud boom of trumpets.

"Queen Lilia the Young," shouted a man, and on a stage outside the Obsidian Castle, Lilia appeared. At the back of the group was Jo, who stared in disbelief at the stage. Alex was next to the stage, since it was the fastest route to the castle. She walked up to a guard who was blocking the archway, and had to think of a way around.

"Look, there's too many people queuing in the bathrooms, so is there any chance I could go in the castle?" she asked.

"Who's asking?" he asked.

"Princess Alexandra Olandine" she replied.

"Of course you can miss, it's the 23rd door on the left," he said, and let Alex through.

Lilia stood on the stage, and the whole party fell silent. However, she was about 100 years old, and looked way younger than Arthur did, considering they were twins.

"Good evening, people of Discoucia, and thank you for attending my humble island party," she said. They all stared at her, and applauded her. "You have come here for one thing: rejuvenation," she said. This time there was a loud cheer from everyone. Jo was looking worried, as she was now beginning to see what Lilia was up to.

"You see, it really isn't a fairytale, I myself have taken off 120 years from my age, and I feel amazing, and I offer this to you," she said. There was a colossal cheer from all the guests, but Jo remained silent; she was hoping that Alex was having better luck.

Alex walked through the corridors of the empty castle. All the guards had presumably gone to keep an eye on the party, and she looked around for any evidence of Lilia's finalised plan. "Where are you?" she said to herself, checking every room. The Obsidian Castle was huge, and was made primarily of an outer wall of obsidian and cobblestone, and there was a dizzying array of rooms that Alex was determined to search. There was a lower corridor that extended like a cross, and Alex had succeeded in searching the lower level of the entrance hall; however, there were three levels above this one, and numerous towers too. She came to the cross of corridors, and didn't know which way to go.

"Um, which way do I go, Archie?" he shouted. Nothing happened. "Come on, you can't be mad at me forever," she shouted. A servant came out of one of the rooms, and handed Alex a piece of paper that had scorch marks.

"This is for you I believe," he said, and retreated back into a room.

'Try Me', it said. "Now you're just acting childish," shouted Alex.

She wandered along the corridor in a straight line and headed for the stairs. At the end of corridor was a magnificent staircase. Alex ran up the stairs and found that she was on the floor where all the bedrooms were. Looking out of the windows, she saw the dark night, and the sea lapping against the harbour walls. Everything in the castle was purple: the curtains, the carpets, the chairs and tables. "I remember that she liked purple, but this is a bit excessive," said Alex, who came to a large ornate door. She opened it, and inside was a large room, and it was only lit by moonlight streaming in from a large window that looked out over the sea. There was a large bed in the centre of the right hand side wall, and on the left hand wall was a mass of papers, though Alex couldn't see what they said. She grabbed a lamp from the bed by the table, and lit it with a match from her pocket. Alex looked at the wall, and saw something slightly disturbing.

The wall was covered in pieces of paper, and all of them had the subject of Sir Arthur Pageon. They were reports of where he had been seen, and they all seemed to be in order, starting from Evermore, and then to Karga, and then to Proceur. The light followed the paper, and proceeded back to Evermore, where she saw that the name 'Archie' was circled many times in red. There was a line that led to another piece of paper that had all the information on Archie that it had. "'Very dangerous, must be avoided at all costs'." read Alex in disbelief. "Number of Discoucians killed as a result of personal actions: 1,785,250," said Alex. "I don't believe it, it can't be true" she said to herself. Alex then read the words 'Eliminate Josephine Olandine, war is inevitable',"

Jo herself was standing behind the crowd, still listening to Lilia's speech. She watched Alex walk off, and continued to watch Lilia win the crowd over. "All I ask is that you give something to me, not gold or jewels, just an agreement," she said. The crowd stopped cheering, and there were murmurs of disagreement. All of the people in attendance had one thing in common, they were all rich, some more wealthy than others, but the mention of something that they couldn't buy with money made them think a bit more.

"On the stage is a piece of paper, and on it are my terms, all you have to do is sign it and you shall be young again," she said, then disappeared leaving the chaos that then ensued.

There was a mad dash for the stage, but the guards formed everyone into a line, and they all signed it. Jo looked for Alex, but couldn't see her. After thinking about her father, Jo saw that this was a chance for him to have a cure, so against her better judgement she joined the queue.

Alex looked out of a window and saw Jo about to sign the contract, and ran downstairs. She ran past a room, stopped and stared inside. There was Lilia, the younger Lilia, that is. "Umm, excuse me" said Alex.

"Are you here to take me home?" she asked.

"You are home aren't you?" asked Alex.

"No you stupid person, I wouldn't live on this Island if you paid me," she replied angrily.

"Then who are you exactly?" asked Alex.

"Who do I look like?!" she asked, losing her patience.

"Your first pet, what was its name?" asked Alex.

"Don't ask me such stupid questions, I don't have time for this!" she snapped.

"What are you doing that's so important?" asked Alex.

"I'm waiting," she replied.

"For what?" asked Alex.

"Jessica the goldfish, Princess Alexandra" said a voice from behind her.

Two princesses imprisoned in a dungeon, I wonder where that idea came from...

Alex turned around, and the real Lilia was standing behind her. She was wearing a purple dress with silver lace pretty much everywhere, purple and dark red hair and dark blue eyes. She looked at Alex for a second, as if she recognised her. "So, you were trying to find the bathroom, but you instead found me," she said.

"Umm, yes, I did get rather lost," said Alex, amazed that Lilia didn't recognise her.

"Well, let me escort you to the main courtyard Your Highness," she said.

"Please, lead on," said Alex.

Lilia took Alex along the corridor and led her to a large window that looked out onto the courtyard. Alex saw Jo being taken into the Obsidian Castle. "What are you doing?" asked Alex.

"I need her, and you I'm afraid, so if you could come peacefully it would be very much appreciated," she said.

"There really is no way out of this is there?" asked Alex.

"No, you're pretty much doomed in every respect. Now I have to ask how you have the amazing ability to be in two places at once?" she asked.

"I don't know what you mean," said Alex.

"I'll explain everything to you soon, now if would please follow me and try not to run. As you are quite aware you are on an island and there's nowhere to go," explained Lilia.

"I could always swim" replied Alex, and she allowed herself to be taken to the southernmost part of the castle, and there was a large trapdoor in the middle of the floor.

Jo was also there, and she saw Alex and couldn't stop talking. "I signed the contract, she's going to invade and there's nothing we can do about it!" said Jo, who was close to tears.

"Calm down sis, it could be worse," said Alex.

"How could it possibly be worse than this?" asked Jo, angrily.

"It could be raining, that makes everything worse. I mean you get your hair wet and along with everything else and it just makes you feel awful," she replied.

"Oh for crying out loud," sighed one of the guards.

"I'm sorry, am I ruining the atmosphere?" asked Alex sarcastically.

"No Your Majesty" he said quickly.

"Yeah that's what I thought, now if you mind not holding my arm so tightly I'd feel better. It's not as if I'm going to run off and I'm sure you could tackle a fragile thing like me" said Alex.

"Umm, I'm not supposed to" he replied.

"Then don't, whatever your name is; don't you wear name badges?" she asked.

"Daniel," he said, but further conversation was suspended when Lilia had begun to suspect something was wrong.

Jo for some reason felt weirdly better, and Lilia eyed Alex suspiciously. "That's a very strange sense of humour you have, Princess, the last time we met you didn't have much of a sense of humour at all," said Lilia.

"I just developed it under the circumstances I suppose, now can we get on with this please," replied Alex.

"Very well, proceed down to the Dank Cellar," said Lilia.

The two were taken down a set of stairs that spun around a circular hole that led down deep beneath the castle. Then they reached a corridor that led off for about 30ft, but then it reached a dead end. There were five cell doors between the bottom of the stairs and the end of the corridor. Lilia took the two of them to a cell and they were chained by their wrist to manacles on the wall.

Lilia sat on a stool that was placed in front of the two chained up prisoners, and for a second she just sat, saying nothing. "So anyway, Jo, how do you feel about the service here? I wouldn't give it a good review, not by any standards," said Alex, who completely ignored Lilia.

"Personally I thought that before you pay the bill it's all perfect service, but afterwards they can't get rid of you fast enough," replied Jo.

"Excuse me," said Lilia, who couldn't believe that her two prisoners were taking such a lax attitude to being chained to a wall.

"Yeah that's true, just make sure that they didn't overcharge you, I've heard that they stick all sorts of stuff on the final bill. Out of city tax if you don't live in the city, unmade beds even though the maids are supposed to take care of that," asked Alex.

"Excuse me!" said Lilia, getting angrier.

"Does that really happen? Most of our bills are taken care of by the servants so I suppose we don't notice. Though I heard that Lady Stephania wanted an artwork from the room she was staying in and they gave her a copy for the price of the original, stuff like that makes you not trust hotels," said Jo.

"Are you two quite finished?" she asked.

"Not yet Leels please don't interrupt. Yes, your servants could be telling them to purposely overcharge and then take a cut of the money; if any of mine did that then I'd tell them to get me in on it since it's never actually my money," said Alex.

"Right that's it, there's only one person that ever called me Leels and that's my brother," said Lilia.

"I give up with this, personally I was anxious and paranoid that you would figure out that it was me and not Princess Alexandra, but it seems that years on this depressing rock have made you slow," said Arthur.

"Arthur?" said Lilia.

"That's my name," he said.

"It's really you?" she asked.

"You were expecting someone else?" he asked.

"What are you wearing, you look beautiful," she said in disbelief.

"Did you have to use that particular adjective?" asked Arthur, slumping down in his manacles.

"Well I haven't seen you in so long, I didn't rehearse this, you know," she said.

"I think that you might have because I certainly did, and I imagined myself in exactly the same circumstances and the same manacles surprisingly," he said.

"Your hair, is it a wig?" she asked.

"It was," he replied.

"May I?" she asked.

"I can't refuse," he replied. Lilia walked up to Arthur and ran her fingers through his hair, while the guards and Jo watched uncomfortably.

"So you're here to stop me from taking over the kingdom; well, you see, that's going to be a little difficult right now," she said.

"I'm manacled to a wall, so what gave you that idea," he replied sarcastically.

"And I see you have a friend, Princess Josephine," she said.

"It's lovely to meet you Lilia, Artie's told me all about you," she said.

"Oh, the pleasure's all mine and I hope it was a pleasant description," replied Lilia. "If I may speak for him, he didn't have a bad word to say about you, though you're showing a different side of yourself by chaining us to the wall," said Jo.

"I have a question Lilia, just one," said Arthur.

"If it's about my battle plans, then I won't be telling you them," said Lilia.

"No actually, I know you're too clever for that so it's something else entirely," he said.

"In that case, ask away," she said.

"Those pieces of paper on the wall upstairs, you circled the name 'Archie', why?" he asked.

"I have been trying to find her; she is the only one who could possibly ruin my plans, mainly because she is a god and also because she seems to have taken a liking to you," said Lilia.

"Oh, OK, in that case you carry on but I'd give me about ten minutes before I break out of here," said Arthur, with a confident look on his face.

"I think I'll put you in my newest creation, and what do I do with your girlfriend?" asked Lilia.

"Do what you want; I don't need her any more. I'm here and that's all I needed her for. I needed a way into Harrha and what better way than using a dim-witted princess?" said Arthur coldly.

At that second Jo's whole world imploded. Everything she knew was wrong, Arthur had just been using her to get here and she meant nothing to him. She was about to cry, but pure hatred and anger did an override of the sadness and she shouted every profanity and swear word she could think of at him. She kicked out at him, and several of them actually landed, and Arthur had to bunch back on the wall.

"You still are the master with women," said Lilia.

"So are you going to move me or not?" asked Arthur.

"Oh no, since you two make such a cute couple I think you should stay together in joyful bliss," said Lilia.

"That's not funny; if her hands were free she'd be clawing my eyes out," he said.

"And her hands will soon be free. You're my brother so I won't harm you at all, it's Princess Josephine who will do that," said Lilia. Jo was so mad that she was still trying to get Arthur, but she couldn't reach him. Then, for both of them, everything went black.

The Mathematical Trap

Arthur awoke in the middle of a square which was underground, as no sunlight was streaming in and it was surrounded by marble columns. He got up, and couldn't hear any sound or see anyone. He left the square and walked off in a northern direction, and saw that the architecture of this little town was that of Evermore, since it was made of sandstone. There were small enclosed streets and houses; however they didn't have second floors, or roofs for that matter. Torches hung from the walls and the place was clinically clean, no signs of life anywhere.

After a minute of looking around Arthur found Jo, who was unconscious on the floor. He was about to wake her, but then he remembered that she wanted to kill him, and then remembered the rope that was built into his dress. He unravelled it and tied her to a column. He then decided to let her cool off and went for a walk. It was ten minutes later that Jo woke up, and taking note of her surroundings she saw that she was alone. She then remembered about Arthur, and began to shout for him.

"Arthur! Arthur! Get here now, you're no longer my friend but you're still one of my subjects," she shouted.

"Don't get your royal knickers in a twist I'm right here," he said, appearing from behind a column.

"Why aren't you tied up?" she asked.

"Because they didn't tie me up, I must confess that it was I who tied you up," he replied.

"Why?" she asked angrily.

"Be honest, if you could run around, all your running would be after me to tear me to pieces and personally I wouldn't dare retaliate, not because you're a princess but because I don't think a friend should hit another friend," he explained.

"Friend? I can't believe you can even say that," she said.

"Look, if I told her not to tear us apart she would have, but this way I could guarantee that we would be together," he said.

"Why would you put me through that?" she asked.

"Could you think of a better way?" he asked.

"Alright, I forgive you, now please untie me," she said. Arthur undid the rope, and Jo smacked him as hard as she could in the face.

"Oww, what was that for?!" he shouted.

"Now I fully forgive you," she said, and walked off for a look around.

"This seems like a healthy friendship," he said, rubbing his face and smiling.

They walked around the town, and the sound of their footprints echoed all over the place. "So, where are we?" she asked.

"No idea, I am completely at a loss to be honest," he said.

"What do we do?" she asked.

"Well, there are some things I do in these situations," he said.

"Like what?" she asked.

"Firstly, we examine the positives, come back with me to the square," he said.

They made their way to the marble square, and sat on the marble bench on the left hand side. "First, what have we got?" he asked.

"A rope. I suppose we could hang ourselves," said Jo.

"And what would that achieve? Besides how do we know this isn't death," he asked.

"Nah, I think the afterlife wouldn't be so clean and there would be other people here. And I was just trying to make light of the situation since once again it seems hopeless," she said.

"We have rope, I also have this," he said, producing the notebook and pencil from his sleeve.

"I have this," said Jo, pulling out a bottle of champagne from beneath her dress.

"I'm not going to ask," he said.

"Is this all we have?" she asked.

"It looks like it, but we do have one thing on our side," said Arthur.

"And that is?" she asked.

"We got in here, so there must be a way out of here," he said.

"Unless they sealed us in," she said.

"Archie! Archie! Help!" they both shouted. There was a puff of blue smoke, and a note fell from it.

"'Sorry, but Lilia is monkeying with time and space here so there is nothing even I can do, but there is a way out and you just have to find the answer'..." read Arthur, just before the paper burst into blue flames. "We have about five days without food or water until we are too weak to move, and from the looks of it Lilia doesn't care about that," explained Arthur.

"So we're on our own, what do we do?" asked Jo.

"Work it out," said Arthur, who walked around the square, and noticed something on the floor.

"Look, it's a huge number five, built into the floor," he said, pointing to the floor. Jo looked too, but had no idea why it was there; however Arthur seemed to.

"She doesn't care, but she has given us a chance to escape the trap," said Arthur, now excited.

"Why are you excited? We're trapped here by your nutcase of a sister, and there's no way out," said Jo.

"Yes there is, and I'm excited because it's a challenge, and I like a challenge" he said. "Then carry on" she said, sitting down.

Arthur looked down a street, and saw something that made him run. After about two minutes of being alone in the square Jo ran after Arthur, and saw him walk through a black doorway at the end of the street and disappear. She ran after him, and they both emerged in another part of the town.

"What happened?" she asked.

"I have to admit it, when it comes to new inventions, my sister is brilliant and she's invented a portal. You see, we go in one door and come out another, though we don't know which one; but we shall soon," said Arthur, who ran back to the square where he retrieved his notebook and the pencil.

"Right, so we know that the number five is of some significance since she put it in the middle of the square," said Arthur.

"She may have chosen that at random," said Jo.

"It's her favourite number," said Arthur.

"Was she good at maths?" asked Jo.

"She was brilliant at maths so I believe that this is some kind of mathematical trap, and the only way out is for us to find a solution to the problem," he said.

"So where do we start?" asked Jo.

"How many doors are there?" he asked.

"Let's go and find out," said Arthur.

They went to look at the doors, and they were all helpfully numbered. "I have a ten, do you find anything higher?" shouted Arthur.

"There's a number zero over here, so I think it's zero to ten," said Jo, who appeared from behind a corner.

Arthur spent the next couple of hours working out the maths, while Jo looked at all the paintings, again and again until she began to see different paintings. She walked back to Arthur, who seemed to have hit a block. "If the number five is a common factor, then where is it?" asked Arthur.

"Well, if you think about it, if you take away most of those numbers from each other, then they equal five," she said.

"I don't understand, write it down," he said. Jo wrote down her calculations, and sure enough they were correct.

"We came in through door number six, and we left door number one, and if you subtract those numbers from each other, then you get the number five" she said.

Arthur stood up, shouted 'Eureka', snogged Jo and ran off to the door they left last time. Jo stood there speechless and then after a second ran after Arthur.

"If I'm right, we should go through door number one, and we will get back to door number six, in the same sense as we started, we just have to reverse it," he said.

Jo was still quiet, as she was still reeling from Arthur's kiss. He took her hand and pulled her into the portal. They ran out into door number six. Hand in hand they ran through door one, and came out again in six. They then made for door number two, and emerged from door number seven. They then ran for door number three, and ran out of door eight.

"We're nearly there, through door four, and out through door nine," said Arthur. They did exactly as Arthur predicted, and then made for door number five, which led them to door number ten.

"Final door; the one that we haven't used yet, it's the door that doesn't make any sense," said Arthur.

"Door zero?" asked Jo.

"That's the one," said Arthur.

They ran through door zero, and around them everything went black. Jo held on to Arthur, who watched as blackness surrounded them, and then there was a white light, and they saw that they were in a small room, with a portal on one side, and a door on the other.

"We're out, so let's find out what's happened in our absence," said Arthur.

"Whatever it is, it can't be good." said Jo.

Arthur opened the door, and saw that they were still in the Obsidian Castle. "There seems to be no one around," said Arthur.

"Look, it's daylight outside," said Jo.

"Then they must have already left," said Arthur. Arthur ran out across the courtyard and down the stairs to the main square. The place was completely clean, like an army of servants had been through and stripped the place bare. He then ran to the huge hangars and looked for any sign of life, but all of Lilia's fleet had disappeared. "This is not good, this is not good at all" said Arthur. He then ran back to the Obsidian Castle and looked for Jo. She ran down the wide corridor from the Sky Port to meet him.

"All of the ships have gone, even the Nostradamus" said Jo.

"I would hope so, I told Corky that if we didn't return by 3.00 he was to fly as fast as he could back to Cesta and wait for us," said Arthur.

"That's a bit of good news, I suppose," she said.

"There must be something we can do," said Arthur.

"Let's get back to the castle, at least from there we can think about what to do," said Jo. They both ran up the stairs and across the courtyard. They then entered the castle to look around more, without the threat of guards.

"There's nothing here," said Jo.

"I'll check upstairs," said Arthur.

"I'll come with you," said Jo. They both ran up the spiral staircase at the end of the long corridor and then to the end of the second floor corridor. They climbed the second staircase and saw that the third floor didn't have as many rooms, or they were much larger.

"I'll look in here, you look over there," said Arthur. He went in one door and she went in another. They continued in this fashion until Jo shouted that she had found something. Arthur ran into the room and a wondrous sight met his eyes.

Inside the room was the largest and most complicated machine he had ever seen. It was so colourful that it hurt his eyes to look at it. In the centre was a control panel, and from out of this were hundreds of brass pipes that ran to blocks of pure diamond, which were so large that they looked like they would be impossible to lift.

"Is this another fog machine?" asked Jo.

"It seems way too complicated, personally I think it's something to do with time, look at the dials in the centre control panel," he said. Jo looked and there was a four dial box which read 0003, and another that read;

YYYYYY-MM-WW-DD-HH-MM-SS-MS

And below these letters were all zeros. "This is a time machine, but I guess that it stops time, but doesn't rewind or fast forward it," said Arthur.

"How can you tell?" asked Jo. Arthur pressed the big red button on the control panel, and he felt a ripple resonate through the room. He looked outside and saw that a starling was suspended in mid air, being chased by an impressive but cruel looking hawk. He opened the window and turned the hawk around so it faced the window. He then walked over to Jo, and saw that she had indeed frozen, and he picked her up and sat her on a chair.

He decided to look outside, and walked up the stairs to the roof. Out on the battlements the weather was still, it was neither cold nor hot, but instead it was in the middle, mild and pleasant. He then walked back in and pressed the big button and the same ripple was felt through the room. At that moment time caught up with itself and several things happened; a starling flew away safely, a hawk hit a window, and Jo looked astonished at Arthur, who had managed to move from one side of the machine to the other in a split second. Arthur looked over at the zeros beneath the letters, and they had changed too. They now read:

000000-00-00-00-00-05-17-32

"What happened?" asked Jo.

"Well you see Jo, this is a time machine and it does indeed stop time, I've been gone for five minutes," he said.

"That's unbelievable, how do you think she was able to create something like this?" asked Jo.

"I don't know but if you look at the first dial, it's gone down from 0003 to 0002 which means that this machine has the chance to stop time only two more times," said Arthur.

"Why would Lilia leave this here? It seems a little odd to have left a time machine here when you've just gone to war," said Jo.

"Yes, maybe she thought that we wouldn't get out in time," said Arthur.

"So what are we going to do?" asked Jo.

"No, not we, Josephine, me. If this has the capacity to stop time then I'm going to use it," said Arthur.

"To do what?" she asked, now worried. Arthur went for the button and Jo shouted for Arthur to "STOOO..." but she was stopped by the ripple.

"...OOPPP," shouted Jo, who expected to see Arthur standing by the machine but this was someone different. They were wearing a burgundy suit instead of a blue dress, and when they turned around, Jo cried at what she saw.

"Hello, Josephine, I've missed you terribly," said the figure, which had a long beard and long scraggly hair. Jo looked first at the small dial which read 0001, and then she stared in horror at the second larger dial at the bottom. She ran at the figure and held on to him, for this was her Artie she held...

0117-06-09-12-16-34-27-14

Discoucia

PART II·

The dreamer, the unwoken fool,
In dreams, no pain will kiss the brow.
The love of ages fills the head.
The days that linger there in prey of emptiness,
Of burnt out dreams.
The minutes calling through the years.
The universal dreamer rises up above his earthly burden.
Journey to the dead of night.
High on a hill in Eldorado.'

Eldorado Overture

Forever is a long way

"Why did you press the button?" asked Jo, still with tears in her eyes.

"I had to, it was the only way," he said, smiling.

"Why are you smiling?" she asked, while Arthur used a handkerchief to wipe away her tears.

"Because I'm back here and I missed you so much," he replied.

"Oh I would have gone with you," she said.

"I know you would have, but I didn't want you to spend over a hundred years without any contact from anyone else. I mean forgive me for saying so but after our little episode in the math trap I didn't want you going mad," he said.

"You've been gone how long!?" she asked, shocked.

Jo walked over to the machine and read the dials, and she saw how long Arthur had been gone for. "I'm so sorry," she said.

"For what?" he asked.

"That you had to do this, my father owes you everything," she said.

"Well you see, I had a long time to think, and I came up with the one thing that I want in this world, but I'm afraid this is something that is between him and me," said Arthur.

"Over a hundred years and you didn't change, what has happened to your sister?" asked Jo.

"I'm so glad you asked, follow me," he said.

"Did you lose your sanity at all?" asked Jo.

"A couple of times I thought I was a tree, but normally I was fine.

Archie didn't talk to me at all and that might be because of the time thing," he replied.

Arthur led Jo out of the room, and she saw that his suit was ripped and frayed at the bottom and at the collars, and was speckled with oil. "So tell me, what exactly did Lilia have planned?" she asked.

"When I caught up with the fleet she was mobilised around Evermore, and there were a lot of craft and she had about 200 black robots on the ground. Then when they were all deactivated I went to Chene, and she had a load of them dressed as tin soldiers which were smashing through windows just as I came there" he said.

"You had to walk?" she asked.

"Yes, the ship wouldn't work for some reason. I suppose the Emerald Levitator Engines wouldn't work, so yeah I had to walk every step of the way but the worst thing was sleeping, since the sun was shining permanently for 117 years," he explained.

"How are we going to sort out all the problems she created?" asked Jo.

"When I removed the all her influence from the major cities, I left a letter explaining that the particular ruler was fooled into thinking that Lilia was younger, but in fact she died in the experiment and her second in command was trying to take over. But since the plan didn't work it won't make any difference. However if you want to keep your dignity and respect intact, then you won't mention this to anyone," he said.

"So Lilia is dead?" asked Jo.

"Legally, yes," replied Arthur.

Walking along the long corridor they reached a large door, which when opened led into a large hall. At the end was Lilia, slumped in her large throne completely alone and not a servant or friend in the world. "Queen Lilia the Young, in her marvellous throne, sits there now, completely alone..." said Arthur.

"How long did it take you to think that up?" she asked.

"About ten minutes," he replied.

"So, here she is," said Jo.

"Sleeping like a baby thanks to my new experimental sleep potion, but I couldn't stick her in Icester like the rest of them so I brought her here in a small boat. I had another conversation with Seashorelle as well," he said, walking up to Lilia.

"How is she? How did she recognise you?" asked Jo.

"Archie told her but she never talked to me at all for all that time, but don't worry I'll see her in Lesiga and we can have a nice chat; but this isn't about her, it's about my sister, and she can tell me what she intends to do now," said Arthur.

Lilia's eyes opened slowly and she rubbed her forehead and felt her eyes sting as she adjusted sunlight. She looked around and saw that Arthur and Jo were standing in front of her; only Arthur now looked much older but Jo was the same. "You used the time machine?" she asked.

"Yes, now 117 years of my life has been pretty much wasted," replied Arthur.

"What have you done?!" she shouted, alarmed.

"Your army is now a thing of the past, or present, I forget which one. Also you my dear sister are now legally dead so no angry leaders of the major cities will be coming after you for vengeance," said Arthur.

"I don't understand," said a perplexed Lilia.

"I think I do, he's saved you," said Jo.

"You may be a complete nutcase but you're still my sister, and I still love you. You could have executed me straight away but you didn't, because I think deep down inside you're not as evil as you would have everyone believe," said Arthur.

"Do you know how hard it is to be feared?" she asked.

"You seemed to be doing a good job of it," said Jo.

"You have to do so many bad things so that people will follow you and do what they are told," she said.

"What's your point?" asked Arthur.

"For years now I've hated the thing I've become, but how could I stop?" she asked rhetorically.

"What do you mean?" asked Jo, with a suspicious look.

"I don't want to be an evil person anymore, but to get the attention of all those stuck up high and mighty snobs there was really no other way, they will never really love you, so being hated and feared is the only alternative," she explained.

"Is this really the problem? Acceptance?" asked Arthur.

"When did Mother or Father really care about anything that we did?" asked Lilia.

"They never did, but it didn't stop me giving up," said Arthur.

"When Father gave me control of Harrha and saw me being merciless, he was so happy and I felt happy," she said, standing up and walking over to a window. Jo watched as Arthur walked with her. "Father thought I was doing the right thing and so I then carried on," she said.

"I think I finally understand everything sis, and that's why I did everything I did, for you," said Arthur.

Lilia turned around in amazement. "What do you mean?" she asked.

"If I made you powerless you would listen, if you would listen then you would talk, and I think you have needed to talk for a while," said Arthur.

"Then tell me what you intend to do with me?" said Lilia.

Arthur didn't say anything; he just hugged Lilia, who went rigid as she hadn't been hugged for years. "I just want my sister back," he said. Lilia finally hugged him back and she remained silent. Jo just watched, and when they were finished she sat on the throne as they both looked out across the ocean.

"What are we going to do?" asked Lilia.

"Firstly Jo is going to change your entire look completely, because if you're deceased then you can't look like you did before" said Arthur.

"I suppose I do to be honest, I'm getting a bit sick of purple," she said.

"I never thought I'd hear you say that. Is there anything else I should know?" asked Arthur.

"You can find that out later on but we need to leave here, have you got a ship?" she asked.

"Mine is back in Cesta, and I told Corky to wait," said Arthur.

"You still have Cornelius driving you around?" she asked.

"I cannot think of a better driver," he said.

"Neither can I, I tried to hire him but he wouldn't leave you," said Lilia.

"He never told me, but that's lovely," said Arthur. There was a puff of blue smoke, and a message floated down into Arthur's hand. "'I think it would be much more feasible for me to meet you in my garden of Vertise, since you will be soon visiting. To get you there I have upgraded your ship so it will be big enough for five passengers instead of three...A'," read Arthur.

"A? Is that who I think it is?" asked Lilia.

"It's Archie; Arthur really annoyed her on the way here and I think that when we see her Arthur should apologise," said Jo.

"You shouldn't mess with her, she is more dangerous than you could possibly imagine," said Lilia.

"More dangerous than you?" asked Arthur.

"I'm tame in comparison to the things she has done, all the people she has befriended in thousands of years she has existed they have all ended up disappearing," said Lilia.

"Then you can ask her yourself when we meet her, I'd like you to join us if you want, and come along on all our fantastical adventures," he said.

"Why would you want me? After all I have done to you?" she asked.

"I think you know the answer to that," said Jo.

"I haven't got anything to give you in return for this," she said.

"Look, Lilia, you don't owe me a thing, if you come with me, and we forget everything you have done, since I understand why," said Arthur.

"I agree, on one condition," she replied.

"I thought so," said Arthur.

"I am not going to be constantly apologising for anything, and I am not your assistant," she said.

"That's two, but fair enough," said Arthur.

"In that case, lead on," she said.

When they had finished talking, there was a thud on the roof, and they all looked up, wondering what on earth that could be. "Follow me," said Arthur, but Lilia was running to a spiral staircase that lay at the end of the hall near a door. She ran up it, followed by Jo and then by Arthur. They reached a small room and Lilia opened the door to reveal the outside of the roof, which was a vast open space, and at the end of it sitting in the sunlight was the Nostradamus, but it had changed greatly.

The body of the ship was much longer and wider, about twice the size that it was before, and the back was very ornate. Arthur didn't see what new rooms were built, and he decided to walk on the ship and find out. He was followed by Jo, and then by a stunned Lilia, who was trying to figure out how a ship had appeared out of nowhere. "It's my ship but it's huge, it's bigger than Yage's ship" said Arthur, climbing up some rigging that was hanging over the hull. Jo followed, but found it difficult since she was wearing such an elegant dress. Lilia found that she had the same problem, but she made a good attempt and jumped onto the deck. It was now very large and spacious, and it had a wooden grate where the hull of the ship could be reached.

Arthur was busy inspecting all the changes that had been made to his ship while Jo pulled Lilia back for a second. "You changed your tune quite quickly, too quickly for someone with a fearful reputation like you," said Jo.

"I don't know what to tell you Jo, I guess it's how committed Arthur is," she replied.

"He is committed, and he's also not as strong willed as you would hope, so please tell me now if you intend to change or you're just doing this to escape," said Jo.

"Why should I explain myself to you?" she asked.

"I love Arthur, and I don't want you to hurt him anymore," said Jo.

"I never wanted to, and I don't intend to," said Lilia.

"Are you two coming?" asked Arthur.

They walked up to the door, which was made of solid oak and had an ornate pattern carver into it, with a large letter 'P' surrounded by ivy. "I see the ship is perfectly tailored for you" said Jo. Arthur just smirked and opened the door. They walked into the sitting room, which was larger than before, and was missing the large amount of bookcases and Arthur's desk. There was a set of stairs in the same place, but they were larger than before, and there was a door in the middle of the back door. Arthur opened it and it was a study, with large windows and a larger desk for Arthur. It had more bookcases and on the wall was a large map of Alavonia, with the different continents there. There was Roltio in the far north, and Colsolia just south of that.

Then there was Discoucia in the centre and to its right was Lesiga, and between the two was the Luminosity Archipelago, where Archie's Island of Vertise lay. Then to the east of Lesiga was the land of Neo Firmania, and even further in the east was Tela Bileiaga, which was a very strange land that was not inhabited; or at least so Arthur thought. Then above this land and Colsolia was Immoratia, a land full of mountains and dark brooding clouds. To the right of Discoucia was the land of Insatia, which was three times the size of Discoucia, but most probably uninhabited too. Finally, at the bottom of the map was Caparonia, an ice waste, which was also uninhabited by people.

"This is a complete map of Alavonia, no one has a complete map of Alavonia," said Lilia.

"Apart from us, but let's carry on looking around and see what is upstairs," said Arthur. Arthur walked back into the sitting room, followed by Lilia, who had to pull Jo away from the map. After reaching the top of the stairs, they walked along a corridor that was a sort of 'T' shape, with the top looking out across the deck, and the middle line went past two bedrooms. "I wonder what happened to my wardrobe," said Arthur.

"Let's look on the second floor," said Jo.

There was a second set of stairs at the end of the corridor, and Arthur went up first. The second floor had Arthur's bedroom, and it was twice the size that it was before, and still in the same position, only the bed was much larger and the wardrobe seemed to be much larger too. When they entered it, though, it was full of boxes, but nothing was on racks. There was a letter on one of the boxes, which Arthur opened and read.

"'I'm sorry that I didn't have enough time to sort this room, but I'm sure that you three can have a good go at it on the way to Portalia, but after that you won't have any time for such trivial things'," he read.

"This is a little strange, I wonder what she meant about not having any time, what are we going to be doing?" asked Jo.

"No idea, it's all part of the mystery I suppose," said Arthur.

"Is this what you do, go around solving mysteries and helping people?" asked Lilia.

"Yes, I know it sounds odd, but we get paid for it, by Jo's father or by the people we help, so it's quite fun," said Arthur.

"Oh, makes sense, how much were you paid on my account?" asked Lilia. Arthur whispered something in her ear, and Lilia's eyes widened.

"How much?! I should try to take over again and we can split the difference," she said loudly.

"Come on, we need to return to Evermore, but first you need to pack," said Arthur to Lilia.

"There is quite a bit, but I suppose one of the rooms downstairs is mine," said Lilia.

"I think that is what Archie meant, and are you going to continue staying in my room? I don't mind," asked Arthur.

"You have a bigger bed, of course I will," she said.

"Carry on, see if your suitcases are under the bed," said Arthur. Jo found that they were, and she followed Lilia downstairs and saw that her room was just as big. It was filled with everything she could possibly need. "Come on Leels, I need to ask you about your time machine" said Arthur.

A Time to Live

"So, how do you plan to turn your Time Machine into a way to help the king?" asked Arthur.

"I have an idea, and hopefully if I do this he won't overreact," said Lilia.

"I think it will be a gesture of goodwill and repentance," said Arthur, carrying a small wooden box up the staircase. It was one of many that were to be loaded aboard the ship, as the Time Machine was being loaded.

"And it gives me a chance to show off," she said.

"Good point, remember you don't have to pander to every royal and aristocrat that you meet, let them watch you and envy you," said Arthur.

"I'll try" she said, sticking the boxes in a pile by the ship, which was being taken aboard by Jo and Corky, who had woken up suddenly and panicked until he saw Jo, who explained everything to him. The side of the ship had an airtight hatch that could be opened out onto the roof. Jo loaded the boxes into the hull. She had recently changed back into her green combat gear, which made it easier to move.

When everything was loaded, Arthur asked Lilia a question that was playing on his mind. "Since you will probably not come back here, what do you want to do about your wealth?" he asked.

"I want to take it with me, we could probably stick it in the hull with all the other boxes," said Lilia.

"How much do you have?" he asked.

"Nine trunks of gold, silver and precious jewels, enough for a little trip around the world," she said.

"Let's get going then Jo! You stay here with Corky and get the ship ready to leave!" shouted Arthur.

"Hurry up then!" she shouted back.

After lugging the nine trunks up the stairs, they were finally ready to return to Evermore. "Why does gold have to be so heavy, and you didn't carry anything!" said Arthur.

"I'm a girl, I don't have to carry heavy things. Maybe you should have stayed as Princess Alexandra," said Lilia.

"Can we please forget about that," he said.

"Nope, that's going to follow you until I mention it at your wedding," said Lilia.

"Sure you will Your Highness," said Arthur.

"Can you handle the new ship?" asked Arthur, standing with Corky at the front of the ship.

"She seems the same, just twice as big," replied Corky. The ship lifted off and flew across the sea. Lilia stood with Arthur in his study, looking at the Island that had been her prison for so long, but was now getting smaller and smaller as she left it for a better life.

Jo joined them after she left the hull. "You have how much gold down there?!" she asked.

"Enough, now what do we know about our path?" asked Arthur.

"Well, we need to get to the Great Rim, which is thousands of miles away," said Jo.

"That path will lead to the south east of Discoucia, to the country of Portalia, which is on the far south east coast," said Lilia.

Arthur looked at the large map, and put his fingers to it. "I wish that I could make this bigger" he said. Suddenly, the whole map changed, and just focused on the group of islands between the coast of Portalia and the coast of Lesiga.

"That's amazing, how did you do that?" asked Jo.

"I have no idea," said Arthur.

"Try it again," said Lilia. Arthur then moved the map all around by sliding his finger and he could see all the places of the world, but again focused on the Luminosity Archipelago.

"This is where we are bound, and it looks a bit different from when I last stayed there," said Arthur.

"What is the capital?" asked Lilia.

"Arkellia, and the Palace of Azahad Sir Nabelle rules, but he has a big screw loose," said Arthur.

"And I assume that all the islands are ruled by Lords?" asked Lilia.

"No, they are all ruled by Sirs or Ladies, who wanted their own islands to rule," said Arthur.

"Oh, how many islands are we visiting?" asked Lilia.

"I don't know," said Arthur.

The ship had now reached the shores of Cesta and it was now dark. "Could you do me a favour Jo?" asked Arthur.

"What is it?" she asked.

"Could you cut my hair please? I want to look slightly presentable when we see the High King again," he said. Jo then went about sitting Arthur on a chair with his back and head across the banister, so all the hair would fall off the edge. When Jo was done, Arthur had the same hairstyle as he always did; only this time it was platinum instead of brown.

"I think platinum is a good look for you, when do you ever see a guy with that colour?" said Jo.

"I hope Archie can change it back," said Arthur.

"I don't know, it depends on how she feels I suppose," said Jo.

Lilia had changed her look completely; she now wore a yellow version of what Jo wore, and her hair was now half purple and the front was now bright red. She felt a lot better to be in the company of friends rather than servants, since they didn't fear her, but she found it difficult doing things for herself when she had originally been given everything she ever wanted.

The Ship had flown across the mountains of Fina and the lights of Evermore were ahead. "Are you nervous?" asked Jo, putting her hand on Lilia's shoulder.

"Not really, I'm prepared for this since he's only a man after all," she replied.

"That's one way to put it but don't go in there guns blazing, my father is quite ill and he may be quite aggressive," said Jo.

"You know your father and I'm here to help him, so hopefully he shouldn't do anything stupid," said Lilia.

"With respect, Lilia, he won't do anything stupid because he isn't stupid," said Jo, standing up for her father who she thought Lilia was attacking.

"Whatever, Princess," said Lilia sarcastically, and she left the sitting room.

The ship docked in the special port that was built outside the great hall, and a path above the buildings below extended to a large door on a balcony. Arthur led followed by Jo, and Lilia slinked behind. Arthur then circled round and walked behind Lilia, making sure that she didn't run back to the ship.

The great hall was lit up as it always was, only this time something had radically changed. There was a huge four poster bed at the end of the hall, and there was a large amount of people crowded around it. Jo ran down the hall, and Arthur with Lilia followed. People stared at Lilia and began to whisper among themselves, and when Arthur noticed he slowed down and stayed close to his sister. High King Olandine was laid in the bed now looking old and frail, nothing like he did when they left.

"Father, what has happened to you?" asked Jo, who was starting to cry.

"Can we have a moment of privacy please?" asked Arthur to the advisors who were clustered around the bed. Most of them shuffled off, but one woman stayed.

"Who might you be?" asked the woman in a rude tone.

"Sir Arthur Pageon, if you must know, and who are you?" he replied. "I am Katarina, advisor to his majesty," she replied.

"Where's Kate?" asked Arthur.

"She has gone on holiday to Portalia," replied Katarina.

"I see, well could you give the High King a moment with his daughter?" asked Arthur.

"Very well, who is the person you are here with?" asked Katarina.

"May I introduce my sister, Lilia" said Arthur.

Lilia's eyes widened since she was to be found out for sure. "It's nice to meet you Lilia, how unfortunate that you bear the same name

198

as the great traitor but thankfully she is now dead and a scourge eliminated from the land," said Katarina. Lilia went red, but kept her anger inside and she refrained from punching Katarina in her stuck up face.

"Yes, thankfully she has gone and we can get back to enjoying life without consequence," said Lilia.

"Excuse me?" she replied suspiciously, but any further conversation was drowned out by the King calling for Arthur.

"Come here, Sir Arthur. Leave us everyone else!" he shouted, and all the courtiers and advisors left the hall.

"So Lilia now that you have nothing, hopefully you will treasure this new part of your life as something better," said the King.

"Excuse me?" she asked, wondering how the king knew, but then thought that Jo must have told him.

"I don't care about the past, it has been and gone and all I care about is the future. There is no heir ready to take the throne, not now at least but if I can survive, then maybe one of my daughters could step up," said the king.

"I have a solution, not a permanent one but until a cure can be found for your affliction then I can stop your illness from progressing any further" said Lilia.

"Do it, not for me but for Discoucia," he said.

"Why am I your heir father and not Alexandra? You said that I would never have to rule," said Jo.

"Alexandra is not ready to take control of the empire, and I said I wouldn't force a kingdom on you since I want you to be free, so I shall not," he said.

"Thank you father, we shall try to find a way for you to be cured," said Jo.

"Sir Arthur, I have heard what you have done for us and I wish to reward you in any way you see fit. Ask anything and I will grant it as best I can," he said.

"There is only one thing I could possibly want, when you are cured and the kingdom is put to rights I wish to marry your daughter Josephine, but only when I can sort my premature age problem with the help of someone," he said.

Lilia looked up at him in disbelief, as did Jo but The King didn't look at all surprised. "I thought that was what you wanted, and I shall give you my consent but only if you can complete this task as you have stipulated," he said.

"Then I shall do my best, since the prize is more valuable than any treasure I can think of," said Arthur. Jo got up and hugged Arthur, and then she gently hugged her father.

"Go now and find me a cure, but first what is your plan Lilia?" asked the King.

"Are you in pain?" she asked.

"No, I just keep getting weaker and weaker," he replied. "I was first hoping for that, but now I'm afraid of that," she said.

"What are you going to do?" asked Jo.

"Well the Time Machine was calibrated to stop time all around the universe, but I can change it so it just focuses in one area," she said.

Over the next two days, Lilia built the Time Machine around the bed, and she covered the area between the bed posts with glass, so no air could get out. The king had about half an hour of air inside, but it had to be airtight for the Time Machine to work. It charged the air particles to stop moving and then in turn it stopped every other particle too. Jo was still very suspicious of Lilia but Arthur told her that Lilia was away from Harrha and would be a completely different person. Jo told him that he should not be blinded by love and to take things slowly.

The King fell asleep and Lilia turned the machine on. It whirred to life, and the king stopped moving. This whole spectacle was witnessed by everyone in the Azure Hall and they were given strict instructions not to touch anything as it could kill the king, since only one charge was left in the machine.

Katarina then unfurled a scroll of paper and ask for Arthur to sign it. Lilia and Jo were interested in what it was, and once Arthur had signed it and then was given a copy of his own to sign, which he was then given by her before she left them. "What was the scroll?" asked Lilia. "My payment for bringing you down, the funds have been transferred to my bank account in Gard where all my money is kept," he replied.

"How much did my father pay you for that?" asked Jo.

"This much," he replied, handing her the scroll.

"You have got to be kidding, how much did I get paid?" she asked.

"That's a joint sum, and just so you know that I didn't ask for money but it's his way of keeping me employed," said Arthur.

Arthur, Jo and Lilia left the Hall and climbed aboard the ship. It started up, and sailed to the south east. It was spring so the weather was cold, but where they were going the sun always shone.

Of course you realise this means Wardrobe

The ship flew past the ruins of the fortress outside Evermore, and then strafed the ridge of the southern mountains. It was flying to the large extension of mountains in the south that split the main body of Discoucia from the kingdoms of Portalia, Tounin and Shoreton, which were ruled by Sir's and Dukes but not Lords or Kings. Then when the ship reached the mountains, it would fly over them and come to the Granite and Sandstone Lands, and then Portalia.

"So, let's get unpacking," said Lilia.

"OK, there's a lot of boxes, so we're going to be here a while," said Jo.

"It's a long way to Portalia, and when we get there I have to sign a load of papers to get us passage across the Archipelago and onto Lesiga," said Arthur.

"What was that mass of papers that Katarina gave you?" asked Lilia.

"The High King wants all the islands and Lesiga to enter a united agreement, and he has given us something to give all the rulers of the islands, a golden bracelet with a precious stone in it," said Arthur.

"I have a question," said Lilia.

"Yes?" he asked.

"All those Ice Diamonds that you took from me, where are they now?" she asked.

"They are in my safe in my study, along with the Snow Gold, why?" he replied.

"I was just wondering, because all of the diamonds and gold that were supposed to be shipped to Harrha on the day of my invasion never actually reached me, so where are those?" she asked.

"Five minute break, we're going on a field trip to my study," said Arthur. Lilia and Jo didn't say anything; they just followed him out of the wardrobe and into the study.

"Now, if you ever need money and I'm not here, there is this, but for the love of Authos, do not tell anyone or go on a spending spree, this is a reserve if we need it," said Arthur, pulling the carpet back from the floor, revealing a metal door with a flat, ornate dial on it.

"I thought that your safe was in the wall," said Jo.

"It was, but now that the ship is redesigned the safe is much, much bigger," said Arthur, doing the combination.

"Is it the same combination as before?" asked Jo.

"Yes, 671967, come and see what is inside," he said.

The door opened and steam wafted out, but it wasn't hot steam but cold, very cold. Arthur swung in followed by Lilia, and then Jo. The girls shivered inside, and when Arthur turned the light on, the room was full of Snow Gold and Ice Diamonds which were all in the same sacks as they were before.

"This is slightly illegal isn't it," said Lilia.

"Well it depends on how you look at it, you see you robbed them from Icester then I robbed them from you. By that logic I didn't rob them from Icester, you did," replied Arthur.

"That's specious reasoning," said Jo.

"It is, and if it gets me off a robbery charge then I'm good," said Arthur.

"How did you get all this stuff if the ship only appeared after you restarted time?" asked Jo.

"I can explain that, you see when I did all the good stuff, getting rid of Lilia's malignant influence and all I went to Icester which wasn't cold. Time had stopped and I looted all the treasure out and wheeled it all the way to Cesta," he explained.

"That must have taken you years," said Lilia.

"It did but I never noticed, since it was all just one day forever," said Arthur.

"That makes sense but how did it end up here?" asked Jo.

"No idea, I loaded all of it in the hull of the original ship but I think Archie decided to put it in a bigger safe," said Arthur.

"Can we get out of here, it's freezing," said Lilia.

Back in the wardrobe the three were busy unpacking boxes and putting clothes on hangers and then onto racks. Jo and Lilia had brought up their suitcases too, and they were putting their dresses and other things onto the racks too. Lilia unpacked a box and found a strange costume: an owl head and a fancy suit. "Where did you get this from?" she asked, putting the owl head on.

"From the Owl House in Gard, strange place, very strange place," said Arthur.

"I'm going to stick a mirror on the wall, that way if Archie is going to talk to us she can," said Jo. As soon as Jo put the mirror on the wall, it began to cloud over just like it did on the way to Harrha.

"Good evening people!" said Archie, who looked a little different than the last time. She had the same hairstyle, but had a beard, a long one that was about two inches long.

"Umm, hello, you seem a bit mixed up," said Jo.

"I am duo-gendered you know, so I can do pretty much what I want," she explained.

"Thank you for the ship, it's amazing," said Arthur.

"That's OK, and do you have anything to say Lilia?" asked Archie, staring at her past Arthur and Jo.

"With all due respect, Authos, I have nothing to say to you," she said.

"Very well, If you think that by being coaxing me into being angry then you are wrong, for you see I am quite patient and I see good in everyone, even you," she said.

"If you say so," said Lilia.

"Anyway if you two could come back to us, we need to talk about the adventure ahead," said Arthur.

"Always straight to the point," said Archie.

"Can I begin by apologising?" asked Arthur.

"No not over the mirror, when you get to Vertise you can say what you have to," said Archie.

"Where are we bound?" asked Jo.

"To Portalia and to the Sea Fort," said Archie.

"I have never been there, what is it like?" asked Jo.

"It's a desert mostly, but the main city is an oasis, a huge oasis," said Arthur.

"Is it beautiful?" asked Jo.

"Yes, very beautiful, especially at this time of year," said Arthur.

"I'm going to pick some flowers, it will be summer by the time you reach me so I'll say goodbye. However if you need me, just call into the mirror and I shall appear," said Archie.

"Thank you, and have fun with the interesting facial hair," said Jo.

Archie swirled out of view, and the lights in the wardrobe brightened up.

"That wasn't very nice, was it" said Arthur to Lilia.

"I don't trust her at all, she seems to be guiding everything here, and don't you think that's a little weird?" she asked.

"I think all those years on Harrha alone have made you paranoid, thankfully we got to you as soon as we did," said Arthur.

"I am not paranoid, I don't rush into things without thinking them over first," said Lilia.

"What is there to think over?" asked Arthur.

"You seem to have fallen under her sway quite quickly," said Lilia.

"I don't like your tone," replied Arthur.

"Hold on you two, if you have any questions for Archie then you can ask her yourself but listen, instead of getting at each other, we should be thinking about cleaning, now apologise to each other," said Jo.

"You must be joking," said Arthur.

"If you can't apologise to your sister in person then how are you going to apologise to Archie?" she asked.

"I'm so sorry Arthur for pointing out your immeasurably gullible personality" said Lilia, in such an overly sweet tone that she was obviously making fun of him.

"I'm sorry too Lilia, it's so good to hear that you remember that word since you will probably need to continue saying it for the rest of your life," replied Arthur.

"OK you two need to see someone, someone professionally trained in family problems, and I think I know the very person who by an astonishing coincidence is on holiday in Portalia right now," said Jo.

Over All The Seven Sea's There Was A Phantom Ship A Comin'!

The night paled slowly into dawn, and the stars one by one disappeared from the beautiful velvet sky that was slowly receding across the desert. Arthur walked out onto the deck and was taken aback by how warm it was. He took off his jacket, and put it on a hook in the sitting room. This would be the last time he would wear a jacket for a while, because the night was nearly as warm as the day here.

"When we reach the city I shall try to find Kate, and she can help you two out," said Jo.

"We don't need any help," said Arthur.

"Yes I'm perfectly fine, I know Arthur has his faults," said Lilia.

"Excuse me?" said Arthur.

"Not now, save it for counselling," said Jo. Ahead in the distance was the City of Portalia, which like all the other cities in Discoucia was named after the country it was in.

The City sat at the edge of the desert, and was built on top of the only mountain south of the massive mountain range at the centre of the southern lands. Gradually the city became much bigger, and the walls of the city were made further out to accommodate the cities size. The architecture here was completely different to Discoucia's, and took on a different style altogether. It was strikingly similar to that of middle age Persia, and the people here were all mixed colours. The people who had lived there the longest had naturally become tanned, but the sailors who fished in the Infinite Sea came from the north or the east, so they were either white or slightly darker.

The city had the distinct aroma of spices, and through the wide streets people walked to the Sky Port to see what had happened the night before. A ship was smashed and its wreckage burning on the main landing. The people came to watch as it was cleared away by the local military, and when the ship tried to land, it was turned away by another, smaller ship.

"I'm sorry, but you cannot land here, but if you follow me to The Sea Fort, you can land there" shouted a soldier from the deck of the smaller boat. Arthur waved, and the Nostradamus followed the small boat across the city. Instead of the city having a castle at the top of it, the Sea Fort actually backed onto the sea itself, in a miracle of underwater engineering. It had several strong-looking towers and a huge building in the centre, which was presumably where the ruler lived. It had six towers, arranged in a rectangular shape, with three on one side and three on the other side. There were large glass windows that sat between the towers, and for a fort the whole place looked quite inviting.

The ship followed the smaller ship to a grassy lawn, but it actually parked on the cobblestone road instead, since landing on the lawn would probably churn up the turf. Arthur ran out onto the deck, and saw that a man was running out of the building to the ship. Arthur leant on the prow of the ship in a nonchalant manner, and awaited the man to arrive.

"Good morning sir," said Arthur.

"Good...morning...Sir Arthur...please...could you come with me, and bring your two friends with you, it's urgent that you come at once," he said.

"OK, I'll just get them," said Arthur, who ran back into the sitting room to wake up the two girls. Arthur banged on Lilia's door, and she appeared with her hair in a mess and wearing a yellow dressing gown.

"Morning, we've been invited to The Sea Fort by Sir Anner, so get ready as soon as you can," he said.

"You do realise it's going to take me a while," she replied.

"Five minutes," he said.

Lilia gave him an angry look, and shut the door. Arthur walked to the top of the stairs, and then retreated back as Jo walked down the stairs in front of him.

"I see you are ready, could you give Lilia a hand since we haven't got long," said Arthur.

"You go outside and tell the messenger we shall be down soon," said Jo.

Arthur ran down to the deck, and climbed down the rigging to the messenger. "They'll be down soon, you know women getting ready and all," said Arthur.

"I know, Lady Camellia takes an hour every evening to get ready," said the messenger.

"So tell me about the Anner family," said Arthur. Sir Stuart and Lady Camellia have two children, Reginald and David, and are protected by their own personal army which is headed by Captain Kystos and Captain Ferno," he explained.

"I see, and what is it that you want us for?" asked Arthur.

"I would rather you discussed that with her ladyship, if you don't mind," he said.

Just as they finished, the girls climbed down the rigging and joined Arthur and the messenger. "Let's go" said Arthur. The messenger led the trio through the main doors and they saw that the inside was just like Evermore, and didn't look at all like the rest of the city. It was wonderfully cool inside the castle, and everything looked perfect which made Arthur wonder what was wrong. They came to a large acacia door which the messenger opened, and it led into a huge hall with a white marble throne at the end, and three smaller thrones either side of it with two on the left and one on the right. In the two smaller chairs were two boys, who both had long blond curly hair. The other two thrones were empty, and when the group reached the congregation at the end of the hall.

Out of the group walked a man in a plum jacket and multicoloured waistcoat. He had curly blond hair like the boys, and a straight dark beard. He held out his hand to shake Arthur's.

"Stu! I never knew you became a Sir!" said Arthur, recognising him straight away.

"Spacey, where have you been?" he replied.

"I've been gone for a while but I'm back again, and I'm heading for Lesiga with my sister and my fiancé," he said.

"You have a fiancé? But I thought that you were..."

"No, I have no idea where everyone is getting this idea from," said Arthur.

"So who did you find to keep up with that weird mind of yours?" asked Stuart.

"May I introduce Princess Josephine Olandine," said Arthur.

"It's lovely to meet you Your Majesty," said Stuart kneeling down on the floor in front of her. Arthur picked him up, and Jo laughed.

"Come on, if she's here with me, then she won't want you to be all formal," said Arthur.

"And is this your sister?" asked Stuart.

"Yes, this is Lilia," he said.

"Wait a minute, aren't you Queen Lilia, who declared war on Discoucia?" asked Stuart.

"Umm..." said Lilia, who was right now very uncomfortable.

"And the one who swore that she would destroy all of the rulers in a hellish firestorm?" he asked again.

"Umm..." she said again.

"It's a pleasure to meet you, I know that you cannot be that Lilia, because she died, but I recognise you as a Lilia that I knew a long time ago," he said. Arthur tried not to laugh, as he knew that Stuart had begun as the son of a farmer in Fina, and they were best friends for the years that they lived there. Lilia didn't know him because she never took any interest in Arthur's life.

"It's a pleasure to meet you too, you have a lovely home here," said Lilia.

"Reg, Dave, Camellia, come over here," he shouted. The boys jumped off the thrones and ran over, and a beautiful woman walked over wearing a white dress that looked cooler than the ones worn in Evermore and Chene. She had long brown hair that was similar to Archie's, which made Lilia suspicious.

"This is my old friend Sir Arthur Pageon, his fiancé Princess Josephine Olandine and Arthur's sister, Lady Lilia Pageon," he said.

"Charmed. Stuart, you need to speak to these fishermen, they need you to tell them about your plan to stop the Ghost of Captain Scurvy," she said.

"The Ghost of the what now?" asked Jo.

"Come with me please, and you shall hear all about it," said Camellia.

The group of fishermen were all arguing loudly with each other, and when Sir Stuart came over they all started to talk to him. "Now hold on, I need to first introduce you all to Sir Arthur Pageon, who will hopefully be able to give us some advice for our problem" he said.

"Do you have any experience with ghosts and monsters?" asked one of the fishermen.

"Well let's see, we went to Karga, and discovered that the monster was a robot. I foiled the Dark Chasm Creature, Jo tangled with the monster in the mountains of Icester which we still don't know about. Then we went to Proceur and discovered that the black monsters were just robots like before. Starfall Academy, and found that the place was haunted by several monsters, but they were just brainwashed kids. Then we went to Cesta and found that the Sea Hag wasn't who everyone thought she was. So in answer to your question, yes, yes we do," said Arthur.

"Ah, right, well in that case I think you are perfectly qualified for the job," said one of the fishermen. "So, tell me about your ghost," said Arthur. "He came about three weeks ago, and he rides a ghostly ship covered in skeletons. It glows in the dark and comes from nowhere and then it disappears as soon as it appeared, only it has destroyed a ship in the process," explained Stuart.

"I see, and how many ships has it destroyed?" asked Jo.

"Five, and that one you saw on the way is the sixth," said Camellia.

"And tell me about Captain Scurvy," said Arthur.

"He is seven foot tall, wears a black coat that's all tarnished, and has a horrific looking face," said one of the fishermen.

"And he is on his own?" asked Lilia.

"No, he has two henchmen with him, and they are both seven

foot tall as well, it's not natural I tells ya," said the other one.

"Well gang, looks like we've got another mystery on our hands," said Arthur.

"How are we a gang?" asked Lilia. "And who says that anyway, it sounds way too corny," said Jo.

"OK, if you say so, I won't say it again," he said. There was a puff of smoke and Arthur grabbed the note, everyone else just looked in awe at the strange spectacle that was unfolding in front of them.

"Please don't ever say that again, I have no idea how you managed to think it up, but for my sake please don't say it again," he read.

"Excuse me, but how did you do that?" asked Stuart.

"It's a long story, but we would love to help you, just tell us what you want us to do," asked Arthur.

"If you could help us solve the mystery of Captain Scurvy, then I wouldn't hesitate to reward you," he said.

"I don't think paying will be necessary," said Arthur.

"Nonsense, take me to your ship and we can plan, just like old times in the tree house," said Stuart. Arthur took Stuart, followed by the girls, and that left Camellia and her two sons with the fishermen and courtiers.

"This ship really is amazing Arthur, how did you build it?" he asked after being led into the study. Jo and Lilia had gone to find Kate, and that left the boys alone. The table was laid with maps, but they were not needed, because Arthur had the amazing map on the wall.

"You see, the ship appears out of nowhere and attacks the fishing boats," explained Stuart.

"And the reason that they are out at night is?" asked Lilia.

"You have never gone fishing have you, the fish here come out at night to feed, and my ships go out and trawl the open sea. We usually send about five ships, so its safety in numbers, but the last couple of times the fishermen have been going out into different areas to catch more," said Stuart.

"I see, so why would the Ghost of what was his name?" asked Jo.

"Captain Scurvy, no idea how he got that name, but he used to prowl the sea and the desert in a ship he stole from Evermore and would rob other ships with rich passengers," explained Stuart.

"Then I suppose we should go out on the sea and wait for him," said Arthur.

"I will go with you, the people are beginning to lose faith in me as it is," he said.

"So how did you end up becoming Sir Stuart?" asked Arthur.

"I saved the High King in a hunting accident, the boar that was coming for him would have certainly killed him but I speared it in time. Which was the best thing I have ever done because I got my own ship and flew for the south, just like I always wanted to do," he explained.

"You got to come down here and you met Camellia I guess, how is she?" he asked.

"Amazing, she has this..." he said, but was cut off by Arthur.

"I didn't mean that, I was asking how she was as a person," he said.

"Oh well that's very different, I was introduced to her by her father who ruled here before, and he wanted her to marry a normal person and not an inbred stuck-up aristocrat," he said.

"I see, well you fit the bill perfectly and I'd like to ask you something," said Arthur.

"What is it?" he replied.

"If I get rid of your ghost, would you be my best man at my wedding?" asked Arthur.

"Of course, when are you hoping to get married?" asked Stuart.

"I have no idea, I was just asking in advance," said Arthur.

"It would be an honour, but how are you going to get rid of the ghost?" asked Stuart.

"If the ship is a ghost ship then it will be impervious to guns, I won't be shooting the captain, just the hull to test it," said Arthur.

"I suppose that would make sense but how are we going to capture the ghost of the captain?" asked Stuart.

"To be honest from that point I will be winging it, but please do me a favour," said Arthur.

"What is it?" he asked.

"Please do not tell anyone, you see the fewer people who know the more chance our ghost will appear," said Arthur.

"I can say that you have decided not to help and are continuing on to Elagos Island," said Stuart.

"Good idea, then we will fly off and hide in the dark out at sea about fifty yards from the fishing ship," said Arthur.

"Then the ghost ship will appear and we can attack," he said, banging his fist on the table.

"Yes, that is all well and good but if you are with us, then people will wonder and ask questions," said Arthur.

"I wonder," said Stuart, who began to think.

Just then Jo, Lilia and a new person walked through the door. The new person wore a white dress which was similar to Archie's, but instead of being part blue, it was all white. She had brown hair tied in a bun with curled strands coming from the sides. She looked like one of the statues that littered the ruins of Tanalos. "We're back and we brought Kate, she is a marriage counsellor and advisor to my father," said Jo.

"I told you, Jo, I don't need counselling," said Arthur.

"Yes you so obviously do, and Kate here will give it to you," said Jo.

"It is lovely to meet you Kate, but I'm sorry that Jo dragged you here, since there was no need," said Arthur.

"I shall be the judge of that," said Kate, in a tone of authority, but not malice.

"Fine, if this is what I was getting into with marriage, then I suppose I'll have to," said Arthur.

"Welcome to the jungle," said Stuart.

"You stay here with Jo and try to think up more of the plan," said Arthur, who walked out with Lilia and Kate into the sitting room.

Arthur and Lilia were sat on the sofa, while Kate sat on the desk. "So Arthur, tell me about your mother," said Kate.

"I can't really remember much about her to be honest, I remember she had long brown hair, and blue eyes, but that's it," said Arthur.

"What about you, Lilia?" asked Kate.

"The same as Arthur, we didn't see her much," she said.

"Do you think that an absence of a mother figure caused you two to lead abnormal lives?" she asked.

"Would you consider my life to be abnormal?" asked Arthur.

"I'm asking the questions if you don't mind," said Kate.

"Carry on; I don't really think my mother had any part in my decisions," said Arthur.

"I think it was my father who decided my course in life," said Lilia.

"OK, but if we examine the time after your father died, then you decided on the reckless course that could have destroyed you entirely," she said.

"I'm aware of that," said Lilia.

"What plan did you have when you had taken over Discoucia?" asked Kate.

"Are you sure we should be talking about this, isn't someone going to arrest me and stick me in Icester?" she asked.

"We can't arrest a dead person," said Kate.

"So who else is in on this little conspiracy?" asked Lilia.

"Me, the High King and Princess Josephine," said Kate.

"I was just going to wing it, I just wanted to rule the place and call myself High Queen, but had no idea how to rule it," she said.

"I understand, ruling a kingdom isn't as glamorous as it seems," said Kate.

"I know, I think that if Arthur didn't come along, then I wouldn't be here now," she said while lowering her head slightly.

"Now Arthur, why did you go to Harrha?" she asked.

"Because I wanted to stop Lilia from taking over the kingdom," replied Arthur.

"And you jumped at the chance to see your sister again," said Kate.

"I did for the kingdom, as much as anyone else would," he replied.

"Really, because I have here a list of times you asked the king for permission to go to Harrha and it looks like you asked him seventeen times," she said.

"How did you get that?" he asked, now worried.

"You asked to come? Why?" asked Lilia.

"You're my sister, how could I not," he said.

"Why didn't you come earlier?" asked Lilia.

"With father in control of the island, I wanted to be as far away as possible, which is why I left Discoucia and flew to Drongo, there I

217

stayed for years," he said.

"You had all that time to come for me and you didn't?" asked Lilia.

"Now look at the positives here, he did wait because your father would have done god knows what to him, but when you came to power and your father was gone, he came for you," said Kate.

"I did ask that many times, but the High King wouldn't allow it, he didn't want to provoke a war otherwise we would be in the wrong," said Arthur.

"Your hands were tied, then?" she asked.

"Yes there was nothing I could do, for the love of god I dressed up as Princess Alexandra for you," he said.

"Yes, that was pretty funny actually," said Lilia.

"He did what?!" asked Kate.

"Seriously, out of everything you know, you didn't know about that?" asked Arthur.

"This is becoming the most interesting session I have ever had, now tell me, after knowing this do you think anything differently of each other?" asked Kate.

"I think I've done a lot for you Lilia, but it's your turn," said Arthur.

"Yes Lilia, tell us how you haven't been completely heartless in this little affair," asked Kate.

"I could have had you executed the moment I captured you. I would have kept Jo as a hostage since she was a princess, but my advisors told me that shooting you between the eyes would be the simplest thing to do. But no, I didn't did I?" she asked.

"No, you stuck me in a space time trap," he said.

"That you escaped, quite easily to be honest," said Lilia.

"Then I had to wander the world for one hundred and seventeen years, alone," he said.

"So you know how I felt, alone on Harrha while you lived on Drongo Island," she said.

"Fair enough, but now we know everything, what do we do about it?" asked Arthur.

"You hug each other, and forget everything that haunts you from your previous life, what you do now is all that counts," said Kate.

Arthur leant over and hugged Lilia, who hugged back, and Kate smiled as she had had another successful session, a very interesting one.

"So Kate, what do we owe you?" asked Arthur.

"You pay me for how well I did the job," she said.

"Please wait here," said Arthur. He walked into the study, and after a couple of minutes he returned.

"Here you go Kate, and thank you," said Arthur, handing her something wrapped in cloth. Kate opened it up, and a blue light reflected on her face.

"Is this an Ice Diamond?" she asked.

"I won't say anything if you don't," said Arthur.

"Thank you, I'll get it put into a ring," she said.

"In that case, have this too," he said, handing her something else wrapped in cloth. She unravelled it and it was a small block of white metal.

"It's cold," she said.

"Some Snow Gold to go with your Ice Diamond," said Lilia, who stood up and stood with Arthur.

"I'm going to have to keep these hidden, since they are nearly priceless," she said.

"Just say you were given them by a mysterious couple," said Arthur.

"I won't say a word, I'll get Descuedus the Smith to create a ring to hold it and I'll wear it when it gets warm," she said.

"We will hopefully see you sometime when we return from Lesiga," said Arthur.

"There was one more question I wanted to ask you; why do you want to go there anyway?" asked Kate.

"To meet my maker," replied Arthur rather cryptically.

"Oh. Well it was a pleasure to help but I must say goodbye to the princess before I leave," she said.

After Kate had left, the group all decided to work on the plan to capture The Ghost of Captain Scurvy. When it was nearly night time Lady Camellia was holding a banquet like she did every Friday. She had begun to get ready and Sir Stuart was seen running across the lawn to the ship.

"We have an hour and the ship is already out, so let's see what we can do," he said.

"She takes an hour to get ready?" asked Jo.

"She does, I don't know why but I don't question her anymore," said Stuart. The ship lifted off past the windows but all the lights were turned off, so it looked like a wraith gliding silently by.

The fishing boat was similar in size to the Nostradamus but a bit more beat up, considering it was used for work and not for pleasure. The ship waited about fifty yards away from the fishing boat waiting for the ghost ship to appear. Arthur and Stuart leaned on the banister watching the ship, like a tiny lamp in a vast empty void. The sea was calm, and everything seemed normal. Then there was a small green light that came from behind the Nostradamus, as if from the shore.

"There it is," said Stuart.

Arthur drew his pistol and he waited for the ship to come closer. He then thought about how Archie despised guns and put it back. Jo and Lilia now walked onto the deck. Jo stood with Arthur and Lilia stood with Stuart. Lilia had become quite taken with Stuart, but since he was married she couldn't say her true feelings.

The ship then got close enough for the four to get a good look and it looked like the Nostradamus, only with skeletons displayed everywhere and ragged sails. As it edged closer they saw the ship's captain. He was a giant of a man with huge hands and a long scraggly beard. His eyes glowed green and he had a large pirate hat on.

There were two other men with him who looked just as mean as he did. One was bald with a long pointy moustache, and the other had a small beard and an eye patch. "Stereotypical pirates aren't they?" asked Lilia.

"Just like something out of a book, but what do you expect from ghosts?" replied Stuart.

"Let's see," said Arthur, who grabbed a rope and abseiled down the hull, and with one arm on the rope, he shot his pistol at the ship. The glowing green wood splintered and new wood was revealed below. Arthur then stuck his pistol in its holster, and with both hands slid down the rope.

"Come on!" he shouted.

Jo needed no convincing; she grabbed a rope and jumped down onto the ship, which had now stopped. The fishing boat had now moved back, since its job as a decoy was now done. Lilia then jumped down, and Stuart followed.

The ship was made to look as evil as possible, and it glowed with a green luminescence that nearly blinded the group. Arthur and Stuart's attention was immediately set on Captain Scurvy, while Jo and Lilia tied the ropes they had swung down on to the banisters of the ship, so it couldn't get away.

"Good evening Captain," said Arthur.

"Get 'em!" he shouted, and the two other pirates ran at Arthur and Stuart.

Arthur dodged a sword strike and smacked the pirate in the mouth. He went down surprisingly easily, which made Arthur worried. He stared at his fist, not knowing that he was that strong. Stuart did exactly the same, and they both let the girls tie up the pirates and went for the captain.

"You need better staff, mate," said Arthur. The captain just growled, and went for Stuart. Arthur put his leg out and the captain toppled.

"Oww" said Arthur, who felt that the captain's leg was made of metal. Stuart and Arthur tied up the captain with the other two, and Stuart commandeered the ship. Arthur stayed with him and the girls went back to The Nostradamus. They then sailed both ships to the Sea Fort, and a large group of people had gathered on the lawn. Both ships landed and it was a strange scene that was unfolding. All the people from the banquet came down as well.

"So, in my past experience, who are we missing?" asked Arthur.

"What do you mean?" asked Stuart.

"All right, let's see who our captain is," said Arthur, who yanked on the pirate hat, and the whole of the captain's mask came off with it.

"Camellia?!" said a shocked Stuart.

"And..." said Jo and Lilia pulling the masks off of the two pirates.

"Reginald, and David?!" he said again in the same tone.

"OK, I understand how but I am a bit clueless as to why" said Arthur.

"You are not like us, Stuart. You are not of our kind," said Camellia, in a snide tone.

"Excuse me?" he asked.

"I asked my father not to marry you but he wouldn't listen, I had to marry a commoner like you!" she said again.

"Oh I see now, but what was this going to achieve?" asked Arthur.

"Stuart is a Sir, not a Lord so he didn't have a position for life, the people could get rid of him," said Camellia.

"So by creating this whole ghost thing you could make the people lose faith in me and then get rid of me, is that it?" asked Stuart.

"Oh good, you're not completely stupid," she said.

"So, destroying ships and terrorising people, how long in Icester would she get?" asked Arthur.

"Criminal damage is five years, and she destroyed six ships, so I'm going with fifty years combining terrorism," said Jo.

"You can't do that, I'm a Lady," she said.

"And I'm a princess, and since I'm higher on the scale that you hold so dear, I say that you and your accomplices need to cool off for a while," said Jo.

"I'll get you for this" she said. "I'm sure you will and I'm also sure that it will make an interesting story one day, but until then, bye" said Jo, who walked off back onto the Nostradamus.

"It was very clever, the whole using stilts to make yourselves look more menacing, but next time come up with something a bit more original," said Arthur.

"Why did she say she was going to get Jo, when she was the one doing the bad stuff? My god it's embarrassing that I'm asking," said Lilia as they walked off.

"Sour grapes, criminal mentality, crash of reality, yada yada yada," replied Arthur.

Kate took Camellia and her two sons with her back to Evermore to face trial which left Stuart alone. "Do you know what you will do now?" asked Jo.

"Not really, I suppose I'll travel for a while," he replied.

"Would you like to come with us? We're visiting all the islands in the Luminosity Archipelago, and you would be welcome to join us if you want," said Arthur.

"No, I would be a fourth wheel," he said.

"I would like it if you came," said Lilia.

"Why would that be?" asked Stuart.

"Because I feel a bit left out," she said.

"It would be a pleasure, with me you won't have any trouble crossing the islands," he said.

"Why is that?" asked Jo.

"The rulers of the islands are all a bit funny, not in good way," said Stuart.

"You can take the room next to Lilia, Jo and I will stay upstairs," said Arthur.

"When do you want to leave?" asked Stuart.

"As soon as possible," said Arthur.

"Then allow me to pack and we can be off, I'll be about an hour and I'll leave control of the city in Captain Kystos' and Captain Ferno's capable hands," he said.

When Stuart came back, the ship was all lit up, ready to leave. "Why are we leaving in the evening?" asked Lilia.

"That way, we should reach Elagos by sunrise, and we can be at Sir Charles' mansion for breakfast," said Stuart.

"Do you know him personally?" asked Lilia.

"I've known him for years, he visits me, and I visit him, he comes from old old incredibly old money," said Stuart.

"Wait a moment, is his daughter Lady Victoria Ridge?" asked Jo.

"Yes, have you met her before?" asked Stuart.

"Yes, Arthur and I have, only Arthur would remember her as Vicki, and she would remember him as Alexandra," said Jo.

"Oh," said Arthur.

"Please explain," said Stuart.

The Demon's of Ridge Mansion

The Island of Elagos is a strange place. It was a sandy, rocky wasteland, but when Sir Charles Ridge's ancestors first settled there, they began work on an oasis of epic proportions. Nine generations down the line, the Ridge Mansion is a white jewel in a green ring of trees that were painstakingly cultivated out of nothing, and the Ridge family are a proud people. Inside the mansion live Sir Charles Ridge, Lady Anna Ridge, Lady Victoria Ridge and Jonathan Ridge, plus the staff. Sir Charles Ridge made a huge amount of money from gold mining, and that catapulted his family into the highest society in Discoucia.

The Nostradamus landed outside the mansion which was an amazing building, and was made from white marble similar to the ruined temples in Tanalos. The gardens were landscaped perfectly, the grass was green, and there were statues all around taken from Tanalos when Sir Charles' uncle explored the place years ago. There was the sound of running water somewhere and from Arthur's bedroom he and Jo could see that there were bridges running over immaculate streams that ran through the trees. Stuart and Lilia were up and they knocked on the door. All they heard was the sound of something being thrown around the room, bashing into the walls and then they heard Jo and Arthur saying something. "That was way too close," they heard Jo say.

"Whatever, I bet we could on every island," said Arthur.

"I doubt it, come on, let's go downstairs," said Stuart, and Lilia nodded with a funny look.

The four poured out onto the deck and they saw nobody about. "There's no one around, isn't someone supposed to be around?" asked Stuart.

"That's usually the way it goes, but for some reason something has happened," said Arthur. Out of the trees burst a horrific looking creature; all green with horns, red glowing eyes, and breathed a horrible stench from its mouth. Then a strange sound was heard, a strange melody, and the creature disappeared, jumping off the ship and running for the woods.

"In broad daylight, I have never seen a monster do that before. At least you have a fog or shadow or something," said Arthur.

"So that's why no one is here, let's follow it," said Stuart, who drew his gun from its holster.

"Keep an eye on the ship girls, and if you see anyone tell them where we have gone," said Arthur.

"OK, be careful men, us women will look after the ship while you go out and do scary work that would be too much for our tiny minds to comprehend," said Jo, very sarcastically.

Lilia just noticed that Jo's hair was comically out of place, with one side all messy and the other nearly perfect. "Did you have a chance to do your hair Jo?" asked Lilia.

"You woke us up in a hurry, I didn't really get a chance," said Jo.

"Oh well, I'm sure that Sir Charles will not notice," said Lilia. Jo looked at her for a second, and then ran into the sitting room and then upstairs. Lilia smirked and sat on one of the banisters.

Arthur and Stuart were running after the demon, and they saw it in the distance. It was a fast runner, and it bolted expertly through the perfectly maintained gardens, and ahead the two saw the desert that bordered the forest. The demon ran out of the forest and into the open. "We've got it" shouted Stuart. Arthur was not so sure, and when the heat of the now open space hit them, they were amazed at how the demon had managed to disappear into thin air.

"Where did it go?" asked Stuart. Arthur remained silent and looked around for something that could be concealing it, but it was just a flat plain that extended off into the distance until it reached the sea.

"We'd better get back, it's amazing isn't it, how it's so hot out here, but cooler in there," said Stuart.

"I'd rather be cool than hot, let's get back to the ship," said Arthur.

Back at the ship, they saw that Jo and Lilia had gone, and they decided to go to the house. Stuart knocked on the door and a smartly dressed man opened the door. "Good morning Sir Stuart, won't you come in and bring your friend with you," he said.

"Thank you Carlswell, this is Sir Arthur Pageon and I trust that Princess Josephine and Lady Lilia are here too?" asked Stuart.

"Yes sir, follow me to the conservatory," said Carlswell.

The House was opulently decorated with a real emphasis on white. There was a cold breeze running through the house which was pleasant for Arthur and Stuart, who after a couple of minutes in the desert felt too hot. They came to a doorway which was open and they walked into the conservatory, which was massive. It had a water pool in the corner and out of the sides ran water into a little river that flowed all around the room. In the centre was a large table, and at it sat six people. There was Jo and Lilia, plus a man, a woman, and a younger man and Vicki.

"Good morning, welcome back to Elagos, Stuart" said the man, who was obviously Sir Charles.

"It looks lovelier than the last time I came," he replied.

"And Sir Arthur Pageon, it's lovely to meet you," said Charles.

"This is such a lovely home, and I must say your gardens are the most beautiful I have ever seen," said Arthur.

"You are too kind, please join us," he said.

Stuart sat next to Lilia, and Arthur sat next to Jo.

"So, Princess Josephine tells us that you had a run in with our resident demon," he said.

"Fast chap, how long have you had a problem with him?" asked Arthur.

"It is a long story," said Charles.

"My favourite kind," said Arthur.

After breakfast, they all sat in the drawing room, and Sir Charles related the strange story that had caused him such upset.

"It all began several hundred years ago, my ancestors came to this Island long ago and they first encountered an alchemist, by the name of

Varellion who lived by the Eternal Spring which is in the south part of the garden. Of course back then there was nothing here, and they told him that they now owned the Island and they wanted him to leave. He then cursed them, and said that a horrible throng of demons would hound the ninth descendent of the family, which happens to be me," he explained.

"Is this a tale that has been passed down from generation to generation?" asked Jo.

"I would assume so, my wife found the tale in an old book written by my grandfather while I was away on the north side of the island checking on the goldmine," he said.

"I was cleaning, I would usually ask the maid to do it but while Charles is away I have precious little to do," said Lady Anna.

"It must be quite lonely here," said Lilia, who was speaking from personal experience.

"I have a lot of servants here so I don't mind that much," she replied.

"Anyway getting back to your problem, what has happened recently?" asked Stuart.

"The Alchemist has returned but he looks more like a magician, and he has been releasing demons left right and centre. He has control over three of them, the green one that you ran into, a red one, and a particularly nasty black one and they terrorise the grounds," explained Charles.

"Oh that is good, we finish with one mystery and we get another one, does the Magician ever get close enough for you to see him?" asked Arthur.

"We don't really venture out of the house, we're actually under siege," said Anna.

"Then it's good we came, I'll get rid of your demons and their malignant magician," said Arthur.

"If you can, then I would forever in gratitude, and whatever we have taken out of the mine this week is yours," said Charles.

"Deal, just send it to my account in Gard when we're done," said Arthur.

"Nonsense, we will do this for you and we expect nothing in return," said Jo, kicking Arthur under the coffee table.

"Sorry, yes what my fiancée said," said Arthur quickly.

228

"Is there any reason you came other than for a simple visit?" asked Vicki.

"Yes actually," said Arthur taking out the bracelet that was given to him by the High King.

"What is this?" asked Charles.

"The High King would like you to become a member of the Discoucian Temple of Lords and with this bracelet you would agree to help him in any way. However he doesn't mean anything bad, it has to be voted to by all the members of the Temple before it goes through and it also means that you would become Lord Ridge" said Arthur.

"If you can get rid of this man, then I shall also agree to the King's terms, but only when you bring him to me," said Charles.

"Do you think you have a chance against him?" asked Jonathan, who hadn't talked for the entire time, and now everyone looked at him and then to Arthur.

"I suppose I have more of a chance than anyone else but I won't be using a gun this time, because if these are real demons then there would be no point. And this magician must be ancient so I'll just have to push him over and that's it," said Arthur.

"We'll see," said Jonathan, who walked out of the room.

"He doesn't get out much and staying here doesn't help," said Anna.

"Why don't you take him with you to your goldmine?" asked Jo.

"He doesn't want to go," said Charles.

"Then tell him to go, he won't change if you don't help change him," said Jo.

"With all due respect Princess Josephine, are you telling me how to raise my children?" asked Charles.

"If you want your empire to continue, then who are you going give it to who is experienced?" asked Jo.

"It wouldn't hurt for him to go," said Anna.

"Alright, when this business is wrapped up I'll take him to the goldmine and show him what to do," said Charles.

"I'm sorry, no one wants advice on raising their kids," said Jo.

"I know, it's OK, you are right, I just didn't want to hear it," said Charles.

Vicki took Jo and Arthur out of the room, and they walked up the stairs and along a long white corridor. They walked past a maid, who was cleaning a painting's frame.

"Good morning Nellie" said Vicki. The maid bowed, and then went back to cleaning. They then entered Vicki's bedroom, which was huge.

"So, you two are now engaged," she said.

"How did you know?" asked Jo.

"Half of Discoucia knows by now," said Vicki.

"Oh no, that was fast," said Arthur.

"So Arthur, it's nice to finally meet you at last," she said.

"You've met before," said Jo.

"I would remember, I have always heard about you but never actually met you," she said, ignoring Jo's comment.

"No, you have met, he was with me on Harrha," said Jo, who was beginning to smile. Arthur began to roll his eyes, as he knew what was coming.

"You were with your sister," said Vicki.

"Could you please not call me Ally," said Arthur in the same voice as when he was disguised as Princess Alexandra. Vicki didn't say anything, she just stared, her mouth gaping. Jo pushed it closed, and began to laugh.

"He was, no," she said finally. Arthur coughed and began speaking again.

"Yes, it's true, not one of my proudest moments, but at least I can be proud of the fact that I mastered running in heels" said Arthur.

"So that story about..." she said.

"Yes, I'm afraid it did happen, but it probably didn't happen the way you have heard it, I'm not that kind of girl," said Arthur.

"Then tell me what actually happened, then I'll clear this up when I go to the Evermore Midsummer Party" she said.

Arthur then explained to Vicki what happened on that fateful day in Chene, and she understood that most of the things that happened were untrue.

"I see now, that makes so much more sense; but I thought you made a great Alexandra" said Vicki.

"Thank you, I still think I should have been an actor," he said.

"So when is the wedding?" she asked.

"No idea, when we've cured my father," she said.

"I heard he was ill, and it seemed that he only had a few weeks," said Vicki.

"He's been suspended in time for a while, and we're going to Lesiga to find a cure," said Arthur.

"What makes you think something is there?" she asked.

"I have a feeling," said Arthur.

"Remember you cannot tell anyone about Arthur impersonating Alexandra, for obvious reasons and because she would probably break his nose," said Jo. Arthur then held his nose, and imagined that to be quite painful. "I won't breathe a world about that, I just hope you can stop the magician," said Vicki.

The day turned to evening, and everything was still. Arthur and Jo went out for a pleasant walk, and they walked past the beautiful hedges and over the running streams. Something was watching them, and it moved behind the hedge and followed them closely.

"So, any thoughts on baby names?" asked Jo.

"That's thinking rather far ahead isn't it?" asked Arthur.

Jo pushed him against a tree, and began to kiss him. Arthur didn't really have a chance to breathe, but eventually saw what she was driving at. Then a rustling made Jo stop.

"Freddy; Archie mentioned it and I kind of liked it," he said, gasping for air.

"Shh, there's something over there," she said.

The strange melody played again, and out from behind the hedge came a small man, with long bony fingers and holding a flute. It had green glowing eyes, and smiled at the two as it began to play. Then out of the dark rushed the black demon, and Arthur stepped in front of Jo. "Good evening, so you like to watch, huh?" asked Arthur.

The Magician growled, and began to play the flute again. The Demon ran for Arthur. He pulled out a pistol and aimed it at the Magician. "Uh? You said you weren't going to use a gun!" it said in a rasping but scared voice.

Out of the bushes came Lilia and Stuart, and with a whack from a spade the two ghouls were knocked unconscious.

Arthur carried the magician, who was surprisingly light, and Stuart came in behind with the demon tied up in a wheel barrow. "I can't believe you did this so quickly," said Charles, who came out of his study with Anna. Vicki came downstairs, and was wearing a pink dressing gown and had her extremely long hair down, which made her look quite different.

"Well, I know who the Magician is; I'm afraid it's your son, Jonathan," said Arthur.

"Did someone say my name?" asked Jonathan, who walked out of the kitchen holding a chicken drumstick.

"If you're here, then who is this?" asked Arthur, pulling off the magician's face to reveal a woman who they didn't recognise.

"That is Verity, my handmaiden," said Anna.

"And her accomplice is..." said Stuart, pulling off the head of the black demon, which revealed the head of the green demon. "This doesn't make much sense," said Stuart.

"Give it another go," said Arthur. Stuart pulled off the green mask, and underneath was the red demon.

"OK, I think I understand, one more time," said Arthur. Stuart pulled off the last one, and it was a sweaty, dishevelled man.

"He is one of my miners, I fired him when he was stealing gold," said Charles.

"It makes sense, keeping you away from the mine and the only way for someone to disappear in the middle of the desert is a trap door, which if we go and look I think we will find," said Arthur.

"But why Verity?" asked Anna.

"This is most probably a relation," said Arthur, pointing to the man.

"And with three different disguises, he could appear to be three demons," said Vicki.

"If he put them on at once, he would look different each time," said Arthur.

"Well, you did it Sir Arthur, and I shall reward you with everything I promised. And you, Jonathan, are coming with me in the morning to my goldmine, and we are going to collect Sir Arthur's reward and will deliver it to Gard personally," said Charles.

232

"What? I'm not going," said Jonathan.

"Yes you are, and that's the end of it," said Charles. Jonathan was taken aback by his father being strict with him, but Anna was happy that her son was actually going to get out of the house.

"OK," he said, and walked up to bed.

"We will be leaving now," said Arthur.

"Thank you for everything," said Charles.

"No problem, pleasure to do it, I think I'm getting the hang of this monster hunting lark," said Arthur.

"Where will you go next?" asked Anna.

"To Escid, I want to visit the ruins of the Old Fortress, and from there I will probably continue to Seone, and deliver the next bracelet," replied Arthur.

"Well good luck, and enjoy your tour of the islands," said Charles.

When Jo had said goodbye to Vicki, they left the house, and the two criminals who would be taken to the mainland by Sir Charles and Jonathan in the morning. The ship lifted off and sped further south, to the apparently empty ruins of the Old Fortress...

Two Lilia's is just two much

The Isle of Escid wasn't that far away from Elagos, so it was still dark when they arrived. They landed on the beach, and the pink moon was so big that it was as light as day. Arthur and Jo climbed out of their window and crawled down the ladder, and Arthur slipped on the last rung and landed on the sand. Jo slipped as well and landed on Arthur. "Oof," said Arthur in a muffled voice.

"Shh, we don't want the other two to hear us," said Jo.

"You do realise that they are probably doing the same thing as us," said Arthur.

"Yes they probably are, but I don't really want to be thinking about that now, come on let's get out of here," said Jo.

The moon was so bright they could see their shadows, and they came to the ruins of the Old Fortress which didn't look that spooky, and Jo dragged Arthur behind a wall. Out of nowhere came a green light, which made Arthur stick his head around the corner. "Huh, what is it now?" asked Arthur, his face covered in lipstick.

"Yeah, what is it?" asked Jo, her hair all a mess.

They were greeted by a ghostly apparition; it was a woman with flowing white hair, a horrible face and a tarnished purple dress. "Why do you dare disturb the ghost of Queen Lilia!" is shouted.

"Lilia, are you playing a joke? Well consider us successfully scared now run along" said Arthur.

Lilia drew a dented sword and swiped for Arthur. He pushed Jo out of the way, and ducked.

"OK, very funny" said Arthur.

The ghost stared angrily with white eyes and went for Jo, but she jumped out of a long broken window and landed on the sand outside. When the ghost turned around Arthur was running away, following Jo since he was being perfectly logical.

The two burst into the sitting room, and Lilia was on the sofa with Stuart.

"Lilia!?" they both said in unison.

"What?" she asked, and was very confused.

"What are you playing at, you nearly cut my head off," said Arthur.

"I have no idea what you are talking about, if you're referring to earlier we've been over that," said Lilia.

"Where did you get that costume from, and how did you get back here so quickly?" asked Jo.

"I've been here the entire time," said Lilia.

"That's true, we've both been here ever since you went to 'get something from the wardrobe'," said Stuart. Arthur and Jo then collapsed in laughter at the same time.

"OK, please explain" said Lilia.

"Would you believe that there is a ghost of you running around the Old Fortress, and they think you're dead," said Arthur.

"Well of course I'm dead, as of now I'm your sweet slightly younger sister that despite all the people who know what I look like have no clue who I am," said Lilia.

"Then we obviously know that it is a fake but I think we should play things a bit differently, so let's wait until morning because I have a fun idea," said Arthur.

"What are you going to do?" asked Stuart.

"You'll see, and when you see you can join in," said Arthur. There was a puff of blue smoke, and a message appeared.

"What is taking you so long?" read Arthur.

"We're having fun foiling phonies," said Arthur.

"Wow, try saying that when you're drunk," said Jo.

"Want to try?" asked Arthur.

Arthur grabbed a bottle of Blue Whisky while he was pulling Jo up the stairs.

"OK, then," said Stuart.

"You know what's funny?" asked Lilia.

"What?" asked Stuart.

"They think they're drinking Blue Whisky but it's merely blueberry juice mixed with a tiny amount of wine so it tastes alcoholic. If they come down here drunk it's the placebo effect," explained Lilia.

"Why would you substitute it?" he asked.

"Because my brother can get really emotional and frankly it's just easier this way. I just hope he doesn't get into the secret stash in the wardrobe," she said.

The Next Morning...

"Ohhh, my head hurts," said Arthur, slinking down the stairs. He walked in on Lila and Stuart, who were still asleep on the sofa under a cover. Arthur didn't wake them, and he walked upstairs to get Jo. They came back downstairs and sneaked past the two love birds, carrying towels. When they got outside, it was about ten in the morning, and they decided to go swimming.

"That was fast," said Jo.

"I never thought Lilia ever felt that way about anyone," said Arthur.

"She was stuck on that island a long time, maybe she was waiting for the right person," said Jo.

"Maybe, but let's go swimming since it's so hot," said Arthur. They both took most of their clothes off, and Jo was surprisingly wearing a bikini, and it turned out that it was in one of the boxes, with a note on top saying 'for swimming'. Arthur was just wearing shorts that he didn't mind getting wet.

They left all their clothes in a pile, and jumped into the water. They swam about ten yards out, and suddenly the sea began to swirl and froth. Jo and Arthur were then pulled out of the water by a huge hand. Then a monstrous head ascended out of the water.

"Seashorelle? Hiya!" shouted Arthur.

"How are my two little adventurers?" she asked.

"We're OK, we're engaged" shouted Jo.

"Congratulations, have you seen Archie yet?" she asked.

"Not yet, we have to go to Seone first, and then we will meet her on Vertise," said Arthur.

"Good luck, do you know that you will soon be getting close to her domain," she asked.

"She has a home?" asked Jo.

"A massive one, the Great Rim houses it and I'm told that it is bathed in perpetual twilight," she explained.

"It sounds lovely," said Arthur.

"Did you expect anything less?" she asked.

"I suppose not. Did you just stop to say hello?" asked Jo.

"Pretty much, I'm swimming over to the Megalithic Trench and it doesn't sound very good," she replied.

"Have fun, we'll tell Archie you said hello," said Arthur, as Seashorelle put them down.

"OK, see you again sometime," she said, and disappeared in a splash of foam.

"We have some strange friends," said Arthur.

"Don't you just love it?" asked Jo, splashing Arthur in the face.

"Yes," he said, splashing her back.

"Ahoy there!" shouted a voice on the shore. Arthur waved, and they both swam towards it.

It was an old man with a long grey beard and bald head, and a younger woman with long brown hair pulled away from her eyes with a daisy flower. They both wore white jackets, although the woman wore hers on top of a pale yellow dress so it was hard to distinguish.

"Good morning," said Arthur, drying himself off.

"Good morning, I am Professor Quake, who might you be?" he asked, shaking Arthur's hand.

"Sir Arthur Pageon and this is Princess Josephine," said Arthur.

"It's an honour Your Majesty, and it's an honour to meet such an illustrious man as you sir," said Quake.

"Who is your friend?" asked Jo.

"This is my assistant Daisy Bloom," said Quake.

"Where are you from?" asked Arthur.

"Our party are from the Hall of Learning in Azahad," he said.

"How big is Azahad?" asked Arthur.

"The city is huge, and is an amazing sight to behold; I hope you will visit it while you are here," he said.

"We would love to, we're visiting all the islands, and we will get to Arkellia soon," said Arthur.

"Good, now would you like to see our work?" he asked.

"I would love to, let me just get Sir Stuart and Lady Lilia," he said.

"Lilia!?" asked Daisy, breaking her silence.

"Now now, Daisy, what did I tell you about mentioning that," he said.

"Sorry, professor," she said.

"Right, I will get our two friends and we will meet you at your camp, where is it?" asked Arthur.

"On the other side of the fortress ruins," said Quake.

"Good so not that far then. See you in a minute," said Jo.

The professor and Daisy disappeared behind the rocks while Arthur and Jo put their clothes back on. They walked back to the ship and climbed aboard. They walked into the sitting room and saw that everything had been returned to normal. They then heard the sound of talking in the study, and went to investigate. Arthur opened the door and saw that the safe door was opened, and the talking was coming from inside. He picked his gun off of the table and walked slowly to the edge.

Lilia and Stuart were sat inside playing cards. "Point that thing somewhere else," said Lilia.

"What are you doing?" he asked.

"It's too hot out there, and it's freezing in here so were staying in here for a while," said Stuart.

"Ah, that is actually quite clever. But could you come with us please, were going to visit the archaeological site on the other side of the fortress and I'm taking bets on who the Ghost of Lilia is," said Arthur.

"OK," said Lilia.

"And why have you put loads of bottles down there?" asked Jo.

"To keep them cool for later," said Lilia.

"Is that just water, so nothing is going to explode down there right?" asked Arthur.

"Just water but now you've given me an idea," said Lilia.

"Come on, tell us later," said Arthur who locked the safe and covered it over with the carpet.

The archaeological dig wasn't that big, and when they came to it they saw that a couple of soldiers were guarding the place. The group was stopped by them until Professor Quake came over and let them in.

"Hello, let me show you around," said Quake. They walked past a variety of rectangular holes with some people in them, who were digging down into the earth.

"So, what is it you are looking for?" asked Arthur.

"The Lost Treasure of Rogera the Pirate," said Daisy.

"Never heard of it," said Arthur.

"Not many people have, that is why we want to find it before anyone else does," said Quake.

"I see, and have you had any luck?" asked Jo.

"Unfortunately not, every time we think were on to something the morning after all of our equipment is destroyed," he said.

"And who is responsible for this?" asked Stuart.

"Now you can tell them, Daisy, I'm going to supervise trench four," said Quake.

"It is the spectral figure of the now dead Queen Lilia," said Daisy.

"OK, let's just examine this from an objective stand point, firstly, what is Queen Lilia doing here? It makes absolutely no sense," said Arthur.

"She visited this Island a long time ago," said Daisy.

"All right, next question is why is she haunting the place?" asked Arthur.

"Does a ghost need a reason?" asked Daisy.

"No, I'll give you that one," said Arthur.

"Why are you asking such awkward questions?" asked Daisy.

"Because if I don't, then no one will," said Arthur.

"Are you going to get rid of her or just leave like most others?" asked Daisy.

"I'll give it a good go," said Arthur.

"You know I did my degree in Psychology, and I would love to practice on you," she said.

"Go ahead, but can we do it in private if you don't mind," said Arthur.

"Come with me to the inner sanctum of the fortress, your friends can look around the excavations while we wait," said Daisy.

Arthur and Daisy left the group, and walked down some stairs into the bowels of the fortress. It was wonderfully cool in the corridors, and Daisy led Arthur through a doorway and into a large room that had two thrones in it, one smaller than the other. "We'll sit here, and I can try to assess you," she said.

"I tell you what, since you came from Arkellia and I will be going there soon, we can do a question for a question," said Arthur.

"If you must," she replied. They sat on the thrones and began to talk. There was light coming in from above, and it was quite pleasant inside.

"First question, what is your idea of a perfect woman?" asked Daisy.

"Princess Josephine. Have you ever seen the Ghost?" asked Arthur.

"Once, when it was above us and was staring out of a window. Do you feel annoyed that the princess is in a higher class to you and this would therefore make marriage to her impossible?" she asked.

"We're engaged actually. When did you hear about Queen Lilia's death?" he asked.

"You're engaged?" she asked, surprised.

"Yes, now answer my question," replied Arthur.

"Oh, I personally heard when Sir Nabelle announced it after he returned from Harrha. Do you think that the Ghost of Lilia is a fake?" she asked.

"I know that she is a fake, and my three friends know that she is. I know my own sister and that is not my sister. Do you think the treasure is up there, or down here?" asked Arthur.

"I think it's in the ruins, but Professor Quake and Professor Gulch say we have to continue digging outside and we don't get to explore here. What is it like being a rich, adored hero that travels the world whenever he wants to?" she asked.

"Well, you see it isn't fun all the time, just most of it. I have enough money to never have to work again but it's a little boring, doing nothing," said Arthur.

"You didn't ask a question," she said.

"No, because you said something that doesn't make sense," said Arthur.

"And what is that?" asked Daisy.

"Well, you said you weren't allowed to explore, yet you knew all this was here. Secondly you should be working right now, but you don't seem to care about that. Thirdly, you came on this expedition but you are a psychologist, no offence but who needs a psychologist on an archaeological dig? Finally, could you please show me which door she has hidden her costume behind, Archie?" he asked, and for a second there was a silence.

Then one of the many doors shook, and Arthur walked over to it. "No, stop" she said. Arthur opened it, and sure enough, there was a trunk inside. Arthur opened it and a green glow illuminated the cupboard. Arthur pulled out the glowing purple dress and the hideous mask with flowing white hair.

"Oh dear, now, Daisy," said Arthur, but she had begun to run, however all of the doors shut suddenly by themselves.

"This place really is haunted!" she shouted.

"No, it isn't. When you're friends with an all-powerful god she really can do anything," said Arthur.

"So what are you going to do?" she asked, when she had calmed down.

"I'm not going to expose you, because I think that you are doing this for the right reason. However I want you to do something for me in return. You see, I want you to scare my friends, and your two professors too if you want," said Arthur.

"Why do you want to help me?" she asked.

"Like I said before, I have enough money not to need it, and I would much rather you had the credit for discovering it since you are much younger than they are, and it will give you a better start than most," said Arthur.

"How did you know that it was me?" she asked.

"I just made an assumption and I ran with it, and I am quite impressed since you nearly decapitated me," he said.

"Sorry about that, but if you were scared enough I hoped you would leave," she explained.

"You know, this is the first time that I have seen the perspective of the villain and you aren't really villainous at all, it's quite refreshing to be honest," he said.

"So what are we going to do?" she asked.

"Have you found the treasure yet?" asked Arthur.

"Yes actually, but I re-hid it again so they would never find it," said Daisy.

"Good, then it can stay there, and tonight we will have some fun. I'll lead them down here, and you know what to do," he said.

"Scare the hell out of them like I did before?" she asked.

"Yep, that's it, but just remember, whatever happens you must not break character, not for anything," said Arthur.

"I'll try," she said, and Arthur outlined the plan to her.

It was becoming dark, and the group were all gathered around a campfire. Daisy wasn't present, because she was so tired from the night before. "So Professor Quake, why haven't you explored the ruins of the fortress yet?" asked Stuart.

"There is more evidence that suggests that it is buried outside the fortress, because that way it wouldn't be found," he replied.

"Are you sure? When I went down there it could have been hidden somewhere," said Arthur.

"Well, we could check in the morning," said the professor.

"Come on where's your sense of adventure, let's go look now," said Arthur.

"It's too dark," he replied.

"It's always dark down there, but I shall go, and discover the treasure myself, finders keepers right?" said Arthur, getting up.

"What about the ghost?" asked Jo.

"Meh, I don't care. It's treasure, so who cares?" asked Arthur, who got up and walked to the door, grabbing the lantern as he went. Jo ran after him, and then Lilia and Stuart followed. Quake and Gulch looked at each other, and ran after them too.

The group moved through the darkened tunnel, and emerged in the throne room. "So here is the throne room, but where do we go from here?" asked Quake.

"You go nowhere..." said a voice in the dark. Arthur dropped his lantern, and the room was filled with a green glow. The Ghost of Lilia burst in through one of the doors, and the two professors ran.

"No wonder they call him Quake," said Arthur.

The four stayed, looking at the Ghost. "I knew that she would be here, but if she isn't a real ghost, she won't be able to stand a bullet!" said Arthur, who drew his pistol and shot. The bang echoed all through the ruins and deafened them. The ghost stood there, still standing despite taking a shot to the heart.

"Get out!!!" she shouted, and the group then all looked at Arthur.

"Umm, I think we should do what I always do in this rare situation," said Arthur.

"What is that?" asked Jo.

"Run!!!" shouted Arthur and they disappeared down the corridor away from the apparently real ghost.

Back at the camp they all congregated. "I was wrong, that thing is real!" said Arthur.

"But you said it was someone in a costume," said Jo.

"That is what I thought, but you can't shoot a person at point blank range and the bullet go straight through them," said Arthur.

"What are we going to do?" said Quake.

"I would go back to Arkellia, it seems that some malevolent force wants you gone, and it's only a matter of time before it gets violent and I don't think any amount of treasure is worth your life," said Arthur.

"Maybe you're right, I don't think that there is anything here," said Quake.

"Well, it was nice to meet you, and when Daisy wakes up tell her we said goodbye," said Stuart.

"Where are you off to?" asked Gulch.

"To Seone, and to meet Sir Thomas," said Arthur.

"His castle is the safest place in the archipelago, so make sure you get there soon," said Quake.

"We will, Goodbye," said Arthur, and the quartet walked away from the camp and back to the Nostradamus. As Arthur walked past the ruins, he looked up to a high window, and saw that the ghost was staring out. He waved, and she waved back. Arthur laughed to himself and caught up with the rest of the group.

The Monster in the High Castle

The ship flew through the night, and far off in the distance the light of the High Castle beckoned them. Back on the ship Jo was questioning Arthur about the ghost. "So, I don't know where to begin," said Jo.

"What do you want to know?" he asked.

"Who was that Ghost?" asked Jo.

"I have no idea, it was real and I shot it," he said.

"That I can't understand, how did you do it?" she asked.

"To be honest my mind has drawn a blank," he said.

"You're not helping," she replied.

"How are you finding our little trip?" asked Arthur.

"I think it's rather fun," said Jo.

"Oh good, where do you want to go for the honeymoon?" asked Arthur.

"I don't know, where is nice?" she asked.

"We could go to Drongo, it's beautiful there, we can ski and swim in the waterfall pools," said Arthur.

"I've never been, surprisingly," said Jo.

"Then it will be a nice surprise," he replied.

The ship stopped and Arthur looked surprised, since her knew that they shouldn't have arrived yet. He walked out on deck with Stuart, and saw that the ship was being kept back by two smaller ships. "What seems to be the problem!" shouted Arthur.

"Who are you!" a person shouted back.

"Sir Arthur Pageon, here to see Sir Thomas Calgius on urgent business from High King Olandine!" replied Arthur.

"How many of you?" they shouted back.

"Five: me, my driver, Sir Stuart, Lady Lilia and Princess Josephine Olandine," he replied.

"Very well, proceed to the dock," said the voice, and the two ships departed back to the castle.

"I love name dropping, it's just fun sometimes," said Arthur.

"It seems to help," said Stuart.

"Anyway, let's get ready to meet our next candidate for being a Lord," said Arthur.

The High Castle was massive and they saw why it had such a name. The Island of Seone had disappeared when the tide came in, and the castle was all that remained. It began as a volcanic island and the huge chunk of rock in the centre was all that remained. A coastal shelf had built up around it causing it to look like an island in the day, and at night the water came in leaving the castle on top of the rock, high above the waves.

The ruler, Sir Thomas, had inherited the island, and liked the sense of security so much that he decided to live there permanently. He has terrible paranoia, luckily so does his wife and they seemed to be a perfect match. He doesn't like visitors, so meeting the group that just arrived would be an interesting experience for him and his wife Mary.

The ship landed in the spacious courtyard high above the crashing waves. "This is impressive," said Lilia.

"Does it remind you of home?" asked Arthur.

"It does actually, though it seems more homely," said Lilia. The Courtyard was sheltered by high walls, and inside it was a large forested area, with trees of all kinds bearing fruit and just generally looking pretty. Then there were the flowers, which were beautiful, even at night. The whole scene looked perfect, a tiny blip of perfection in the chaos of the Infinite Sea.

There was a cobblestone path that led past a set of ornate windows that let out some yellow light, but the inside couldn't be seen. "I'm tired, I'm going to sleep, I'll see you in the morning," said Arthur.

"I'll come with you," said Jo.

"I thought you might," said Lilia.

"Excuse me?" said Jo.

"Nothing, you two go upstairs, and we'll go for a walk in this dreamy forest," said Lilia.

"Just make sure that you don't go too far, we're on somebody else's island," said Jo.

"I'm not sure I'm comfortable with this conversation," said Lilia.

"Neither am I, go get 'em kid," said Jo, who ran up the stairs after Arthur. Out of a window, a man looked down onto the courtyard on the ship that was parked in his courtyard. He closed the curtain, and wouldn't be seen until the next day.

Stuart and Lilia walked hand in hand to the edge of the castle walls and they saw the sea crashing beneath them. It was a spectacular sight but it wasn't the sea that made them stare. It was the green luminescent creature that was soldiering through the waves towards the castle. "What the...?" said Stuart.

"It's probably someone in a dopey costume," said Lilia.

"Don't you think it's strange that every island we visit has a monster or some kind of ghost, which always turns out to be someone that we've met previously?" asked Stuart.

"To be honest with you I'm having the time of my life, it was a sad story before but ever since I've joined my brother, it has become quite fun," said Lilia.

"In the time that I've been in his company, I've lost my wife and my two step-children," said Stuart.

"A wife and two children that didn't think you were good enough," replied Lilia.

"I don't like to think about it that way, but I guess you're sort of right," said Stuart.

"Of course I'm right, but if you don't want me to, I won't mention it again," said Lilia.

"So what are we going to do about that Sneaky Sea Creature?" asked Stuart. "In the morning, I'm too tired to do anything now," she said.

"OK, let's go," said Stuart, who escorted her back to the ship.

The sun rose over the High Castle, and the small forest awoke with a burst of songbirds that flew up to the eaves of the great hall. Arthur awoke to find Jo almost comatose on the bed. He poked her to see that she was OK, and an angry murmur confirmed it.

"OK then, you sleep and I will have a proper look round," said Arthur. Arthur walked downstairs and met Lilia, who was the only one awake.

"Morning," he said.

"Hello, sleep well?" asked Lilia.

"I never do, and I don't think you do either," he said.

"It's true. I never dream, I wonder what it must be like," said Lilia.

"No idea. From what Jo tells me, it's either horribly scary, or beautifully amazing, but you never know which it will be," he said.

"I wouldn't mind dreaming, but how do we do it?" she asked.

"We could ask Archie," said Arthur.

"I don't know about that," said Lilia.

"When are you going to trust her?" asked Arthur.

"Do you?" she asked.

"Of course, but only because she has shown me enough things to make me believe," he said.

"I see, I'll tell you what, if she can make me dream, then I will believe," said Lilia. There was a puff of smoke, and a note appeared, which Lilia grabbed.

"'I will hold you to that'," she read aloud.

"There's your answer, I just hope that you will think that this is a good wish," said Arthur.

Arthur and Lilia then went for a walk through the forest, since no one was around and it was still quite early in the morning. "Do you remember when we were taught about the six gods when we were younger?" asked Lilia.

"I almost forgot, but you took great pride in remembering their names," said Arthur.

"There was Authos, Seashorelle, Ignatio, Evere, Altatia and Persus," said Lilia.

"I don't remember Persus, who was that?" asked Arthur.

"From what I can remember, Seashorelle is female, as is Altatia.

Ignatio and Evere are male, which left Authos to be both, and also Persus. They could freely change their gender to fit any situation," explained Lilia.

"It's funny that Archie has never mentioned Persus, when they are obviously opposites of each other," said Arthur.

"I remember that when our teacher Mr Dale taught us about them, he seemed to be disgusted at the idea of a duo-gendered deity," said Lilia.

"Whatever happened to him?" asked Arthur.

"He was thrown out of a window by dad when I told on him," said Lilia.

"What did he do?" asked Arthur.

"Nothing, I just didn't like him," said Lilia.

"Just like you I guess, and it must have burned you every time I was told on but he did nothing," said Arthur.

"Yes, even that time in mother's wardrobe when you..." said Lilia.

"That's enough, can we change the subject? Did you know that our perception of the god system is completely out of whack?" asked Arthur.

"What does it matter? Anyway Stuart and I saw a Sneaky Sea Creature last night swimming through the water and underneath the castle," said Lilia.

"To be honest I'm getting a little tired of this whole fake monster thing, I want a day off," said Arthur.

"So we're not going after the monster?" said Lilia.

"No, I'm just going to glaze over the whole thing; Sir Thomas can sort it out himself" said Arthur.

"We're just here to give him the bracelet from the High King, and that's all," said Lilia.

"And that is all we shall do," said Arthur.

They wandered out of the seclusion of the small forest and were met by a guard, who looked them up and down suspiciously. "Are you Sir Pageon?" he asked.

"That be I," replied Arthur.

"Would you please accompany me to see Sir Thomas," he said.

"Of course, lead on," said Arthur. Lilia went with him, since she wondered what the guard might do if she went back to the ship. They entered the great hall, which wasn't spectacularly huge like the ones they had visited but was cosier, with fine oak panelling and beautiful stained glass windows. At the end of the hall was a man sat at a table reading a large book.

"So Sir Arthur, from what I've read you are quite the adventurer," he said.

"Well, I get around a bit I suppose," said Arthur humbly.

"And you Lady Lilia, I cannot find any reference of you anywhere, what is your last name?" he asked.

"Duncannon. I was married once but I still remain Arthur's sister," said Lilia, who was amazed at how she came up with a name so quickly.

"So, Lady Lilia Duncannon and Sir Arthur Pageon, it's nice to meet you. I am Sir Thomas," he said, stretching out his hand to shake Arthur's.

"It is nice to meet you too. We are on urgent business from the High King and I wish to offer you something in his name," said Arthur.

"Oh a gift, you upper class types are always doing that," he replied.

"Well it is more of a gesture of goodwill," said Arthur.

"So a gift," replied Thomas in a deadpan tone.

"If it makes you happy, then yes it is a gift," said Arthur, producing a red silk bag from his jacket pocket. He handed it to Thomas, who examined it and then laid it on the table.

"So what do I receive this gift for?" he asked.

"The High King would like to have your allegiance, and if so you would become Lord Thomas of Seone," said Arthur.

"Only if I can meet Princess Josephine," said Thomas.

"Very well, she is asleep on my ship," said Arthur.

At this point Thomas changed his look. At first he was gradually beginning to like Arthur and when he heard that he could become a lord, he became even happier, but now he was slightly annoyed. This was not because Jo was asleep, but because he loved had her ever since he saw her as a child in Evermore.

Sir Thomas came from a long line of money managers in Gard. They all attended to Lord Yage's immensely huge pile of wealth as best they could, and now because of them the treasure pile was in order. Large bars of gold were being forged instead of coins, that way there was more space for jewels and gems in the vast treasure hall. It was a sight that Arthur would see in the future, but the amazing sight would be lost on him because his mind would be on other things.

When the Calgarian family were wealthy enough, they bought the island of Seone from the High King and set about turning it into a sort of paradise above the waves. Sir Thomas Calgarian had a daughter who was being schooled in The Temple of Earthly Wisdom on the island of Ailu; however he never really loved her mother Lady Mary, but still loved Jo. When he was attending an archery contest he saw her for the first time, and at this time Jo was only 104, and was seven years older than him. When they actually met, it was at the after party in the Olandine mansion just outside the main walls of Evermore...

Several Years Ago...

"Hello, I'm Jo, what is your name?" asked Jo to the young boy who couldn't stop staring at her.

"I...I..." But Thomas couldn't answer, he was too scared to.

"OK 'I', it's nice to meet you, is there some reason that you keep staring at me?" asked Jo.

"Umm," he replied, but was still too tongue tied to say anything.

"Come with me, we can go out onto the veranda and you can tell me all about yourself," said Jo, taking Thomas's hand.

Halfway through the main room that was full of people, they were stopped by the High King. "Josephine, where are you going?" he asked.

"I was taking 'I' here to the veranda, to see if the air improves his vocal ability," replied Jo.

"I see, well first I would like you to meet Lord Logious Pageon, he is here from Fina with his two children," said the king.

"It's nice to meet you sir," said Jo.

"It is nice to meet you to my lady, you shoot very well for a princess," he said.

"Thank you very much; you do a lovely job of pointing out my gender and heritage as something that should be taken into consideration when discussing my shooting ability," said Jo, who walked off and left her father to apologise to Lord Logious.

"That was brilliant," said Thomas.

"I'm not scared of anyone, they are all just people, just like me and you," said Jo.

They reached the veranda, and outside were two other children, one a boy with short brown hair, and the other a girl with red hair that grew down to her shoulders. "Good evening," said the boy.

"Hello, who might you be?" asked Jo.

"Arthur, and this is my sister Lilia," replied the boy.

"Are you Lord Logious' children?" asked Jo.

"Yes, are you Princess Josephine?" asked Lilia.

"I am, it is nice to meet you two, what are you doing out here?" she asked.

"I don't really like talking to people, and neither does my sister," said Arthur.

"Oh, I'm sorry to hear that," said Jo.

"Why are you out here?" asked Arthur.

"I'm here with young Thomas, who seems to be gaining his voice back," said Jo.

"Aww that is cute," said Lilia.

"Hold on Lilia don't be mean, we all were that young once and think about what would happen if we met Thomas here in the future?" said Arthur.

"Hah, flashback humour," shouted a woman in the crowd, who disappeared as soon as she had appeared.

"I don't know what that was about, but tell me Thomas what your surname is?" asked Arthur.

"Calgarian," said Thomas in a sheepish tone.

"Oh, so you're of the book keepers of Gard," said Lilia sneeringly.

"I don't know, it must be a very interesting job, seeing all those gold and jewels and putting them in the right order," said Arthur.

"Why do you insist on ordering things?" asked Lilia. "Maybe you have an obsessive compulsion to order things?"

"Why do you have an obsessive compulsion to disorder things?" asked Arthur.

"OK, maybe you two should calm down," said Jo.

"Yes Princess," said Lilia.

"Don't mind my sister, she is a little bit of a nutcase." said Arthur.

"It's alright, but we are leaving you out Thomas, Thomas?" she asked, but he had gone.

"He wandered off a couple of minutes ago," said Arthur.

"Oh, he seemed rather pleasant," said Jo.

"Anyway, I'm going to get something to eat, would you like to join me Josephine?" asked Arthur.

"I would, and I bet I can eat more than you can," said Jo. They ran inside and from behind a curtain, the docile and subdued Thomas watched the two, his heart filling with jealousy for the first time.

Back on Seone Thomas had just remembered all this, and he looked at Arthur and Lilia differently. He didn't say anything about what came into his mind and still wanted to see Josephine, so decided not to say something that would compromise the situation.

"Sir Pageon, if you would be kind enough to fetch the princess I shall agree to your terms," said Thomas.

"Very well," said Arthur, who left with Lilia out of the room and walked back to the ship.

"Look, I don't know if you remember but Thomas was that guy we met at Jo's archery tournament," said Arthur.

"I remember, I don't think I was that nice to him," said Lilia.

"Like everyone else, I think that's a reasonable assumption," said Arthur.

"What are you going to do?" asked Lilia.

"Protect my fiancée," said Arthur, who climbed up the rigging to the deck followed by Lilia.

Jo was in the sitting room with Stuart, and they both were having tea. "Where did you get the tea from?" asked Arthur.

"Anyone who is asking that question is thinking too much," said Jo.

"Alright, alright, but I need you to do something, something that will seem really odd but don't treat it as such," said Arthur.

"Does this have anything to do with what you asked me to do last night?" she asked.

"Honeymoon, Jo. No this is much different, come with me upstairs," said Arthur, and they left Stuart and Lilia in the sitting room.

Jo emerged about ten minutes later, wearing a white nightgown and with her hair in a mess. "I'm not going to ask," said Lilia. Arthur came down as well, and led Jo out onto the deck. When Jo got out she saw that Sir Thomas was standing by a tree, watching her as she left the sitting room. When he saw Arthur, he changed his expression.

"Good morning, Thomas," she said.

"Good hello Princess, it's lovely again to see you," he said, obviously very nervous. Jo remained on the deck, as Arthur had told her to stay there.

"I see that you have beaten your shyness," said Jo.

"I see that you look as beautiful as ever," he replied. Arthur didn't really know what to do, and he turned around to see that Lilia and Stuart had gone up to his room and were watching out of an open window.

"I was wondering if you would stay for dinner," said Thomas.

"I'm afraid not, we were only here to carry out my father's orders and we must leave now for Vertise," she said.

Thomas now had become angry, because when his family had moved here he got everything he ever wanted, but the one thing he truly desired was in front of him and he couldn't have it. "Very well, once again the influence of our parents dictates our lives," said Thomas.

"I'm sorry, I hope you will agree to the proposition of my father," she said.

"Yes I think I will, being a Lord has its advantages like being able to visit Evermore," he said.

"Goodbye Thomas," she said, and the ship's engines started up and it lifted off. Jo walked back inside with Arthur, and they began their journey to Vertise, almost.

The ship was about a quarter of a mile from the high castle, and it suddenly stopped, and descended. Arthur walked to the flight deck, which had windows so clear that it was like they were not there. "Why have we stopped?" asked Arthur.

"It looks like a sea creature is in a spot of bother," said Corky.

Sure enough the Sneaky Sea Creature was struggling to swim, and in broad daylight it looked quite silly. "Land in the sea, we're going to pick this one up," said Arthur.

"Yes sir!" said Corky, who brought the ship down onto the calm sea next to the creature. Arthur walked onto the deck and looked over the banister. The sea creature grabbed onto the rigging with webbed hands and panted from exhaustion.

"It looks like you are in need of assistance," said Arthur, who climbed down and held out his hand.

"Thank you," it said, and took Arthur's hand. Arthur hauled it onto the deck, and it rested with its back on the banister. It had a large mouth, and two evil looking eyes, and a long tail. The green scales glistened in the sunlight, and with its feet stretched out it looked almost human.

"OK. This has never happened before so I'm just going to come out and say it, who is it that I have the honour of addressing?" asked Arthur.

The creature took its head off; and Arthur saw that it was a woman, with long black hair and brown eyes. "Lady Mary Calgarian" she said.

"The absent Lady Calgarian I see," said Arthur.

"Are you going to take me back to him?" she asked in a proud voice.

"Oh no we're not going back to Seone any time soon, you're with us to Vertise at least," said Arthur, sitting next to her.

The ship lifted off, and a spray of water filled the air as it rose steadily into the sky. It then continued on its course to Vertise, the garden island and the shrine of Authos. "So tell me, Mary, why you would want to leave such a nice well balanced individual like Sir Thomas?" asked Arthur.

"I take it from your wording that you could already guess," she replied.

"I think that we are doing you a favour, because anyone who would want to leave someone bad enough to swim across the open sea must be desperate," said Arthur.

"You guessed it; I was heading for Vertise because one of my family is a gardener there, and he could help me," she said.

"What was he doing to make you want to leave?" asked Arthur.

"He had a shrine to Princess Josephine which I accidently discovered, and when I confronted him about it he got violent. I said I wanted a divorce, and he imprisoned me in the bottom of the castle," she said.

"That part seems to make sense, but how did you get this costume?" asked Arthur.

"It was given to me, by a strange woman who visited my cell," she said.

"I thought so, she said that she would influence things," said Arthur.

"Who are you talking about?" she asked.

"Would you believe Authos?" asked Arthur.

"No, I'm afraid not," she replied.

"Oh well it is pretty unbelievable, but at least you are safe," he said.

"Thank you," she said.

"This is what you want, what you really really want?" asked Arthur.

"Yes, you got me out of a loveless marriage and when I tell my father about this, he will get me a divorce straight away and then he will ruin him," she said.

"Remember Mary you have a daughter, and I don't think you should subject her to her father being ruined. Secondly, he couldn't help it that he loved someone that he could never have. When a person truly falls in love nothing will ever really erase that feeling, they can have all the most beautiful people thrown at them but that spark that first ignited their heart will never be extinguished, and you unfortunately married a man who was already sparked," said Arthur.

"That's a lovely way to put it, but it doesn't make me feel any better and imprisoning me wasn't a normal thing to do," she said.

"I know it sounds like I'm defending the guy here, and he does have an unhealthy obsession with my fiancée which I will let slide because he couldn't help it. Getting back to your imprisonment, his world was crumbling around him and people do things that they later regret in those times, and I think he will to. I would suggest that you take a break from him, he will see that imprisoning you didn't work and that you are not an object that is under his control, and that you are free," said Arthur.

"And what if he doesn't change?" she asked.

"Then at least your father knows he will be able to help, who is your father anyway?" asked Arthur.

"Squire Peter of Alkenwedge and Tanalos," she said.

"I see, well he can give you all the help; you need and it's a pity he isn't closer," said Arthur.

The Garden of Authos

The ship was now in sight of Vertise which looked like a tropical paradise even from a mile away. In the centre was a massive stepped pyramid, and on its various tiers trees and plants grew, so it looked like a mountain. "It looks incredible," said Arthur.

"It does, doesn't it," said Mary.

"You can go into my sitting room and take off your costume, Mary, Jo will find you something to wear," said Arthur.

"Thank you, you're very kind," she said.

"Yeah, it's what I do," said Arthur, brushing his lapel.

The ship landed at the base of the pyramid, which had small steps leading all the way to the top. "I think she wants us to climb to the top," said Arthur.

"The worst thing is, I think you are right," said Jo. The five of them had congregated on the deck, and just stared up at the colossal structure.

"Couldn't we fly up?" asked Lilia.

"Something wrong with your feet?" asked Arthur.

"But that's effort," she replied.

"Yes, yes it is," said Arthur, who jumped off the boat and began to climb.

It was midday and the further up they climbed, the hotter it became. "I have to admit, she picks the perfect places in the perfect times," said Arthur.

"Who does?" asked Mary.

259

"Archie, or as you would know her, Authos," said Arthur.

"I still don't believe you," said Mary.

"You'll see," said Jo, who was struggling to keep up with Arthur and Stuart. They got about halfway, and then decided to stop. They took a detour to the side, and walked off around one of the many forested tiers of the pyramid.

"I like it here, she hasn't got something that shows off but something that works with nature," said Jo.

"I think it looks like a mountain," said Lilia.

"Maybe that was what she was going for," said Arthur.

"CORRECT!" boomed a voice that seemed to be coming from everywhere.

"I think we better continue upwards," said Arthur.

"There's something I don't understand. Spacey" said Stuart.

"And that is?" asked Arthur.

"Why did Jo have to wear a white nightgown and have messy hair when she was already up and dressed?" asked Stuart.

"I thought that she should look normal, since it seems that Sir Thomas wanted Jo just as she had been before, regal and perfect. Of course I can't erase one of those things, so I went for normality to soften the blow," explained Arthur.

"I see, so you tried to make her look less desirable on purpose?" he asked.

"If that is even possible," replied Arthur.

"Thank you," said Jo, who was catching up with the two men. Lilia was behind with Mary, and the two seemed to be having fun bashing how stuck up Sir Thomas was.

They finally reached the top, and on the large stone plain that lay around them was a simple throne in the centre, and someone was sat on it. "Archie!" shouted Arthur, who ran to her. Jo was amazed that Arthur had any energy left, but she tried her best to run after him. Stuart waited for Lilia and Mary.

"You finally got here, what took you so long?" she asked. Archie was wearing a different colour now; she was wearing a red and white combo that was similar to her previous one but the colours were simply different.

"Captain Scurvy's Ghost, The Ghost of Queen Lilia and The Sneaky Sea Creature," replied Jo.

"Ah, I see. Well, now that you are here we can leave and go to The Temple of Earthly Wisdom," said Archie.

"First, I just wanted to apologise," said Arthur.

"No need, walking around with platinum hair must have been punishment enough," said Archie.

"It was actually, is there anything you can do about it?" asked Arthur. Archie put her hand on Arthur's and his hair clouded over and became brown, although this time it was a bit lighter.

"Happy now?" asked Archie.

"Thank you, it's finally back to normal," he replied.

"Not quite, you are 337 and Jo here is 220, which is one heck of an age gap so I'd like to return you to normal," said Archie. Stuart, Lilia and Mary witnessed Archie levitate off the ground and then Arthur did the same. He was enveloped by a bright light, and then he returned to the ground.

"You know, it is brilliant that you two carried on your relationship despite the age difference," said Archie.

"You can't put an age on love," said Jo.

"Good, you two seem to be doing fine and I believe that Lilia needs some convincing," said Archie.

She walked over to the group, and they all fell silent. "So Lilia, tell me what I can do to prove my authenticity," she said.

"Can you grant wishes?" asked Lilia.

"Of course I can, but every Discoucian gets one so remember that," she replied.

"You can ask for dreams," said Arthur.

"No, I have only one wish, I want to marry Stuart," she said.

"No I can't do that," she said.

"Why not? It's selfless, and it will bring me true happiness," she replied.

"I can give you a very good reason why, because that is already going to happen, and only you will leave the story now, and will not be involved in it anymore. If you wish to marry Sir Stuart, then it will mean your departure," said Archie.

"Can I have a moment with Stuart to think about this," she said.

"You have all the time in the world," said Archie.

After about five minutes Lilia and Stuart returned, as the sun was beginning to set. "We have decided that we will leave, let Arthur and Jo continue on and we will return to Portalia," she said. Arthur looked most hurt out of everyone.

"I don't want you to go," he said.

"I have to, you brought me out of hell and I will always love you for it. Now I will hopefully brighten up Stuart's world the way you did mine," she said.

"I got you back and now I'm losing you," said Arthur.

"No you are not, and you can come and see me anytime, just please love me enough to let me go," she said.

"OK, but look after her Stuart, not that she needs it," said Arthur.

"I will, thank you for helping me get over losing my wife," he said.

"I think this one will love you for who you are," said Jo.

Archie was standing with Mary, as they didn't have anything really to contribute. "It's weird watching this from outside," said Archie.

"I feel sorry for Sir Pageon," said Mary.

"He will be fine, a lot of adventures lie ahead for him and his wife," said Archie.

"How do you know that?" she asked.

"My god so transparent," said Archie.

"OK Archie, you can prove to me that you are benevolent, and give me the power to dream," said Lilia.

"Is that your one and only wish?" she asked.

"I want to fall asleep and go to strange and amazing places, meet strange and amazing people while it's all inside my head," said Lilia.

"Come here then," said Archie. Lilia walked over to her, and Archie put both her hands on her head.

Lilia felt her mind race, as it was filling with the most amazing things she had ever seen. She fell to the floor, and her eyes were glazed over with a rainbow of colours. They looked like two kaleidoscopes, both moving in tandem. Lilia blinked, and then got up. She then did something unexpected. She hugged Archie, and was brought to tears.

"Thank you, thank you," she said.

"Don't mention it, just try not to be so xenophobic in the future," said Archie.

"I don't know what that word means," said Lilia.

"Never mind," said Archie, who clicked her fingers and in the distance a light appeared.

"There is your ship, ready to take you to Portalia," said Archie. Stuart shook her hand awkwardly and they left, flying off towards a new found happiness. Mary climbed down the stairs to find her relative. She returned to Alkenwedge with her cousin and the whole affair with Sir Thomas was quietly forgotten.

"So the three of us, back together again, sort of," said Jo.

"I do prefer it when you are around," said Arthur.

"Come on let's get going, we have to be in Ailu before sunrise as I need to see Lady Christa on urgent business, and there are reports of her mother's ghost haunting the Temple," said Archie.

"Another ghost," said Arthur.

"This one is a little bit different to the ones that you have faced before," said Archie.

"How so?" asked Jo.

"You'll see," said Archie cryptically.

The ship floated up to the top of the pyramid, and landed on the massive open space. "Shall we go?" asked Archie.

"Of course, ladies first, then duo-gendered and then me," said Arthur.

"Funny, but I'll take it," she said. They boarded and the ship flew to the south-east, to the Island of Ailu.

The Wilting Magnolia Flower

The Temple of Earthly Wisdom was founded by a group of members of the Order of the Tangerine, who were not happy with the way it was run. They left for the island of Ailu, which at that time was uninhabited. With a quarry of pink marble and several magnolia tree seeds, they founded the Temple of Earthly Wisdom, with the largest library in the whole of Alavonia, six hundred million books, which were mostly copies of the rare books that the sisters copied from the private libraries of Discoucia. The sisters of the temple are comprised of rich children who aren't rich enough to attend the now defunct Starfall Academy. However the children there are intelligent but become complacent, whereas at the temple they become more diligent and attentive.

The Nostradamus now flew faster, for some unknown reason even Corky couldn't explain, but he now had the power to fly faster. Back in the study the three were sitting in the safe, which was now referred to as the freezer. "You know the more I hang around with you, the faster the time will go so I need to do something that will sort this problem out," she said.

"Archie, I know this is a little off topic but have you ever been in love?" asked Jo.

"To be honest with you Josephine, I wouldn't know love if it smacked me in the face. Sure I had some flings in the past with mortal but that only complicated things. Nowadays I simply keep myself to myself," replied Archie.

"Everyone has to have somebody," said Arthur.

"Not me, I just shepherd other people like you two, but I don't think there is any danger of me falling in love," she said.

"No offence, but that's a pretty lonely existence," said Jo.

"I know, but there isn't really much I can do about it," she replied.

"Also I was wondering if you could slow down your effect on time?" asked Arthur.

"Well, I could put it into the story line that I clicked my fingers and time went back to normal," she said, clicking her fingers. The ship began to slow down and Corky was as perplexed as ever.

"I don't know how you did that," said Arthur.

"I'm like a living Escher print," replied a cocky looking Archie, who opened the door to the deck since she knew they had arrived.

Sure enough they had, and the sight that met their eyes was beautiful. The whole area seemed to be landscaped with pink blossom trees all around, and flower beds that were in full bloom. And the small rivers flowed like millponds through pristine white avenues. There were red wooden bridges across these small rivers, and lanterns on the end that were lit up in the dark. At this time of the day, anywhere would have a hint of evil or gloom, but not here. The ship had landed outside the temple which had a ten foot wall made of pink marble, that was pristinely clean as much as the rest of the island.

"This place looks like heaven," said Jo.

"I got the idea from a Japanese garden, but it's a pity that you don't have koi carp in Alavonia because they would have been perfect," she replied.

"Japan is a country in the other world?" asked Arthur.

"It is and at one time this is what most of it looked like, I'm just paying homage to it here because I was inspired by it," said Archie.

"Tell us more about it," said Jo.

"You have watermelons here, right?" asked Archie.

"Yes, though they are quite rare," replied Jo.

"In Japan they have created square ones that are in a cube shape," said Archie.

"That's incredible, what else?" asked Arthur.

"Strawberries, they have blue ones there," said Archie.

"Do they taste any different?" asked Jo.

"No idea, I've never tried them," said Archie.

"I have a question about Lilia," said Arthur.

"Do you want to know about her dreams?" asked Archie.

"Yes please, what will she see?" asked Arthur.

"Since you cannot dream normally I cannot compare it to anything, but you Jo would understand," said Archie.

"Explain it to me, and I will try to then explain it to Artie," she said.

"Have you ever had a dream which..." said Archie, but she was stopped by a floating ghost that appeared on the deck.

It was wearing a pink dress that was ragged and frayed at the base, and she wore long white gloves and had long white hair. The thing that worried the trio was the fact that she had no face, no legs or feet, and between her the end of her gloves and the beginning of her dress, there was nothing there either.

"Good evening, we were just discussing the flora of Japan," said Archie.

"Leave my temple," is said in a menacing tone.

"What is your name?" asked Arthur, who had begun to get used to the routine.

"Lady Magnolia, ruler of the Earthly Wisdom," it said, with the voice coming from nowhere.

"OK," said Archie.

"What?" it asked in surprise.

"You want us to leave, we will but you have to give us a reason why," said Archie.

"I wasn't ready for a follow up question," it said, before disappearing behind a cherry blossom tree.

"So we just saw Lady Magnolia's ghost, let's go to sleep and we can check out the suspects in the morning" said Archie. Jo and Arthur went upstairs to bed and Arthur had another night of no dreaming, the same as he always did, and then, just before the sun rose, he had a five second dream. He saw a swimming pool surrounded by girls of all ages. He awoke the same as Jo; they both woke up in tandem.

They got dressed and met Archie on the deck. "Come on then, let's wrap this one up quick, make sure you bring the bracelet for Lady Christa" said Archie.

They climbed down onto the path and walked up to the door. Archie gave it a loud knock. It was made of black oak, very old and very rare. The door was opened by a young girl with blonde hair tied in a bun.

"Good morning, Sir Arthur Pageon here to see Lady Christa," he said.

"Come in," she said; letting the three in, she closed the door and locked it. The inside of the temple was even more beautiful than the outside, with four rivers running into a central pool, and all the girls that Arthur saw in his dream were there, all sitting on the perfectly maintained lawn.

A woman in a silver dress walked up to them and introduced herself as Lady Christa. She has long silvery blonde hair, and was about 450.

"It is a pleasure to meet you Sir Pageon, welcome to our little slice of paradise," she said.

"I have to admit, this place looks like a utopia," said Arthur.

"Who are your friends?" she asked.

"This is Princess Josephine Olandine and this is Miss Archaelia," said Arthur.

"It's a pleasure to meet you Princess, I hope you approve of our humble dwelling and I am afraid I am not familiar with your name, Miss Archaelia," she said.

"I know, it is a bit odd but I was born with it and that's all that can be said," said Archie.

"Would you like a tour?" asked Christa.

"Of course, and then later I would like to talk to you about some business," said Arthur.

"If you so wish," she said, and led them to the lawn.

The first four girls looked quite young. "This is Sara, Jeshica, Felicity and oh no not Susan, what are you doing here, you're supposed to be out in the grove collecting fruit," she said. Susan promptly ran off and they moved off to the next group. The next lot of girls were older.

"This is Talia, Catalina, Cordalia and Louisa, they are our best mathematical scholars," said Christa. They now moved around the pool to a larger group of girls that were in all sorts of acrobatic positions.

"This little conflab consists of Eloise, Galicia, Valeria, Iris, Virginia, Farah, Razia, Maria and Sernia," she said. Arthur and Jo were amazed at how Lady Christa remembered all the names.

They finally reached the group of much older girls, and there were four of them. "And at the top of our school, we have Melody, Symphony and Harmony, and our head girl, Lady Alicia May," said Christa. Alicia May was about 220 with white hair that seemed to reflect the sun, and she wore a simple green dress with black lace that matched her deep emerald eyes.

"You have a lovely temple, and so well tended," said Jo.

"Who is this?" asked Alicia.

"This is Sir Arthur Pageon and his two companions Princess Josephine and Miss Archaelia," said Christa.

"Are you here to deal with the ghost?" asked Melody.

"Now Melody, I don't want you talking about that," said Christa.

"We met the ghost last night and she seemed an interesting character," said Archie.

"Do you have any clues about it?" asked Harmony.

"None, except she is most probably a resident of this temple though I can't think of a motive," said Archie.

"Neither can I, but can I talk to you about that business, Lady Christa?" asked Arthur.

"I have to show you the grounds first," she said.

They were taken through the immaculate grounds that were kept perfect even though the weather was so hot that ordinary grass would wither and die. "How do you keep the grass so green?" asked Arthur.

"One of our previous students has become an eminent botanist and she managed to create this grass that could withstand any kind of heat, and will still remain lush and green," she explained.

"That was lucky," said Archie, as they walked past a group of girls who were meditating in a circle under the shade of a large willow tree.

They reached an ornate door which was circular and painted red. Christa opened it and they came to the Library which extended down underground as far as the eye could see. "So this is where you keep the millions of books you have," said Jo.

"If we ever get a load more, we dig and add another level; it's kinda like a reverse skyscraper and we're going down instead of up," she said.

"I love the idea but why would the ghost of Lady Magnolia haunt the place?" asked Archie.

"We have some students here that don't want to be, they are sent to us by parents that wish to travel instead of take care of them and we inherit those issues," said Christa.

"You think that it is a student playing a joke?" asked Jo.

"I do and frankly I'm willing to look the other way until they get bored. Now what is that business you wanted to talk to me about, Sir Arthur?" asked Christa.

"Is there somewhere private we can go?" asked Arthur.

"Allow me to show you to my study, you two are free to move around the grounds as you wish," said Christa.

"What do you think we should do?" asked Jo.

"Wait for nightfall and then trap the ghost," said Archie.

"What if this like Lilia's ghost and a trap has no effect?" asked Jo.

"Look, Jo, there is only one place where you are going to find real ghosts and that is my domain, but thankfully they are the people that don't spend their time scaring other people," said Archie.

"Am I ever going to see your domain?" asked Jo.

"One day, very soon," said Archie.

"Let's go and capture a ghost," said Jo.

They went back to the ship, and rigged up a complex net trap above the deck, and several girls were watching with avid fascination at the two women that were setting up such a complex trap. Melody looked out from behind the black oak door and sneered. Harmony was up a tree, and she also saw the trap, and she sneered too. Symphony was pruning a magnolia tree when she saw the trap, and she laughed.

"Are there any real ghosts or monsters in the world?" asked Jo.

"Of course there are, ask any crypto-zoologist and they will tell you that there are some things in this world that science can't explain now, but will probably be able to in the future," replied Archie.

"And how would somebody explain you?" asked Jo.

"They wouldn't, because that would be downright rude to go into my physiology and find a reason for why I'm so special, but other than that I try to live in blissful ignorance of my own existence," replied Archie.

The day turned to night and the girls sat on the banister, waiting for the Ghost to appear. Arthur still hadn't returned and they waited anxiously for him. Jo at least was worried about her fiancé, but Archie was much more interested in the ghost. They heard the rustling of some leaves and looked behind them. There was nothing there and they turned back. The ghost stood in front of them, waiting for them to scream. Archie pulled on the cord that activated the trap, and the net came for the ghost. She slid back into mid -air before the trap hit her, and stood triumphantly on the banister.

"Did you honestly think I was that vulnerable?" she cackled.

Arthur then climbed aboard and was quite drunk, then knocked over and fell on the ghost. They both landed in an undignified heap.

"Oh God...Iiii'm so sorry," he said, before falling unconscious.

"So, the award for best costume goes to..." said Archie who grabbed hold of the ghost's hair, which came off in her hand.

"It's a wig, but what about the head?!" said a very confused Archie.

The knocked-down ghost did a very strange thing: the costume deflated and all that was there was an old dress, a pair of gloves and a wig. "I have no idea what just happened" said Archie.

"Neither do I," said Jo.

"I'm dying!" said Arthur.

"Come on, let's drag this little negotiator inside and get out of here and bring the costume too, I want to examine it," said Archie. When she got to the study she wrote a letter to Lady Christa explaining what had happened and posted it through the oak door. The ship took off and everyone met in the wardrobe to check out what was going on.

"The costume has obviously been worn by someone, since it's still warm and we heard it talk," said Archie. They left Arthur downstairs in the study asleep, and were trying to figure out what was going on.

"But the person who was in it is gone and their identity still a mystery," said Jo.

"Indeed but I don't think that it matters anymore, with the help of Discoucia the island will be a little less isolated now," said Archie.

"So we're just going to let this one go?" asked Lilia.

"Like with your ghost, yes we are," said Archie.

Pageon of Persia

The ship sped towards the largest island in the Luminosity Archipelago, the Island of Arkellia. This was also the capital and its Palace of Azahadria was a wondrous sight to behold. It was built of sandstone much like Evermore was only it was a darker red, and since Arkellia is mostly flat and desert terrain the walls needed to be higher. They were built higher and inside the palace walls was a garden and lake that were regarded enviously. Sir Nabelle was a descendent of one of the previous rulers of Gard who used his money to live in splendour like a king. However, Sir Nabelle is a little unhinged and loves to compete and win in the most irregular ways, as Arthur will find out.

The ship landed with a bump that woke up Arthur from his drunken slumber. He didn't have any visions this time and looked around for water. He couldn't find any, and when he saw the huge marble lake outside the window he ran outside as fast as he could. He stuck his head underwater, and for a few seconds he had forgotten that he had to breathe, but he felt so good that he didn't care.

When he brought his head up, he had several ornate spears pointing at him by heavily armoured guardsmen. "Good morning, I'm sorry but I was so thirsty," said Arthur.

"Come with us sir, we are taking you to see Sergeant Crippler," said one.

"Well, he sounds delightful," said Arthur sarcastically, who was pulled to his feet and taken inside one of the buildings.

Arthur was thrown into a chair, and left in a room on his own. He straightened his bow tie, and then his jacket. He wiped the sweat from his brow and tried to look presentable. A man walked in, who was rather nasty looking.

"Who have we got here then?" he asked in a menacing tone.

"Sir Arthur Pageon at your service, do I have the honour of addressing Sergeant Crippler?" asked Arthur.

"You do, and Sir Arthur Pageon, well, I see that you are one of our high profile guests," he said.

"Look I'm sorry for drinking out of the pool, I didn't realise there was an etiquette that had to be observed," said Arthur.

"Is this an apology?" he asked.

"Well yes, water is probably a precious thing here and I'm sorry for drinking it without asking," said Arthur.

"Well, in that case consider yourself to carry on with your business," he said, suddenly nice and happy.

"Huh? What happened to the whole tough guy act?" asked Arthur.

"Oh, well I get quite a few posh snobs that would rather get me fired than apologise. They never can, but you are the only one that has apologised," he explained.

"Oh good, I'm glad to hear it," said Arthur, shaking his hand.

"What is it that you are here for?" he asked.

"I am here to see Sir Nabelle on some business from High King Olandine," said Arthur.

"Oh, that may be a problem," he said.

"Why?" asked Arthur in a concerned voice.

"Sir Nabelle is in a funny mood and he just read a book he got from Ailu, called the Prince of Persia, and I hope you didn't have anyone with you," he said.

"Miss Archaelia and Princess Josephine Olandine," he said.

"OK, now I am going to explain to you frankly what happened and please don't run after them. It won't do any good, your only chance is staying with me as with me we can free them," he explained.

"That's my best friend and fiancée and if he's hurt them...!" said

Arthur, getting angry.

"No he hasn't, they are probably imprisoned in the treasure room at the top of the Violet Tower," said the sergeant.

"Then let's go," said Arthur.

"OK, but it isn't going to be easy, it's all to see if you are as chivalrous as the character in his book," he said.

"Not an issue, come on then," said Arthur.

They checked the ship, and saw that the girls had indeed gone and they walked up to the main door and it opened up into a large entrance hall. "Which way?" asked Arthur.

"To the left," he replied. They followed a corridor with a burgundy and black carpet with the most amazing patterns, but Arthur wasn't concerned about the decor.

They then ran into the first of their obstacles which was another corridor, which had bits of the floor missing. "I'll go first," he said. Arthur watched as he ran through the corridor by jumping side to side with considerable ease. Arthur followed almost exactly as the sergeant had done. They were now beginning to climb and when they reached their next obstacle, they saw why.

They had emerged in the hall of learning which had stacks of books, though not nearly as many as The Temple of Earthly Wisdom. They were quite high up and they saw the doorway on the other side of the room. It was a balancing act across the top of bookcases and wooden beams. Arthur found that when he thought of Jo, he summoned up enough courage to keep going.

They finally reached the doorway and continued along a darkened corridor. Arthur was beginning to get ahead of himself and overtook the sergeant, who pulled him back just before he was about to fall into a shadowy pit. "Jump" he said and Arthur watched as he sailed over the pit to the other side. Arthur stepped back and then jumped to; he landed in the dark onto the floor in what must have been one of the scariest moments of his life.

They saw a light at the end of the gloomy corridor and followed it until they emerged into a courtyard, which had three levels. Arthur looked up and he could see the Violet Tower rise up behind the courtyard, and this only strengthened his resolve. He climbed up the courtyard in stages and this reminded Arthur of the courtyard that he and Jo had climbed up in Evermore.

The sergeant was amazed to see how adept Arthur was at climbing.

"Where did you learn to do that?" he asked, being a level lower than Arthur.

"Princess Josephine taught me in Evermore," he said as the sergeant scrambled to the top level.

"You must love her very much," he said.

"I do, now, we don't have a moment to lose," said Arthur, who walked down the next corridor cautiously. They entered a large room with a glass ceiling which was made from purple, pink and blue stained glass, and through it they could see the Violet Tower.

"We're almost there," said Arthur.

"Here is where we split company, my friend. There are two separate towers that open the main door to the Violet Tower. You activate one and I will activate the other, and we meet back here," he explained.

"Thank you for helping me," said Arthur.

"Don't mention it, all it took was one sign of decency and I'll help you with anything, sir," he said, and disappeared down the right corridor.

Arthur went down the left corridor which was well lit, and seemed to have no mechanisms or traps. Arthur then walked to the interior of the tower which was filled with mechanical apparatus of every kind. There were chains linked to giant wheels, which were all motionless. Arthur looked up and saw that the switch he looked for was at the top of the tower.

He set about climbing the tower. He began by climbing a ladder to a platform. He then climbed precariously around a wheel, and achieved his objective of getting to the next platform. He looked up and saw that there were about four more floors to the switch, but he couldn't see a way to go.

After looking around for a while he saw a small switch built into the wall which he pulled down. It clicked and some chains began to move in between the gap that led from one side of the platform to the next. Arthur ran and grabbed it. He waited for the chain to take him to the third level. On this level he ran up some steps to the fourth level.

"Two levels to go" he said to himself. Arthur pulled another switch on the wall, and saw that the next way was a straight diagonal way up that was now moving in out of the wall. Arthur waited for it to go in and then started to run. As it came out he began to run up it, and that gave him the maximum amount of time to get up.

Arthur had ample time and he got up to find a way to the last level. He found it. It was a set of cut-outs in the wall and they went up in a diagonal fashion before they reached the switch on a terrace at the top of the tower. Arthur carefully stepped along the cut-outs and managed to finally get to the switch. He then saw something other than a switch on the terrace.

It was a gleaming sword, ornately decorated, and Arthur regarded it as a thing of beauty. He picked it off the stand it lay on, and Arthur also found a sword belt that he attached to himself. He put the sword in its sheath, and pulled the switch. The machinery began to whirr to life, and the whole tower came alive. Arthur now felt more powerful with the sword, and he jumped down to the sixth level. Then he jumped down and rolled onto the fifth level, and did a similar routine to this on the fourth, third and second levels.

He then reached the wheel that he had used to get to this floor, and found that it was furiously spinning. "I wonder what I do now," he thought to himself. He found a part of the level that didn't have any machinery and simply swung down to the first level. He then climbed down the ladder and walked triumphantly down the corridor to meet the sergeant.

Sergeant Crippler was waiting for Arthur in the room that they had left. "Sorry did I keep you waiting?" asked Arthur.

"Not at all, I'm surprised you made it," he replied.

"It's worth it, now let's carry on," said Arthur, who opened up the big doors to the Violet Tower. They walked along an extremely ornate corridor and emerged in a circular room with a large outer spiral staircase that extended up to the top of the tower.

"Come on, let's get going," said Arthur who ran up the stairs as fast as he could. He felt quite dizzy when he reached the top as did the sergeant, and they emerged at the top of the tower.

It was a large circular room with a series of widows that were stain glass in extremely ornate patterns. The treasure that littered the floor was what drew their attention first, but Arthur was only interested in finding Jo. "Jo!" he shouted. "Over here, in the cage!" she shouted back. Arthur ran up a pile of gold, and slid down it. He saw that there were two large cages, Jo was in one and Archie was in the other. Archie was wearing a more summery version of her dress, and was sitting cross-legged on the floor reading a book that she most probably had magically pulled out of nowhere.

"You got here then," said Jo.

"It wasn't easy you know, but here I am, and where is our host?" asked Arthur, who was trying to unlock the cage door.

"I am here Sir Arthur; and congratulations for beating my palace," said Sir Nabelle, who had appeared out of nowhere.

"Could you please unlock the door?" asked Arthur.

"Now is the time when I give you a choice, you can either have all the gold here, or your trapped companions," said Nabelle.

"Take the gold, Arthur, and I'll tear the place apart," said Archie.

"Hmm give me a millisecond to think about that, I would like to have my friends please," said Arthur.

"What!?" asked Nabelle.

"Get my friends out of here if you don't mind," said Arthur.

"Very well," said Nabelle, who proceeded to unlock the cages and let the girls go.

"Thank you. Now I have a request from The High King, he asks for your allegiance," said Arthur.

"I'm listening," said Nabelle.

"If you agree to give him support and help if he needs it, then you will have help from anyone else in the kingdom and you would be known as Lord Nabelle," said Arthur.

"This is only in a crisis," said Nabelle.

"Yes, if we are in war or if another island needs evacuation because of a small war or natural disaster, something of that kind," said Arthur.

"You don't seem to be the normal stuck up official, why are you doing this?" he asked.

"So I can marry Princess Josephine," he replied.

"That seems a worthy thing to do and I will not stand in the way of love, so by all means I will ally myself with Discoucia," he said.

"Excellent, here," said Arthur, passing a bracelet to Nabelle.

"Thank you, you were a worthy challenger, and I will allow you to take one piece of treasure with you," said Nabelle.

"May I choose?" asked Archie.

"Of course, White Maiden," said Nabelle.

"Your people originally came from Sorro didn't they?" asked Archie.

"Yes, how did you know? People believe that we are from Gard because we have so much money," asked Nabelle.

"I like history," said Archie, who was looking around the treasure pile.

"What is it you are looking for?" asked Arthur.

"Hold on," said Archie, who dug into a pile of gold and pulled out a large clear fist sized gem.

"I would like this," said Archie.

"How did you know about that?" asked Nabelle.

"Well, you see, I need this; I cannot explain why, but may I please have it?" asked Archie.

"Of course. I'm sorry I put you two in a cage, dramatic effect and all, you know," he said.

Archie clicked her fingers, and gestured for them to go out on the balcony. They all walked out, and the ship appeared. "It was nice to meet you," said Arthur to Sergeant Crippler.

"You go get em'," he shouted. The ship flew away from the beauty of the palace, but unfortunately the beauty was lost on them.

It's a stone cold shame

Professor Cordelia Paradise was the complete opposite of Archie, and her real name was Persus. She began by causing misery to those who deserved it, which could be seen as being amoral; however she took it to a major extreme that made Archie want to foil her at every possible opportunity. She has her secrets as much as Archie yet she didn't seem to care as much about keeping them, since according to her it was too much work to be nice. Her daughter did her best to follow in her mother's footsteps but didn't possess complete godly powers, which was the result of having a mortal father.

This wasn't always so and Archie used to be her partner, back in a time when it called for it. Archie herself contained the Element of Water, where Cordelia contained the Element of Fire and she had a temperament to go with it. They both did some amazing things but their friendship came to an abrupt end when they disagreed over how to deal with a particularly strange fairytale villain. Cordelia wanted to chop her head off while Archie wanted to send her to Icester.

As far as looks, Cordelia was a contrast to her personality. She had bright pink hair and in her own realm wore a bright purple dress with red heart designs all over it. She looked like a fairytale princess since she preferred the Middle Ages over the more Celtic Paradise Archie had surrounded herself with.

Archie had taken her costume off, and had put in the trunk with the rest of them that Stuart had made for her. She had changed back into her plain blue and white dress. The ship needed to stop off on the island of Larntone because it was steadily running out of fuel. Archie said she could just re-fill it but Corky needed to clean the whole thing out, which meant that the ship needed to stop.

Larntone was a rocky island, similar to Omean but with more mountains and high cliffs. On the island at the moment was a small team of archaeologists also from Arkellia, only they were excavating the ruins of Sunrise Temple in the Dragon Valley. The ship landed rather bumpily in a secluded area above the valley and Corky began to fix the engines. "When do you want me to fill them up?" asked Archie.

"When I've cleaned her; You may as well go for a walk, when she's clean you can fill her up and we can leave," replied Corky.

"OK then," said Archie.

"If you can make fuel appear then I'll eat my hat," said Corky, who had been playing along with Archie up until this point.

"I'm a trans-dimensional super being and you're a driver, though none of that matters because you don't have a hat," said Archie.

"Exactly," he replied.

"You're a funny guy," said Archie who left the ship and joined Arthur and Jo on the ridge, looking down at the ruins of the temple.

It was a large open space and sticking out of the floor like jagged teeth were the ruins, columns and broken walls, and a camp with people milling around in the centre. Their ship was at the other side of the valley and with the sun rising so high, it was baking hot. "Are there other people doing the same as us Archie, you know, adventuring and such and such?" asked Jo.

"It depends on what you mean, when your tale is being read it's happening, so by that logic Bilbo is on his travels with the dwarves, Frodo is taking the ring to Mordor, Harry is sitting in his cupboard under the stairs feeling slightly dejected, Sinbad is fighting a Cyclops with a genie and Bugs Bunny is avoiding Daffy Duck. These adventures are all happening at once because people are reading them, it's the beauty of stories," explained Archie.

"Are all these stories in books?" asked Arthur.

"Yes they are, well most of them," said Archie.

"Are they in your library?" asked Jo.

"They are all there, just don't mention their names or The Evil Lord Copyright will get you," said Archie, who half smiled but continued to look down at the valley with a telescope.

She saw something that obviously caught her attention, and she gave the telescope to Arthur and then went back to the ship for some unknown reason. Arthur then looked down at the camp, and saw that a woman was standing in the centre, and she wore a white dress and had a white headscarf that obscured her hair and only showed her face.

"Who is that?" asked Jo, who took the telescope after Arthur.

"No idea, I've never seen her before," replied Arthur.

Archie returned with her hair tied back and carrying a back pack slung over one shoulder. "Where have you been?" asked Jo.

"Gearing up for war," replied Archie.

"Who is that woman?" asked Arthur.

"You'll find out, but we're going down to have a word," said Archie, who ran down the stone path to the valley floor. When they reached the bottom of the valley, they walked through a crumbling arch and into the excavation.

For once they were not set upon by guards, and were instead greeted by one of the professors, who introduced himself as Professor Manjaro. He was happy to see Archie for some reason and she couldn't understand why.

"Good afternoon Miss Archaelia, and you too Sir Pageon, Professor Bloom is here and she will love to see you again," he said.

"Sorry, but who is Professor Bloom?" asked Arthur.

"Professor Daisy Bloom," he replied.

"Oh Daisy, yes, I know her and I would love to see her again," said Arthur. Jo coughed, and Archie nudged her. Arthur just looked blankly at them both and then carried on talking to Manjaro.

"And who is the head of your excavation?" asked Arthur.

"Professor Cordelia Paradise," said Manjaro. Arthur and Jo both looked at Archie, who didn't look very happy.

She didn't say anything; she instead just walked into the centre of the camp where Paradise was sitting at a table, her back to Archie. "Good Afternoon Archaelia, it's nice to see you again," she said, not turning around.

"I wish I could say the same, but then again I really couldn't," replied Archie.

"I hope you don't mind but I am really busy here," she said.

"Doing what?" asked Archie.

"That is of no concern of yours, why don't you go back to paradise and don't bother me," she replied.

"Whatever you are doing, it can't be good and I want you to stop, even though I don't know what it is I still don't trust you," said Archie.

"Why do you insist on foiling my brilliant plans at every turn?" asked Paradise.

"Because you are an evil and malignant person who delights in inflicting torment on others, and frankly I know what you're really like," said Archie.

"I see that you have found some new companions, and I wonder if they will be as friendly if they knew the real you," said Paradise menacingly.

"I think that you just need to leave my world and once you are gone, I can be happy," said Archie.

"Do you want to have another duel, and if you win I will leave, but if I win then I will continue to stay for another one thousand years," said Paradise.

"Very well Persus, what is the competition?" asked Archie.

"I challenge you to collect the fourteen gems of Discoucia, and without any powers, we will both give those to Phoebe in the hills above the ruins of Tanalos," she explained.

"I knew that I would be collecting gems, but I already have two," said Archie.

"I know you do, and they are now in the vault on Harrha; I couldn't give you an advantage now, could I," she said in a mocking voice.

"Look I don't want you to really go if you would just be constructive for once," said Archie, changing her tone it what could only be described as swings and roundabouts.

"Oh come on, do you really think this world needs us again? For crying out loud, you'll be trying to convert my daughter next," replied Cordelia.

"I've never actually met your daughter," said Archie.

"Is that so?" asked Cordelia, sipping her tea.

"Oh, and Hyperion asked that if I saw you to tell you that he has begun to build the Constellation CP065xrT in the alien city somewhere in Hypaxxion. As much as you think I am a bad person that you always need to bring down, he might destroy the planet," said Cordelia.

"He went to Chargunthi-Khlora and tried to resurrect that stuff, is he insane?!" asked Archie.

"Well I guess he just wanted to get to know how our parents lived, it's been so long since we had a visit from them huh?" she asked.

"There's no empirical evidence that we gained our powers from alien life and we both know that we had retrograde memory loss when we all woke up. Everything just kinda formed around it and here we are," said Archie.

"One day they are going to have to know, the world will have to know that their comprehension of the planet is skewed and that there is a deep dark secret below Seraphale Island that I may never set foot on. Oh and by the way I have to ask you if you think bright pink gothic Victorian is something I should attempt," she said.

"I wouldn't wear pink in a million years, unless I was disguised as an old person again but that ain't gunna happen. And gothic is supposed to be dark and depressing you know," replied Archie.

"When our contest begins, I'll be the one looking fabulous while you simply run around in that tattered old thing," she replied.

"I like this dress, and what you wear looks so uncomfortable and probably took you ages to put on anyway," said Archie.

"What happened to us? I know that you think the worst of me but I at least had fun doing what we did," asked Cordelia.

"I don't want to start this again, you can't stand me because I believe in making people happy without asking anything in return and I can't stand you because you believe in punishing people to such an extent that it destroys both them and other innocent people," replied Archie.

"I don't have a problem with what you do, I just don't understand why you do it," said Cordelia.

"Are you trying to get out of the bet?" asked Archie.

"Are you trying to be funny?" asked Cordelia.

Arthur and Jo had already met Daisy, and they stood watching the intense confrontation between the two people. "You will do everything in your power to stop us won't you?" asked Archie.

"Of course I will but since we won't be gods for a year, our power will be significantly reduced," said Paradise.

"None of your usual pre-preparation, well you know what I mean," said Archie.

"No I won't be doing a thing, you would know about it as much as I would," she replied.

"You're right, I would, and you know that what we promised must happen if either one of us wins," said Archie.

"Of course and I'll be waiting for you, all four of you," said Paradise.

Archie then shook hands with her which made the air around them go a peculiar clash of pink and blue, then she walked up to Arthur and Jo. "We're leaving, now," said Archie.

"Why?" asked Arthur.

"Because we cannot stay, please, we have to leave," said Archie.

"Very well, goodbye Daisy," said Arthur.

"It was lovely to see you again," said Daisy, who hugged Arthur, and shook Jo's hand awkwardly. They walked back to the ship and when Archie clicked her fingers, the ship started on its own. Corky was half asleep and he struggled to control the ship as it flew north, away from the ruins and away from Larntone entirely.

"OK, what happened?" asked Arthur.

"I met Persus, and I have a chance to be rid of her forever," said Archie.

"How can we help you?" asked Jo.

"You're going to help me?" asked Archie.

"It's what friends do," replied Jo.

"Well, God Girl will be joined by her three companions in a battle of good against evil," said Archie.

"Who is God Girl?" asked Jo.

"That would be me," said Archie, and there was a flash of smoke.

Archie changed into God Girl, and she looked like a strange superhero with an equally strange costume. She had dark patches where her eyes were, and the torn strips of fabric that made her look like a wraith in a kind of poncho, and her wrists were now banded with black fabric on white. No skin could be seen, and Archie now had a black hood with white lining. "Oh, right," said Jo, wondering how it ever came to this.

"Where did you get that style from?" asked Arthur.

"I don't think they want me to say," said Archie, and Jo felt the same way as Arthur did watching Archie talk without actually seeing her talk.

"You know, this might be a little over the top and I'll look at something else in The Twilight Vale. I can be anything and everything, maybe even a war hero" said Archie, switching in a puff of smoke to her .

"You hate war, it seems a little bit hypocritical," said Arthur.

"We can get it in editing," replied Archie.

The ship flew to the north, and then suddenly stopped. Arthur, Jo and Archie walked out onto the deck, and the volcanic island of Starkellone was in eruption. Corky had stopped so that everyone could watch the amazing spectacle. The ship then dropped, and landed on the water, which sent a spray of water into the air.

'It's raining all over the world'

The island of Availa is situated closest to the blue sand shores of Lesiga, and is home to Penguin Beach Resort where people come to see the penguins. The Island is ruled by Sir Richard who is probably the most sensible ruler in all the islands, and lives in a large mansion on the north side of the island. It was originally just flat land but it was converted with walls and lowered gardens to accommodate trees. It was from the islands that most of the timber was cut and shipped to Discoucia to build houses before stone was found to be a better material. After all the trees were cut down, the island was left a barren wasteland, but penguins from the southern continents still migrated there.

The ship landed with a shake next to a large stone wall just in sight of Sir Richard's mansion. It was a spectacular building with an imposing brick wall built around it. The roads on the island were raised and below them were the acres and acres of sand dunes that stretched as far as the eye could see.

"I'm going for a walk, it isn't every day that you get to take a trip across miles of sand dunes," said Arthur.

"I'll come with you," said Archie.

"I want to see the penguins, so you two can come back to the resort when you're done and we can have dinner," said Jo.

"I am hungry, it's like we haven't eaten in chapters," said Archie.

"What do you mean 'chapters'?" asked Jo.

"Nothing, I sometimes say things that are just in my head and that don't really mean anything," said Archie.

"Well you carry on with that," said Jo, who jumped down the rigging and walked off to the south.

"Come on, we can have a nice chat about things," said Archie.

"There are a few things that I want to ask you," he said, as they walked down from the road and onto the dunes. There was grass growing everywhere, but it was a thick matted grass that had sand in odd areas. It carried on like this for miles.

"Shall we walk to the sea?" asked Arthur.

"Why not? Anyway, what did you want to ask me?" she said.

"What is your domain like?" he asked.

"It's more of a place for the eyes and its eternal majesty and beauty cannot be described in words, but I'm sure I'll give it a good go soon," she said.

"And what can you tell me about Persus?" asked Arthur.

Archie then looked very serious and stared at Arthur in a way she hadn't done before. "I can't, she is someone who I would rather forget about than discuss but if you really want me to, then for you I will," she said.

"Go on then," he said, now intrigued.

"The god system in Alavonia works very simply. I am the elemental god of Water and my legendary familiar is Seashorelle. Then there is Cordelia who is the elemental god of Fire and her familiar is Ignatio. After that is the pleasant Phoebe who you would know as The Misty Morning Rider, she is the elemental God of Earth and her familiar is Altatia. The last is the somewhat unhinged Hyperion who controls the Air, his familiar is Evere and he does some silly things" she explained.

"Right, so you four run around causing all kinds of mayhem to us mortals" he asked.

"Hey, you wouldn't believe what some of us go through and sometimes what we look like wears out," she said, making a gesture over her whole body.

"Is what you look like a disguise?" asked Arthur.

"Yes and no, I don't think you have ever seen what I really look like," said Archie.

"Can I?" he asked.

"No, I'm afraid that if you saw me as I truly was it would give you a heart attack, but don't let it put you off," said Archie.

They decided to return to the ship and Arthur changed the topic of conversation. "When you said that you gave us wishes, is it any kind of wish or do you have limitations?" asked Arthur.

"Yes; I tell you what, try a wish and I will tell you if it is possible, and this doesn't count as your wish," he said.

"OK, I would probably wish to have a nice retirement in a huge stately home, with Jo at my side and three kids," he said.

"No, that I can't grant because like Lilia's wish it has a good chance of coming true without me," said Archie.

"It's going to happen?" he asked.

"Look at it this way, you have enough money to buy anything, you have a fiancé who loves you and three buns in the oven," said Archie.

"Wait a second, Jo's pregnant?" he asked.

"Oh, umm, congratulations!" said Archie, who didn't know what to say.

"I can't believe this," said Arthur.

"Look I didn't mean to tell you, but yes she is and I want you not to say anything, promise me you won't," she said.

"I'm so happy, I can't not tell her," he said.

"I know, but she won't notice a thing for the next nine months, and then the second nine months is when the babies will begin to give her one heck of a time," said Archie.

They reached the path, and by now it was late afternoon. The Ambro Restaurant was situated in the south and overlooked the penguin beach. Jo was sat at a large table and was stuffing herself with bread rolls. "I see you've already started, sorry we're a little late," he said.

"It's OK, I haven't seen anyone I recognise and I haven't seen any monsters running around either," she said.

"Dinner time, I suppose," said Archie.

"They have everything here and it's all sea food too," said Jo.

"I'm in the mood for all you can eat," said Archie.

"So am I, I think they have one of those contests here," said Jo.

"What kind of contest?" asked Arthur.

"You have to beat the champion at an eating contest, and if you can you get a trophy," said Jo.

"I'm up for it, who is the eating champion?" asked Archie.

"You're looking at her," said Jo.

"You?" asked Arthur.

"I went here once with my father and I beat the previous champion, now you don't get the trophy unless you beat me," she said.

"You kept that one quiet," said Arthur.

"I know, apparently it's not ladylike to be the champion at eating huge amounts of food," said Jo.

"Nuts to the Penguin Mutant, I challenge you, Princess Josephine," said Archie.

"But you're a god, I can't beat you," she said.

"Well, I do have an organic body like you and limits too, so no opening voids inside me so the food goes elsewhere," said Archie.

"Okay then, consider this a battle of food," said Jo.

There was a table set out in the centre of the restaurant, and a group of people crowded around the two. Jo was sitting confidently staring her opponent down. Archie was sat nonchalantly picking her multicoloured teeth with a toothpick. "Ladies and gentlemen, we have now a battle of titanic proportions: the champion has returned, and she is challenged. Miss Archaelia of The Great Rim wishes to challenge Princess Josephine Olandine of Evermore in an all you can eat contest," the announcer said.

"You're going down," said Jo. "Sure I am, and if you believe that then at least one of us is severely deluded" replied Archie.

"The first wave of food will be a starter, one hundred deep fried prawns each," he said. A huge pile of deep fried prawns were placed in front of Jo and Archie, and they looked at them with interest.

"They look amazing, but can I have some sweet chilli sauce?" asked Archie. A chef dumped a big bowl that was full of the sauce, and it had to be big since Archie would be doing an awful lot of dipping.

Archie took a relaxed approach to eating but Jo was ravenous, and demolished fifty prawns in ten minutes. When Archie was finished,

Jo was waiting for the second course which was a huge pile of scampi, the pile was about two feet tall, and Archie then did something that everyone looked at with confused looks. She threw them into her mouth, one by one in rapid succession, like tasty bullets. She repeated this until all the scampi were gone. Jo was starting to feel a slight strain but she continued on, as she wasn't going to let Archie forget about this when she had won.

They finished the second course and out came the third, a big bowl of paella. "This looks lovely, and I am going to enjoy it," said Archie.

"Come on Jo, you're eating for four now," shouted Arthur.

"What?" she said back to him.

"Nothing, good hustle kid," he shouted back.

Archie shot him a venomous glance and he tried to avoid it. They slowly finished the course and the waiter brought them two large drinks. Archie downed it in one go and Jo struggled to lift the glass. "We are half way through and now comes the fourth course," said the announcer.

It was three large fish that were battered in breadcrumbs.

"Excellent, finally we have real fish they look amazing" said Archie who was unfazed by eating such a large amount of food. Jo had now gotten her second wind, and she set about eating the fish as fast as she could. Archie just stared at her and then giggled, because Jo's belly had begun to poke out of her shirt, and looked quite funny. "Yes I know, though if I am going to beat you I have to concentrate," said Jo.

When they had finished the round of fish, it was time for the fifth course.

"Ladies and gentlemen, the two challengers have now eaten four courses of food and now have two courses left, the next one nobody has finished not even our champion because she has beaten all opponents before this stage," said the announcer.

The next course appeared, and it was a huge bowl of fish soup. Jo stared at it for a second and shakily picked up a spoon. Archie called a waitress over and whispered something in her ear. She walked off and everyone wondered what she had said. The waitress came back with a large straw and Jo's eyes widened. Archie then did the unthinkable, and actually slurped the soup up through a straw.

The crowd watched in horrid fascination at Archie drain the bowl of soup and then wipe her lips daintily with a napkin. Jo watched with her mouth wide open, she didn't have a chance. "Give up, Josephine?" asked Archie.

"If I did, then I wouldn't be a very good role model," said Jo.

"Then you carry on, I need to ask Arthur to fetch me something from the ship," said Archie.

She walked over to Arthur and gave him his instructions. Arthur was to go and get his business over with Sir Richard and retrieve something from the ship that wasn't there before, and bring it back. The two people carried on eating after Arthur walked through the crowd and out the door. After Jo had nearly choked on the last bit of her soup, she leant back and groaned. "This is incredible, our two challengers have eaten five courses and we now have the last course, which is the hardest course to finish out of all six," said the announcer.

From out of the kitchen came two carts and on them were large bowls, about a metre across, and they both had a cloth covering the contents. "This is something new invented by our chefs and they have yet to be given a name, but it has been agreed that the champion of this challenge will give them a name" said the announcer. The bowls were placed in front of the two, and the cloth was taken away. Inside was a mass of chips, and Archie was surprised that the people here didn't get the memo that they were called chips.

"What are these exactly?" asked Jo.

"They are cut like wood chips but they come from potatoes, as mentioned in Asterix," said Archie.

"She is right!" said the announcer.

"Go on then Jo, now that you know what they are go ahead and dig in. Shall I fetch you a spade?" asked Archie.

"I'll be fine with a fork, thank you," she replied.

Jo set about attacking the bowl. She had faced monstrous robots, a snow monster, an impossible trap, but there was no easy way out of this. "It's funny when you think about it, but were being rewarded for being gluttonous and the fact that you, a princess, are being cheered on is brilliant," said Archie.

"Why is it brilliant?" asked Jo, in a strained sarcastic voice.

"Socially you have escaped a Dark Age of repression and your technology has become advanced, and your morals are well balanced with the right combination of fun and restraint. Though you know what happens to perfect worlds?" asked Archie.

"Is this a trick to win?" asked Jo.

"No not at all, I just hope that Arthur brings me back what I asked," replied Archie, who had nearly finished. Jo desperately crammed chips into her mouth which was now coated in soup from the previous course, and she had not bothered to clean it.

They finally finished and the whole crowd cheered. "Ladies and gentlemen, our two challengers have both finished and it is up to them if they wish to call it a draw," said the announcer.

"What do you think Jo? I don't mind, this way we're not second to each-other and we're both as good as each other," said Archie.

"Since I'm probably going to explode, I agree," she said. They were both presented with a trophy and thankfully they didn't have to pay, since they had finished the whole thing.

The Book of Dreams

Arthur walked back in to find the two nearly lying on their chairs and in his hand he held a large book, with a blue cover that had a strange symbol on it.

"What exactly is this book?" asked Arthur.

"I refer to it when I need guidance, you see my domain is a little different from yours, when you see it you will understand," said Archie.

"You didn't really explain it," said Arthur.

"Did you get allegiance from Sir Richard?" asked Archie.

"Yes, he is a great friend and he owed me a favour, and now that I'm done I am free to search for a cure," said Arthur.

"Good, then I'm afraid that I must leave you, you need to make it to my home on your own but here, look at this," she said, reaching into the cover and handing Arthur a map.

She literally pulled it out of the solid book cover and Arthur placed it on the table. It was a map of Lesiga and the island of Availa, which had a small ship on it, presumably the Nostradamus. "So tell me about the book," said Arthur.

"Inside this book is every dream that I have ever had and from these you guys were born, your whole world and everything in it so if anything happens to you, the record is here," said Archie.

"You created the world?" asked Jo.

"I had a hand in it, creating the oceans and all water. Now look in the book," replied Archie.

"Is anything going to happen to me?" asked Arthur.

"Let me see," said Archie.

She opened the book and inside it was nothing, just a swirling void of many fantastic colours. "This is what dreams look like?" asked Arthur.

"No, something here is terribly wrong, the book is in a flux which means that something bad is about to happen, all the harmony and balance in the world won't hold for long, you need to get to The Great Rim as soon as possible," said Archie, and she began to fade along with the book.

"But how do we get there?" asked Jo, but Archie had disappeared completely.

"Ohh, I think I'm having a food baby," said Jo.

"I'm not saying a thing but were leaving for Lesiga now, we've lingered in this archipelago for too long, let's go," said Arthur.

"I can't move," said Jo.

"Then I'm carrying you, you can either make me look like a hero or walk," said Arthur.

"You can be all the hero you want, a free ride is a free ride," said Jo, who stretched out her arms for Arthur to carry her. He walked out with her and with much cheering from the other diners.

Back on the ship Arthur tucked an already asleep Jo into bed and went downstairs. He couldn't sleep, so much had happened. He was going to be a father and Archie had gone. He'd lost his freedom and his safety net in one day, and now ahead of him was the home of a god and the untold wonders that lay inside. He tried to get his head straight but nothing could work, so he opened his safe and looked at the bottles that Lilia and Stuart had left. They were all the same, all bottles of a purple substance. Arthur then saw that a note had been left on them.

'Thank you for everything brother, here's something that I know you will like, it's a drink I distilled on Harrha called Purple Sunshine and it tastes out of this world, only don't drink more than a glass in a day, it's so sweet that you would probably turn into a nice person... Love your favourite sister, Lilia'

Arthur picked up a bottle and took it out of the freezing safe and out into the warm of the study. He closed the door of the safe and a wisp of cold steam puffed from the floor. Arthur covered the door

298

with the carpet and stuck the bottle on the desk. He pulled the cork and a sweet smell instantly filled the room. Arthur then felt that he was in a dreamy atmosphere and he found that he felt surprisingly uplifted. All of his problems didn't feel like problems anymore, but instead they felt like opportunities.

He poured the drink and drank about half. All around his head he could hear several different noises. At the bottom of both ears was a steady thumping sound and above that was the up and down sound that wasn't as heavy as the first. Then in between that he heard a lyrical sound like a violin that undulated up and down at odd and irregular intervals.

Then he heard something new; he heard someone singing. It was a male voice, heavy and distorted and he couldn't tell what the person was singing about, or the words. But then he heard three words, the only ones that were at all decipherable, 'can't come in'. The relentless beat went on and on, and it was so infectious that Arthur didn't want it to stop.

Discoucia didn't have many musicians and the best were all in the employ of Lords and Ladies for their personal entertainment. Arthur walked over to the window and collapsed on the windowsill, barely being able to keep himself up. The sky was on fire, and he saw rainbows and clouds of a thousand colours and hues all flowing around the magnificent scene that greeted his eyes. Arthur then collapsed onto the floor, which he found amazingly comfortable.

He slept there until the morning, and when Jo came downstairs, she shook her head in disappointment. "Drinking again, I think you're turning into an alcoholic," said Jo, but then she found that Arthur had drunk only a small amount of the bottle, and that he seemed so peaceful, not like he was before. She tried to pick him up and his eyes jolted open. He stood up, and seemed more alert than he had been in a long time. "No hangover?" she asked.

"No, I feel amazing, I have no idea why but I feel extremely refreshed and I want to go for a swim, are we nearly in Lesiga?" he asked.

"We're there, Corky has landed the ship by the river, where it joins the sea," said Jo.

Like lightning Arthur ran out of the study, through the sitting room and as he ran he ripped his clothes off apart from his underwear, then threw open the door. He ran across the deck and he saw all around that Lesiga was amazingly different than what he expected. He stopped on the deck as a slightly cold chill had hit him, and looked around at his surroundings which were all considerably different from what he expected.

"You haven't been taking hallucinogenic concoctions, have you?" asked Jo.

"No, that would make me as bad as the people your father's government imprisons," said Arthur.

"And how do you explain this?" asked Jo, holding the bottle.

"It isn't anything serious and it made me feel so happy," he said.

"That's as maybe, but I don't want to lose you since I know how easy it is to get addicted. Archie told me what I did on Inimosisle and I don't want to be embarrassed like that again," said Jo.

"I'll bear it in mind," he said, walking back into the sitting room.

Scenes From a Childish Fantasy

From where Arthur was standing he could see that they had landed on a vast plain, with irregular hills and tufts of grass poking out in odd places. This continued as far as the eye could see but then the view was blocked by a bank of fog, and behind that they could see nothing. There was what had once been a deep stream but now it was dry, and in the centre was a line of blue which was strange against the sandy coloured silt.

"OK, I'm going to change and we are going to sail up stream to the source, which is where I think we will find the entrance to Archie's domain," said Arthur. He walked inside and after ten minutes the ship lifted off and began to sail up the dry stream, towards the ominous looking fog bank.

"So what are we to expect in Lesiga?" asked Jo.

"Well, the rulers live in a fabulously huge castle, and they are King Charles and Queen Georgina," said Arthur.

"Oh I remember, they live in the Astral Castle in fabulous wealth while the rest of the people live below in squalid conditions, I visited it when I was little," said Jo.

"There is also a large house between us and the castle, and if I remember rightly it's called Danis Hall," said Arthur.

"A bit of a lonely place to have a home, how big is it?" asked Jo.

"About the size of Evermore, the grounds that is, but the house is built upon the highest point of the southern moors and it looks out over the various farms and villages that are spread across the continent," said Arthur.

"Are we going to run into any monsters?" asked Jo.

"I don't know, but the place is a very spooky setting so who knows. As long as we have the ship we'll be safe," said Arthur.

Just after he finished they heard a blood curdling howl echo through the fog, and it sounded so horrific that Jo was gripped with terror. She grabbed Arthur and buried her head into his arms. "Oh dear, that doesn't sound very pleasant does it," said Arthur.

"Another thing I love about you Artie, you never panic," she said in a muffled voice because she didn't want to look up.

"I'm going outside to see if we can see anything," said Arthur.

"There is no 'we', Arthur; I'm not going out there, not by a long shot," said Jo.

"Fine stay in here, it was probably just one of the farm dogs a mile away and the sound echoes through the fog," said Arthur in a calm voice.

"You can't honestly believe that, when is that ever the explanation?" she asked.

"Good point, but I'm curious," he replied and walked into the sitting room.

It was quite nice in the sitting room with the lights on; it was nice and bright in comparison to the dark fog outside. He looked outside and couldn't see a thing, the light inside made it darker outside and since it was midday, he was amazed that there was no light coming in from above.

Arthur walked out into the gloom and was amazed at the stark change that had occurred to the landscape. He looked in the direction from which the howling came and couldn't see nor hear a thing. He looked back in the direction of the sitting room and Jo was looking at him through the window. The silence was terrible; when there was a sound of some far-off creature the land had seemed alive, but now all that was left was this dense fog and nothing else.

Then Arthur heard it again, a howl from out in the darkness but this time it was closer, much closer and inside the howl was a undertone of growling, which took away the notion of it being a farm dog as they are not that big. Arthur ran to the spotlight that he had rarely used, pulled off its cover, and turned it on. The light buzzed into action and Arthur pointed it out into the gloom.

What Arthur saw next played on his mind from that point on. He always knew that there was no such thing as real monsters, and that he had been trying to find an explanation for the snow creature ever since they had visited the Icicle Mountains. He aimed the light out to the bank of the river and he saw a black shape running out of the light. He had no idea what it was, but the more he thought about from then, the more the image changed in his mind.

"What was it? What did you see?" Jo asked as Arthur walked back in.

"I don't know what I saw, but I'll be telling Corky to stop the ship at Danis Hall for the night, I want to ask Sir Edward about a few things," said Arthur.

"Can't we just keep going, it would make so much more sense," said Jo.

"No, it annoyed me that I never figured out what the snow creature was so I'm not letting this one go," said Arthur.

"I'm going into the wardrobe, so I can find something nice to wear, and since your wardrobe has no windows it seems to be the safest place," she said.

"Our wardrobe, Jo," he replied.

"Yes, that's going to take a while to get used to," she said.

"Well wear what you want, it's all ours," said Arthur. Jo ascended the stairs, and Arthur walked out onto the deck and down the stairs into the hull. The hull of the ship was a large space, even for a small ship like The Nostradamus and had all of Arthur's guns and gadgets in boxes and several crates of emeralds and rubies, for powering the ship. They were all sizes, and shapes.

Arthur just blithely walked past them and knocked on Corky's door. "Enter" was the reply. Arthur walked into Corky's room, which was large, and well lit. The front of the ship's hull was glass, most of it at least, and this how Corky could navigate. All across the walls were maps and posters, and in the corner was a small bed. It seemed to be very cosy, in light of the conditions outside.

"Did you hear the howling?" asked Arthur.

"Yes sir, I reckon something's trying to scare us but I know you don't believe in such things," said Corky.

"Neither do you, but in the circumstances we're going to Danis Hall for a short stop, and with its battlements and high turrets it should be safe there until we have solved the mystery, how are we doing on fuel?" asked Arthur.

"Fine, I think we should do a full check on the ship before we push on to the Great Rim, who knows what we shall encounter," said Corky.

"Then set a course. I think we should bear to the east, the fog is so thick that we have to rely on maps," said Arthur.

"I'll get us there, you go and attend to your beloved," he said.

"Aye aye navigator," said Arthur, who closed the door on his way out.

Jo was looking for something new to wear, but nothing felt right. Arthur then walked in, and Jo turned around expecting something horrible to walk through the door. "Oh it's you, what's happening?" she asked.

"We're on course for Danis Hall and it's nearly dinner time, so get something nice" said Arthur.

"I can't find anything that looks right," she replied.

"I'm sorry, but I'm no expert in this situation," he said.

"I thought that you were," she replied.

"What's that supposed to mean?" he asked.

"I'm going to be your wife, so I think I should know everything about you," she said.

"Hold on a second, now that were bringing this subject up I want to ask you something, I have never actually heard about your mother," said Arthur.

"I don't like to talk about it" said Jo.

"The first time I met you your mother wasn't in sight, but I didn't notice anything because my mother was comatose in bed from the night before so I thought that was normal," said Arthur.

"She just wasn't around," said Jo.

"Is your mother dead?" asked Arthur.

"She died when I was 185," said Jo.

"Then where was she when I saw you first?" he asked.

"The same place as your Uncle Phillip, that's why he recognised me but I said he was mistaken," she said.

"Your mother was in Hemlock Asylum? I'm so sorry," said Arthur.

"She tried to slit Alexandra's throat and sacrifice her to Persus, she belonged in there," said Jo, in a voice of anger that thinly veiled her sorrow.

"Why didn't you tell me?" he asked.

"I don't think that you would find me much of a future wife when I had screwy relatives," said Jo.

"Mine are worse than yours," he replied.

"We both have chequered pasts, but let's hope that we can make our family more of a beacon of happiness," said Jo.

"I think we will, learning from the past and all that," said Arthur.

The ship stopped, and they both went to the deck to see where they had landed. They were next to a large house, and they could see that the lights were on inside, and they looked quite warming in the fog.

Arthur was waiting downstairs and Jo joined him in an elegant and refined dress from Discoucia's 'Neo Firmanian' period of fashion. "Your mother had excellent taste, this would suit anybody perfectly," she said.

"Huh? Oh that wasn't my mother who owned that, it's a backup for the blue one that I bought in Neo Firmania," he said.

"This is yours?!" asked Jo.

"Can you please not look at me like that?" he asked.

"I'm not surprised really, and you don't have to be ashamed about having a feminine side," she said, sitting next to him and leaning her head on his shoulder.

"Come on; let's go introduce ourselves to Sir Edward and see if he can put us up for the night," said Arthur.

"Maybe he can tell us more about the monster out there," said Jo.

Just as she said it, there was a howling but it was far off in the distance, but it was enough to make Jo run out the door and over to the banister, climb down and bang on the front door. "Hold on, you're not making a good first impression," said Arthur, following Jo down to the front door.

The Ghoul at the Hall

The door was opened by a smartly dressed woman who was about 250, and wore a plain maid dress. "Good evening sir, how may I help you?" she asked.

"Sir Arthur Pageon and Princess Josephine Olandine to see Sir Edward," he said.

"On what business shall I say you are here on?" asked the maid.

"Monster removal ad royal business," said Jo. At this the maid's eyes widened, but her general expression didn't change.

"Very well I'll tell him you've arrived, please wait in here," she said.

The inside of the hall was beautifully ornate, with shields and sword decorating the wooden panelled walls. There were also paintings and tapestries with people and scenes from battles long ago. There was a large solid oak table in the centre with three large silver candelabras, with red candles flickering in a cross breeze that could have been coming from one of the many ornate leaded windows. There was a crest on each of them in stained glass with a lion and a mermaid, and as Arthur was looking at it, Jo was looking at a painting that seemed to transfix her. It was a painting of a man, who had long grey hair and a horrific expression on his face and an angry look with blazing eyes. It was the dog by his side that Jo was staring at; it was a brown hound with pricked up ears, eyes that matched its master and fangs dripping with blood. Beneath its blood stained paws was a lamb that had been slaughtered.

"That is my great, great grandfather Sir Daniel, the Mad Sir Daniel" said a booming voice that shattered the tension of the room. At the end of the hall was a staircase, a straight one, and it led to a landing that looked out over the hall.

"Cheery bloke," said Jo.

"Yes you could call him that, do I have the honour of addressing Princess Josephine Olandine?" he asked.

"Yes, it's nice to meet you Sir Edward," she said.

"And you must be Sir Arthur, are you expecting to see something out there?" he asked.

"You tell me," replied Arthur.

"So you've heard our little ghoul out there on the moorland?" he asked.

"It seems a little bit of a cliché, a monster out on the moorland and you only hear it and not see it," said Arthur.

"I have seen it, and I never want to see such a thing again," said Edward.

"If you could explain yourself what you saw, then hopefully I can build up an answer to your problem," said Arthur.

"What problem is that?" he asked.

"The problem of a ghoulish hound terrorising you," said Arthur.

"I'm not worried, it doesn't come into my house so why should I be worried?" asked Edward.

"I wasn't really prepared for that, you don't want us to solve the mystery?" asked Arthur.

"It would be a waste of time, plus it seems to be adding a bit of mystery and suspense to the place," he said.

"In that case, would you be able to put us up for the night?" asked Arthur.

"Of course, dinner will be served in an hour and I can show you around the estate while we wait," said Edward.

"I would be delighted, come on Jo," said Arthur, who took Jo's arm and followed Edward through a door beneath the landing.

They walked through a corridor as ornate as the hall, and it seemed to be full of antique memorabilia from past wars and past occupants. There were paintings of different kings and queens and at the end, the way split in two. There was a large painting of an elegant woman, who wore a shimmering blue dress and had short wavy hair.

"Who is this?" asked Jo.

"That is one of my ancestors, her name has been long forgotten so she is only know as 'The Danis Girl', and she bears the likeness of my father," said Edward. As Edward walked down to the right, Jo and Arthur looked at it a second longer and Arthur noticed something in the picture that Jo didn't.

"I don't think Edward knows that this 'girl' has an Adam's apple" said Arthur.

"Don't you think it's strange that we think that the first Discoucian was called Adam, how would you possibly know that," said Jo.

"I think it's best not to think about it, and don't mention to Edward that his father may have had an interesting private life," said Arthur, who followed Jo to where Edward was waiting.

There was a red door that was very ornate, and when Edward opened it, it led to a strangely designed room that didn't seem to fit in with rest of the architecture of the house, but it was decorated the same. It was built like a cellar, so that the glass ceiling was at the same level as the ground. It wasn't a flat ceiling and seemed to be more like a conservatory. There was a large table in the middle, and the diners could sit below the glass roof.

"This is a new way to eat," said Arthur.

"Yes it is a modern arrangement but I like it, now we can have a talk about what is going on in Discoucia these days," said Edward.

They sat down and a simple dinner was served, a steak of questionable origin. "What is in this?" asked Jo.

"It's a speciality of my cook, it's a swordfish steak," he said.

"I don't think those two words should be put together" said Arthur.

There was a puff of blue smoke, and a piece of paper flew into Jo's hand. "'Tell me about it'," she said. "It looks like Archie agrees with you."

"So, on another topic, what is the land around here like?" asked Arthur.

"There are a number of farms and there's another stately home west of the Astral Castle, but it's been in a state of ruin for years and no one lives there. On a clear night you can see it from the tower room, and fortunately enough the fog looks like it's just about to clear," said Edward. He was right, the fog had cleared and the sky was now full of tiny stars everywhere.

"I would like to go and have a look, if you don't mind," asked Arthur.

"Of course, it looks extra creepy at night, and with the moon out it should be as light as day," he replied.

Arthur and Jo followed Edward down the corridor past the now slightly comical picture of The Danis Girl and up a set of stairs. They then went down a dark corridor and up a spiral staircase. This led to the tower room, which was a circular room with a large closed window. Edward opened it and the cold air blew in, but it didn't affect Arthur as he had three layers on. Jo shivered but tried to hide it, however Arthur took off his jacket and put it around her and she was silently thankful. Edward pointed out across the landscape, with its rivers, and random trees that bordered roads and fields. They saw farmhouses, all dark, since it was late at night. The whole scene took on a blue and grey hue, and the starry sky made it look beautifully lonely.

"There is the farm at Marsh End and if you go up from there, is the next farm at Earthydown," explained Edward. Then Arthur and Jo's attention was focused on a clump of old trees, and the black dome and many chimneys of a large old house. "That's it, the old Tenebra place, empty for years," said Edward.

"Forgive me for the silly question, but why is there smoke coming from the chimney," said Jo.

"By Authos, that's strange, strange indeed," said Edward.

They heard the howling again and this time it came from the direction of the Tenebra house. "I wouldn't mind going to have a look, tomorrow at least, investigation and all that," said Arthur.

"I will too, I own the land from the borders of the Sersitio Forest to the sea and if someone is squatting I want to know," said Edward.

"Then that's our plan for tomorrow, but I'm afraid we can't take my ship as it's being prepared for the journey ahead," said Arthur.

"The farmers around here don't like flying ships so we'll walk;

it's only about a mile away. And Princess, could you please do me a favour and entertain my wife, she gets so bored in the autumn when there is nothing to do," said Edward.

"No problem but I hope you two will be careful, that place looks a bit freaky," said Jo.

"It's probably haunted or bewitched or some such fiddle faddle," said Arthur. There was another puff of smoke, and Arthur read the note aloud.

"'I think now is the time to say it but this was my favourite part of One Hundred and One Dalmatians, and I wished it was longer so you are living my wish, have fun. All credit to Dodie Smith and the good people at Disney'," read Arthur.

"She's getting worse," said Jo.

"I'm not in the mood for her nonsense, I just want it to get light before we go and explore that place," said Arthur.

They left the tower room and retired for the night. Arthur slept in one room and Jo in another. This was not an arrangement that they had decided, but they had no other choice since it was in the huge and walled house that they felt safe. Jo dreamt of that old house and the horrors within. Arthur dreamt that the Danis Girl was throwing oranges at him, and Edward dreamt of dalmatians, loads of them.

The morning came, and Jo went in to wake Arthur up. "Did you sleep well?" asked Jo.

"Not really, I don't know if I like it here," said Arthur.

"Me neither, just get your little pleasure jaunt over and we can leave. I don't want to be separated from you again," said Jo. Arthur tussled Jo's hair, and got up to look out of the window. The morning had not improved the look of the landscape. Arthur could see the tracks of many carts that had churned up the roads leaving gouges that were now filled with rain water. There was smoke rising from the chimneys of the farmhouses they saw last night but the Tenebra place looked quiet, and as ominous as it had done the night before.

"I'll get dressed and meet Sir Edward for breakfast, will you join me?" asked Arthur.

"Do you mean will I eat food? What do you think the answer to that is?" asked Jo.

311

"Point taken," replied Arthur.

"Are you sure you want to go?" asked Jo.

"I have to but there is something I want you to do, if I don't come back then don't come after me," said Arthur.

"What are you talking about?" she said.

"I don't want you to get into any unnecessary harm," said Arthur.

"Aww, you're concerned about me," she said. Arthur put his hand on Jo's arm, and looked really concerned. "I'm serious, go to the Astral Castle and then go with Corky to the Twilight Vale, you'll be safe there and I'll join you as soon as I can," he said.

"Don't be serious, I don't like it," said Jo.

After a hearty breakfast Arthur and Edward were ready to leave. They left Jo and Lady Lucy; the wife of Edward in the hall and walked down the track to the gate. Edward didn't seem to be very talkative, and as they passed through a clump of trees, they caught sight of the Tenebra house sitting like a silent creature within a ring of trees. They followed the muddy track but stayed on the side of the road because the verge was much firmer. After a quarter of a mile they reached the first farm, which Edward identified as Marsh End. At this time of year there wasn't much activity, but some animals could be heard behind the high walls.

"Come on, we get about six hours of light in the autumn," said Edward.

"OK, you lead," replied Arthur, and they continued to make their way along the sodden path. After about half a mile they reached the second and last farm on their way to the old house. "This is Earthydown Farm, a little bigger than the one down at Marsh End, but they both have large and high walls as much as each-other," said Edward.

"Is that to keep someone out?" asked Arthur.

"Someone or something," said Edward.

"We're nearly there I assume," said Arthur.

"See for yourself," said Edward.

The road went uphill, and there were several dead trees at the top blocking the view but now they saw the Tenebra house in much more detail. It looked half like a ruined castle, and seemed to have many smashed windows and crumbling fixtures. They were about a hundred yards from the trees that surrounded it, and through the trees Arthur caught a glimpse of the decaying walls with wrought iron spikes. The whole place didn't look inviting at all. They walked through a field which had been recently ploughed to allow the frost to kill the weeds, and had a fence bordering the perimeter. They entered the copse of trees, and they were all gnarled and weather worn. Nothing seemed to grow here, apart from the clumps of mushrooms at the base of several trees.

The walls were about seven foot high, and had ornate stone bowls on the top of pillars that partitioned each section of the wall. The trees looked like long bony fingers ready to snatch a passing sparrow, and the calling of a crow could be heard somewhere above them.

"This makes a change from the usual settings I've encountered," said Arthur.

"Be careful where you step, there are a lot of holes around here, the cellar was rather extensive but the masonry wasn't so keep an eye out," said Edward. They walked along the old track and finally came to the gate, and Arthur caught his first sight of the old house.

It was built just like a fortified manor house, and in the garden in front of it was a stone banister with pillars at the end of it. There were plant pots on the pillars, and the roses that were planted there had grown wild over time and now sought to choke the stone that contained them. There was a kind of dense fog carpeting the floor, about half a foot deep, and this made the idea of pot holes a much more intimidating concept. They stared at the hulking mass of decaying brickwork, crumbling turrets and smashed windows for a while, and it suddenly seemed to get dark. The whole scene just seemed to become dull and lifeless, even more so than before.

"What time is it?" asked Edward. Arthur looked at his watch and it was only half past noon, so the change in light couldn't be accounted for.

"Do you think we should go in and check out where the smoke was coming from," said Arthur.

"Of course, we don't want our women folk to find out we ran away scared do we?" asked Edward.

"My fiancée doesn't care about me being scared, since we've come up against so many terrifying creatures and adventures in the past," said Arthur.

"Is Princess Josephine your fiancée?" he asked.

"Yes, she is actually," said Arthur.

"You lucky guy, but won't she end up ruling Discoucia?" asked Edward.

"No her father promised that she would be exempt from that, her sister Princess Alexandra will become High Queen Alexandra when her father passes away," said Arthur.

"We're just stalling for time, aren't we," said Edward.

"Yes," replied Arthur, and with that they both walked into the grounds of the Tenebra estate.

The house seemed to be staring at them, and they walked carefully across the ground, feeling the ground for any holes. Edward led and Arthur followed, and they reached the front door, which was scary looking piece of architecture, and seemed to be swinging on its hinges.

"Were there really holes in the ground?" asked Arthur. Edward picked up a piece of broken brick from the floor and threw it into the fog. There was a silence, and a smash as it hit the floor.

"Sorry, but I had to prove that," he said.

"And you gave away our position too," said Arthur.

"Ooops," said Edward, in a mixture of embarrassment and worry.

They pushed on into the house, and closed the heavy oak door behind them. The fog swirled after the jet of air that was created from closing the door. The House had now swallowed up Arthur and Edward.

A Very Big House in the Country

Jo had finished breakfast when Arthur and Edward were about to leave. Arthur gave her a kiss goodbye and joined Edward outside. She followed the maid who took her to Lady Lucy's room; she had been very ill recently and had stayed in bed. Jo sat on a chair at her bedside, and for a second there was a little bit of awkwardness.

"So, Princess Josephine, by what fortune do you grace my humble home?" asked Lucy.

"I doubt that your home qualifies as humble, it is actually quite beautiful," said Jo.

"Thank you, but you did not answer my question," she replied.

"We got lost in the fog, and we saw your ghoul on the riverbank," said Jo.

"Oh yes, I have heard it out there on the moorland, but it doesn't frighten me," she said.

"As I can clearly see, you're all tucked up in bed behind a locked door and a large wall," said Jo.

"Exactly, it's good to be rich," she said.

"I really don't know how to reply to that," said Jo.

"You're much richer than I am, but you insist on taking the moral high ground, why?" asked Lucy.

"I don't put much importance on money and wealth, if I lived with Arthur in a hut then I would still be the richest person on Alavonia," she said.

"I in turn do not know how to reply to that," said Lucy.

"Are you really ill, or do you just not wish to get out of bed?" asked Jo.

"Could we please talk about something else?" asked Lucy.

"Very well, tell me about the Great Rim," said Jo.

"It is a massive range of mountains and at the top is a massive blue dome, no one knows who built it but it is too high for anyone to climb," explained Lucy, who had now gotten out of bed and walked over to the window.

"What are you looking at?" asked Jo.

"There in the east you can just see the mountains, they are so high that on a clear day even the tops cannot be seen," she said.

Jo walked over to look, and she did see the mountains, which were immense by anyone's standards. "So that is the Great Rim, and how do you know of a blue dome if no one has been able to climb that high?" asked Jo.

"There is an observatory in the Astral Castle, not as big as the one on Tomo but with it the skyentists could see up into the mountains, and they saw that the dome exists and it is incredibly huge," explained Lucy.

"Is there an entrance to the mountains?" asked Jo.

"There is only one; no one has ever been in, come with me to the library and I shall show you," she said.

Lucy got dressed and took Jo into the huge library that was full of multi-coloured books of all sizes. Lucy found the book she sought quite quickly; it was bound in blue leather and had some beautiful gold binding. "The Legend of the Twilight Vale by Sir Alfred," read Jo out loud.

"This is one of my favourite books because it sounds like such an amazing place, even though it couldn't possibly exist," said Lucy.

"Why couldn't it be real?" asked Jo.

"It's too impossible, the place is safe all the time and it can only be entered through the Gates of Destiny, which are made of solid granite and are impenetrable. Then there is the account of what it looks like inside, blue everywhere. Only problem is that the one person to write about the inside says that it is like a dream and he has no empirical evidence to support what he claimed," she explained.

"What would you do to visit it?" asked Jo.

"I would stay there forever," she said.

"What about your home and your husband?" asked Jo.

"I hate it here, it's cold all the time and there is something that I have never told anyone," said Lucy, pulling up her sleeve. She had several bruises on her arm, and they looked quite painful.

"How did you get those?" asked Jo.

"How do you think?" she asked.

"No, that cannot be true," said Jo.

"I have wanted to leave here for months, but Edward wouldn't allow it," said Lucy.

"So he did this to you?" asked Jo.

"In the summer I'm an accessory, but in winter I'm a burden," she said.

"Why can't you leave?" she asked.

"I'm in the middle of nowhere, what can I possibly do? And I have thought about it for a while, but I don't even have anywhere to go. My mother and father are dead, my home is now owned by Lord Yage for one of his wives, all I have now is this life here," said Lucy.

"If he is bruising you like this, then you need to come with me," said Jo.

"Where to?" she asked.

"The Twilight Vale," said Jo.

There's no Hound Around, not a Sound, and it can't be Found

The foyer of the house looked as bad as the outside. At the end of the room was a large door, and on either side was a staircase, that led to different rooms. Arthur gasped, when he thought he saw a man in the corner, but it was actually a suit of armour. Arthur walked up to it and inspected it. The helmet was dark, and the rest of the body was made of a dull metal, that had long since lost its sheen. There were rotting green drapes hanging from the crumbling plaster walls, and inside the windows let in very little light.

"Where do we check first?" asked Edward.

"Where would the smoke be coming from? You know the place better than I do," said Arthur.

"Let's try the main sitting room," said Edward. They walked over to the door, and Edward opened it carefully. Some falling crumbs of plaster fell on his hair, and when they opened the door they strained their eyes to see inside. The sitting room was large, with the same plaster and fixtures as the foyer.

"This place has seen better days, who were the last owners?" asked Arthur.

"The Franklyn family, they were trying to turn this into the biggest fortress west of the forest, but they ran out of money, peasants," he said. Arthur then felt rather awkward; the rich people in the Discoucia were much more polite when it came to their treatment of less well off people. But Sir Edward seemed to be different, an arrogant country sort who had space enough to develop his own opinions of the rest of the world, and could inflict them on the poorer farmers that he allowed on his land.

"So tell me Arthur, what your opinion of the lower classes is?" asked Edward.

"I think that money isn't a blessing but instead a chock that divides people, to be honest I have more money than I will ever need. However I don't count my self-worth in how much I have, it's what I do with my life that will determine my character," explained Arthur.

"Very nice speech, you have your opinions and I have mine," he said, and they pushed on through the house. They came to a room which was obviously the kitchen, and they found the source of the smoke.

The stove had been burning from the night before but Arthur noticed that something was missing, but he didn't say anything as it was something so glaringly obvious. However Edward didn't seem to notice, which made Arthur even more suspicious. "So this must have been what was causing the fire, but it doesn't actually answer any questions," said Edward.

"No not at all, but I think we should split up, you go upstairs and I will check the cellar," said Arthur.

"Very well, yell if you get into trouble," said Edward, who headed through a door at the back of the kitchen.

Arthur walked back into the foyer through the sitting room, and found that there was a door below the staircase and Arthur opened it. The door didn't creak like he expected it to and when Arthur felt the hinge, it was covered in oil. "Something about this doesn't make sense" said Arthur, who pressed on down into the cellar. He then found his answer in the cellar room.

It was a dark place, which had a small amount of light coming in from the holes in the roof, and the floor was covered in grey dust. Arthur walked over to the back wall, and on it were chained two figures. One was a skeleton, with rags from where the clothes used to be. The next figure was a woman, who looked quite old, with long grey hair and ragged clothes. She seemed to be asleep.

320

"Excuse me, but what are you doing down here?" asked Arthur.

"I...I...who are you?" she asked.

"Oh my lord, you're alive? Sir Arthur Pageon here from Discoucia, let me help you down," he said.

"I'm so cold," she said. Arthur looked around for something that he could use to get her off the wall, and instead found what he thought was a pile of fur coats. In fact it was a costume, of the ghoulish creature...

Arthur then found a crowbar in the corner next to a pile of other tools, which just added more answers to the mystery. Arthur broke the chains off the wall and got the woman down. "Who are you?" asked Arthur.

"I am Lady Elisa Franklyn, and the poor soul you see on the wall is my late husband," she said.

"You must be freezing, put this on," said Arthur, handing her the hideous looking costume.

"I can't wear that!" she said.

"Look, it's either this or my jacket, and that isn't very warm," said Arthur.

"Oh well, if I must I must," said Elise weakly. Now Arthur was standing next to the ghoulish creature, which stood staring with horrific red eyes, and jet black claws. They made for the stairs, but out of the gloom came Edward, holding a gun.

"I see you've discovered my little secret," he said, walking them back and he stood beneath a shaft of light coming through the floor.

"I guessed it for a while, a stove without any food, you knowing exactly where you are going and the whole ghoul routine but please fill me in with the details of why," asked Arthur.

"One simple thing, control," he said.

"Control of who?" asked Arthur.

"The stupid farmers, they think something is out to get them at night so they stay in and don't get out of line, and Lady Franklyn here just got in the way. I needed a ruined house to conduct my business from and this one was the easiest. Ruining her family and her home was easy," explained Edward calmly.

"So what happens now?" asked Arthur.

"You are going to stay here, I'll tell the princess that you were mauled to death by the monster and Lady Franklyn will continue her life down here much as she has done," said Edward, in a horribly calm voice.

There was a puff of pink smoke, and a piece of paper landed onto the floor in front of Edward. "Is this a trick to distract my attention?" he asked.

"No, but I think that you should read it, it is from Persus of course," said Arthur. Edward picked it up, not once taking his eyes of Arthur and Elise.

"People like you deserve one thing, help from above," he read. Edward looked at Arthur with a puzzled expression, and Arthur smiled.

There was a silence, and then Edward looked up. He saw a small black object fly out of a window and sail down at him. He was so mesmerised by the object that he failed to get out of the way, that the object then came into contact with his forehead. It was a brick and it knocked him completely senseless, which made him crumple to the floor in a heap.

"Run," said Arthur, who grabbed Lady Elise's paw and pulled her past Edward and up to the top of the stairs.

"I can't run," she said.

"Then I'll carry you," said Arthur, who picked up Elise and carried her through the garden while carefully avoiding the holes in the floor. They made it out of the ring of trees and were greeted by an unexpected sight. It was nearly dark and in the field was parked the Nostradamus, and Jo was pacing up and down the deck.

"Start her up, Jo, we're leaving for the Twilight Vale, screw the Astral Castle, let's just get to safety!" shouted Arthur. Jo never asked about the fact that Arthur was carrying a horrible creature, but she had since learned not to question such things. The ship lifted off and blasted towards the Great Rim and it wasn't a moment too soon, because Sir Edward had begun to wake up...

Voyage's End

The Great Rim was invisible at night and from the deck of the ship Arthur saw in the distance the lights of the Astral Castle. He wished that he could go and see it, as his lifelong dream is to see all the wonders of Alavonia. The ship sped across the flat land that lay between the forest and the mountains, and Arthur returned to the sitting room where there were three women inside.

Lady Franklyn was asleep on the settee with a blanket covering her. Jo was sat on a chair, as was Lady Lucy. "Edward is not going to be happy, but I don't think this could happen to a better person," said Arthur.

"I'll drink to that, if I had a drink," said Lucy.

"Oh no, I have no idea what we are going to encounter ahead but we should be in complete control of our faculties nonetheless," said Arthur.

"The book says that we should land the ship in the sheltered cove above the main door, and that way it will be safe from anything coming towards us," said Lucy.

"You know an awful lot about this, don't you?" asked Arthur.

"It's my favourite subject, so you're in my territory now, boy," she said in a cocky voice.

"Well we have never actually been formally introduced, it's nice to meet you Lady Lucy," said Arthur.

"It is nice to be here, thank you both for taking me away from Sir Edward and I'm sure Lady Franklyn here will agree with me," said Lucy.

"I'm sure she will, poor woman, what he did was barbaric," said Jo.

"I hope that Archie will be able to help, I know it is unfair for us to bring her someone to take care of," said Arthur.

"If everything she has said is true, then I think that she will be more than capable to cope," said Jo.

The ship got about a hundred yards from the mountain face, Corky stopped the engines and Arthur went down to his room to find out what was going on. "I can't go any further sir, I don't want to harm the girl," said Corky.

"We do have lights, you know, and I think we should use something we haven't used in a long time; drop the anchor," said Arthur.

"All the way?" he asked.

"No, till it's about a metre from the floor, then I'll get out and guide you to the cove," said Arthur.

"What cove?" he asked.

"There is a sheltered cove that you can park the ship while we are inside and there are shops around the Astral Castle if we are gone for too long, so you can survive without us," said Arthur.

"Are you going to be gone long?" asked Corky.

"No idea, this is going to be a bit different, you see we're going in to the mountains, all four of us, and we don't know how long it will take," said Arthur.

"Well you be careful lad, and make sure you and your missus get back in one piece," he said.

Arthur smirked and walked out of Corky's room. When Arthur was on the deck he let down a rope and tied it to the banister. Before he climbed down he saw Jo and Lucy laughing through the window, and he felt happy that Jo had found another friend. He climbed down and the ground was very rocky. After walking over to the anchor which was hanging down from the ship, he pulled it up the small slope around the still unseen door. There was a group of rocks that Arthur wedged the anchor in, and Corky turned on the ship's floodlights. The whole area was illuminated and Arthur saw the door, which was huge, about twenty feet tall, and was such a simple looking door that it could have been missed by the normal rock climber.

The ship landed in the sheltered area above the door and they looked out across the dark and empty landscape, and then up at the invisible tops of the mountains. "Come here Arthur, I want to show you something, have you got a sledgehammer?" asked Lucy.

"I think you know the answer to that," said Arthur, who walked down into the hull and reappeared with a large hammer.

Lucy took it, and she walked over to an outcrop of rock, and swung the hammer so hard that when it hit the rock, Arthur and Jo thought that there would be a spray of rock, but that never happened. The hammer smashed into the rock and bounced off. Lucy had to steady herself when the recoil came back through the hammer handle.

"What type of rock is this?" asked Arthur.

"It's Blue Granite, so hard that the only mine in this whole range is only six feet long," said Lucy.

"She has definitely fortified herself well," said Arthur.

"Do you honestly believe that Authos lives in there?" asked Lucy.

"You read the book, didn't you?" asked Jo.

"That was just a romantic fantasy, it couldn't possibly be true," said Lucy.

"I'm going to sleep," said Jo.

"I'm not, we've come so far already and I want to carry on, and I don't think you would allow me to go alone," said Arthur.

"No I wouldn't, and I can stay up if we must go," said Jo. Lucy was looking out into the void and she saw a small light out in the darkness that didn't seem right. It was a mild night and it was quiet, way too quiet.

"What are you looking at, Lucy?" asked Jo.

"I don't know, that tiny light out there above the trees, I don't like the look of it," she said.

Arthur walked into the sitting room then into the study, and retrieved his brass telescope. Arthur looked out across the landscape and focused on the light. Lucy and Jo watched him as he scanned the surroundings, then he shuddered. "Umm, Lucy, did your husband have a ship of his own?" asked Arthur.

"Yes, but he hasn't used it in years," said Lucy.

"Here he comes," said Arthur, who passed the telescope to Lucy, who also shuddered.

Arthur then acted fast; he ran to the banister and climbed down to the ground. Jo ran with Lucy and they followed Arthur down to the door. They stood in front of the huge granite door, and didn't know what to do. "Archie, could you please open the door!?" shouted Arthur.

"It's not going to work," said Lucy.

"It has to, otherwise we'll have a gunfight on our hands," said Arthur. The door stayed still and nothing moved. There was a silence, then something happened which made Lucy change her whole outlook on the situation.

The door started to hum, and part of it lit up. Four circles glowed with a faint green glow, and there was a faint hand print on each. Arthur put his hand on one and the door shuddered. Jo put her hand as well and it shuddered again, only this time much more. Lucy put her hand on too and the door nearly opened, but the last place was not filled and Arthur knew how to fill it. He took his hand off and ran back to the ship.

The light was getting closer and Lucy contemplated running up the black mountainside in an effort to escape her husband. Arthur came back carrying Lady Franklyn, who put her hand out sleepily and joined with Arthur in putting their hands on the wall. The whole door lit up with thousands of intricate patterns. The door then opened up and a warm breeze blew out from the cave inside. Arthur carried Elise and Jo was pulled by Lucy inside. The doors then slammed shut, just when Edward's ship came into view out in the dark. The group now had one choice: they had now entered heaven but they just didn't realise it yet...

The Sanctuary of Blue Light

The cave wasn't dark since there were several crystals sticking out of the wall, and they gave off a dim light that lit up enough to see where things were. "So, we're here inside the Great Rim, it must have taken ages to make this tunnel," said Lucy.

"I like it here," said Elise, the first words that she had said in a long time.

"You spend most of your time chained underground in the dark and you like it here?" asked Jo.

"It feels warm, snug and secure in here," said Elise.

"Plus, these walls are made of granite, so the tunnel is as secure as my safe," said Arthur. There was a whooshing sound outside the door followed by a muffled sound of someone shouting.

"Shall we push on?" asked Arthur. The floor was covered in sand and it felt warm when Elise felt it. She had begun to feel much better ever since she was freed and didn't know how to thank Arthur for what he had done for her.

"It is quite strange, this whole situation I mean," said Lucy.

"I try not to think about it," said Arthur.

"I just go with the flow most of the time," said Jo.

"I have a question for you Lucy, what is your maiden name?" asked Arthur.

"My full name is a little long," she said, as they passed more crystals in the tunnel.

"You're among friends here," said Jo.

"Very well, my full name is Lucinda Drexel Constance Theodosia," she said.

"Ah, we're going to probably stick with Lucy," said Jo.

"I thought you might," said Lucy.

"I've never heard of the name Theodosia," said Arthur.

"It isn't very common, I'm actually the last Theodosia," she said.

After walking up what felt like a hill, they entered a large room which seemed like an amphitheatre only there was no one in it, and it seemed to have no top. There was just the dark; but what attracted their attention was the large hole in the wall. There were stalactites and stalagmites blocking the hole slightly, but Arthur saw that he was able to climb through. He was followed by Elise who struggled to get through, and was severely weakened from it. Jo and Lucy followed and they were greeted by an amazing sight, so amazing that they couldn't fully take it in.

A dark blue sky, like a beautiful shade of midnight and stars as immeasurable as sand on a beach. The land was lit up by glowing crystals of red, yellow, pink and purple, and light blue orbs flew gracefully through the air. The forest in front of them was dark, but not evil looking and in fact looked quite peaceful. It was made up of ancient oak trees covered in a beautiful looking blue moss.

The whole area was saturated in colour and a vague sound echoed through the trees that sounded like a lullaby. There was an overpowering sense of placidity and peacefulness that entered the minds of the four travellers that made them forget everything and put them at ease instantly. They felt as though they had crossed over a threshold to another world and now they were in a dream, a living dream that was so much better than anything else the outside world could offer.

Elise collapsed and lay peacefully on the soft grass verge. Arthur ran over to her and was taken over by tiredness which made him fall onto the verge too. Jo and Lucy also began to fall under some kind of magic spell and they fell onto the verge as well. Just as Jo closed her eyes she thought she saw Archie, just for a second, but then the whole world went black.

Arthur awoke first and saw that the place had not changed. He was feeling quite healthy and invigorated, and saw that the girls were collapsed in a pile sleeping soundly. He pulled them over to the verge where they were in a more dignified position. He then walked over to the entrance of the forest and decided to climb one of the ancient trees and get a much better view of the palace.

It was so beautiful that Arthur couldn't believe that such a place really existed. Arthur then took out a smaller version of his telescope and looked across the sea of blue trees to the palace. "She really has style, and knows how to overdo it," said Arthur.

"Are you going to stay up in that tree all day?" asked a voice from below. Arthur lost his footing because he thought that he was alone, and he slowly drifted onto the grass.

Arthur expected to be hurt but for some reason he didn't feel a thing, it was like there was no pain here. Archie stood looking at Arthur with an ashamed look. Arthur got up and saw that she had changed dramatically since their last meeting. She was wearing an elegant dress with every kind of gem and design on it. Her hair was so long that it was being lifted by what looked like glowing birds, only they were smaller and gave off a funny glowing dust. Then she smiled and Arthur felt that everything was good and right in the world.

"So you are finally here, welcome to my home, the only safe place in Alavonia," said Archie.

"It is more beautiful than I ever imagined," said Arthur.

"And it is here that you will discover everything that is to come and the answers to any questions you may have, but first you must introduce me to your new friend," said Archie.

"Don't you mean friends?" asked Arthur.

"I'm afraid not. Lady Franklyn is now a resident of my world since she passed away about five minutes ago. Quite peacefully, actually, and now you have brought her here to heaven, she can join my people," said Archie.

"She's dead?!" he said.

"I'm afraid so, you see she couldn't keep up, and she finally gave up in her sleep," said Archie.

"Did she suffer in death?" asked Arthur.

"No one ever suffers here, you're in heaven, Arthur, and there's no pain, no possible chance of attack since the walls are a mile thick and you have to see my palace; the builders may have taken ten thousand years constructing it but they really outdid themselves," said Archie.

"How much did it cost?" asked Arthur.

"Money doesn't work here. I mean it's true that I am unbelievably rich. I could buy and sell Lord Yage's gold plated backside and not make a dent in my wealth, but gods don't usually mess with current affairs," said Archie.

"OK, but how much would it cost?" asked Arthur.

"I forget how your money system works, explain it to me again" said Archie.

"The bottom of the scale is brass coins and they are called pennies" said Arthur.

"Just like in the other world, what about the copper?" asked Archie.

"They're called Corbs," said Arthur.

"So when it comes to silver I remember that they are called Interis," said Archie.

"And then there is gold which are called Kigcoses," said Arthur.

"I have no idea where you got that name, but isn't there a platinum coin?" asked Archie.

"Those are few and far between, mostly for commemorative occasions and people don't normally have them and they are called Eulokos," said Arthur.

"OK, in that case the price of my palace is one hundred million Eulokos or one hundred billion Kigcoses," said Archie.

"What have you got in there?!" asked Arthur.

"You'll see, a lot of stuff to make sure that I never get bored here, I'm unbelievably rich but what does it matter," said Archie.

"How does it feel to have all that money?" asked Arthur.

"It feels great...ask a silly question," said Archie.

Archie led Arthur back to the clearing, and he saw that Elise had gone. Jo and Lucy still remained sleeping on the verge. "I think you two should wake up," said Archie. And with that they did wake up and Jo jumped up to hug Archie.

"Yes yes it's nice to see you too," said Archie.

"Your home is amazing," said Jo.

"Thank you very much, I hope you enjoy your stay," she said.

"Excuse me," said Lucy.

"Yes, a warm welcome to you too Miss Theodosia," said Archie.

"Hello, what is Archie short for?" asked Lucy.

"Archaelia, if you must know my full name is Archaelia D'Angelo Mysterioso," said Archie.

"You know I have never heard your full name, though I suppose it's not your real name," said Arthur.

"Oh no of course not, I can't tell you that since it would give way too much away," said Archie.

"You're not really a god, are you?" asked Lucy.

"Yes, I have the power to crush Alavonia into powder, and then do something with that powder that will send me to all the other planets," said Archie.

"Prove it," said Lucy.

The four then whooshed through the air and landed on a street, outside a large mansion. In the garden was a large pile of suitcases and more were being moved out of the house. Sat on the boxes was a girl of about 175, with a black hair band and shoes that were way too big for her.

"This is my home," said Lucy.

"It was, but now you are moving out and soon you will be married to Sir Edward in Evermore and then you will move to Danis Hall until you are rescued by Jo here," explained Archie.

"Are we back in time?" asked Arthur.

"I told you I can do anything, but don't move because if you do the whole image will shatter, and we will zoom back to the Twilight Vale," said Archie.

They watched for about five minutes until Lucy intentionally stepped forward. Everything blurred and they all found themselves back in the clearing. "Why did you do that?" asked Arthur.

"It was too upsetting for her, she didn't know when she was that age how bad things were to be and wanted to get rid of that image of hope since there really was no hope at all," said Archie.

"OK, I believe you, you're a god, it's all true. So where do we go from here?" asked Lucy.

"Up there, to my throne room," said Archie.

She pointed to a large stained glass window in the centre of the palace, which was so large that it could be seen from the clearing. "Before we go I heard a whooshing sound outside the door after it closed, what was it?" asked Arthur.

"Oh that, well Sir Edward was extremely annoyed when he couldn't find you and blow your brains out, so he decided to burn the ship down" said Archie. Arthur's eyes widened. "What!?" he shouted.

"Then the whoosh was me plucking it from the ground and placing it on a higher ledge where he could never find it," said Archie.

"He is never going to leave us alone is he?" said Lucy.

"No, I think that Sir Edward will have a further part to play in your tale but I want you to know that this is only a repercussion of bringing Lucy and Lady Franklyn here. He believes that the good Lady will testify that he killed her husband and nearly killed her, then there's what he did to you Lucy," she explained.

"But he did everything bad, why doesn't he just leave?" asked Jo.

"Trust me evil villains never do that, they will do everything in their power to stave off a service of time in Icester. But you're safe here so try to put it out of your mind," said Archie, who led them down a trail through the forest.

"How many people live here?" asked Arthur.

"About ten thousand, they are all the souls of exemplary good people that the Misty Morning Rider delivers to me every now and again," said Archie.

"You know the rider?" asked Lucy.

"I sometimes play Chrysso with her while her horse rests in my stables, plus she allows me to visit her lost island sometimes," said Archie.

"Do you have servants?" asked Jo.

"Yes I do, but they don't consider themselves as such and neither do I. They are mostly made up of servants from your Lords' and Ladies' estates, and they love their job so much, that it doesn't feel like work," said Archie.

"It's a pretty nice set up you have here," said Arthur.

"I just wanted a sanctuary free from the torment and danger of outside, and when I called this place heaven, I lied," said Archie.

"I knew it, Heaven can't exist on Alavonia," said Lucy.

"I know this is a little abstract, but you tell Belinda Carlisle that," replied Archie.

"So what is this place?" asked Arthur.

"The middle I suppose, you have the real heaven at the top and you get there by not murdering anyone, it's as simple as that. Then you have Hell where the murderers go, and the Misty Morning Rider knows so there's no getting away," said Archie.

"So this place is in the middle?" asked Jo.

"Yes, if you're an exemplary Discoucian then there's a chance you end up here," she replied.

"Archie, I don't know if you've noticed but rather a few people have made a transition on account of me," said Arthur.

"Oh I know, but you've saved Lucy and you saved Lady Franklyn from an agonising, lonely and hopeless death. And what of the hundreds of souls that you have saved before, and will go on to save after her?" said Archie.

"Where will she go?" asked Lucy.

"She will come here, she never hurt a soul, and she was an amazing gardener, hard to tell I know but I could use someone to tend to the vast palace gardens," said Archie.

"So she had a happy ending after all, what about her husband?" asked Jo.

"Great miner that guy, made a fortune in the silver mines of Drongo and he will start with all the other new miners over in the east part of the Vale. Then most probably rise up to be a foreman or manager," said Archie.

"So they're together again?" asked Arthur.

"Yes, yes they are," said Archie.

They came to a beautiful river which seemed to be a running flow of mist. There was a bridge across it, an ornate white wooden structure that was wide enough for all of them to cross. They then arrived at the gardens of the palace.

"So what do you call this palace?" asked Jo.

"The Moonlight Palace" replied Archie.

The palace loomed up above them, and it was twice the size of Evermore. The gardens had well cut grass and flowers of only one colour, blue. They walked along a path of polished granite with borders of blue orchids. Archie led them up a set of stone stairs to a large patio where a large fountain pleasantly poured water into a crystal pool.

"Is this a dream?" asked Lucy.

"It might very well be but you can never tell when you are actually in one. Everything seems safe and surreal, nothing like the real world and you feel like you are surrounded by a soft light fuzz that keeps you from being hurt by anything. The temperature is at a constant which means that your sense of temperature is turned off, so I can understand that you would think so but I assure you that this is all physically real," explained Archie.

"OK, I believe you, this is real," said Lucy. Archie took them to the archway that led into the palace. There was a large chandelier above them as they passed into the main foyer.

It was the size of a great cavern though one thing it was missing was a set of stairs.

"How do we get to your throne room?" asked Jo.

"Through that door," said Archie. Arthur went first, and then Jo and then Lucy. The door then slammed shut behind them. Archie was in front of them in the small room.

"I don't know how you did that," said Arthur.

"You now have to make the ascent to my throne room so that you can prove that you are worthy of the task I have for you," said Archie, who faded out of sight.

"She's nuts," said Lucy.

"I think she's nuts in a good way," said Jo.

"Well then, I reckon we better get going," said Arthur.

The Great Ascent

The three looked around the room and saw that there was a spiral staircase hidden around the wall. They entered through a small door on the other side of the room. It was so cramped inside that they had to crawl through. When they thought that they had been travelling forever, they emerged on a balcony. Arthur looked down to see how far he had come, and they had probably travelled about twenty feet up. Then he saw something horrifying. The floor was carpeted by some kind of fog, and it was slowly rising.

Arthur decided to do an experiment while the girls climbed out of the cramped tunnel. He opened his belt buckle and took out a reel of string. He tied a pencil from his pocket to the string and lowered it down. The ledge he was on was big enough for a child, so he carefully let the girls pass him and carry on through the tunnel upwards. Jo looked confused at what Arthur was trying to do but she just let him carry on. Arthur dipped the pencil in the fog, and there was a hissing sound. He pulled the string back up, and all that was left was a melted end. "Acidic fog!" shouted Arthur, who put everything back and followed the girls up.

When they had cleared the side tunnel they came to another ledge, and this time there was no tunnel to continue up.

"Where do we go from here?" asked Lucy.

"We jump across," said Arthur. On the other side of the circular room was another ledge and Arthur jumped from one side to the other and landed precariously, but held on to the ladder that was built into the wall. It was made of the same blue stone as the rest of the walls and most probably resistant to the highly acidic fog.

"I can't jump that far!" shouted Lucy.

"I have an idea, throw me that rope that's on your back Jo," shouted Arthur.

Jo did, and Arthur tied it to the ladder. He then threw it to Lucy who tied it to her waist, but didn't feel any safer than before. She took a run up and jumped across the divide. She screamed as she went, but she made it. Arthur untied her and she climbed up the ladder. Jo then jumped as well, and found the whole experience rather fun in a strange way. They all climbed up the ladder to the second area, which was through a door at the top of the ladder.

They entered a room which had a circle of pillars and they were all different heights, presumably for climbing. Arthur saw the door to get out of this room about twenty feet up and he told the girls to go first, and to go as fast as they could. He then walked back to the doorway above the ladder, and looked down at the room that was filling up with fog. He stared for a while, hypnotised, and then ran back to the girls. They had already reached the top, and were waiting in the doorway. "Come on!" shouted Jo. Arthur then expertly climbed up the pillars, and jumped across the wide gap to the doorway, and ran ahead of the girls to the next room.

Arthur expected the next room to be straight after the first, but instead he ran up a long corridor which switched to the left, and then to the left again and so on, so it felt like he was running around in circles. The girls were coming fast behind him, after seeing the fog flow into the pillar room and after about a minute of blind running he emerged into the next room.

It was a small square room which didn't seem to have much in the way of challenges. The trio ran through the doorway on the other side of the room and into another room that was identical to the first. They then ran through another door which led to a staircase. The staircase went up then switched back into a room that was presumably above the one they were just in. They looked over and there was another set of rooms exactly the same as the ones below. Arthur was perplexed about why they were like this, but he just wanted to get away from the fog that was slowly creeping in from below. The rooms were lit by small crystals that also seemed to be immune to the fog, and lit the rooms with a dim light that didn't really show any detail of them, but prevented Arthur, Jo and Lucy from walking into any walls.

They then entered a huge room that must have been at least one hundred feet wide, and extended up as far as they could see. "What were all those other rooms for? They didn't really hinder us at all," said Lucy.

"I have a feeling that they were not to hinder us, but to hinder the fog. At least that's what I hope which means that this whole situation may not be completely hopeless after all," said Arthur.

"How do we get up?" asked Jo.

"Those notches, they go around the wall in a circular pattern. I think it might take a while but that's what those other rooms were for," said Arthur, who ran over to the wall and inspected it.

"Right, Jo first, then Lucy, and then I'll go last," said Arthur, but Jo and Lucy had already started to climb. Arthur grabbed the notches and followed them.

The course they were taking seemed to be the slowest one but this didn't really affect them, because the thought of being melted didn't seem too inviting. The one thing that was happening to the three that they didn't really notice was that they were beginning to tire. The sleep in the clearing may have made them feel better, but it still didn't help that they had not eaten or drunk since they had entered the Twilight Vale.

Another thing that they had not counted upon was that there was nowhere to rest as they moved around the massive tower. "I can't go any further," said Lucy.

"You have to," said Arthur.

"I can't, I'm exhausted," she said.

"Well you can stop if you want, but you will be using up half your energy holding on and when that's used up, you're gonna fall. So keep going and that hopefully won't happen," said Arthur. Lucy then took a deep breath and carried on going; she caught up with Jo and they moved on.

They were about half-way when the floor began to turn white, ever so slowly but it had the same effect on the three clinging to the wall. Lucy began to panic and nearly mowed Jo out of the way, but Jo also panicked and moved much faster. Arthur was quite calm, and followed them around the tower.

They finally reached the top and it was a flat ledge. Jo and Lucy collapsed from exhaustion and Arthur nearly did too, but he checked the next room first. There was a timer in the room and a lever, which Arthur didn't pull until he carried Jo and Lucy into the room. He pulled the lever and the door closed, and Arthur heard the timer ticking. He looked up and the room had a spiral staircase running around it, and there was a bright light above which obscured the top.

The door clicked open and Arthur saw that the door shut for five minutes, and then opened to stop the fog. "You two rest, and I'll keep an eye out for the fog," said Arthur.

"I love you," said Jo, who closed her eyes and fell asleep. Arthur then had a better idea; he picked up Lucy and carried her up the stairs, and then dropped her off at the top. The top was just a bright light, and Arthur couldn't see a thing. He placed her on the floor, and ran down to pick up Jo. He lifted her up in his arms, and carried her heroically up the stairs. When he reached the top, the light seemed to become less bleached and began to recede, and Arthur saw where he was standing.

He was standing at the top of the stairs of the foyer, and was confused beyond belief. The corridor that they were in was so beautifully decorated that it didn't fit in to the rooms they were in before. Arthur walked doggedly down the corridor to a huge room that had four statues of figures on each side, all on white marble plinths. On the left side was a gold one, then a black one, then a blue one, and lastly another gold one. On the right hand side was a black one, then a silver, then a green and then a red. At the end was an incredibly huge throne made of marble, and sat on it was Archie, who actually sat with her feet on one arm rest, and her back on the other. She was reading a book but it was hard for Arthur to see, since the room was so big.

"What just happened!?" he shouted.

"Oh good, you're here, it took you long enough," said Archie.

"We were just in a tower with fog, where did it all go?" he shouted.

"Come here," replied Archie. Arthur walked doggedly across the room, and as he got closer he saw that Archie had much longer hair. She sat properly now, much more elegantly.

"A throne seems to fit you very well, being in control of everything and everyone," said Arthur.

"Do I detect a hint of derision in your voice?" asked Archie.

"What was all that about?" asked Arthur.

"You made it here so you should be proud," said Archie.

"Proud? What would have happened if Jo had fallen, my future wife and children could have died," he said.

"Arthur, she could have died so many times before she entered here but she didn't, believe me, it isn't her time yet," said Archie.

"And that's another thing, you know when we are going to die, it isn't a good thing and you said you couldn't see the future," said Arthur.

"I couldn't agree more, but I'll tell you the truth here and now. I don't actually know when you are destined to die, the same with Jo, I just know that you are not destined to die now by my hand," said Archie.

"Then you are not all knowing," said Arthur.

"Correct, but if all of us deities come together we can answer all the questions in the universe. Only Astrae never comes and frankly we're all happy about that," explained Archie.

"Can any other gods come here?" asked Arthur.

"Just Phoebe, she is always welcome here. Then again she can walk through walls, so she is technically welcome anywhere," said Archie.

"Does Astrae have something against you?" asked Arthur.

"In a sense, yes, she doesn't like the fact that I have such a lovely realm and hers is full of fire, lava and smoke," said Archie.

"Is she from the other world like you? I mean you've alluded to it enough throughout our strange time together," asked Arthur.

"Yes she is, and that makes her more dangerous and hopefully this whole new adventure will bring her out of hiding, though it's a long shot," said Archie.

"So we are the bait for a deity I've never heard of?" asked Arthur.

"Yes you are, there is something I need you to do while you're attracting attention to yourselves," said Archie.

Jo and Lucy woke up and followed the sound of voices, and saw that Arthur was talking to Archie, who sat on her throne as elegantly as a King or Queen would. "Hello, we made it," shouted Jo.

"Yes, you did, and not a moment too soon. You have another adventure in front of you, as do I, but first you will stay here for a while as my guests" said Archie.

"So this is the end?" asked Jo.

"This part of your journey is over, but as far as your future goes there is a lot to come," said Archie.

"But this isn't the end of the book, I haven't shown you around my home yet, then we can do all this ending stuff," said Archie suddenly.

The Last Chapter

The Palace was enormous and Archie led them to a long corridor with hundreds of portraits in it. They were all important-looking people, though the three couldn't recognise them. Archie opened one door and inside was a cavernous room, which was a study, and its window looked out across the vale. It looked like the study of Lord Aquatine, though much larger and with more books.

"Have you read all of these books?" asked Lucy.

"Once or twice, I have a lot of time on my hands and I've turned my palace into a place where I can distract myself," said Archie.

"If you're going to be a godmother to our children then you won't need any distractions," said Jo.

"I have no idea what to do," said Archie, who closed the door and continued to the next room.

"Neither do I, I'm just planning on winging it," whispered Jo into Archie's ear.

They then came to a door with waves carved into it, and Archie pushed it open. Inside was a swimming pool, a massive one with water slides and waterfalls all built into the walls and flowing through rockeries with exotic looking plants.

"This place looks so beautiful, I would love to go swimming here," said Lucy.

"And so you shall, we're going to have to wait two months for January the first and that is when we will leave here and go out on your greatest adventure," said Archie.

"Show us around before we go swimming," said Arthur.

"I would love to," said Archie, who closed the door on the perfect scene for another.

They walked down the corridor and above they saw that there were bridges with red fences, and they were presumably for floors that were higher up.

"I'm starting to get a headache," said Arthur.

"The place does that, the Vale has a different type of air which makes it look dreamier but the headache will go in a while," explained Archie.

"I don't feel a thing," said Jo.

"Neither do I," said Lucy.

"For some strange reason it doesn't affect women hence why I'm staying in this form," said Archie.

"Excuse me?" asked Lucy.

"I'm not filling her in, one of you two can do that," replied Archie who took them into a room with a huge staircase that circled around the wall, and up into what seemed like forever.

"Come on my bedroom is on the fifth floor, actually it's the entire fifth floor," said Archie.

After walking for what seemed like five seconds they reached the fifth floor. There was just one room and it was what seemed to be a foyer. "You have a foyer to your bedroom, and I thought Evermore was ostentatious," said Arthur.

"Your foyer to your bedroom is bigger than my whole bedroom," said Jo.

"I know but this is such a large palace after all, and I am a god so I have a godlike bedroom, simple as that," said Archie.

"It's alright for some," said Lucy.

"You think this is good, you should see my actual bedroom," said Archie, who led them to the huge door.

She met a man who seemed to come out of nowhere, literally nowhere, and he looked happy to see her. He had white curly hair and wore a blue tuxedo similar to the one originally worn by Arthur.

"Sir Wishheart, these are my new friends Arthur, Jo and Lucy," said Archie.

342

"It's nice that you are back, my lady; your room is all prepared," he said before disappearing again into nowhere.

"He seemed nice," said Jo.

"The first person to come here, I helped him like I helped you and he was a brilliant guy," said Archie.

"Is that where we are destined to come, here?" asked Arthur.

"That won't be for a long time, just don't do anything to jeopardise it like going on a killing spree. Because only I can take moral souls from Phoebe, not immoral otherwise there is nothing I can do," said Archie.

"What constitutes murder exactly, are all the people who fought in previous wars damned forever?" asked Lucy.

"That is where it gets technical. It is judged by the Rider if the people killed were senselessly killed or not," she explained.

"How would she know?" asked Lucy.

"She does a forensic examination of all the evidence and then decides on what the verdict is," said Archie.

"And if they are good they come here?" asked Lucy.

"No not exactly, you see back in the beginning, I think it was the rocking 50s. The year was 10050 since it took me ten thousand years to help build your world. Then it took us fifty years to assign the gods each their two forms and their elements. Then we decided to take three different realms. I took here since it was the safest place I could possibly think of and Phoebe took the alternate dimension of Jalhenna, which is the name that we are giving the realm, Arthur, not Erthyana," explained Archie.

"Why do you call it the 'rocking '50s'?" asked Jo.

"I suppose you had to be there. But as I was saying, Phoebe got Jalhenna, because she was in depressed teen mode which I believe she now regrets. Then she became the Misty Morning Rider who wants to be alone, so she lives one second after us and as a result I hardly ever see her. She gets days off however and that's when I meet her on her island," said Archie.

"Are we going to see your bedroom or what?" asked Jo.

"Come on then," said Archie, who opened the door and revealed the splendour she lived in almost all the time.

343

It was incredible, how all this that they saw before them could be one bedroom. It had massive windows that looked out across the vale, and the floor was carpeted with an azure colour that looked like a sea. The room was set up with two levels. The one they had started on was a lower level, and a set of marble stairs led to the second level, which was like an inside terrace.

Columns held up the roof and they lined the wall between the first and second level. Inside the wall were bookcases, and they were full of books which looked well read, since they were the only things in the room that were not immaculate. They walked across the large open space and they climbed the stairs to the second level, which was on the right since the windows were all on the left.

On the second level of the room was Archie's bed which was about four times the size of a normal king size bed. Jo was astonished that such large beds existed, and the sheets must have needed a very long washing line. "This is where I sleep, you will all have the guest bedrooms and I will see you in the morning" said Archie.

"How do we know if it's the morning here?" asked Arthur.

"Unfortunately I cannot make the sun rise here, which I know makes the place sound depressing, but since it's perpetual twilight out there I would suggest closing the curtains," said Archie.

"What's for dinner?" asked Jo.

"I have no idea, let's go and find out," said Archie.

The group followed Archie and as they passed around a corner Arthur noticed that someone was missing. "Where's Lucy?" he asked.

"She's gone?" asked Jo.

"Oh dear, she must have gotten lost," said Archie. A pale woman walked up to them and Jo was quite shocked to see that she had a bullet-hole through her forehead and a dim blue light seemed to be emanating from it. Jo thought that she shouldn't stare and looked down at her eyes, which were emanating the same kind of light.

"I'm sorry to disturb you, my Lady, but a package has appeared in the foyer that is addressed to you, we have no idea how it managed to get here," said, the woman and noticed that Jo was staring at her head.

"Very well Barbara, I'll see to it while you look for Lady Lucinda," replied Archie.

Outside, in the Dyavolt Inn, Corky sat with drivers of other noble families as they chatted about what they disliked most about their employers. The door swung open and the rain swept in, causing everyone to yell. A person wrapped in a green cloak walked in and slammed the door. They scanned the area and focused on Corky, walking straight to him.

Back in the Twilight Vale, the group had arrived in the huge main foyer again after passing through many new and wondrous rooms; the large polished oak table in the centre of the white marble floor had the package on it. It was a present, a pink box tied with a purple silk bow.

"Where did that come from?" asked Arthur.

"No idea, I don't know who delivered it," she replied and looked at the label, and on it was a poem.

'Just a present to you dear friend, who life very soon will come to an end. The time will come, and that is soon, when you and your friends, will all go boom..." read Archie.

"Is that package supposed to be ticking?" asked Arthur.

Archie picked up the package, and sure enough it was ticking. Archie listened to it, and then it suddenly stopped, then clicked. "Oh dear..."